Alexandria

Spin It: Book One

Angera Allen

For questions or comments about this book, please contact the author at authorangeraallen@gmail.com.

Printed in the United States of America

Angera Allen
www.authorangeraallen.com

Editor Lisa A. Hollett at Silently Correcting Your Grammar
Editor Emma Mack at Ultra Editing Co
Cover Design by Kate Newburg at Bad Star Media
Formatted by Kate Newburg at Bad Star Media
Cover Photographer by Jessica Quintal at Shine by Jessica
Cover Model Angera Allen
Proofreaders: Marlena Salinas & Andy Barba

Alexandria / Angera Allen. -- 1st ed.
ISBN 978-0-9986829-1-4

Dedication

This book is dedicated to my secret woman's group on FB.
This group has been such a huge support in my crazy life.
The sisterhood is unbreakable, and I am blessed to be a part of this loving community. I don’t think I would be publishing this book right now without these ladies. So, to all my Smuffin Sisters,
I love you and thank you!

prologue

Alexandria

If five years ago, I would've known sneaking out of the house with my best friend would change my life forever, I probably wouldn't have done it. But I'm sure anyone who has ever been violated says these exact words. If I… If only… I should have… But the end result is, I *did.*

Remembering the events of my ordeal has the hairs on the back of my neck standing on end. Being raped and not remembering is just as terrifying as if you did remember. They usually say if you see your attacker once, you see them everywhere—in your dreams, a glance of someone with the same features—but my problem is I can't put a face to the person in my nightmares.

I was eighteen years old and living with my mamá in New York, while Papá was in Europe working. A few individuals from Spin It, Inc., the record label my parents own, my best friend, Stella, her mom, Abby, Mamá, and I went to the local music festival. We'd been at the festival all day, and Mamá was tired, making us leave before the evening events even started. I wasn't too happy about leaving, so after she went to sleep, I snuck out, meeting up with Stella and a group of girlfriends. That's where I made my first mistake, and now I think, *I never should have...*

Our group stayed together the whole night just dancing, drinking, and having fun, and there were so many good DJs that the music was unbelievable. There were a couple of groups of boys dancing around us. I don't remember any one guy paying me attention. I love to lose myself in the music, and all I wanted to do was dance. I remember being so happy and thinking how I couldn't wait to be on stage someday playing my music.

Stella and I had always been raised to watch our surroundings and never trust anyone we didn't know. Our group was drinking, half of us underage, but we trusted everyone and knew who we were with, so being drugged was the last thing on anyone's mind. But that's where I was wrong. Again, you think, if only...

The last thing I remember is getting soft drinks at the bar and moving my way back through the crowd. Sipping on the drinks so they wouldn't spill on me, I noticed the bathroom line wasn't long, so I decided to go before heading back. I had finished one of the drinks, and I remember giggling to myself that I was going to have to get more drinks after waiting in line. I was bouncing around in the line laughing because I had to pee and was feeling drunk. I don't remember going to the bathroom or leaving. The next thing I remember was waking up in the hospital.

From what Stella told my mamá and the cops, she found me on the ground passed out near the bathrooms. I had a faint pulse and was "dead weight," but I didn't look hurt or anything. When Stella and our group couldn't get me to respond at all, they panicked and called my mamá.

By the time Mamá got there, I was surrounded by festival security and the police. She went crazy, having our security team question everyone, from the group of girls they found me near to the people at the booth, putting the fear of God in all of them. They were all concerned that I had been drugged and took me to the hospital.

Once I got to the hospital, still unconscious, they pumped my stomach, hooked me up to an IV, catheter, and heart monitor. Not knowing what I was given, they treated me like I'd had a drug overdose.

The doctor told them that I was indeed drugged with what was commonly known as the date rape drug. The drugs are powerful and dangerous. They can be slipped into your drink when you are not looking. The drugs often have no color, smell, or taste, so you can't tell that you've been drugged. They can affect you very quickly, and they cause victims to become weak, confused, and even pass out. The doctor informed my mamá that I was given GHB and a good amount of it. That I was lucky they found me when they did. While they examined me, they noticed blood between my legs, and to everyone's worse nightmare, my virginity had been taken from me.

Finally, after several hours, I woke up to my new reality. Waking up to my mamá crying next to me in a hospital bed, I had never been so scared in my life. All the feelings came rushing over me: shame, anger, guilt, shock, and most of all, fear. I know it wasn't my fault, but I still tell myself, if only I hadn't gone out… Everyone's life changed that night, not just mine. I went to our house in Spain, where I recovered and started to put my life back together, which included me barricading myself in my room.

After a lot of therapy, my therapist and I think the guy must've known me, liked me, or just didn't want to hurt me seriously. It seems he took what he wanted and let me go. I had just a few bruises, no scratches, and he even put me in a safe spot where my friends would find me.

I thank God every day that I didn't get pregnant or contract any STDs. I don't remember anything, and that really messes with your head. I'm thankful and somewhat lucky because some of the girls in my group therapy weren't so lucky, and listening to their stories breaks my heart. My biggest fear is that I don't even know what he looks like and that he's still out there.

I keep hoping that one day I'll remember a face or something, anything. Because not remembering anything makes me paranoid. So many things still run through my head, like, did I know him? Did I fight him? How did he get to me? There're just so many unanswered questions, and I'm confident that's why I'm still having anxiety and panic attacks. The music scene has its good—and its bad.

My parents have always been protective of me. But after the attack, you can say I lost all freedom and privacy. I'm never alone unless in the studio or my house; even then, usually someone's around. I haven't had any serious boyfriends besides a couple of guys I went on dates with in college. I even made one have sex with me so I could get over that phobia. It was okay, nothing like my books say or even my girlfriends.

Listening to my girlfriends talk, I think I was just too young and stressed with wanting to get it over with so I wasn't this broken girl anymore. Of course, it didn't help we had to hurry since I'm always watched. I've only told my girlfriends about Mark Kast, my first boyfriend. I was more embarrassed than anything, but I got it over with and I had sex. I know I can be with another man and that I'm very sexual, but I'm waiting for "the one." The one who makes me stop breathing—and not in the panic attack way. I want something like my parents have, but being sheltered with my bodyguards always watching makes it pretty hard to meet men.

At least I know that men are not the issue. Shit, I would love to find someone to be with, share intimate things with, and feel that complete security. The incident itself wasn't traumatic because, honestly, I don't remember anything. It's the aftermath of knowing he's still out there. That is what I have nightmares about—the unknown and being violated by someone who hasn't been caught. I know I sound like a broken record, but five years ago next month changed my life forever, but I will be damned if I let it ruin my life.

Alexandria

Music vibrates through my body like blood pumping through my veins, making me move to the beat. With my eyes closed, I feel it in my soul. If every day could be like this, I would be in heaven. Suddenly, a hand slides around my waist, pulling me from my sedated state. Mmm, a hard, muscular chest pressing against my back, feeling a hand swiping my hair to the side with warm breath on my neck makes my nipples harden in arousal. My body starts to tingle all over, wetness building up between my legs and making my panties stick to my bare skin. When I feel lips on my neck, I try to turn to see who's behind me. But I suddenly feel as if my body is in slow motion and I can't move, only feel. Fear…

In a panic, I bolt straight up in bed, sweat beading on my forehead and looking around the room to realize I am home alone in my bed. "Dammit."

Frustration starts to take over the fear I was feeling, and

I'm questioning myself as to why I'm having these nightmares all of a sudden. I use to have them every day, but through the years, they have become less and less. That is, until a month ago, when I started preparing for my move to the States.

I put my hands over my face, trying to calm my heart from beating like it's going to explode out of my chest. After a few moments, I gain control of myself. I lie back, closing my eyes with a deep breath. *Please, God, one day, let me remember*. I can't keep going on like this, and I'm pretty sure the nightmares are because I'm stressed about the move back to the country where it all happened.

Letting out a frustrated breath, I know I won't be able to go back to sleep, so I get up. I shake my head, trying to clear away the bad dream, and run my hand through my thick brown hair, readjusting it on top of my head in a loose bun.

Exhausted, I tell myself, "Seriously, Alex, get it together."

Needing to get my mind off my dream, I head to the only place I have peace, the studio. If I'm going to be up this early, I might as well be productive and make some music. Music has always been therapeutic for me, and it's when I feel the most carefree and relaxed.

After that day, I never really left the house, or my room, for that matter. I threw myself into music and withdrew from everyone. I was so in my head, struggling with myself over not being able to remember anything, and I couldn't take the looks of pity either. So I swallowed myself up in my passion, which wasn't hard with the family I have.

My papá, Lucas "Luc" Mancini, is an international DJ and goes by DJ Luscious Luc. He met my mamá, Maria "Mia" Lopez, when he was in Ibiza playing for a weekend music festival. They had me young, and you would think it would've put a kink in his plans to become an international star DJ with his own record label, but it just made him push harder.

They are the reason music is in my soul. For as long as I can remember, I've always been in the studio. Being the daughter of two international icons, I guess it was in my genes, but there's always the pressure of being as good or failing them.

Since Papá's from the States and Mamá's from Spain, we have two homes now and travel between the two. I've stayed here in Spain for most of my life. After the incident, I became more withdrawn, not wanting to leave. I took online college classes for a while, but eventually finished at the nearby university.

A few years after I was born, my parents started a record label called Spin It that was based out of New York. But they mostly lived in Spain with my mamá's family while I was growing up. She traveled with him as much as she could. I know it was hard on them for a while, going back and forth, but Mamá always felt better being with her family while Papá traveled doing shows.

I received a business degree, but my love is producing music. For the most part, I've been kept in the background of my parents' fame, and they shield me from the craziness of the politics, fans, enemies, and most of all, men. Really, all I can say is I've lived a sheltered life.

Since Mamá can sing, my papá used her vocals to make a couple songs, which turned them into international superstars, with the songs hitting number one worldwide. You can tell my parents are madly in love with each other and enjoy what they do. I love music and have always known I would be in the music business somehow.

Closing my eyes and listening to the beat, I clear my mind and start to relax.

The opening of the door to the studio pulls me from my trance. Feeling the strain on my eyes from staring at the computer screen, I look up at the clock, realizing I've been here for over two hours. Pinching the bridge of my nose to relieve some pressure, I glance over to see Brant, my personal bodyguard, standing in the doorway, so I turn in my chair while taking my headphones off before I acknowledge him. "Good morning, B."

He leans against the doorframe. "I saw you on the monitors. Can't sleep?"

Turning my head slightly toward him, I keep staring at the monitor and reply tiredly, "Yeah, another bad dream."

Not wanting to see the worried look on his face, I keep looking at the screen when he responds with a concerned voice. "Want to talk about it? Is it the same one?"

I feel sorry for worrying him. Brant Bolton—I call him "B"—was assigned to me after my unforgettable night five years ago and has become a permanent fixture in my life. He's a good-looking guy, but more like a brother than a bodyguard. He's only three years older, and we've learned to trust each other and have matured tremendously together since he goes everywhere with me. Brant's much more than just a bodyguard, he's family, which has made our bond unbreakable. I call my security team our brutes since all of them are big, badass boys.

Before I reply, I lean back in my chair. I turn my head to face him again with a half-assed smile as I try to convince him I'm all right.

"No, I'm okay. It's the same one. I think I'm just stressed about the move."

"Well, if you need to talk, I'm up and around."

"Okay. Thanks, B."

With a nod, he closes the door. I think over the last year I've truly tested our friendship, or should I say, his job. When I took a year off after graduating college to travel Europe, it was hard on him, my parents, and our security team.

A year ago, I traveled with my best friend and a couple of girl DJs to Europe for my parents' label. It was the best thing for me, a year of freedom with no parents or my grandmother. During this time, I feel I really found myself. Thinking about the girls and the bond we all shared this last year warms my heart. It was a huge eye-opener for me to be on my own to experience the music scene, or rather, life without my parents' influence. This last year has been the best time of my life and the scariest. Being sheltered all those years and then jumping right into life was exhilarating.

After saving my work, I close down the computers and I stretch, deciding I need to start my day. I have so much to do before I leave tomorrow. I'm pretty excited about having my own place in New York. I've shipped most of my stuff there already. Mamá's getting everything settled for me, so I don't have to deal with all that once I arrive.

For as long as I can remember, I have been kind of a recruiter for my papá when it comes to music. I'm always on my computer, downloading or searching for new music. Two years after my incident, Papá had me start going through music for the label, telling him what I thought of certain DJs or singers. Working with him started to pull me from my seclusion. That is how they got me to start taking trips back to New York, using music for me to meet people I recruited for him.

I'm excited to be working with my parents full time. I miss being around them, and it's become harder and harder to leave them after my short visits. I have started to love being in New York, though I'm anxious about working at the label. I usually just stop by the office with Papá, but I tend to prefer working from the safety of my own home. I have always been more behind the scenes with the music, although these last few years, my papá has tried to pull me more into the business side of the label.

It was a shock to both my parents when, at the end of my college education, I told him I was going to come back to work for a record label and travel for a year. I think they were more shocked I wanted to travel than the working part. Papá lost his shit at first, but thankfully, Mamá stepped in, reminding him I'm a grown woman and he needed to treat me like one. In the end, he decided since I was going to be traveling with my girlfriends as they went on their European music tour, I should start off managing them.

After breakfast, I head out to the pool to relax while going over emails and work stuff. Our house in Spain is the most beautiful place on earth. Our estate is a very secluded property, tucked away in twenty acres of vineyards, on the outskirts of Zaragoza, Spain. My parents bought the Spanish estate when I was ten years old, moving my grandparents in with us. The estate is massive with six bedrooms, but Papá made two rooms into a state-of-the-art music studio, along with an office. My grandfather passed away a few years later, when I was just a teenager. So it was mostly just my grandmother and me who lived there full time, along with the staff, of course.

Going over my emails, I notice Brant stalking toward me, looking completely stressed. I can always tell when he's uneasy by the way he walks. His shoulders are tense, which makes them even more massive than they already are, but most of all, his jawbone is clenched. If he doesn't have on sunglasses, his hazel eyes will give away all his emotions. Brant's eyes change when he's pissed off. He's a hulk of a man next to me at six foot two inches, with a body builder type of body and massive shoulders, along with thighs to match. I tried to get him to grow his hair out, but he says it's easier to keep short.

Trying to hide my amusement, I lift my hand to use as a visor to look up at him through my sunglasses. "What's up, B? You seem stressed."

"Well, I sent in my report for last month. Just thought I would let you know I had to say we went to Club Monico. Maybe you can contact Beau so he won't mention it to your father, but I'm sure he will. Even though nothing happened, he'll probably say something."

Beau is the owner of our security team, BB Security, and

my father's best friend.

"It's okay, B. Papá can't keep me from everything. He'll be more upset I found out more about his past than he intended me to. Don't worry, I'll take full responsibility for going to the nightclub. Just say I forced you or tricked you."

I laugh as I say the last part since that has become Brant's and my motto this last year.

He would always tell my parents I was throwing a tantrum or that I wouldn't listen to him. We came up with that one after I went to my first after-hours party. I had an anxiety attack, but we both got through it. Papá flipped out, but I told him he needed to get over it, that I'd be going to more big clubs, after parties, and events. I still haven't been to a music festival since that day. So why not make the first one I go to special by going to the same music festival where my virginity was stolen five years ago? After that night in New York, I've only been going to small events and nightclubs for the label, but I need to move on by going to a big festival to overcome this anxiety.

Just thinking about it makes my stomach turn. I get anxiety attacks when I'm in crowded places, but usually, I can control them so no one knows. Brant probably can tell, but he just watches me, seeing if I will need him. I haven't since the first few times going into the clubs.

When I have an anxiety attack, it ripples through my body, making it so it's hard for me to breathe. I remind myself that I'm in control, that nothing will happen to me. I had only one full-blown panic attack this year where I passed out in a club, but it was because so many people were in the club and then a fight broke out, sending me into an attack. I just felt like I couldn't breathe, that someone was watching me, or that they could take me again.

I get those feelings all the time, like someone's watching me. When I told Brant, he just laughed and said, "Yeah… Alex, you have at least four bodyguards watching you at all times." But I know the difference.

Brant waves his hand in front of me, looking more irritated than before as he spits out, "Hello, Alex. Daydreaming again? Just let me know what you tell Beau or your father. That way I don't lose my job."

I reply, in my sassiest voice, "Like you would lose your job. B, you're stuck with me for life or until you quit this arrangement. I'm sure I'll be getting a call from one of them."

Before he turns to walk away, he barks out, "Just try not to get us in too much trouble, Alex."

When we're here at the estate, Brant can be more relaxed. He usually just hangs out with me. It's nice to have him around in a casual friend way, not like some of the other guys who just stand around watching. Brant heads to the end of the pool while taking his shirt off, showing his dark, hairless chest, along with his six-pack. The man's a machine with every muscle tight and lean. I just have to admire him.

In the last couple of years, he has fully filled out. I think we both look completely different from how we did a year ago. He's even bulkier since we changed up our workouts, or should I say, I started to work out. That entailed him working out even more than he usually does. His chest is about twice the size now, along with his arms that are the size of my thigh. While I've been toning my body, I shrunk two sizes.

Being away from my grandmother's cooking for so long shows. I stand at five feet four inches and have way too many curves. My butt's a little too round for my liking, with my breasts on the larger side, along with a tiny waist. I had weighed about one hundred and fifty before we went to Europe, but I came back at one hundred and twenty. I never actually paid attention to my weight, but touring with three girls who were crazy about their weight as well as with what they wore made me think about it myself.

I changed my workouts and what I wear. I used to be in jeans or shorts with flip-flops and a baggy T-shirt. Now my friends have me in sky-high heels and designer clothes that fit my form and show off more than Papá would probably like. This last year when I was away from my family, I found myself. Everyone back home in New York will be surprised to see how much I have changed. I'm sure of it.

I continue to watch Brant as he pulls himself up out of the pool to sit on the side. He looks over, catching me looking at him, and it makes him smirk while wiping away the water from his face. "Did you send the rest of your stuff, or do you have more shit for us to send?"

"No, I sent everything I'm going to send. Everything else will stay here for when I visit. I just have my suitcase."

With a nod, he leans back so the sun shines on his face. Mimicking him, I throw my head back, letting the sun beat down on my own face. I'm going to miss this place and how quiet it is. Things are going to change for me and I'm excited, but I'm anxious about it as well. I don't like the unknown.

One month prior – Madrid, Spain

When she enters the club, my body senses her before I even

see her. Instinctively, I pull my Kangol hat down lower on my face, adjusting my sunglasses, and allowing me to stare at her without being noticed.

Alexandria Mancini…*mi belleza*. She is my beauty and my obsession.

I fought with myself for hours, telling myself not to come, but I can't seem to stay away from her. The connection we have is indescribable. I know she feels it too because when I get close, she seems to tense up, looking around.

I try to disguise myself so no one can recognize me. The last thing I need is groupies trying to maul me while I'm watching her. I'm only here to make sure she is okay and just watch. I fight with myself, knowing she is protected, but I still need to watch her. I don't know why I do it or why I don't just go and talk to her, but then I tell myself it's not the right time, that I need to make a grand gesture when I first get introduced to her. Plus, with her being so protected and having a wall of men guarding her, I need to plan. Just a little bit longer.

I watch her slide her hand over her voluptuous breasts gracefully, grasping her silky brown hair and shifting it over her shoulder. She tilts her head back, laughing with her friends, and it has my cock jumping to life. My mouth waters just thinking about sinking my teeth into her flawless neck.

Fuckin' hell, she is beautiful and mine!

Yes, I need to find a way to plant myself permanently in her life because Alexandria is my future. I can feel it in my bones.

Alexandria

The next morning, I lie in bed trying not to get emotional about leaving today. It'll be a while before I come back. With taking on a full-time job at the label, along with the festival coming up, it'll be hard to get away.

The sound of the house phone ringing jolts me from my thoughts. I look down, seeing it's my mamá.

A smile spreads across my face when I answer the phone, speaking in Spanish, "Mamá, how are you?"

With excitement, she replies, "*muy bien, mija!* Are you all set?"

We speak Spanish to each other most of the time unless other people are around. "*Sí, Mamá*. I'll be in New York by early evening."

Mamá hesitates before replying. "Okay, well, Papá and I will be at the office then we'll go straight to dinner."

"Okay, I'll see you soon. Love you, Mamá."

"Have a safe flight, *cariño*. I love you too."

Looking at myself in the mirror as I get ready, I see her. We look like we could be sisters. She had me at twenty, and from what I know, it wasn't an easy pregnancy. She is so petite and is still stunningly beautiful. I'm a mix of both my parents if you look close enough. I have my papá's crystal blue eyes and full, heart-shaped lips, but overall, I resemble my mamá. He towers over us at six foot two inches with his muscular build and dark wavy hair. He's all chest, with broad shoulders and some tattoos. Like my friends say, "All Italian."

Mamá, on the other hand, is a little shorter than me at five foot two. She has olive skin, with long curly brown hair to her waist and the most beautiful light hazel eyes with the longest eyelashes. She's super slim with just enough curves.

Since my long hair takes forever to dry, I just put it up in a loose bun for the flight. Knowing I'll be stopping at the office before dinner, I slide on some skinny jeans that hug my ass, fitting just right but not too tight, and a red button-up shirt with matching red heels. I try to look professional but casual just in case.

My papá's family comes from money and owns the building that Spin It is located in downtown, and we occupy the top four floors. The top two floors are where all the suites and offices are located. The next floor down contains the studio and conference rooms. I haven't been on that floor in quite some time since I usually use the studio at my parents' penthouse. The next floor down are our security offices, where BB Security's main office is located.

Brant's speaking to me when I look up, dazed from my thoughts. "What did you say, B?"

He's irritated. "You need to quit daydreaming, Alex. Are

you ready to head to the airport? If so, I'll call to have the car pulled around." I nod my head yes.

With my iPod blaring one of my mixes, I settle in on the plane then start to look at my calendar for the month. I'll have a busy month being back and taking on a full load, along with the festival.

I like doing this job, being in control of people, or rather, planning their events. Being in charge of a performer includes me making sure they have transportation, arranging their flights, hotels, car services, and so forth. I need to make sure the event or club has the right equipment for them to perform. I also set up security and review the contract with whoever wants to book them, like time, date, cost, and any requests from the performer.

Brant touches my arm, making me jump in my seat, so I pull my headphones down to hear what he's saying. Brant apologizes, letting me know we're close to New York. I smile, nod my head, and put my headphones back on.

As I walk off the plane, I notice a black SUV along with a limo in the hanger. I automatically think my parents are here, so I start walking over to the limo when its back door opens, and Papá's golden boy Emmett slides out, making me stop in my tracks.

"Emmett? E, is that you?" I am both shocked and amused at the same time. *This can't be Emmett Tate?*

Emmett looks just as shocked. "Damn, Alex, look at you. Jesus, you look stunning."

I start walking toward him while he holds the door to the limo and smiles at me. "Holy shit, Emmett? Did you do some steroids or eat half the county in the last year? You're huge."

The Emmett Tate I knew was at least fifty pounds lighter and a computer geek. The man standing in front of me is no geek, more like a professional football player with his enormous chest and muscular shoulders. *Uh...definitely not a geek anymore.*

His gray shirt makes his green eyes pop, while the shirt shows off his well-defined upper body and ripped abs like it's a second skin to him. His baggy jeans hug his lean hips, yet strain around his thighs, letting me know they are just as firm.

In a baritone voice, he says, "Shit, girl, I think since you lost so much weight I look even bigger. I think both of us have changed since the last time we saw each other. We are not kids anymore, baby girl."

Emmett has been working under my papá, kind of like a protégé. When I was at the office with Papá, I got to know Emmett pretty well. He was such a computer nerd, always helping me, but since I've been gone, we haven't seen much of each other. From what I know, Papá thinks he's the next up-and-coming DJ.

When I reach him at the limo, Emmett stands up, towering over me, and he leans down to embrace me. I squeak, "Jee-Zus, E, your arms are like vise grips." I hug him back, and then he pulls away to look at me.

"Turn around and let me see you. Damn, you look *fucking hot.*"

My cheeks redden at hearing his comment. Man, has he

changed since I last saw him. I pull away, disconnecting our touch. Looking a little puzzled, I ask him, “No offense, E, but what are you doing here? Where are my parents?”

Emmett grabs the door to the limo. “I’m here to pick you up and take you to Club Spin where your parents are.”

Blank-faced and without thinking, I start rambling off questions like some spoiled brat having a tantrum. “Wait…Club Spin? Why are my parents there and not at the office? Why didn’t they just text me?”

I close my mouth, realizing I just sounded pretty pathetic. Glancing over my shoulder, I see Brant coming up beside me, so I turn my gaze to the SUV where our security team is. This is just too weird, very unlike my parents.

Brant feels my anxiety and leans into me, “Alex, get into the limo. We will be going to meet your parents now. Would you like me to ride with you?”

I still don’t move but turn back to face Emmett. “No, B. I’m good. I just hate not knowing.”

I proceed to get into the limo with a smirking Emmett in my wake. Brant gets into the front seat of the limo, and then we’re off to meet my parents.

Once settled inside, Emmett throws his head back, laughing a full-hearted laugh while he puts his hands on his massive thighs. “Well, baby girl, at least some things haven’t changed.”

Baby girl? Maybe he thinks I’m still some spoiled brat—or maybe he has spent too much time with Papá—since he is the only one who calls me baby girl.

Feeling embarrassed after my outburst of questions and not wanting to show it, I try to settle more into the seat like I’m still getting comfortable.

His smile reaches his eyes and he continues, "I guess they altered your plans."

He leans back in his seat as if he's waiting for me to flip out like some little girl again. He has that arrogant smile on his face like he knows what's going on and isn't telling me. Emmett has known me for many years and has seen his fair share of my tantrums.

Letting out a huff, I pull out my phone to dial Mamá's cell. When she answers, I can barely hear her over the music in the background.

"*Mija*, I'm glad you're home safely. Did Emmett make it there yet?"

Trying to act normal, in a sweet voice, I reply, "Yes, Mamá, he's here and…" I pause. I can tell he's staring at me with that goddamn smirk on his face. I get an uneasy feeling in my stomach then shake it off, telling myself this is Emmett we're talking about. He just looks different, but then again, I look different too.

Focusing on my call, I try not to sound irritated by keeping my voice pleasant. I ask another barrage of questions, but this time in Spanish so only she understands. "We are on our way, but why did you send him? Why am I meeting you at the club and not the office?"

She laughs softly. "We sent the car to pick up Emmett to come here, so we just had him swing by to get you first. Papá wanted you here tonight so we can support Emmett while he performs tonight with two of our rookie DJs."

I start to rattle questions off in my head, but I don't want to say them out loud. So I try to focus, letting out a long breath while saying nothing. I look to Emmett, who's still smiling and staring at me.

When I don't say anything, Mamá laughs, "I'll see you soon, *mija*." Then she hangs up.

Looking down at my attire, I start to feel uneasy. I'm not dressed for a club, but this is just not like my parents. I take another breath to try to relax. *I hate not knowing what I am doing.*

Club Spin is my parents' club. They purchased the massive venue just three years ago, and it's become one of the hottest clubs in New York. I haven't been there in over a year.

I look over at Emmett with no expression on my face, still trying to put my finger on how I'm feeling. This isn't the same reclusive, geeky, timid, Emmett I knew. Instead, he's larger, more confident. I guess we have both grown up this last year.

I fold my arms over my chest. "So, you're headlining tonight. You've made impressive progress, I see, from producing to headlining. I guess I've missed a lot."

While I'm speaking, his eyes roam over my body, stopping at my chest. Realizing that I'm pushing my breasts up with my arms crossed, I unfold my arms. I look back at him and see he's now looking in my eyes with excitement radiating off him. It makes his whole attitude change from cocky guy to a bright-eyed, beaming kid. "Yes, it's a big night for me. I need to prove to your pops I can rock the house with this size club so I can move on to the next level. I'll be performing all month before the festival, hoping to fill a spot."

I tilt my head to the side with a devilish smile on my face, chuckling. "I see." I know Papá and his "levels."

First, a performer needs to submit his demo. Then our team weeds out the train wrecks from the good ones. I have been doing this for Papá since I was little. He then listens to the ones we think are good, and when he hears something that intrigues him, he brings in the DJ. He puts that DJ in various gigs around New York or wherever they come from. After they're in the nightclubs, he moves them up based on the size of the club or the event. Emmett has been with us for a while now. He's always with Papá, so I've never heard him play. But I know he's a great producer and works a lot with Papá on miscellaneous stuff for the record label.

I reach up, turning on the overhead light. I pull out my compact to inspect my appearance, letting my hair down from the loose bun it has been in since this morning. It's almost dry, so I try to fix it to avoid looking like I just got off a plane. My long, thick curls fall down my back, while I adjust my bangs to the side. That's when I hear what sounds like a growl come from Emmett.

Did he just growl at me? Emmett makes another noise.

Oh. My. God. That was definitely a growl.

My body tenses up, but I try to ignore him while I apply some makeup. The overhead light shines right in my eyes, so I can't see his face across the limo. Usually, I don't wear too much makeup. But since we're heading to the club, I apply more so I don't look so jet-lagged. We don't talk while I fix myself up. I feel his eyes on me, staring me up and down, taking in all my new curves and making my body tingle. Once I'm finished, feeling a little bit better about the way I look, I turn the light off and put my stuff back into my purse so I don't keep fidgeting.

Crossing his arms over his chest, Emmett puffs it out so it looks even bigger than it already did. "Baby girl, you look gorgeous. Quit fidgeting. Your hair's longer, you've changed so much, you're even more breathtaking than I remember.

Your Europe trip seems to have done you a lot of good."

Silence. *I've changed? Shit, more like, he has changed. I'm used to the shy, quiet Emmett.*

With a smile, I reply, "E, I am the same person you text and email with. Nothing has changed."

Emmett lets out a rush of breath. "Naw, you look *way* different."

Finally getting my thoughts together, I change my expression to look a little playful as I correct him. "Emmett, who are you, and what've you done with my friend E? What's up with the nickname 'baby girl'? You must have been hanging around my papá too much since he is the only one who calls me that. You know I go by Alex, and yes, I had a fantastic time. Thank you."

There's silence for a few minutes while we stare at each other, both trying to figure the other out. I see him looking me up and down again. I want to panic like a spoiled little brat, but I've come a long way these last few years, trying to keep my tantrums to myself. It doesn't take a lot to bring out my Spanish temper.

Emmett leans forward with his arms resting on his thighs, and of course, he has that fucking cocky-ass grin. "What, you don't like the new me, Alex?" He pauses with a devilish smirk before continuing. "I've done a lot of changing over the year, and maybe I have been around your pops too much. Or maybe I like calling you baby girl."

A feeling of nervousness and irritation takes over my body. My hands start to sweat, and my body feels hot and cold. Being an only child, I get my way and I'm a hot-headed girl, so I'm trying to keep myself in check. I'm not used to being around guys unless my bodyguard, my parents, or my girlfriends are with me. It is very rare that I am alone with someone. I reply in a sassy but sarcastic voice. "Well, I'm not sure if I like this—" I put my hands up to make a quote sign "— 'new you' since I'm so used to the shy E. It's just catching me off guard."

Why do I feel so testy? This is E we're talking about. Who cares if he has totally changed his looks and attitude? He's still E, right? I mean, I have changed everything about me as well.

Feeling his eyes still on me, I look down to make sure all my shirt buttons are closed. I then look out of the window, trying to distract myself from his stare. I notice we're close to the club, and as I look out at the city passing by, I see how much it has changed since I've been gone. Anxiety starts to stir in my belly.

Breathe, Alex. Change is good, just breathe.

Glancing at Emmett, I see he's still looking at me. His intense stare lets me know he's having his own conversation with himself. He actually looks a little stressed or even sad, and I can't put my finger on it.

"E, are you okay? Getting nervous?"

He seems to snap out of whatever he's thinking. "Hell no, I don't get cold feet."

There's that pretentious grin that I want to slap off his face. He finishes arrogantly. "This is what I do, I'm good at it, and I love it."

I laugh out loud. "Cocky, are we?"

Emmett replies in a calm voice. "I have changed a lot over the last year. I am tired of being that shy little guy who is walked all over and taken advantage of, so I am taking what I want and making a name for myself."

I pause, thinking about what he said before I reply. "Well, that makes two of us, now, doesn't it? I am just not used to you being so...so outspoken."

Emmett turns, looking back out the window, "I think it is about time we both get what we want."

Alexandria

Without saying anything, I watch him staring out into the night, wondering what he is thinking. With the streetlights going by, I notice his blond hair's longer too, and he still has flawless skin and a square jawline. The veins in his neck pop out, then he flinches like something outside is making him mad.

He turns to move to the seat next to me and asks, "Are you ready?"

Ready for what? He looks like he is getting ready for a fight.

Right at that moment, the dividing window slides down with Brant yelling over his shoulder, "Alex, stay close. They just messaged me that the club is at full capacity inside."

Brant turns, giving me his serious look. It stresses him out when it's big crowds because of my hatred of being confined, still one of my biggest triggers after the rape. Lately, I have been okay and trying to work it out in my own head, but sometimes I freak out. I don't leave the VIP area, and if I do, I'm with a group.

When the car comes to a stop at the front entrance, Brant gets out, heading toward my door. At the same time, Emmett's out on the opposite side, motioning for me to slide out his door and wearing that damn smile again. I can't help but feel the excitement beaming off him, which brings a smile to my face.

After I pull myself together, I look in the mirror one last time before getting out on Emmett's side. He steps toward me, making me lean back against the doorframe and pinning me. He pulls me even closer to him by sliding his arm around my waist.

Leaning into my ear where no one can hear, he says, "Alex, I am so happy you're back. Do you know how long I've wanted you?"

Before I know what is happening, he gives me a quick kiss and then, without hesitation, turns away, grabbing my hand to pull me with him.

What. The. Hell. Just. Happened?

I'm stunned. No one has ever been so blunt with me or had the balls to do that to me before. It was so fast, I still can't believe it happened. I'm still in shock when Emmett slows our movement, releasing my hand and moving his to the small of my back, guiding me toward the security team.

Seriously. Did Brant see that? What the fuck does Emmett mean how long he's wanted me?

I know I have a dumb-ass look on my face, but Brant doesn't say anything to me. He's on my right then I notice two more guys from our security team walk up, nodding at

Brant. Maybe it's what Emmett just did or all the security huddling around us now, but I start to panic.

I stop in my tracks, trying to gain control of myself. Brant comes up to my side, saying, "Breathe, Alex. I got you."

I need to get over this fucking crowd phobia.

Emmett turns to grab my hand and is pulling me to follow him again. I guess Emmett's getting security too tonight. I follow him into the nightclub, anxiety bubbling up in my stomach. The club is loud and the music's thumping.

I'm still trying to deal with my panic attack when my hands start to sweat and I feel tense all over. Knowing Emmett can feel my hand sweating, I close my eyes for a second, taking a deep breath and listening to the music. Even with my anxiety, I start to pull energy from the nightclub with the music and the people laughing. I let the atmosphere consume me, taking over my anxiety. It is my most favorite thing about an event. With the lights, the music vibrating off the walls, and the energy of the crowd, I feel so free and in control. It helps to suppress my anxiety, and I start to feel alive. I focus on the music while I look around to see anyone I know.

Walking into Spin, you enter a big lounge area with couches lining the walls and a set of restrooms located off to the side. After the lounge, you enter the main room where there are two bars on either side of the building. If you walk straight, you will take a couple steps down to the massive dance area with the stage directly in front of you. Next to the bars are the VIP booths, lining the walls on both sides of the building, all the way up to the stage. The VIP booths are raised higher so you can see over the mass of people on the dance floor. Each booth is secure with its own bouncer and cocktail waitress. The booths give me the security I need to be able to have fun and enjoy the music without the crowd.

Once the VIP area comes into view, I notice all the people.

What the...

I gasp, "*Santa Maria.*" *Oh, my God.*

I hear Mamá squeal and scream from the back of VIP, *"Mija!"*

Everyone in VIP starts yelling, "Surprise! Welcome back, Alex."

My body freezes before I get to the stairs. Emmett turns to stand at my side before he leans in, whispering into my ear, "Surprise. Welcome back, baby girl."

I pretty much tune him out, trying to overcome the surprise mixed with my anxiety. Still not moving, I feel Emmett's hand on the small of my back, guiding me forward. A huge grin instantly appears on my lips, welcoming the greetings from people I know and some I've never met. They all compliment me on how I look or how excited they are that I'm back. Feeling the love and excitement from everyone, I start to relax.

Spotting Papá toward the back, I pause for a minute, taking in my surroundings. I'm intrigued by the DJ who's playing because he's killing it right now on the decks. The crowd loves him. The opening set's hard because a lot of people are not there yet, and if they are, they don't have enough drinks to get on the dance floor. This guy has the floor packed with people dancing, which is what we like to see.

Suddenly, someone's grabbing my hand. Looking to see who it is before pulling away, I realize it's Emmett tugging me toward my parents. I glance back to see Brant not far behind with a not so happy look on his face.

Once we reach Mamá, she notices right away that Emmett's holding my hand. Smirking, she goes to hug Emmett. Without letting go of me, he hugs her with one arm, keeping ahold of my hand.

Okay, this is weird.

Mamá then pulls me into a hug, turning me and making us break our connection. I think Emmett is going to protest. But instead, he heads straight to Papá. Releasing me from her hold, Mamá cups my face to kiss me on my cheek before speaking in Spanish, "What was that all about?"

Noticing she's a little too happy about Emmett holding my hand, I laugh, shrugging my shoulders. "Who the hell knows? He has been acting weird, making me feel testy since he picked me up. Which by the way, you could have given me a heads-up that he was picking me up."

She laughs while giving me a big hug, and she tells me she has missed me.

We walk over to where Papá's talking to Emmett. Once Papá sees me, his face lights up with the biggest smile that shows all his pearly white teeth. He's a very attractive man with short, curly brown hair and blue eyes that match mine. Warmth fills my heart every time I see that smile; it makes me feel so special.

Taking two strides toward me, he embraces me. The first thing out of his mouth is, "Hey, baby girl, stay close to Brant or one of our guys. It's crazy in here tonight. I don't wanna worry about you."

I missed his New Jersey accent. With how heavy it is, you would think I would talk more like him. But by living in Spain for the majority of my life, I'm fluent in both Spanish and Italian, but I favor Spanish.

Here we go. Here comes my lecture.

I look straight up at him since he's so damn tall. Sarcastically, I joke, "Yes, *Dad.*"

I laugh at the expression on his face because he hates when I call him Dad instead of Papá. He gives me his *"I'm your papá"* look before saying, "Don't give me lip. You're my baby girl, and nobody's gonna get near you tonight."

Letting go of his embrace, I laugh, turning to walk toward Mamá, shaking my ass. Over my shoulder, I say, "But what if I want them to touch me?"

His face gets red, frustrated with me, but he doesn't say anything when he turns around to Emmett—who is looking at me with a strange look I can't put my finger on yet. Maybe irritation? Anger?

As the night continues, everything goes great. I'm having a great time with my parents and the people from the label. Everyone can't get over how much I've changed in appearance and how much I've grown up. Emmett keeps staring at me and brushing up next to me, trying to touch me any chance he can.

Noticing my girls aren't here, I turn to Mamá. "Where are the girls?"

"It was short notice when we decided to do this today. Ginger and Izzy have gigs, Stella is still out of town, and Eva couldn't make it last minute."

Not giving me a chance to respond, she tugs me on to the dance floor. I think Papá will flip out since this is the first time I've danced with Mamá at a club, but when I look over at him, he's all smiles. My parents love to dance, and they're both exceptionally good at it. He loves when we dance and sing around the house.

I see Papá coming up to us, and he puts his arms around

Mamá. I turn and keep dancing next to them when I feel a pair of arms wrapping around me. It triggers a flashback from my dreams, and I freeze, slightly panicking, I feel lips next to my ear then a whisper. "Relax, Alex. I told your pops I was going to dance with you."

Sweat beads on my forehead, and I'm still tense as I try to take deep breaths to calm down. This is Emmett. I'm safe. *Goddamn triggers.* I'm still frozen and not moving when Emmett pulls me in closer with my back to his chest. Trying to relax, I take a few breaths, telling myself this is Emmett and not my nightmare. It's just that this position with some-one behind me freaks me out. Breathe. Let the music take over. I'm in control. Shit, I'm still tense, and I try to suppress my fear.

Relax. Breathe.

I look over to see Papá giving me a nod with concern in his eye, and then he puts his head back into Mamá's neck. *Okay, this is Emmett. My parents are here. Take a deep breath, try to relax.*

I start to move to the music with Emmett attached to me. It feels good but just so weird to be in someone's arms. I can feel his chest on my back. Usually, my security would have already had this guy off me. But since it's Emmett, I guess it's okay. He pulls me in tighter. One arm wraps around my waist, while the other moves up and down my thigh. His breathing on my neck brings a wave of heat through my body and be-tween my legs, and my sex starts to ache. I'm so into the music I even think I feel a kiss on my neck.

The music picks up, sending us to the edge right before the vocals drop, which is my favorite part of the song. That's when I feel his erection press against my lower back, and I tense up. The crowd goes nuts, and I try to move away from Emmett, but he pulls me back against his chest. Again, I feel his erection rubbing up against my back, making my nipples harden. I've turned away from him so he can't see how aroused and tense I am. It's like my body and mind are fighting each other, with my thoughts winning.

It just doesn't feel right, so I try to get some space between us by looking over my shoulder and saying, "Let's head over to the VIP. Don't you have to go on in ten minutes?"

Emmett murmurs into my ear while letting out a deep breath, "Yeah, but I want to finish this song with you. I like feeling your body next to me."

The feel of his breath on my neck sends goose bumps down my arms. Not knowing what to say, I just keep moving to the song. Feeling eyes on me, I glance over to my parents, who are staring at us with smiles on their faces.

I don't understand why my parents are looking at me funny. I wonder if they actually want me with Emmett. I wish I knew what was going on. I feel weird suddenly, and Emmett must sense I'm still tense. He takes my hand in his and leads me off the dance floor toward the VIP area.

Before entering VIP, he swings me around, pulling me into his chest while sliding his fingers under my chin and softly pinching it with his thumb, forcing me to look into his emerald-green eyes. His voice is tight like he is struggling. "Baby girl, I'm going crazy watching you dance. The way you move your body makes me so fucking hard. Do you know what you do to me?"

Umm...

Closing his eyes and taking a deep breath before opening them, he leans into me, then continues. "I've waited so long for you to come back…to me. Like I said in the limo, I am going after what I want."

Before I can answer or pull away, he kisses my cheek and pulls me into VIP, leaving me speechless again.

Seriously. What the…

I just can't make my mind decide how I feel. I'm in so much shock I feel like I've been sheltered because no one has ever spoken to me that way.

Still holding my hand, he leads me over to where his music is, releasing me to get his things together. I just stand there looking at him stupidly. I feel totally naïve. If my girls were here, E would've been put in his place and tonight wouldn't be such a cluster fuck or confusion.

Even in college, the guys I dated only told me I looked good or beautiful. They were always polite, with proper manners, nothing as sexual or passionate as Emmett has just been. I have always been in control, the dominant one. I've even had drunk guys come up to me before, but nothing like this. I've read this kind of stuff in books, but I never had it happened to me. I just don't know how to feel about it.

Next thing I know, Mamá is coming up to me, saying she has to go to the bathroom. I'm still in shock, just watching Emmett get his stuff, so she pushes me with her.

Mamá starts rambling off questions in Spanish. "*Cariño*, what's wrong with you? What did Emmett say to you? You look like you've just seen a ghost."

She looks concerned, probably because I have this dumbfounded and shocked as hell look on my face.

I start to laugh so hard I lean over with my hands on my knees.

I reply in English, "Emmett just kissed me again."

Shock spreads over her face. "Again?"

Still laughing, I stand up. "Yes, he kissed me on the cheek getting out of the car, I think on the dance floor, and my cheek just now...again."

When I finish, I take a deep breath to calm myself down from laughing.

She gets a smile on her face. "Well, at least your papá likes him, and he has some big balls." We both start laughing.

I don't tell her I don't feel that way for him. I know my body reacted—who wouldn't respond to a hot guy touching you? —but my mind keeps saying no. I still see Emmett as the geeky, shy boy, but it's just the first day back. Maybe I need to give it some time.

Once I'm back in VIP, I feel eyes on me. I look behind me to see Brant staring at me, pissed off but talking to Eli, Mamá's bodyguard. I walk over to him to see what is wrong when I see he's done talking to Eli.

"B, what's up?" I start to look around anxiously.

With a straight face and without looking me in the eyes, he says, "I don't like that guy."

I look around to see who he's talking about, but I don't see anyone in particular. "Who?"

Brant turns to me, puts a hand on my elbow, and walks me to the corner of the VIP area. He turns me to face him. "I don't like that Emmett guy. I don't like how he's touching you or the way he's looking at you. It's like he's a creeper."

I take a deep breath, putting my hands on Brant's massive biceps. He's so overprotective of me. I guess, being my bodyguard, he's supposed to be. Though sometimes, he goes overboard, even worse than my papá.

Cracking a smile and trying to hold back a laugh, I reply,

"B, he's harmless. I've known him…"

He puts his hand up to stop me and rants on. "I know you've known him for a while, but I never liked him even when he was a scrawny geek. But now that he's all buff boy, I really don't like him."

I try to control my laughter inside. Brant's like an older brother with his protectiveness, but he makes me feel safe when he gets that way. We've had our issues this last year with men trying to touch me or dance with me. My security made it hard for any man to approach me. I've felt sorry for B the past few years since I've started going to clubs. I've told him several times I can handle myself now. I've taken enough self-defense classes, I think. I just need Brant to stand watch in case something goes wrong. But when a guy comes up to dance with me or talk to me, I don't need him pouncing on them.

Usually, I don't let too many people touch me, so he doesn't have it too hard. He knows my facial expressions and knows when I'm panicking or in distress. For him to act and say this is uncommon.

"B, you see I can take care of myself. Emmett's just Emmett, even with his new looks and attitude. No need to stress, big guy."

As I smile at him, he gives me a fuck-you look. He folds his arms over his chest, looking even more pissed off and like I'm not taking him seriously. I notice his eyes are golden brown.

Oh shit, I pissed him off.

"Did you not just have a panic attack on the dance floor when he came up behind you? Did you not just freeze when he embraced you? Believe me, Alex, I am being relaxed, but

I'm telling you I don't like him. I know you're a big girl and can handle yourself. Hence why I haven't taken him down and beaten the shit out of him for kissing you. But I can read you, and you didn't like it."

Oh, God. Who else saw Emmett kiss me?

"B, I know this is hard for both of us, but I'm okay. I understand what you are saying and am listening to you. I've taken in your warning, and if there isn't anything else, let's head back over to the stage where Papá is hanging out."

He just nods his head again, still looking pissed off.

I turn away from him, walking back over to the stage to meet up with Papá and watch Emmett's set. The crowd goes crazy when Emmett drops his first song. Standing to the side of the DJ booth, all I can see are arms moving together in sync, in a completely insane rhythm. I love how the music just makes people come alive.

I have a huge grin on my face when Papá comes up to me. He has a big smile. "What did I say? He's good, yeah?"

I laugh to myself, still with the cheesy grin on my face, "Yes, he is, but then again, he watches and learns from the best."

Papá grins down at me. He puts his arm around my shoulders, pulling me into an embrace while he leans in. "Uh-uh. Nah, this boy has his own way of doin' music."

Neither of us says anything. Instead, we just look at Emmett and the crowd. I watch his style of mixing, listen to make sure he hits the beats and how smooth his transition into the next song goes. His style's real big vocal house with some progressive tribal.

Nice. Very. Nice.

I love when a DJ knows what his crowd is feeling by the

way he looks to them and plays for them. Emmett's kicking ass tonight. I'm moving my head to the beat, embraced by my papá. I feel my body absorbing the music, making me so happy that I slip into my music daze, as I call it. Where there is nothing around me but the sound of music, it's like my soul speaks through the beats.

Papá turns me to face him but leans into me, speaking near my ear so no one else can hear him. "I'm sorry I had E come dance with you. I saw you tense up."

I look up at Papá, seeing his concern in his eyes. I smile my baby girl smile for him and reply in a playful way, "It wasn't a big deal. I was more concerned about you wanting to kick his ass than him dancing with me."

At that moment, Papá throws his head back and laughs, pulling me in for one of his big bear hugs. When he halfway releases me, I see his face turn from laughter to seriousness. "I know I need to let you be a woman and all that, but it's hard. I know you're smart and don't take crap from these DJs or any man, for that matter. This is our business, so I need to trust you to do the right thin'. That includes you becomin' a woman and livin' your life. I can't keep you locked up forever. I need to let you grow up, baby girl. Which is why I'm gonna have you shadow me these next few months."

When he's done, he leans closer, kissing me on my forehead. Speechless with tears building up, I don't let them fall, I just hug him. "Thank you, Papá. You know music's our life, and I love being here in the club with you and Mamá. I want to move forward and be more involved."

We keep hugging when he replies, "I'm tryin'. It's hard with both my girls in one place. The thought of someone touchin' either of you makes me go crazy inside, especially with everythin' goin' on."

I look at him with a puzzled look, even though I kind of know. "What do you mean, with everything going on?" The look in his eyes reveals an understanding that he's said too much.

Turning to look at Emmett, he says, "Nothin' to worry your little head about, baby girl."

"No one will ever physically hurt me again, I promise you that. And I guarantee my brutes will say the same thing. No one will touch me that I don't want touching me. I love you."

We hug and my eyes drift over to where Emmett's mixing. At least, he should be mixing. But instead, he is staring at us with a look to kill. His jaw is clenched, and his veins look like they are going to pop out. I step back from Papá, still staring at Emmett, who leaves the decks and walks over quickly.

Looking straight at me, ignoring Papá, he asks, "Are you okay?"

I look at him like he has lost his marbles. Papá smiles with an arm around me. "She's fine. We're just havin' a heart-to-heart. Now get back on the decks and finish your set." Emmett looks at both of us with concern, but he walks back to the decks.

With amusement on his face and half laughing, Papá says, "Well, it looks like you have an admirer with some really big balls."

In a flat voice, I reply, "Mamá and B said the same thing. But he's still geeky E to me."

He watches Emmett. "Baby girl, so much has changed, and you have a lot to catch up on. That's why I want you with me, learnin'."

Both of us keep watching Emmett, who never misses a

beat. Not once does he lose the crowd, making Papá happy.

I walk back over to the VIP where Mamá is talking to the rookie who had the opening set. He is a good-looking guy, a bit taller than me. When I'm almost to them, he shakes her hand and walks off before I can introduce myself.

"Jeezus, Mamá, where are we getting these DJs from? He is too cute."

She has a questioning look on her face, and I laugh, continuing with a devilish grin. "Are we going for the world record of hottest DJs?"

She gives me a sweet, motherly look, putting her arm around me. "We're trying to find you a good match." We both laugh a good hard laugh at her joke.

The night is a huge success for our record label. When I head out with Mamá, it's around two thirty in the morning and I'm exhausted. Emmett's finishing up his set, and our closing DJ is getting ready. Papá is going to stay with Emmett and the closing DJ to make sure everything goes smoothly and everyone gets paid. I don't get a chance to say good-bye to Emmett since he is still on stage. We leave with Brant, and as soon as we get in the car, I fall asleep, exhausted from being jet-lagged.

I wake up startled, with someone's hands on me. I hear Brant say, "Easy, Alex. It's me." I look up when he is lifting me from the limo.

"B, I can walk."

He puts me down, and we all walk to the elevator. Everyone follows me to my new home, and after doing a quick run-through, they all leave, with Mamá kissing me goodnight and welcoming me home in Spanish. "*Bienvenida a casa, mija,*" she says then heads back to the elevator.

Alexandria

The next morning, still jet-lagged, I wake up in a panic, forgetting where I am. Taking in my surroundings, I realize I'm in my new home. With a deep breath, I lie back and relax until I'm fully awake. And then I start to get excited. *I'm in* my *new home. Mine. Just* me.

After taking a long shower, I'm less stressed, especially since I spent extra time taking care of myself. I feel like I can start my day. I put on one of my mixes, and when the song "Da Bump" by Mr. V featuring Miss Patty starts blaring over the sound system, I close my eyes, take in a deep breath, and smile. *I'm home.* Music flows through the speakers, filling the house, and I bounce around. I continue to dance while organizing my place to my liking.

Mamá and I had planned and gone over where I wanted most of my stuff, and she set pretty much everything up and organized most my belongings. But I unpack my suitcase, reorganizing my personal things.

Halfway through the day, after a visit from Mamá, I look at my phone and see a text from an unknown number. I click on it.

> **EMMETT**
> Thank you for the dance. The night couldn't have been any better. I'm glad you came out to support me on your first night back. Your kisses made it even more special. When can I see you again?

Thinking this could get interesting, I text back.

> **ALEX**
> You're welcome for both the dance and the support. You stealing kisses from me was unexpected. You definitely rocked the house last night, and I was very impressed. Getting settled in my new place and ready for my first day of work tomorrow. I'm sure I'll see you soon. It'll be good to have a friend around.

There. I put out there that he was a friend to me. Hopefully, he gets the hint and lays off the intimate shit.

My first day was overwhelming, to say the least. Papá wasn't lying when he said he was going to throw me into this job. I have five performers that I'll oversee, and with the festival coming up, it's crazy around here. Over the next few weeks, performers will be coming into town for various events leading up to the music festival. Everyone's stopping by to say hello, welcoming me back, or just introducing themselves to me.

I'm knee-deep in contracts for my DJs and the events we have lined up for them when my personal assistant, Eva Lewis, walks in with all the demos that have been turned in this month from rookies.

Eva's one of my close friends and one of our posse of five girlfriends. Eva has been working for Spin It for almost two years, and I'd met her a few times while I visited New York. We hit it off immediately, becoming good friends, and once I knew was coming to work full time, we demanded that she be my personal assistant. My parents loved the idea, and now she works with me.

Eva's very beautiful, petite all around. Thick, blunt-cut black hair to her shoulders makes her face look square. She's just a tad bit taller than I am. Oh, and hell-on-wheels crazy.

Seeing what she's carrying, my eyes bug out, looking at her like she's crazy. "Seriously, you're handing these to me today on my first day here? Don't you see I'm head to toe in paperwork and calls?"

We're close and usually tell each other how it is, but she doesn't say anything. She just looks at me with a "fuck you" smirk and sits down, holding all the demos.

"I'm sorry. I'm under a lot of stress. With it being my first day, I'm a little overwhelmed."

She sets the demos down with a look of concern. "Didn't you get enough rest before coming here? What the hell, Alex?"

I just look at her with tired eyes, "Well, I was rested till my parents dragged me off to Club Spin for a welcome home party till two thirty in the morning after being on the plane all day. I slept some yesterday, but I think I'm still jet-lagged."

She stands up, looking surprised. "Shit, that's right. I'm sorry I couldn't come, it was short notice. I had something with my parents, and since I've been gone so much with you traveling, I couldn't miss it. How did it go?"

I begin to explain to her about the evening's events, along with my conversation with Papá about letting me live my life, but I leave out the parts with Emmett in them.

She stands with her hands on her hips. "Wow." Still looking shocked about Papá, she grabs the demos, turning and leaving with them. She calls over her shoulder, "I'll go through these and give you my opinion to help you narrow it down."

Without another word, she's out of my office. I love how we're so close that she can read me. I think she knows me just as well as Stella does, and we've known each other since we were babies. I turn back to my work, burying myself back in the contract I was working on.

Wednesday rolls around, and it's still a madhouse at the office. Everyone's excited for the event at Club Touch tonight. I'm getting into the swing of things and loving it here. I never knew living alone would make me feel so free; the feeling is amazing. Seriously, no bodyguards, no grandmother, no parents, and no girlfriends. Just me. This last year has made me grow within myself, giving me the power to move on and let the woman inside me out. I like this new me. Well, the *me* I've had inside my head all these years but have been too afraid to let out.

Emmett has stopped by every day with a cup of coffee to say a quick hello. Thankfully, he doesn't hang out too long, but it's nice of him to come by, letting me warm up to his cockiness. I knew I'd love it here with all the people and being around the music scene. Every week leading up to the festival, we have at least two big events. This week, the event are tonight and Saturday night. Tonight, I'm going with the girls. They had come home after we traveled for eleven months, while I went back to our house in Spain, in order to get some rest before my move to New York.

Papá has REX, the rookie from the other night, and Emmett performing. It's supposed to be a huge night. This club's three levels are supposed to be unbelievably beautiful since the renovations.

Around lunchtime, I receive a text:

EMMETT

Baby girl. Looking forward to seeing you tonight, I've missed your smile.

ALEX

Yes, see you there. A-L-E-X, not baby girl. You sound like Papá.

EMMETT

I like calling you that. Save me a dance, and I want

> another good-luck kiss from you. See you tonight.

What the fuck's wrong with him? I feel the tension in my shoulders, and I think I need to have a talk with this "new" egotistical Emmett.

> **ALEX**
> If you quit calling me baby girl, I might save you a dance. We should probably talk tonight about this stealing kisses shit. See you tonight.

Feeling proud of myself, I go to put my phone down when another text comes through.

> **EMMETT**
> A-L-E-X, I WILL have a dance with you, no matter what. Your kisses are my good-luck charm. I can't break the streak. Your lips are mine tonight.

That little shit. Maybe *I have* lived a sheltered life…

I've only ever heard about men speaking to women like this in books or movies. My security team usually intimidates everyone, and I don't generally make myself available for men to approach me. To be honest, I'm often trying to get my anxiety under control. I probably look like a bitch, but really, I'm just freaking out. These past few years, I have been working on myself and becoming the stronger woman that I am now, so men were never really on my agenda. Well, tonight Emmett and I are definitely going to have a talk.

I finish my day's work to try to get home so I'll have enough time to get ready and pick up the girls before heading to the club at ten this evening. I'm excited for tonight. I've been thinking of Emmett all day and trying to figure out how to handle this situation with him. Maybe I'm not giving him a chance. I think about Saturday night and how my parents suddenly forgot they were going to the club. And then at the last minute, they had Emmett pick me up. I think they're up to something, possibly playing matchmaker. I get it, though. Emmett's hot as hell, and Papá really likes him. Maybe tonight I should just have fun and relax. Forget what my mind says and go with the flow. I really need to get laid, I think. I'm twenty-three years old, for heaven's sake.

Alexandria

The girls want me to wear a dress and I was thinking cute little dress shorts, but instead, I think I'm going to go for sexy tonight. I pull out a slinky black dress that I bought on my trip, and I love it. Only having worn it a couple of times in Europe, I'm excited no one here has seen me in it yet. It is very formfitting, to say the least, but it covers all my important parts. It has a deep V-cut in front, showing off my large breasts, but it holds them just right. The back drops down to below my waist, showing off my muscular but petite body. The skirt hugs my hips and is above the knee, so it isn't too short. The girls said it was made for me, and I love the way I feel in it.

Now… What to do with my hair? I decide to throw it up in a loose bun with some strands falling deliberately, then swoop my bangs to the side. I know I will want to dance and get sweaty, plus having my hair up will show off the back of my dress.

Seeing myself in the mirror, I get excited, but I still have to reassure myself it's okay to wear this outfit around my family and remind myself it is club attire. I usually don't dress like this around them, so I'm feeling a bit self-conscious.

As I finish up getting ready, Brant walks in the front door right on time, yelling, "Alex." Brant has a key to my place here, but he only walks in when I've texted him to be here at a certain time. We are both excited to have our own places here in the building, and we are on the same floor. When we lived in Spain, he lived in the house behind our main house. That's where the security team lived. When I walk into the living room, he stops in his tracks and just stares at me. My face turns red, feeling uncomfortable with the intense stare.

"What? Is something wrong with what I have on?"

Brant pulls himself together then shrugs. "No, but do you think that's what you should wear with your father around?"

He knows Papá too well, but I'm a woman now, not some little girl. I'm living my life.

I sound a little pouty. "He told me he was going to let me grow up and live my life. He needs to be able to be around me wearing stuff like this. We're starting to go to the same events and clubs." I pause. "Plus, I'm twenty-three years old and not a kid anymore." I feel stupid since I come across a little like a spoiled brat having a tantrum.

Laughing, Brant says sarcastically, "Don't know if you're trying to convince yourself or me, but we'll see how long that lasts."

The doorbell rings before I can come back with a smartass remark. I head to my bedroom to get my clutch ready so we can leave.

"B, can you get the door? It should be Gin."

Ginger Wolfe—I call her Gin, but she goes by DJ Gin-Gin—also lives in the building, just a floor down. She moved here from West Virginia because Beau knows her father, who's just as overprotective as Papá. Beau's the only reason Ginger was allowed to move up here. Her father is the president of a motorcycle club down there, and he wanted her to be able to experience her music career but with protection. Beau was the best option; I guess they go way back. I don't really know too much since she doesn't talk a lot about her life back home. I do know we are kind of alike in the sense she is running from something. We just don't push each other about personal shit unless we need to talk. Otherwise, we just focus on music and being single girls.

Ginger and I have become really tight over the last year, and I consider her one of my closest friends. Stella is really the only friend who stuck by me throughout my life and is more like a sister. Well, until I met Eva, Gin, and Izzy through the record label. Now I don't know where I would be without my posse.

When I traveled to Europe, it was almost always four of us girls. Stella and Eva took turns traveling with me, then there were Ginger and Izzy, who were the two DJs I managed. Ginger is rising to the top and fast. She has a style that no other girl has right now, producing her own stuff, which I think is what put her on the level of international status. Once she realized that I knew my music, how to mix and produce, she freaked out.

I remember that day like it was yesterday.

Ginger yelled, "Whoa! Shit, girl, you can mix. Why the fuck do you not mix or have your music out there? You're good, Alex."

I shied away from the question. "I don't know, just never had the opportunity and never pursued it."

Not many people know I can mix or produce, but when you used to be with your papá every day, you catch on to it, and my love for music just makes it easier.

That was the day Ginger and I became even closer, bonding over the love of producing.

When the door opens, I turn to see her walking in with a smile. But by the look on her face, I can see she's uneasy, and that's when I notice she's not wearing her normal attire.

Smiling, I look her over from head to toe then tease her. "Nice legs, Gin."

She's always in jeans, a cute T-shirt, and Converse. But tonight, she's in dress shorts, a tight shirt, and heels, not Ginger's usual look. She was born a biker girl, and I guess you could say she's a tomboy at heart and never shows her body too much. She's very attractive with her bangs and long, straight jet-black hair that falls to the middle of her back, light green eyes, and pasty skin. I think she has the most well-proportioned body out of all of the girls—when she shows her assets that is—and she's skinny as Eva but with larger breasts and a round booty. Out of all my friends, I think I have the most curves going on.

Ginger looks at me then her eyebrows shoot up. "*Damn…* Hel-low, boobs."

We look at each other and both start laughing. While we are both laughing, I see Brant is behind her totally checking her out with hooded eyes, not even caring if he gets caught. Not wanting to bring any attention to him, I start for the door.

"Well, let's get this party started."

After picking all the girls up, we head to the club. I am so happy to be back with my girls. The confidence and self-esteem I feel when I am around them are like night and day. It's like I am more empowered with them at my side.

When Brant lets us out at the club, he grabs my arm, pulling me to him so he can whisper in my ear. "Be ready. It's packed like sardines inside. If you need me, just give me a look."

I nod my head in appreciation and start to prepare myself. When we go to new places or clubs, I need to brace myself for being squished together. I notice we have three other security guards walking up, making me wonder why. I look back to see Brant helping Ginger out and saying something in her ear, which also seems fishy, but I don't say anything.

When our team is in place, we head in. As always, Brant follows behind the group and me. He's like me and wants to be in control and see everything in front of him.

Once inside, the place comes alive. "Satisfaction" by Benny Benassi blares through the speakers. A big smile crosses my face when I notice all of us girls are moving to the beat, our heads bouncing while throwing our shoulders side to side, in sync with the music. The lasers start flashing all over, lighting up the club and making my anxiety subside. Usually, when I'm with my girls or my parents, I feel safe. I feel more relaxed with my small group. I still feel the anxiety at the bottom of my stomach, but I suppress it and ignore it. My heart starts to pound with excitement, and I let my body take over and move to the music. Beams of light are flashing everywhere. I feel the energy building up inside of me. I want to dance. The new sound system in here is truly amazing. Grinning from ear-to-ear, I look around to see if I notice anyone.

Suddenly, someone grabs my arm, and I look over to see it's Jason Hughes.

Jason Hughes of Jas Entertainment is our leading promoter. I love working with Jason. I met him a few years back, and we hit it off instantly. He's so upbeat and crazy. Over the last year, I've been in communications with him off and on regarding the label.

It has been forever since we've been face-to-face, but he looks the same, if not better.

"Jason!" I squeal while hugging him.

He pulls away to look at me with his sparkling hazel eyes. "Shit, Alex, I barely recognized you. You look stunning."

I blush. "Still a flirt, I see."

Someone calls his name from behind him, and we both turn while still embracing. After telling the person one minute, he turns back to face me. "Beautiful, I have to go talk to these people. But I promise I'll be over to your booth once I'm done." He squeezes my hand and is off before I can blink.

He's great eye candy with his lean build, blond, surfer-style hair, and beautiful hazel eyes, but most of all, it's his award-winning smile. I love that no matter where he is, he's always smiling. He treated me like a queen when I attended a couple of his events before we left for Europe. He's always flirting with me through text messages or emails. He even asked me out when he knew I was coming to NYC for a visit, but I told him I don't mix business with pleasure. His events are local, always a big deal with a couple of our DJs from our label playing for him, like tonight.

My group is waiting for me—we never leave a girl behind—and we start heading to VIP again. I see my parents in the booth, and the girls make me go up first. Probably to see my papá's expression when he sees what I'm wearing, but it's my mamá's face I see first, which makes me feel much better about what I'm wearing. After giving me a big hug, she spins me around, looking at my outfit. "I love your dress, and you look so beautiful, *mija*."

I hug her again. "Thank you, Mamá."

I smile, turning to Papá, who's already staring at me. Once he sees me looking at him, his face lights up, but his eyes tell me everything. He's not happy with my dress. He does the same as Mamá. Hugs me and then turns me around to look at me. I'm waiting for the lecture. He stands there and leans in. "You look so beautiful. You're all grown up. I love you, baby girl."

Shock spreads across my face. He smiles, leaning in again to say, "If you leave B's side, I'll ground you, though." We both throw our heads back laughing, then he pulls me in for one of his big bear hugs.

I turn around to face Ginger, who's staring at me. I walk over to where she's standing with a look of, "How did it go?"

I laugh, throwing my hands in the air. "Let's get a drink."

Eva squeals with her high-pitched voice. Everyone knows I won't get drunk and that I don't take drinks from other people. I've had a phobia of public drinks unless there's a lid or cover since that day five years ago. I usually only like to do shots or drink bottled water. I don't trust too many people giving me drinks, and I won't even take a drink from a bartender.

Usually in VIP, we have bottle service where I'll pour myself a shot. If someone's going to slip drugs in the whole bottle, then I won't be the only one passing out.

We take a couple of shots of Patrón then head to the dance floor. The crowd is insane. We can barely move so we decide to go back to VIP to dance around there.

Ginger grabs me by the arm. "Let's go on stage. I want to see what these guys are playing on." I nod then head that way.

Papá's on stage with Emmett when we walk up. When Emmett sees me, his mouth is firm with no expression, but his eyes squint together and he looks irate.

Shit. Don't panic.

The look he gives me is so intense I have to take a couple breaths before I get to them. I introduce Emmett to Ginger, but they already know each other, and I make a mental note to talk to her about it later. She didn't look happy to see him. I brush it off, thinking they both work for us, so I'm sure they see each other in the studio or have played together before.

Emmett hugs me, his hands sliding down my arm to the small of my back, and he pulls me into his chest. Taking a breath, he says in my ear so no one can hear, "Fuck, Alex. How am I supposed to DJ with my cock stiff as a rod with you looking so fucking good?"

I pull away from his embrace, trying to process what he just said to me. I don't say anything but try to hide the emotion on my face.

Why am I always shell-shocked? Why can't I say anything or react to him?

Papá is staring at us. Not wanting to cause a scene, I just smile. Papá finishes his conversation then heads over to stand behind our rookie DJ, who's DJing right now. Ginger heads over to check him out also, and once she is in conversation with Papá, I'm jerked back into Emmett's embrace. Before I can even think to move, he pulls me to the side of the stage, behind a huge speaker.

I squeal, "Emmett."

His voice is pained. "Alex, Jesus you look so…" Standing still, I just look at him, speechless. Emmett is looking like he is trying not to lose control and he continues. "…so fucking good, I'm having a hard time controlling myself. Fuck… I can't even think straight right now."

I'm still shocked, but I start to get pissed when I can't move, so I try to push him off again. This time, Emmett lets me have some space, but he doesn't let me go completely. Flushed and red as hell, I look up. "What the hell, E? What has gotten into you? We are friends."

He has one hand around my waist holding me to his chest, and the other is at the nape of my neck, halfway in my hair. I straighten up to pull away some more. Still sounding pained, he growls, "What if I don't want to be just friends anymore? I've sat by for so long doing nothing, but you're back here now, and I want to date you, Alex."

Before I can respond, I hear a familiar voice. "Alex? You all right?"

Thank God.

Brant is standing to my side, so Emmett lets go of me but doesn't move away. Before I turn to Brant, I take a deep breath to gain control. But when I speak, my voice comes out weak, giving away my state of emotion. "Yes, B. I'm fine, just a conversation between old friends."

Quickly, I walk away from both of them. I feel Emmett's intense stare on my back telling me to stay and talk, but I don't look back. I just keep walking with Brant right on my ass. Once out of Emmett's sight, Brant grabs my elbow, pulling me to face a very pissed-off man.

He looks like he is going to explode, and I can see in those golden-brown eyes that he is not happy. "What the fuck was that, Alex?"

Santa Maria, *he's pissed.*

"What the fuck just happened, Alex? Do I need to put him in his place?"

Still stunned at how angry Brant is, I don't reply. But instead, I just look up at my brute. His eyes change from hazel to golden brown when he's pissed, and right now they are pretty brown to me.

Shit.

He continues. "He had his hands all over you, and you were pushing him away. I was going to come beat his ass, but I know you are friends with him and he's close with your father, but still, he was pushing pretty hard, Alex." He keeps holding my elbow, which keeps me close to him.

I come to my senses, "B, I'm okay. He was just talking to me. He wants to date me. I told him no, that we're just friends. Relax. You're right it took me off guard the way he was acting, but he's a friend. Plus, you can't go beating up every guy who approaches me or wants to date me."

Pulling myself away by my elbow, I break free of his hold. I hear him take a deep breath and see him closing his eyes, trying to relax. When he speaks, I can tell he's trying to control his anger. "Alex, it's one thing for a guy to come on to you, and another thing when he's manhandling you. I'm here to protect you, not let men assault you. Regardless if he's your friend or not, he needs to respect you. If you want to be with him, I'll back off. But otherwise, *he* needs to back the fuck off."

Jesus, he's really pissed.

I put my hands on his shoulders, hoping to calm him down more, and I speak in an understanding, soothing voice. "Yes, B, I understand. I'll talk to him tomorrow when we're not in a club screaming at each other. I agree with you one hundred percent."

My mind is going a million miles a second with so many questions spinning around. I head back to VIP where the other girls are. They take one look at me, and Ginger exclaims, "What the fuck happened to you?"

I proceed to tell them about what Emmett said and how he has been acting from when he picked me up at the airport to our embrace just now. They all have their mouths open in shock because I don't do kissing, and I don't let any guys near me. I hug people, but that is pretty much it. Eva's always the one to mouth off first. "What the fuck?"

Ginger is folding her arms. "Shit. Alex, what are you going to do?"

That is when all of them start talking at once. Feeling overwhelmed, I can't help but burst out laughing. "Fuck it." I shrug my shoulders.

The girls are all saying variations on, "Who are you, and what have you done with Alex?"

I don't know how to feel, so this is all new to me. In Spain, I experienced independence but never really explored dating or men. I was having too much fun just being me without my parents. Don't get me wrong, men approached me or asked me to dance, but nothing so blunt and straightforward as Emmett is doing. The girls talk about men and sex regularly, but shit, this is intense.

Alexandria

Toward the end of Emmett's set, all of us girls are facing the stage dancing when I feel a hand wrap around my waist, pulling me into a firm, muscular chest. On instinct, I panic, freezing up. When a hand slides my hair aside, I feel a breath on my neck, and that's when I try to gut whoever is behind me with my elbow. I hear, "Well, hello, sexy…" Whoever it is, is cut off when my elbow connects. Then I hear, "Jesus, Alex."

Still in panic mode, I turn to see Jason bent over, holding his gut. "Shit! Jason, I'm so sorry." Taking a deep breath, I try to get my panic attack under control. "What the hell are you coming up behind me like that for?"

Fuck. Breathe, Alex. I start telling myself over and over again, *It's just Jason…*

He stands up holding his stomach and looking like he's hurt. I go to touch him, apologizing repeatedly. When I touch his arm in concern, he grabs me into a bear hug, laughing.

"Damn, Alex, who knew you could strike like that? Next time, I'll warn you first."

I squeal and try to laugh it off, but I still feel the panic in my stomach. "Jason, let me go."

Jason puts me down, seeing I'm still upset. "Shit, Alex. I'm sorry. I didn't mean to scare you, really."

Feeling bad, I give him a half smile with a chuckle. "No worries. I just don't like people grabbing me from behind. You're lucky I didn't hurt your private jewels."

Jason holds me at arm's length to see if I'm okay, looking me up and down. His award-winning smile spreads across his face, and he makes me turn around for him to see my outfit, while whistling. I feel the blush creep into my cheeks from his flattery. His face lights up. "Damn, Alex, you're looking hot tonight."

Trying to hide my embarrassment, I say in a teasing voice, "Oh, stop, Jason. I'm not going to go out with you just because you say I look hot." I push him teasingly.

He stops dead in his tracks. His face changes to serious with no smile. "Alex, I'm not joking. You look amazing tonight. Why won't you let me take you out?"

Suddenly, I feel the energy in the room change, and I sense someone staring at me. When I see Emmett, he is staring daggers at me from the stage. He isn't bouncing around or doing anything but sending death looks my way. I smile at him then turn back to Jason. "Jason, you know I don't mix business and pleasure."

His face is strained, and he looks like he's thinking about something serious. He rubs the back of his neck while putting his other hand in his pocket. In a stern voice, he replies, "Well, I guess I need to tell your father I won't be doing business with him anymore." And he walks away.

Oh. My. God. What the fuck? He's really serious.

I go after him, screaming over the music, "Jason! Wait!"

Jason turns to me, putting both hands in his pockets and looking serious. He is always smiling, and this is such a different look, one I haven't seen before. "What's wrong? You can't stop working with us."

He looks me straight in the face and speaks with a neutral voice. "I've been asking you out for almost two years now. I haven't seen you in over a year, and the feelings I had before are still there. Alex, it gets harder and harder each time I see you. I want to take you out and get to know you outside of the club."

Shock spreads across my face, my lips form an "O," and I'm speechless.

What do I say to that? I'm so lost...

I stay silent, and he reaches out and grabs my arm. "Look, Alex, I have to get back to the group and pay people out. I'll call you this week. Just think about it, and maybe we can do lunch?"

He leans in and kisses me on my cheek before walking away, leaving me stunned. I have been back less than a week, and two men have kissed me. What the fuck?

What just happened? My happy Jason just got real with me. I leave for a year, and come back to madness.

Standing there having a conversation with myself in my head, I see Izzy bouncing up to me with a half grin on her face. "What was that all about?"

Before I can say anything, tears are filling my eyes. Izzy sees I'm about ready to lose it, and she grabs my elbow, pulling me to the bathroom. We pass by Brant, and before he can stop us or say anything, Izzy holds her hand up to him. "B, we need to use the ladies' room. She's okay. Just girl stuff, I promise."

Isabella "Izzy" Rogers is the complete opposite of me with her five foot nine, slinky supermodel body and shoulder-length strawberry-blond hair, which is always in some kind of crazy updo. Her blue eyes stand out, but more than anything, her smile is what catches your eye, along with her upbeat personality. The girl is crazy and plays some sick progressive electro house music, but most of all, she doesn't take any shit.

He looks at her then to me, and after I nod that I'm okay, he moves out of our way. Brant knows to keep his distance because he has seen me freak out and throw tantrums. He knows when I'm truly in distress and when to intervene. Once I'm in the ladies' bathroom, the tears start to fall. I try to get it together while Izzy just sits there looking at me while handing me a tissue.

After blowing my nose, I clear my throat. "Izzy, I have no idea what is going on with all these men. All of a sudden, they don't want to be my friend, they want to take me out."

God...I feel like such a childish brat.

Izzy smiles down at me. "Alex, they've all wanted you for a while. You're just now making yourself available to date and letting them pursue you. Plus, your father is letting you off the leash so they can at least get near you. Over the last year, you've come out of your shell to the point where men can be near you without anyone freaking out."

I think about what she says and wipe my eyes. "I just don't know what to do. I really like Jason, but I think as just a friend. My body feels like it's on overdrive and horny, but my mind is saying no." Starting to laugh, I finish wiping my eyes.

Izzy rubs my back to comfort me. "Alex, you don't have to pick one guy. You can date multiple guys. You don't have to fuck them. Date and have fun. Believe me, you will know when it's the right person." Feeling better after hearing her say that, I clean my face up and hug her.

I don't know where Emmett is, but he has finished his set. I'm sure he's somewhere by my parents. Izzy and I start to dance some more, but with all the emotions going on in my head, plus the shots I had earlier, I'm exhausted. I tell Izzy I'm going to head home, so I start over to let the girls know I'm going to have Brant drive me home and the car will take them all home when they want to go.

When I'm on my way to tell Brant I want to leave, I run smack into Emmett. He pulls me into a hug while picking me up.

I laugh, "Let me go. Put me down."

Emmett puts me down. "Where are you going?"

"I'm heading home, I'm tired."

Emmett pulls away, standing straight up stiffly. "So are you going to leave with that Jason guy I saw you with?"

I try to ease my way out of his embrace, but I don't get very far since his grip tightens around my waist.

"What the fuck are you talking about, E?" I spit out. "I'm going home alone."

Emmett's face is hard with his jaw clenched. "You don't want to be with me?"

Irritation rushes through my body, but I'm too tired to deal with this shit. I put my hands on his chest and say in a calm voice, "E, I'm going home because I am tired. I've hung out with you a couple of times already. I just got back, and I'm not even settled yet. I think of us as friends because that's what we are. Just call me tomorrow so we can talk about this."

Sliding my hands down his chest, I push off him and he releases me. Emmett looks like he's fighting himself from within. His brows are pulled tight together with his jaw clenched, and he runs his hand through his hair, rubbing his neck. When I think he's going to say something else, he shoots daggers over my shoulder. Turning to see what he is looking at, I realize Brant and Ginger are behind me, both looking pissed off.

Something is going on.

Brant takes a step toward me. "Alex, you ready to head out? Your mom is going to ride home with you too."

I nod my head. "Yes, B. I'll be right there." I turn back to Emmett. "Look, E, I've had a long couple of days. Don't think too much of me going home early. I'm exhausted, so call me tomorrow."

I turn to walk away, but Emmett grabs my arm, pulling me back into his shield of a chest for a big hug, and buries his face into my neck. "I'm sorry. I just want to be alone with you so bad. I've waited so long for you. Have a good night's sleep, baby girl. I'll call you tomorrow."

Before he can try to kiss me, I pull away. I don't want Jason or anyone else seeing him try to kiss me, which makes my mind start to wonder… *Do I have feelings for Jason since I'm worried about Emmett kissing me?*

Right when I think I'm free of his embrace, he pulls me back in to kiss me, but it's a quick peck on the lips, and then he's gone.

I try to turn to leave, but I just stand there for what feels like hours but is probably only minutes, when I feel Brant grab my arm to pull me toward the exit.

Once outside, I see my parents by the car. The fresh air helps me clear my head, calming me down and helping me get myself together. Papá kisses Mamá goodnight and turns to me. “How was your night, baby girl?”

I know I look tired, but I put a smile on my face and answer as cheerfully as I can. “Really good. I’m just exhausted and feel a bit buzzed.”

Papá just smiles down at me, pulling me into a big bear hug. “I love you, baby girl. See you tomorrow.”

Once in the car, I lay my head in Mamá’s lap. I love her for the simple fact no words are needed to be comforted. She just pulls me into her lap and runs her fingers through my hair.

Alexandria

When I wake up after hearing something, I look around the pitch-black room. Fear and panic start to form in my stomach. My body freezes and I don't move.

Did I have another dream? I'm at home...

My phone vibrates, and I jump at the sound. I flick the light on next to my bed to grab my phone. Opening the text to read it, I take a deep breath, knowing I must have woken up from my phone vibrating.

EMMETT

Alex, I'm sorry for getting so upset, but I lost it when I saw you with Jason. I don't like the guy, and I've heard some pretty shady things about him. I want to date you, and maybe we haven't seen each other for a while, but I like you a lot. Maybe it's because I talk to your pops every day, and we talk about you all the time. Please don't be mad, please give me a chance. I don't want to be with anyone else. Please text me in the morning. Have a good day at work, baby girl.

I'm exhausted from thinking so much, and my mind starts to fight with my body. He's a good-looking guy. I'm obviously attracted to him since my body responds to him. But I think my body is craving any man's touch. *Why do I care who sees me kiss him? I'm just looking for a soul mate, love at first sight.*

I've known Emmett for a while, but never personally. You would think if it were love at first sight, I would've been with him a long time ago. Frustration building inside of me, I lie back, taking a few more deep breaths.

Get it together, Alex.

I text Emmett back.

ALEX

I'm not mad at you, I would say I'm more on the confused side. Why all of a sudden can't you be without me? Let's talk when I have some time. I'm in meetings most of tomorrow, but I'll text you so we can chat. Have a good morning.

EMMETT

Why are you still awake? You don't get up this early for work, do you? What are you doing?

ALEX

I was asleep and just woke up to your text. No, I don't get up this early. I was sleeping.

EMMETT

I texted you an hour ago. What are you doing awake right now?

Seriously. What the fuck? What does he think I'm doing? Um...control freak. Now I'm just straight-up annoyed and irritated with Emmett.

ALEX

E, I just woke up to my phone beeping. Don't know when you sent it, but it just woke me up. I'm going back to sleep, and I'll talk to you later.

EMMETT

Oh, sorry, was just worried about you. I'll chat with you soon.

I seriously need to have a talk with him tomorrow because this is getting out of hand.

Lying back down, I try to fall back to sleep. But clearing my head of the dream and Emmett is almost impossible until exhaustion takes over, slipping me back into the unconsciousness.

Thursday and Friday are insanely busy at the office with nothing but late nights working. Emmett still stops by the office with coffee or food, but I make excuses why I can't leave with him. I've been texting both him and Jason, agreeing to go to lunch with both men outside of the club. I'm sure I'll be seeing them there, but they want to see me outside the club on an actual date. I haven't been on a "date" since I was in college.

I'm overwhelmed with work and my new life here in New York. I need to get my feet under me before I start dealing with dating men. Half of me doesn't want to settle down, but I don't see what is wrong with going on dates.

Tonight, I'm going to Club Spin with Papá to oversee a bunch of international headliners. Emmett is spinning at another club where Jason will be promoting, so I'm in the clear tonight just to have fun with no stress. I'm excited that tonight will just be Papá and me at the club. He wants to show me a couple of DJs, and he has a surprise for me.

I dressed up for tonight since we'll be entertaining international DJs. I have my hair pulled up in a loose bun with soft curls hanging around my face. I only put on a little bit of makeup, doing my eyes darker. I wear another little black dress that fits me like a second skin, with a halter top holding my top parts in and showing off my back. Red heels to match my red lips, earrings and bracelets. I must admit I'm looking pretty fucking fabulous, and I hope Papá doesn't freak out. At quarter to ten, Brant comes through the door, stopping dead in his tracks. His face turns into what I call a big brother look of concern.

"Jesus! Alex, you're going to give your father a fucking heart attack. What the hell?"

Turning my back to him, I grab my clutch off the kitchen table.

"Oh, relax, B. He did okay with my other dress." I turn back to face him, only to find him in the same spot by the door, and now I feel slightly unsure of my outfit. "Do I look okay, or is it too slutty?"

Brant furrows his brow. "No, Alex, you look hot, but you're making my job fucking harder each time we go out. You don't notice all the men who want to devour you, but I do." Pausing, he runs his hands through his hair. "Just stay close to your father or me. We have a lot of foreign people we don't know coming who will be in our VIP area."

I smile while walking over to him to give him a hug. Half hugging me, he turns toward the door to leave.

When the town car arrives at the club, I see the line around the corner and wonder if I know the DJs who are playing tonight or if Papá has brought in someone I may have seen in Europe.

When we exit the car, Gus walks up to me with his face turning bright red, almost the same color as my shoes.

Looking pissed off, he barks out, "Bloody hell, Alex. Whatcha wearing?"

I blush. "What?"

Brant shakes his head with a smile. "Welcome to my hell, Gus."

Without a word to me, Gus turns to Brant. "Be wide. It's black in there. Alex, yer da is in VIP." He's telling Brant to be cautious and that it's crowded in there. Gus's slang is probably the hardest I've had to get used to, and still sometimes, I have to ask what he's saying.

He doesn't wait for me to answer before he turns, yelling at me. "Stay close ta me, Alex." Brant comes up behind me, laughing while we walk into the club.

Aengus "Gus" Stone is the head of security when Beau isn't around. Gus is one large man, and it would be hard to miss his six foot three, lean-built body, with broad shoulders and all muscle. He's an Irishman with red hair and pasty skin, but since he's been in Spain most of the last three years, he is darker than most Irishmen I know.

As we hit the door, I feel the anxiety in the bottom of my stomach. *Will I ever get over this feeling?* I push it down, and I feel Brant's hand on my lower back, pushing me to move on. The flash and strobe of lights blind me at first. The beat is bouncing off the walls, making the vibrations run through me. The beat is more trance progressive than what is usually playing for an opening DJ. When I recognize the song as "Like a Roller" by Tomcraft, I start bobbing my head, trying to get into the music and relax.

Once we hit the VIP, Papá sees me and, as always, his face lights up, making my heart swell with love. He pulls me in for one of his bear hugs before turning me around in front of him to look me over with a strained smile.

"Jesus, baby girl, you're goin' to send me into an early grave, but you look stunnin'."

With a smile, I reply, "Thank you, Papá."

I look around to see who's DJing, but I don't recognize him. Papá puts an arm around my shoulder, pulling me into his side.

"Alex, I brought you here tonight so you could see how things go when we have DJs that aren't on our label—free agents. Also, I've got other promoters here, and I want your opinion on them. Not to mention I wanted some alone time with my baby girl." He squeezes me while I respond with a smile.

Turning to look at me, he continues, "I've been in contact with this DJ from Europe, Maddox Maxwell, goes by the name DJ Mad Max. You heard of him?" Before I can reply, he keeps going. "He says he saw you before at one of the clubs in Spain. He'll hopefully be comin' on to the label soon. I wanted you to meet him, see if you recognize him, also to see what he has to offer us and if you like him."

With a smile and a whole bunch of sarcasm, I reply, "Hmm, I don't think I know a Mad Max. If he saw me, I doubt he could have gotten close to me with all my brutes nearby."

Papá squeezes me harder. "Oh, yeah. Well, I'm relieved to hear that, even if you're bein' sarcastic."

I throw my head back with a laugh then turn to look around, "Well… Where is this DJ Mad Max?"

"He's not here yet. Since he's the main DJ tonight, he'll be here later. He has a huge followin' and a big entourage with him, so I'm sure we won't miss him when he arrives. They'll be in the VIP across from us. I'll introduce you when he gets here."

Letting me go, he turns toward the booth. "Do you want somethin' to drink? Then I'll introduce you to some more people. *Capisici*?"

Following him over to the booth, I take a seat next to

him, looking around at the crowd.

"No, I'm good for now, thank you."

He narrows his eyes that are identical to mine and says, "What you can't have a drink with your papá, but you will with your friends and your má?"

I smile at him. "Papá, it's business tonight, you said. I don't usually drink when I'm with new DJs or doing business. Plus, you know I hardly drink."

With a stern face, only a smirk letting me know he isn't serious, he hands me a shot anyway. "Here, have a shot with me and relax." *Well, shit. Shots it is, then.*

Alexandria

The night progresses with ease, even with the place packed and all the VIP areas full. We're in one of the VIP areas off to the side of the stage. Since we don't have any DJs with us, we take a spot farther away, leaving the other booths for the DJs. Brant is stressed out due to a few fights in the club, but he knows my father is right next to me at all times.

I don't leave the VIP area except if I have to use the bathroom since we are not in our regular booth. The night is going great, I'm feeling relaxed, and after a few Patrón shots, I head to the bathroom. Waiting for Brant to look over at me, I get his attention with a head nod then motion I'm heading to the restroom near the front door. Once I'm making my way out of VIP, I stop with a panicked feeling, and that's when I hear a commotion coming from the front door. Anxiety rises in my chest with all the people pushing toward me. I look behind me, and I grab my chest, feeling a panic attack coming on. I look for Brant, but I can't find him. There are too many people pushing to get by me. Hearing my name being called, I try to look around, but I'm pushed into the flow of people being moved toward the front floor.

Shit, is there another fight heading this way? Calm down, breathe, Alex. Don't have a full-blown panic attack, your papá is here. Get it together, for fuck's sake. Shit, I can't breathe.

I finally stop to bend over, clutching my chest and trying to take a deep breath. I look up, and just a few feet away from me I see the most beautiful gray eyes I've ever seen staring over toward the stage. Maybe they are blue, but I'm pretty sure they are gray from here.

Letting out a deep breath, I stand up straight, letting go of my chest and trying to gain control of my body while staring at him. The pain ceases.

He's beautiful.

I just stand there staring at this gorgeous specimen of a man while everyone pushes and crowds around us. I take in all his beautiful features and his black hair pulled back into a low ponytail with a few strands loose around his face. He's perfect with his long, dark eyelashes, perfectly manicured eyebrows, and his strong jawline. Fuck. My heart starts to pound in my chest, making my breasts heave.

Wow. Just. Fucking. Wow.

Feeling my panties become wet, I let out another deep breath, and my nipples harden against my dress, sending tingles down my body. He must feel me staring because he turns his head in my direction, and our eyes meet. It's like everything around us stops, and it's just the two of us. His brows shoot up as he recognizes me.

Shit. I totally just got caught eye-fucking him. Holy hell.

Not breaking the connection we have, he makes a move toward me when a hand comes around my waist, yanking me to the side. I scream, losing eye contact. Feeling the loss of his gaze, I try to get away from whoever has a hold of me.

The crowd pushes the gorgeous man, who now has security around him, toward the dance floor while I'm pulled the opposite way. I let out another scream when Brant yells in my ear, pulling me out of my daze. "I got you, Alex. I got you…just breathe."

Brant speaks into his mouthpiece, letting the other guys know he has me. Once the crowd moves away, I turn to Brant. Trying to look like I'm not freaking out, I put my hands on my hips.

"What the hell? Who was that? Where were you?"

Brant stares with a strained face, looking perplexed. "That was DJ Mad Max, the guy from Europe that your father has here. I lost track of you when you bent over, and the crowd pushed you away before I could get to you." Nudging me to lean up against the wall, he looks me over. "Are you all right? What happened? Did you have a panic attack?"

Not answering, I bend over at the knees again and try to gather myself.

Was that a panic attack or anxiety? It started out as a panic attack. Shit. The guy, damn. My body came alive, responding to him. Good God. My body is still on fire.

Thinking of the gorgeous gray-eyed man again sends a wave of heat rushing through my body down to my core. While straightening back up, I slip my hands over my face to calm myself then take a deep breath.

When I regain control, I turn to Brant. "Okay, I'm okay. I

think it started out as a panic attack with the crowd, but I got it under control when I looked at that guy. I'm okay now. Let me go to the bathroom. Wait here for me." After a concerned nod from Brant, I turn toward the bathroom.

Suddenly, I stop, turning back to Brant. "Thank you, B. I don't know what I would do without you." Looking a little more relaxed, he nods his head, motioning for me to use the restroom. I can tell he is trying to get control of his shit.

Jesus, I need to get it together.

Once back in VIP with Papá, I'm still feeling off. I try to clear my head when I start to feel pressure on my chest again. Shit. The hairs on my neck rise, making me look around. Even in the crowded club, my gaze instantly finds him, this DJ Mad Max from Europe. He's in the VIP area across from us, staring at me with the most intense glare. He has probably twenty people around him, making it hard for me to see him fully. Most of the group is women, on the slutty side, I might add. He has a woman on each side of him, sending a jolt of jealousy running through my body and making me tense.

What the hell? I don't even know this man. Shake that shit off. Get it together Alex. Lust, jealousy, need, and desire. I've gone crazy.

I'm fighting a war inside my head over this Mad Max guy. He is so damn gorgeous in a bad-boy way, making my body crave to touch him. He is having a conversation with people, but he never takes his eyes off me. Not wanting to break the connection, I lean into the railing in front of me, clinging to it for support. Just looking at this man makes my body ignite. My nipples are as hard as rocks and aching to be touched. As I shift on my feet, I feel my panties rub up against my throbbing sex, sending goose bumps over my body. All these feelings are foreign to me.

God, I need to get a grip, but he is so fucking hot. Yes, sir…he has my attention.

Out of the corner of my eye, I see Papá come up beside me, looking at where I'm staring intensely.

With an amused look, he smiles, "Hey, so you do know Maddox? He's a big thing out there, I hear."

I reply without breaking eye contact with Maddox. "No, I've never seen him before or heard of him." Jerking my attention away from this gorgeous man, I break the connection first, feeling pain in my chest. "Did he say where he saw me?"

Papá leans on the rail and turns his body to face me. While he crosses his arms, he raises an eyebrow with what I'm assuming is amusement. "Nah, he just said he saw Gin and you in a club in Spain."

I look back to where the magnificent man was, but he is gone. My heart stops for a second, but then I feel his eyes on me. I scan the crowd and find him just outside of his booth. I let out a gasp as the air in the room becomes charged, and I feel a pull toward him. Noticing that he is coming straight toward us, I start to panic inside, trying to keep my face expressionless.

The way he stalks over to me, it's like an animal would after its prey. *Shit.* That would mean I was his prey. My hands start to sweat, and I hold the railing for support. He lets his hair out of his ponytail, and some of it drops down on his face, making him look even more dangerous than before.

God was generous the day he made this good-looking man. He's wearing black cargo pants with black biker boots and a dark gray T-shirt that is pressed to his enormous chest with tattoos peeking out of the sleeves. He looks more like he belongs on a SWAT team instead of in a DJ booth. This man reeks of bad boy, making me weak in the knees.

Watching each step he takes toward me, I tell myself, *Fuck me. I'm in trouble.*

Feeling sharp pains in my chest, I move my hand up to rub it. *Shit, what's wrong with me?* The air lodges in my throat, making it hard to breathe. With a blank face and trying to mask the emotions boiling up inside, I just stare at him when he approaches. He has four guys with him, which I'm sure are his bodyguards. At least he didn't bring any of his sluts with him.

Wow, where did that come from? Seriously, Alex. Jealous much?

I still haven't taken my eyes off him, and he approaches with a smirk on his face like he knows what he's doing to my insides. We break eye contact when Papá extends his hand to greet Maddox. I feel the loss of his stare as he accepts Papá's hand. He speaks with a husky voice that makes my mouth water.

"Hey, Luc. Thank you for having me here tonight."

Oh, my God. What kind of accent is that? British? Italian? Jesus, it's hot.

I think I just came in my panties. I can't get over how my body is reacting to this man. Never have I lusted over someone, needing to touch him. Yes, I have wanted to touch a man before but never this needy feeling that I have.

Watching him, I try not to fidget with all the energy running through me. My body defies me when my nipples harden again. *Dammit.* I pray he doesn't notice since he is down in front of the VIP on the other side of the railing. Feeling the heat rise between my legs and making my sex throb, I try to hold my emotions tight, knowing if anything were to touch my nipples or my clit, I would combust.

While they speak to each other, I just take in his full heavenly appearance. Close up, he is even more beautiful, with smooth, dark skin and very masculine features…and those eyes. Oh, lord, those eyes. They look silver now that he's nearby, not gray.

Seriously hot.

Watching his plump, lickable lips move makes my mouth water. I try to concentrate on the accent, but I fail horribly because all I'm thinking about is kissing those scrumptious lips. Licking my own lips sensually, eager to taste him, I bite down on my lower lip to gain control of myself. I need to suppress my urge to jump over the rail and attack him.

Damn, what has gotten into me? I'm never like this. But I have never seen a fucking guy like him before. This man makes me feel alive. Fighting with my subconscious, I just stand there, not moving.

My body reacts like nothing I've ever felt before, leaving me feeling disheveled over my reaction to this unknown man. When I hear Papá go to introduce me, I pull my eyes from his lips up to his… Fuck me. Silver eyes. I thought they might even be blue, but no, they are silver.

With a twinkle in his silver pools, he snaps his gaze to me. Making eye contact, he gives me a half smile, like he knows I was just eye-fucking him. Extending his hand to me, he says, "Alexandria." Without hesitating, I reach my hand out to greet his. When our fingers touch, I get shocked, making me jump. Every nerve in my body ignites and I gasp. *Did I just get a static shock? Why didn't he jump?* The way my name glided off his lips with that fucking accent. I don't know if I can stand up much longer, which in turn, makes him smile back at me, showing me his fucking dimples. Could he get any more goddamn irresistible? I mean, seriously, dimples?

God help me.

Every nerve in my body feels like it's on fire with my sex pulsing against my now soaked panties. I can't mask my emotions much longer with our hands touching. I'm going to lose it soon. His touch is rough with calluses, but he's gentle with my hand.

Papá clears his throat, snapping me out of my lust-induced trance. In a weak but seductive voice, I say, "Maddox, it's so wonderful to meet you." The sound of his name off my lips makes my nipples tingle, sending a shiver through my body. Maddox looks me over from my eyes to my mouth, then down to my chest and back to my eyes with the sexiest fuck-me smile I've ever seen.

Wow... Holy Mother-Of-Hotness.

Still holding my hand, he pulls it in to kiss the top of it. My face flushes, making my knees go weak again, so I have to grab the railing with my other hand for support. Heat rushes through me to my core, making me let out a deep breath I didn't know I was holding.

I pray to my God in a whisper, *"Dios Mio!"*

Maddox just smiles when he straightens up, never taking his eyes off me. *Shit. Did he hear me?* Papá must sense I'm unable to speak because he steps in and begins to tell me that Maddox contacted him regarding coming to the States to play. Maddox releases my hand, sending a pain to my chest, but he keeps his intense stare focused on me. I just keep nodding my head with a smile, trying to follow along with what Papá is saying. We finally break the connection when one of Maddox's guys comes up behind him, whispering something in his ear. Maddox's jaw tenses, and his face is strained. His eyes go from light silver to a charcoal gray within seconds. Obviously, something his guy said made him mad.

He turns to Papá. "Luc, I'm needed on stage regarding something with my equipment before I start my set. Please excuse me."

When he turns to me, his face changes back to being relaxed, showing me his dimples. A tingle erupts in my belly, spreading through the rest of my body before he bends to pardon himself. "Alexandria." The way my name rolls off his tongue sounds so sensual, even erotic, especially with his smile and those damn dimples. It almost makes me think he's trying to get a reaction out of me. Well, mission fucking accomplished. Standing straight up, he still has a devilish smile on his face, leaving me breathless.

That fucking smile should be a crime. No, wait. That smile is what the girls call a panty-dropping smile. Jesus, I feel like a teenage girl with my hormones raging. What's wrong with me? I never lose control of my body like this. This man leaves me breathless. I want to do naughty things to him. I can't help but feel this connection between us like we are fused together when he touches me. Lord help me.

I bite my lower lip, smiling back. "Maddox." He takes a step closer to me with such an intense glare, but he stops himself. Appearing to change his mind, he turns without a word and leaves us.

The way he moves away from us with such confidence also gives me a chance to check out his ass. *Holy shit, is there anything not godly about this man?* Once he's out of sight, I turn to Papá, laughing in a sassy voice, "Jesus, Papá, that man is way too good-looking. What's up with us contracting every good-looking person out there?"

Papá turns to look at the stage with a chuckle. "Ah, you have no idea what's in store tonight. Just wait and see, baby girl."

I'm still looking at Papá when I notice his mischievous smile. He must be up to something.

Alexandria

Turning my attention to the stage, I keep my eyes on Maddox moving around getting ready for his set. I feel like I'm in a trance and he's the only person in the club. I even catch him looking at me several times, stealing my breath each time. It's like we have a piece of string connecting us, or at least, that's how I'm feeling.

Suddenly, the lights go out and lasers shoot everywhere with fog pushing out on the stage. That's when I see him. *Santa Maria.* Maddox took his shirt off. The bass drops and the lights blast all over. He mixes in his first song, and my insides explode with waves of excitement.

"Oh, my God, Papá."

In a trance, I take in all of his massive body with both of his pectorals covered in what look like intricate tribal tattoos. The tattoos wrap around his massive shoulders, sliding down his biceps. He looks like a football player wearing shoulder pads, but instead of pads, his shoulders are covered in tattoos, leaving his washboard stomach clean of any marks. *Holy fucking hotness.*

Wait…this song. What the fuck? I know this song. It can't be, but it sounds like…

Without taking my eyes off Maddox, I speak to Papá. "Papá, isn't that? No, it can't be…" Standing still and holding the rail with both hands, I keep my eyes glued to the stage. I can't take my eyes off him. This song sounds so much like my parents. Maddox has his headphones on, pushing his hair out of his face and giving me a clear shot of his heavenly features. Both his hands are on the mixer, messing with the knobs. When he looks up and right at me, our eyes connect, and that's when it happens.

I let out a squeal. "Good God."

I hear Mamá's voice drop into the song, making me gasp and put my hand over my mouth. Papá laughs at my reaction to Maddox's song. He leans into me, "Ah, I guess you can say this's one of the surprises." He puts a hand on my back, rubbing me for comfort or maybe it's excitement. Who knows? All I can do is stare at the spellbinding man on stage.

I'm speechless. Maddox remixed my parents' song, and it is fucking amazing. I turn to Papá, finally breaking the intense stare Maddox and I are locked in.

"Papá, when did he… How did he… Holy crap. He is good."

Damn, he's not just fine as hell, but he's talented too. The way he switched the beat and moved her vocals, making it more progressive, is something I never would've thought to do. This is completely crazy.

Papá still sounds amused as he crosses his arms over his

chest. "Well, he contacted me, sayin' he saw you in Spain, heard who I was, and remixed our song for me. He wanted to know what I thought and if he could come out to DJ for us."

Looking at Papá, I can't figure out what to think or feel because it's just so overwhelming. My thoughts and emotions are going crazy. Taking a deep breath, I let it out slowly. "Has Mamá heard the song?"

"Ah, yeah. She loves it." Excitement pours off him, and he unfolds his arms, putting both hands in his pockets and rocking on his feet like a little kid.

I glance back toward Maddox, and he's bouncing behind the decks with his hand in the air. Then he points to me, and I hear my mamá in the background singing, *"Mi Amor."*

Jesus Christ.

I want to run onstage and jump into this man's arms. But instead, we lock eyes in a trance again. I can't turn my head away from him, and I have the biggest grin on my face. This song, this man, this connection I have with him is freaking me out. I need to know more, but I can't seem to pull myself together to speak when he's around. My mind is running a mile a minute, my body is still on fire and filled with lust, and I'm so aroused by him and his music I feel like I'm going to explode with all my senses on overdrive.

The crowd erupts, going into the next song. I look over the crowd, just seeing the movement of sweaty bodies going crazy. After taking in everything, I look back at Maddox. Jesus, he's fucking great. I think I just fell in love. Moving to the music, I stare at him like a young girl with a crush, needing to be near him so I can do deliciously naughty things.

For the next two hours, I don't move from the railing. Instead, I just stand there staring, wondering how I could have missed seeing this man in Spain. When Maddox is close to the end of his time slot, Papá grabs my hand. "Hey, are you ready for your next surprise of the night?"

I'm on cloud nine in a state of bliss and I don't know how tonight can get any better, but I reply with a girlish smile. "Yes."

I notice Brant coming up behind me to follow us to the stage. He doesn't look too happy, but I'm sure that has to do with the massive number of people tonight as I haven't left the VIP area since Maddox went on stage.

Once I'm near the stage, I start to freak out. *Shit.* I am going to be seeing Maddox again. I need to pull it together because I don't want to come across as some crazy teenage fan or make a fool of myself. I feel the pain in my chest again. *Dammit.* Maybe Maddox is giving me a panic attack with this connection we have. Does he feel this magnetic pull too, or am I just reacting to the hottest man I've ever fucking seen?

When we turn to head up the stairs, I hear my name with a scream. I look up, seeing my friend Sasha from Spain.

Freaking out, I squeal half in Spanish and half in English, "*Dios mio,* Sasha! What're you doing here?" I pull her into a hug.

Sasha is a DJ and one of the promoters I had the pleasure of working with in Spain.

Papá yells, "Surprise!" throwing his hands up in excitement.

Breaking the embrace, I try to rub away the aching pain in my chest. Not knowing what to say, I look from Papá to Sasha. "What's going on? How did you…"

Sasha interrupts me, bouncing up and down and speaking with a thick Spanish accent. "Well, after you left, I was so intrigued with you and the girls, I needed to come see how DJ life was over here. So I contacted your papá, and here I am." She grabs me into an embrace again.

Before I can say anything, she whispers into my ear before pulling away. "Wish me luck. We'll chat after my set." Then she takes off toward the other side of the stage.

I turn to Papá, putting my arms around him. "Thank you, Papá. Tonight has been unbelievable, to say the least. That song, along with my girl Sasha, tonight couldn't have been any better."

Papá laughs, pulling me into a big hug, "Welcome home, baby girl." Totally excited to see my friend, I start to bounce around in his arms, hugging him tighter.

When Papá releases me, he moves to greet someone behind me. Before I turn around, the hair on my neck rises. When I do turn, I am face-to-face with Maddox. A very tall, very sweaty, very massive tattooed chest, and holy fucking hell, very pierced nipples with barbells. How did I not see that earlier? Shifting my weight to release some pressure, I let out a moan and hope they didn't hear me.

Breathe, Alex… Jesus, he's hot! Breathe, Alex, but fuck, he's hot.

Papá talks to him from behind me about his set, but I can't concentrate with his naked chest in front of me. I can't take my eyes off Maddox and him wiping the sweat off his face, his chest, and those fucking lick-me-suck-me-please nipples.

God, he's so fucking lickable. Running my tongue over my lips ever so slowly before biting down on my lower lip, I keep myself from moaning. *Jee-zus*. I can't help thinking what it would be like to nibble on his pierced nipples or to use my tongue to lick the sweat off his chest by tracing the tattoos over his pecs.

Fuck me…

Shifting to shake off the tingling running down my body, I try to pull myself together, looking back and forth between the two men. They tower over my short-ass frame with Papá a full foot taller than me, and Maddox a couple of inches taller than Papá, closer to six foot four.

When Maddox finishes talking to Papá, he looks down at me, catching me eye-fucking him, *again. Dammit.* I can't seem to make eye contact with him when his tatted-up chest is right in front of my face. I hold my breath and finally look up. I hadn't realized the height difference earlier when I was on the steps in the VIP and he was on the dance floor in front of us, but now that we are so close, he towers over me.

Letting me know I've been caught, Maddox shines his panty-dropping smile on me. "Did you like my…" He pauses with a devious grin while raising one eyebrow. "…um, set, Alexandria? What did you think of the song?"

Damn, that accent makes you question his heritage along with those lips. Fuck and those piercings. He can't be for real. Lord help me.

Someone calls Papá, and he excuses himself, pulled away with another DJ and giving me enough time to respond. Feeling nervous—as it's just the two of us—I push a piece of loose hair from my bun behind my ear. Making eye contact, I smile. "I loved the song. You did a great job." Pausing to think, I bite my lip. "Um, your set, it was mostly all your production. I would like to hear some more of your stuff sometime." *Okay, that sounded professional enough. Great job, Alex.* I mentally give myself a high five.

Eyes still locked on mine, he throws his shirt over his shoulder before placing his hands in his pockets, making his chest flex. I let out a moan before snapping my mouth shut. Maddox laughs at my reaction. "Yes, Alexandria, you have a good ear. My set was mostly all my own music. I've heard you have some original music of your own? Maybe we can talk production sometime soon. Maybe tomorrow?" One eyebrow rises like a challenge.

Wait, what? Tomorrow? He knows I have original music of my own. But how? Oh, my God, he wants to see me tomorrow.

I start to do a happy dance in my head, but it's short-lived because when I open my mouth to say something, a group of girls walks up, calling his name. He doesn't look away from me when one of his bodyguards comes up behind him and whispers in his ear again. I close my mouth and just stare at him.

Maddox breaks our connection when he moves to slip on his shirt, so I take in a deep breath that I desperately need.

Once his shirt is on, he moves closer to me, saying in a husky voice, "I should head back, but it was very nice to meet you, Alexandria. Finally. Officially." Taking my hand, he kisses it again. Electricity zips through my body again with a wave of fire from head to toe, making my cheeks blush. His touch does crazy things to my body. This connection ignites our souls when we touch; he must feel it too.

Not releasing my hand, he asks, "Can I see you tomorrow?"

Shit…today, tomorrow, fuck, any day.

Standing there holding hands, I whisper, "I have studio time scheduled…"

Maddox cuts me off, bending down and leaning into me, still holding my hand. He kisses me on the cheek, sending my heart into overdrive. Heat rushes throughout my body, leaving my face lit up like a Christmas tree.

I'm frozen in shock, and he pulls away smiling. With his beautiful dimples that I crave to kiss on display, he says, "Don't answer. Just think about it, and I'll be in touch tomorrow morning. Until tomorrow, Alexandria." He releases my hand, and I feel a sharp pain in my chest again with the emptiness from the loss of his touch. I let out a gasp in protest.

Before I can speak, he's gone, with his entourage following behind him. I can't believe the pull this powerful man has over me. I just feel like something is pressing on my chest, making it hard for me to breathe. *What am I going to do tomorrow?*

We finally leave after Sasha's set is over around two a.m. and all the DJs are paid out. Brant is beside me, guiding us girls out of the club. Sasha and I catch up, promising to meet up tomorrow with Ginger to do some studio time. Ginger and I had studio time scheduled, so it will be exciting to surprise her with Sasha. Butterflies ignite in my stomach thinking about Maddox and how he wanted to see me tomorrow. Just thinking about him makes me feel all warm inside and turns my cheeks hot.

Sasha notices the smile on my face and asks, "What's that big smile for?"

I shrug. "Tonight was one of the best nights ever. You're here and spending time with Papá."

I don't mention Maddox because I don't know what to say. She's in town until after the festival. Hopefully, I can talk her into working for the label as one of our promoters. Her entertainment company is based out of Europe, so it will be a tough sell, but she did so well and the crowd loved her.

Alexandria

The beat of music, the breath on my neck, and then pain in my wrist.

I scream, *"Help!"*

I bolt up, screaming. Sweat is dripping off my face, and I look around, realizing it's my room.

"Goddammit." Breathing hard, I try to calm my heart rate.

Breathe, Alex. You're in control. Relax.

Feeling scared, I realize that was the first time in my dream I felt pain or heard myself cry out for help.

Did I scream for help?

Maybe my mind is trying to remember or tell me. *God*, I wish I could remember. I've been over and over this night, but still nothing.

Maybe I did yell for help. Why would I dream it if I didn't do it?

Maybe this festival coming up is bringing up old memories. I wonder if I'll remember being at the festival? Maybe the suppressed images will finally come back to me? Feeling tired, I lie back and try to sleep for a few more hours.

When I wake up the next morning, I'm still tired and drained from the nightmares. I turn my phone on, and it starts beeping, letting me know I've got text messages and a voice mail.

Shit.

JASON

Thinking about you. Wishing you were here with your group tonight so I could see you. Talk to you soon.

Ok sooo I'm drunk txtin U. I was so excited 2 see u, and I've missed u. I haven't talked 2 u 2 day. Please call or txt soon

And…

EMMETT

Are you home yet? Is Jason talking to you? Are you awake?

Sorry for bugging you. I just miss you. I hope you had a good night with your pops. I can't wait for our lunch date this week.

Okay, these guys are getting a little too crazy. As my girls would say, they are stage-five clingers. Since meeting Maddox, I haven't even thought about them, which makes me think my feelings for them are as just friends. Neither of them makes me feel like I felt last night. Shit, no one has ever made me feel like that.

The last text is an unknown number, and my heart skips.

> **UNKNOWN**
> Hola, hermosa! It's Maddox from the club. What time do you have the studio scheduled? Can we maybe have an early dinner? Let me know when you wake up. MM

How did he get my number? He called me beautiful!

I start to feel happy and nervous at the same time when my mind starts to go crazy. Am I going to be able to hang out with him and still function? I can't even speak to him without eye-fucking or freezing up. What will we have to talk about? Should I meet him with the girls or after they leave? I could have him meet me here. Will Papá let me use his studio?

Still unsure, I need to call Mamá, but then I remember I have a voice mail.

Ginger's voice comes through the phone. "Alex, you have some serious admirers and maybe even a clinger. I've been asked by three people where you are today. I'm excited for our studio time and hearing your new stuff. Call me, girl."

Shit. I wonder which one she thinks is a clinger?

After listening to the voice mail, I store Maddox's name in my phone and text him before I can talk myself out of it.

ALEX

Hey, Maddox. I'm glad to hear from you. I have the studio scheduled today from one to four and tomorrow from three to five with my girlfriends. I do my studio time at my parents' penthouse in Papá's studio. We had plans to take Sasha out to dinner tonight after our studio time, but let me see what I can do. Yours, Alex

I start pacing with nervousness.

Can I go through with this? Why am I so nervous? Can I be alone with him? Should I have him come to the office with the girls?

All I can think about is getting him naked. My hormones are on overdrive when he's around. Panic starts to build up in my chest. Then my phone beeps.

MADDOX

Good morning, mi belleza. Since you're in the studio so long today and I don't want to interrupt your plans already, maybe we can just do dinner and studio time tomorrow. How about I come at the end of your time tomorrow with the girls, say at five o'clock? We can figure out if you want to keep working on music, or we can just go to dinner. How does that sound? MM p.s. I like how you say you're mine. ;)

Mi belleza. He called me his beauty. Wait, I'm his…

Smiling to myself, I look at my text and realize I signed it with "Yours, Alex" like I would on a letter. Butterflies take flight in my stomach, leaving me light-headed. He likes me saying I'm his. This man does such crazy things to my body, and I've never had this feeling before. Taking a breath to release the stress, I reply.

ALEX

Five tomorrow sounds perfect. Thank you. p.s. I like saying it too. See you tomorrow. ;)

"Oh, my God." *Lord help me. I can't believe I just did that.*

MADDOX

I'm just looking forward to spending some time alone with you so we can get to know each other better. See you at five, beautiful.

ALEX

Don't you need the address?

MADDOX

No, I know where you live.

Letting out a deep breath I didn't know I was holding, I fall back on my bed then start to bounce around like a little kid, feeling so alive. Adrenaline running through my body gives me a huge high. I jump up to start my day.

My house phone rings after I get out of the shower.

I see on the caller ID it's Brant calling. "Hi, B, how is your Sunday?"

His voice is still thick with sleep, "Good, just checking in with you. Are you and the girls still working on music at your father's studio?"

"Yes, that is still the plan." I sound way too chipper for my own good. I don't mention Maddox to him yet. I need to talk to my girls and see what they think.

"Sounds like someone had her coffee this morning. Okay, if you need me, just call. Maybe I will swing by and see you all in a few."

"Okay, sounds good. Get some rest and have a good day if I don't see you."

Right at noon, the front desk calls to inform me Ms. Mendez is here. I tell them to have her come on up. Maddox has me all twisted up in knots. I'm so nervous about meeting him tomorrow that I don't even think about making music.

I look in the mirror one more time to make sure I look okay. My hair is down in loose curls, I applied light makeup to go with my white tank top, I'm barefoot, and I'm wearing my favorite pair of skinny jeans that make my ass look perfect.

Also, I'm feeling nervous because I don't usually do studio time with too many people. If it were just Ginger, it would be one thing. But Sasha and I just started getting to know each other on a personal level. Freaking out about Maddox is one thing, but adding studio time only has my anxiety twisting in my chest. I don't want her thinking I'm some girl obsessing over Maddox. Plus, I still haven't established if she knows him from Spain.

I need to tell them. What if Sasha knows Maddox?

"Breathe, Alex."

Opening the door, Sasha bounces in, hugging me good morning. I relax immediately, wondering why I was worried in the first place about telling these girls anything. It's just my inexperience and self-doubt talking to me. After I greet her with a hug back, I tell her to come in.

As we enter the living room, I glance over at her. "Would you like something to drink? Gin should be here anytime, and then we can head over to my parents' place." Sasha is looking around, taking in my place.

Once you walk in the door, you can pretty much see the whole inside of my place except the bedroom and bath. The living room is sunken, so you have to take two steps down to where my sectional couch is facing a fireplace with a big, flat-screen TV above it. One whole wall is floor-to-ceiling windows overlooking the city, and there's an open plan kitchen that has an island with matching barstools. The kitchen table is off to the side next to the window looking out at the city. Overall, I love my new place, very modern décor with my Spanish accessories.

Sasha is stunning with her smile that seems never to fade. "You have a beautiful place, Alex. How do you like living in New York compared to Spain?" She sits down on my couch, making herself comfortable. I follow behind her, sitting on the other side of the couch and pushing my hair back from my face.

"I love it here, but Spain is so much more… Hmm, how can I say this? Not so busy." With a shy smile, I continue, "What about you? Do you love it here compared to back home?" Folding my hands in my lap, I try not to fidget.

Sasha starts rambling about being in New York and comparing it to her home, getting comfortable by turning with a knee slightly bent on the couch and an arm across the back so she can face me straight on. I love that she is so at ease and confident. The more I'm around my friends and people I am comfortable with, the more I feel the confidence that I have inside starting to show. After being sheltered most of my life, I think I am finally starting to break out of my shell. I've always been more of an introvert, and I was always alone. Nodding my head and smiling at her while she talks, I try to focus on what she's saying.

Sasha must notice I'm not paying attention because she stops midsentence. "What's wrong, Alex? You seem quiet or like something's wrong." Tilting her head, she evaluates me with a long stare.

Shit.

Smiling, I lean forward, saying nervously, "I have a date tomorrow, and I'm totally freaking out. And once you get to know me, you'll know that I don't date… like N-E-V-E-R…" I try to laugh off my shyness, but I feel the heat on my cheeks.

Sasha squeals, clasping her hands together. "With who? Is it that Maddox guy from last night? I saw how you two were looking at each other. He's one mouthwatering man, that's for sure." We both throw our heads back laughing. It's easier to relax since Sasha is so easy to talk to.

Before I can respond, the doorbell rings. When I get up to go answer it, Sasha bounces up, following me. "Don't think you can get out of telling me who you have a date with, chica."

When I open the door, Ginger walks in not looking happy at all, but she says hello, hugging me. When she sees Sasha, she yells, "What the fuck? Sasha? Oh, my God." Grabbing each other, they squeal and laugh. Once Sasha tells Ginger what happened and why she is here, Ginger hugs her again and we all get so excited. "That's so awesome of Luc."

Standing with my arms folded over my chest watching the two of them interacting with each other, I just smile, feeling the love in the room. We seem to be growing our little posse of girls. Sasha was a huge part of our Europe trip, but we never really had one-on-one with her outside of the club, which makes this time special.

We all head out to my parents' penthouse, chatting it up about Sasha's stay and where she'll be playing. I'm glad the subject changed from talking about Maddox and my date. We say hello to my parents, and my papá sets us all up and tells us they'll be back later, leaving us girls alone to work on music.

Right after my papá leaves, we all sit down, and I'm thinking about what song I'm going to let them hear when Sasha turns to me, breaking my thoughts. "Okay, chica, tell us who you have a date with and why you're so nervous."

Ginger's face goes blank as she yells, "Seriously, Alex. I don't go out with you for *one* night, *one* fucking night, and look what happens. Details *now*. Who is it? Emmett? Jason?"

Laughing, I throw my hands up in defense. "Easy, ladies. It just happened, and I don't know what to think of it."

Ginger puts her hand up. "Hell no. Who is he? Details now."

I turn red. Just thinking about him again makes my body ignite. Biting my lip, nervous to tell them, I whisper, "Maddox Maxwell. Or you might know him as DJ Mad Max." Both girls let out a scream of excitement and start rambling.

Sasha points at me, "Eh! Chica, I told you he was into you. I saw how you two devoured each other last night."

Ginger leans back in her chair, smiling a full smile. "Alex, you little devil, you. *Finally,* you're coming out to play. I'm so happy for you. Where're you two going? What did he say? Info, please..."

Turning to the computer screen, I tell them about my night, his song he remixed, how he made me feel, and why I'm scared shitless. When I refer to my incident, Sasha doesn't say anything or ask what happened. She just nods her head and keeps listening. I feel so good about getting this off my chest. My feelings for Maddox are just so foreign to me compared to how I've felt around other men or the couple of men I've dated. Nothing compares to the connection I feel, and that's what scares the hell out of me. When I'm done ranting and venting, both girls are just sitting there listening with encouraging smiles. *What?* When neither of them says anything, I get self-conscious, asking, "What?"

Both girls look at each other, but Ginger leans forward to speak first. "Look, Alex, I've got no room to talk, but you need to live a little. I think I have more fun and experience than you do, and I'm boring. You did so well when you were away from your parents. Now you're back, and you've gone back into this shell and you need to branch off. Your bodyguard and parents should listen to *you*... You're old enough to make your own decisions, and Maddox seems like something you want to pursue, so you should. Even if it's a one-night stand, Alex, you can do whatever the fuck you want. You need to quit being scared and live life. Look at me. I finally left my family and came here to start a life for myself. I didn't know one single person. Granted, I had your family, and you're now one of my best friends. But you have to take chances, girl, or you will regret it." Ginger sits back, still smiling, and continues. "I'm just glad it isn't with that Emmett guy. Total- fucking- tool, if you ask me."

What the hell. Seriously?

As I get ready to ask about Emmett, Sasha chimes in, turning my attention to her. "Chica, you're so beautiful and have too much going for you to live in the shadows. You deserve the best, and if you make mistakes along the way, so what? It's your life, and you need to love as much as you can. If he's right, you'll know. And if he isn't, then you move on. But you should try at least. Get out from under this mask and show your true self, not the self you think your parents want you to be." Standing up, she moves in front of me, swiveling my chair to face her. She crouches down. "I know you can mix and I know you can sing, so I want to hear what you've got. No holding back, I want to see the real you. Now let's listen to some of your stuff." Swiveling my chair again to face the computer, I let out a breath. *They're so right. Who cares if I mess up or if Maddox is all wrong for me. Oh, well. It's my decision.*

Feeling more confident, I play my most recent song, while both girls pull their chairs next to me and listen.

Maddox

I feel anxious for tomorrow because I don't want anything to go wrong. I want this girl, more than I've wanted anything in a very long time. I want her more than I'd like to admit. I keep telling myself it's just an obsession. The connection we had was something I've never felt or experienced before, making her number one in my mind and fantasies.

Ethan yells at me from the other room, interrupting my thoughts.

Ethan Jameson, probably the most important guy on my team, is my IT guy, or "go-to" guy. He's tapping into Alexandria's life right now. I know it's wrong, but I need to know more about her and what she likes, how she thinks, and who she is. I need to know more so I can understand why I'm obsessed with her.

Since the night I saw her at the club, I haven't stopped thinking about her with her silky olive skin, long brown hair that cascades down her back, hugging every inch of her sculpted figure, and most of all, her angelic blue eyes. My body felt her before I even saw her in her VIP booth. All I've thought about since seeing her is making her mine. Especially now after last night and the electricity that ignited between us when we touched. It took everything in my power to not take her right then in front of her father at the club.

I walk into the massive hotel room which has been turned into an office with screens, monitors, and recorders everywhere. When Ethan notices me, he points at the big screen, saying in a very cocky voice, "Who's your man? If you didn't know, that would be me. Dude, her father's studio is linked into the BB Security system, and voilà. There she is with her girls, talking about you, bro."

"What the fuck?"

Seeing her with her girls sends an instant shock to my crotch, making it throb. *Down dog, not time to play yet.* It has been too long, and I need to release some tension—but only with Alexandria, no one else. Other women are nothing compared to the way I feel about her. A woman I've never even had a conversation with until last night. *Fuck me.* I lean into the screen. "Rewind it all the way so I can see and hear what is going on."

Ethan rewinds the video to the beginning. I grab a seat, pulling it up next to him, not saying a word or taking my eyes off her. I'm so entranced by her beauty when I hear one of the girls say, "Who is it? Emmett? Jason?"

I growl, snapping my head toward Ethan with a piercing look. "Who the fuck are Emmett and Jason? Find out now."

Ethan nods his head and pauses the video with a smirk. "Already did, brother. Both of them work with the label. Emmett has worked with her father for several years now, and his background comes up clean, but I've got some red flags on it. It's too clean for my taste, and I think there is more to him than his record."

"Motherfucker." Tension instantly settles in my shoulders. I cross my arms, gripping my biceps to ease the madness that is storming inside of me. I don't want anyone near her.

Goddammit. "What do you mean, more to him than his record?"

An evil smile spreads across his face, making him look more like a scary son of a bitch than the boy next door. I know I wouldn't want to piss him off. He might not look lethal, but this fucker would mindfuck you before he beats the shit out of you. He's so damn smart and is wicked on a computer.

He puts the folder down, leaning back in his chair with a chuckle, "Well, Madd Dog, I've been breaking into files almost all my life. This record looks like someone made it look too perfect. I'll do some more searching, but I wanted to get as much as I could before you got here. So far, I only know about his work stuff and that he is seriously infatuated with your girl."

I can't just sit here listening to him talk about these men wanting my girl. With a growl, I stand up. "And the other fuckin' pissant?"

Ethan laughs. "Okay, so far Jason comes up clean too. From a rich family, seems like a laid-back guy, and he owns Jas Entertainment, which is one of Spin It's number one promoters. I will dig deeper on both of them. Tap into their life and see what I can find." He goes to stand up with a shit-eating grin. "Both are pursuing her as we speak."

I feel my skin heat with the amount of rage burning inside. I turn back to face my girl, fisting my hands to relieve some of this tension. "Not for very long if I have anything to do with it. She's mine. Push play."

We both sit there listening to the girls talk when I hear what I think is Alexandria whispering my name. "Maddox Maxwell, or you might know him as DJ Mad Max."

My heart starts to beat faster. Without looking at Ethan, I say, "Turn it up, I can't hear."

Relief begins to wash over me when I hear the girls start to talk about me, but then Alexandria starts telling them how she felt the first time she saw me, our connection, and how I made her feel.

"Fuck me." My nipples harden around my barbells, sending a jolt down my body. My cock throbs even harder against my jeans. Watching her move her hands over her chest while talking about me, I look at her lips and think about her beautiful mouth slowly slipping over my cock, suctioning down. *Jesucristo...*

When I hear her say she is scared shitless of how she feels and something about an incident, it pulls me from my lust-filled haze. *What incident? What the hell is she talking about?*

I stop breathing and lean in more to see if I heard her correctly, but she goes on about our connection.

Taking a big breath, I turn to Ethan. "Did you hear that? What do you think she means 'incident'? You pulled everything on her, correct?"

Ethan nods his head yes, grabbing her file. "I even looked it over again. There is nothing...no car accident, no injuries, nothing that I can see would be an incident that would make her scared to be with you."

Fuck... "Did she maybe pull my record?" I'm a hundred percent sure all my stuff is wiped clean, thanks to Ethan. My mind starts racing over all the things she could mean by that. *Dammit.*

I keep listening to the girls talk while they try to help her not to be scared about our meeting tomorrow. My nerves start to build inside me, throwing so many questions around in my head.

When I hear her drop her first song with her vocal, I growl, cursing in Italian. I lean forward to see her face. "She's so red like she's embarrassed. Why? Fuck, she *is* that fuckin' good." I have so much emotion running through me, and again I ask myself how can she be single, so shy, and why has she hidden her talent. She's like a goddess.

Ethan breaks into my thoughts, whispering to me, "I agree. She truly is amazing."

I bark, "She's mine. All fuckin' mine."

Ethan laughs but doesn't say anything, and we both just sit there listening to her play her music for the girls. My mind just goes crazy with butterflies bouncing around in my stomach. *Shit.* I've had plenty of women and never felt like this. It's like my heart is going to explode. Her voice is nothing like her mother's, and she can mix. The girls encourage her to play more, and I see her coming out of her shell.

Hmm, music is the key to making her relax once you get past her shyness. I just sit there looking at my woman... Well, she doesn't know it yet, but she'll be mine. Thank God no one has claimed her but me, which brings me back to those two pissants. I let out a growl but don't say anything.

Ethan and I sit quietly for what seems like an eternity, listening to her play her songs, and by the time her girlfriend moves in to start playing, my dick's hard as a rock. *Fuck,* I feel like I'm going to bust out of my jeans. Just seeing and hearing her gets me so worked up. I feel alive just looking at her, and her voice is so angelic. I start to move around, too much energy is running through me, and my mind is going a mile a minute. I need to go to her right now. I need to feel her touch, that connection, again and soon.

I must look frantic because Ethan stands up and turns to me with his arms folded. "Dude, you're starting to freak me out. I've never seen you this wound up before, Madd Dog. What's going on in that head of yours? Talk to me."

I stop pacing and turn to my friend. "So many fuckin' things, I can't even think straight. I need to confirm my meeting with her father, and I need to know what she meant by the incident. But most of all, I need to be with her and make her see that she is going to be mine."

Ethan's expression doesn't change. "What do you need me to do?"

I take two steps toward him, putting my hand on his shoulder with a smile. "Keep doing what you're doing. I want her monitored, and if you hear anything else important, text me. I need to hit the gym to relieve some of this tension."

Alexandria

Monday morning came and went slower than a turtle running for his life. Seriously, I can't get Maddox off my mind, and I even dreamed of him last night. My excitement is outweighing my nervousness. I'm sure once I'm at my parents' studio working on music with the girls I'll start to freak out again, but right now, I'm just in heaven thinking about him.

I even Googled him to see what I could find out about him. All the social media sites show where he has played and links to his songs. I found nothing in regards to his family except an article about his father's accident, leaving Maddox a very rich man. Nothing on past relationships, except in all the pictures posted of him, he is always with beautiful women or fans—but never the same woman, leaving me with so many questions.

Around three in the afternoon, I meet the girls at my parents' studio. The girls promised me they would make sure I'm okay and stay with me until he arrives. Since my parents aren't here, I don't have the stress of Maddox meeting them. I'm hoping we'll be out of here before they come home. I did tell my mamá he was coming over to listen to my music and we were going to dinner. She was beside herself with excitement.

The whole time the girls are with me, we chat, barely working on music. When the girls are getting ready to leave, I finish up, saving the stuff we worked on, when suddenly it becomes quiet in the studio. My stomach gets tight, and I panic when I hear Papá clear his throat.

Shit! Fuck!

Standing up, I turn around, only to come face-to-face with Papá *and* Maddox—who is half an hour early, of course—standing beside him looking, if at all possible, even more gorgeous today in daylight than at the club.

The studio is so quiet you could hear a pin drop before Papá says, "Alex, look who I found downstairs. Maddox is here to see you and take you to dinner?"

It's more like a question than a statement coming from Papá. The girls both have grins from ear-to-ear, and they speak before I can muster up words. Ginger goes first. "Hi, Luc. We didn't know you were here."

She speaks to Papá but is walking toward Maddox. "And… It's nice to meet you, Maddox. I'm Ginger."

She holds her hand out for him to shake with Sasha following suit. "Hi, Luc. Maddox, we've met before."

Wait. What? Has Sasha met him before? She didn't say anything.

"…I played after you last Saturday, but my name is Sasha."

A wave of jealousy crashes over me. *What the fuck?* Maddox shakes both the girls' hands, greeting them with a hello, only to return his eyes back to me. Papá clears his throat, getting my attention. I look up at him with a full grin on my face, "Yes, Papá, I'm sorry I forgot to tell you he was coming over. I hope it's okay." I'm still stuck in the same spot, not trusting my legs to move, so I clasp a hand on to the closest chair for support.

I can't read Papá to know if he's pissed off or what, but to my shock, he turns to the girls. "Well, girls, I hope you enjoyed your time here today. If you need any more time in the studio and the office is booked, just let me know."

The girls take their cue and head out, speaking with Papá. Once Papá reaches the door to the studio, he turns back, looking straight at me, "Your má will be home in a little bit. If you need anything, I'll be in my office."

Oh, my God... Holy Shit.

Realizing I haven't replied, I smile even bigger at him. "Papá, I'm fine, thank you. I'll come say good-bye before we leave." With that, everyone goes but us two.

When Maddox shuts the door, I let out a deep breath. I try to focus on his face, not letting my eyes wander down his immaculate body. He smiles at me, and when our eyes lock, I look into the most beautiful silvery eyes I've ever seen. And then there are those dimples I want to touch so damn bad.

I speak in a somewhat mellow but cheerful voice, trying not to sound overly excited. "Hey, Maddox. Please come in and have a seat."

Breathe. Just don't think about his eyes or face or chest, and definitely, don't think about his godlike body. Fuck, I can do this.

"Hola, hermosa. Gracias." He moves toward me, breaking up the little pep talk I was having with myself in my head. That's when I smell him, all freshly showered with a slight scent of cologne. My mouth starts to water, and I feel my sex pulsing. Maddox brushes up next to me to take a seat, and he wraps a hand around my elbow before leaning into me, giving me a kiss on my cheek. I feel like I just got electrocuted with sharp tingles zipping through my body.

Ay, Papi!

Maddox strides right by me with grace and confidence radiating off him, letting me take in his full body now that I can watch him without getting caught. He's wearing dark blue jeans that hug his hips and are formfitting around his massive legs, along with a plain white T-shirt that fits him snug enough to show off all his glorious upper body muscles and letting his tattoos peek out from where his sleeves end on his biceps. *Jesus, this man is so damn sexy.* He turns, catching me eye-fucking him again. *Dammit.* My mouth is slightly open like I'm going to say something…or maybe I want to eat him. Either way, my mouth is open.

"Alexandria, do you like what you see?" He puts his hands back in his pockets. While I'm looking at him, his hair falls into his face, making me want to touch him and run my fingers through it.

God, I feel so needy with him, like I need to touch him.

I get a boost of confidence I didn't know I needed. With a sexy grin on my face, I answer seductively, "Yes, Maddox. I do." I turn, taking a seat in my chair and trying to hide that I'm freaking out.

Shit.

When I turn back around, Maddox is still staring at me

with intense eyes and an expression I can't quite put my finger on. I smile at him, gesturing to the seat.

Maddox sits with confidence and goes right into talking about music, what he likes and where he gets his inspiration. I start to relax since we're discussing my favorite topic, and I enjoy making small talk with him.

Maddox seems totally at ease and is very upfront with me, telling me all about him. I learn he's four years older than me, is Italian on his mother's side, British on his father's side, and speaks five languages, including being fluent in Spanish and Italian. When his father died in his early teens, his mother moved them back to Italy where her family is from until he turned eighteen. Then he started moving around, but he currently lives in Spain.

It explains why his accent is so different, having so many languages mixed together. It's intriguing to hear him speak with such a combination of accents. I tease him about how he says "Fuckin' hell" instead of "Bloody hell," like most British people do.

We don't exchange too many details about ourselves, just the basics. I want to ask more questions, but I know it will mean he will have the right to come back at me with more questions, and I'm not ready for all my secrets to be out there just yet. We laugh for what seems like hours. Maddox is so easy to talk to, it's like we've known each other forever.

My body is still on high alert with all his slight touches here and there. He makes me feel like he needs my touch as much as I need his. I'm so overwhelmed with how it feels so right being with him compared to any other man, that I keep playing with the computer, messing with music, trying to keep busy and not look so nervous.

Maddox pulls me from my thoughts. "When I saw you at the club, you took my breath away."

Should I know where he last saw me?

Trying to mask how he is making me feel with his intense stare, I smile. "My papá mentioned you saw me at a club. Where did you see me?"

Looking amused, or maybe it's annoyed, he replies, "I was at Club Monico when I saw you and your friend Ginger."

Okay... so he knows where I live and contacted Papá.

"Hmm, I'm sorry, I don't think I saw you because I would've remembered you." I give him a mischievous smile.

"You didn't see me. I was in one of the VIP areas, and you were...well, let's just say, you were surrounded by your security. You didn't look like you wanted to be bothered."

When I don't say anything, he continues. "Alexandria, I'm not going to beat around the bush with you. I find you very attractive, and ever since I laid eyes on you, I've not been able to get you out of my mind. I've set a lot of things aside to come see you. I want to be with you, or I should say, I want to get to know you. Would that be okay?"

He's looking at me seriously, complete dominance radiating off him and making it hard for me not to show how affected I am by him.

Oh, God. Does he want me? Did he really just say that? I don't know if I should be pissed or excited.

My body is telling me to jump him, while my mind is telling me to hold up. With all these questions running through my brain, I can't think. I watch him with a straight face as I lean back in my chair, moving my hands to rest on each of my thighs and trying to calm myself down. "Maddox, I'm flattered. It sounds like you went through a lot of trouble to see me. What if I would've had a boyfriend?" I raise one of my brows to challenge him.

He fires back, sounding amused, "When I want something, I consider all avenues, figuring out how I can make it mine. So you can say I've looked into you. I found out your name, then realized who your parents were, where you lived, that you just graduated from college, and are now working for your family's label. I also know you write and produce music, and you even know how to mix probably better than half the DJs you have on the payroll on the label."

Shit. Does he know about my rape?

Shocked and overwhelmed, I still don't say anything, and he continues, "I also know you're very passionate about music, your father is very protective of you and your mother, and last but not least, I know you've never had a boyfriend except for a couple of dipshits you dated in college."

Oh God, he knows.

Maddox never moves, showing no emotion when he speaks to me. Only when he sees my reaction does a sexy grin creep across his flawless face. Realizing I'm not going to talk and taking in the shocked look still on my face, he pushes his hair out of his face and leans forward to grab my chair, pulling it so we're facing each other. *Oh, God.*

In a soothing voice, Maddox tries to calm me down. "Please don't be alarmed. I'm no sociopath. I'm sure you Googled me as well. I just like to know who is occupying my mind. This is something new for me, but I assure you I'm no stalker. Well, maybe a little bit, but you're safe with me, so please don't look scared. Plus, your father's right in the next room."

Don't panic. Breathe.

I realize my face is showing my thoughts. *I am freaking the fuck out.* I'm so turned on by him, I can't see straight. The dominance in his tone and the directness of what he wants from me have my sex throbbing between my legs and waves of lust seeping through my body. I feel the anxiety in my stomach, but it is nothing compared to how aroused I am by him.

The whole time he's talking, all I can do is think dirty thoughts about him and look at his plump, kissable lips. They are so full. Jesus, this man is like a god sent from above, but with tattoos. My nipples harden, and I squirm in my seat to soothe my sex from pulsing.

Seconds go by while we just stare at each other. Moving my eyes to his lips, I lick my own lips, wondering what it would be like to suck on his.

Wait... What?

Maddox is staring at me because when I look up from his lips, a huge smile spreads across his face. "Alexandria, you obviously feel the same way I do. I see it in your eyes and in the way you look at me."

Snapping out of my lust-induced trance, I stand up to put some much-needed space between us. "Maddox, I don't even know you. Yes, I Googled you. Yes, you scare the shit out of me. And yes, you're very straightforward, but—" I turn to speak to him, but in a blink of an eye, he's by my side. He wraps one arm about my waist, while the other arm reaches up, grabbing my neck under my hair, pulling me to him and forcing me to look up.

I gasp at his sudden closeness, giving him the opportunity to bend down and press his lips to mine. Every time he touches me, I feel electricity run through me, followed by waves of heat. I melt into him, and he's teasing my lips with his tongue, waiting for permission to enter my mouth. When his hand slides over my ass, I moan, giving his tongue the passageway it was begging for.

He tastes like mints, and without thinking, my hands shoot up around his neck into his hair, needing to touch him. I slip my tongue into his mouth, teasing him and giving him full access. My tongue dances with his, pushing his farther into my mouth and making both of us moan. He pulls me tighter, making our bodies press harder against each other and letting me feel his massive erection pushing up into my stomach. I pull on his hair, bringing him down closer to me to deepen the kiss. Maddox growls something fierce, sending goose bumps over my body.

What am I doing? Shit. This feels so right. God help me. I should stop this. Fuck, it feels so good.

Breaking the kiss, he walks me back over to our chairs where I pull away from him. I look over at his lust-filled eyes, panting as I say, "I don't even know you. I've never done this in my life." I run my hands through my hair, pushing it back. "I mean, with some stranger. Regardless if you know everything about me, I don't know anything about you."

I feel relieved now that I've expressed my concerns, and I sit back, staring at his beautiful face. Without saying a word, he grabs my thighs, pulling me closer to him. He leans his head back, maintaining eye contact with me. "Alexandria, I am sorry for pushing you with that kiss, but I have thought about those lips for so long. We don't have to do anything. I'm just telling you I want to be with you and see you as much as I can while I'm here. You can't deny we have a connection that is drawing us to each other. I know you feel it too. I'm sorry for rushing you."

Shit. He feels it too. What do I do?

Leaning back in my chair, I take a deep breath and look at the computer. "It's okay, the kiss was amazing. You're right, I've never felt this way with someone. When you touch me, I feel like I'm on fire, and I get pains in my chest when you're not touching me. Let's just take it slow. Is that okay?"

Feeling insecure but needing to see his eyes, I turn back to see his reaction. He smiles the most fucking amazing smile ever at me. "Yes, of course, Alexandria. If you're mine, we can do whatever you want…as long as I can keep kissing you." Then he kisses me while bringing my chair even closer, pulling me in for a deeper kiss.

Oh God, he can kiss.

Maddox breaks the kiss with a moan. "Alexandria, can I hear some of your music now, please? I really would love to hear some before we leave to eat."

Pulling away from each other, we both turn to the computer, and I don't know why, but I dig out songs I've never let anyone hear. Songs that have me singing in the background. What I played earlier for the girls was commercial stuff, but what I'm about to play for him is my heart. I load up one of my favorite songs.

When I was back home in Spain, I had a lot of time on my hands. With my parents here in New York, most of the time I focused on music and school. A majority of my songs have a story or some feeling behind them, so I think that is why I don't share them with anyone. This one is about trying to find love and being alone. When I push play, I sit back, looking straight at the monitor so I don't see his reaction. I wouldn't be able to handle it if he didn't like it, so I just stare at the monitor while it plays.

When I hear Maddox whisper something, I look over. "What?" He shifts my chair, turning it to face him and pulling my legs in between his massive thighs so we are as close as we can get.

"Mi robas mi aliento."

I take his breath away. It's more like he takes my breath away.

Maddox reaches out his hand, brushing his thumb over my lips then pushing my hair behind my ear. "Alexandria, you have the most beautiful voice like your má. Why don't you let people hear this? You could make a lot of money, plus keep your family name going."

His words of affirmation make me blush, and butterflies take flight in my stomach and I feel light-headed. I swallow hard, trying to clear my throat. "I make music to make me happy. Most of my music is from my heart, usually telling a story or describing a feeling I'm having. Music is in my soul. It's kind of like therapy for me." Laughing softly and feeling stupid for confessing my feelings, I try to look away from his intense stare.

With his hand on my chin, he tilts my face back so I can look into his eyes. He smiles, showing me those dimples I'm coming to love so much. "Alexandria, you're very talented, and you should let people hear your stuff. Why don't you DJ or perform? I can't believe your parents haven't pushed you. You can't keep this a secret forever."

With his full-on flattery, a wave of heat rushes through me, and I blush again. His gaze has me in a trance. Without thinking, I whisper, "I'm afraid I'll fail. Most of my music, no one has heard, even my parents. I don't want to let my parents down. I know I would be compared to them, and I don't think I'm that great, so I keep my music to myself."

Moving both hands to cup my face, Maddox pulls me forward so our foreheads are touching. In his husky but sensual voice, he says, "Alexandria, with that song I just heard and with all your other songs, *you will never fail.* Don't deny everyone your talent by keeping these to yourself." Brushing his lips against mine, he whispers, *"Dios mio, eres hermosa."*

There he goes again, calling me beautiful. I don't think I can deny this man, and it scares the shit out of me.

As he releases my face, I hear my mamá coming down the hall. Feeling like a kid who just got caught, I push my chair away and turn back to the computer. Maddox laughs. "Are we not supposed to be next to each other?"

I know I sound a little nervous as I say, "No, we can be. It's just I haven't been like this with a man before with Papá around. He usually scares everyone off. Hence the shock earlier when he left you alone with me."

I smile at him with my sweetest smile. "My papá is very protective, as you might know. I didn't tell him about today because I thought he would freak out and not leave you alone with me."

Shrugging an oops, Maddox lets his head fall back and laughs just as my parents walk into the studio.

Papá is midsentence when he walks in. "Baby girl, you two—" He comes to a halt when he sees Maddox right next to me, touching me. Papá looks shocked, but he continues, "You're still here?"

I'm trying to see if Papá is mad or not, so I just stare at him with a smile. Maddox stands up to greet him with his hand out. "Alexandria was just letting me hear some of her music she made."

At the same time, Mamá walks in the door, stopping to assess the situation. She then strides between the two men, pulling Maddox into a hug. "Maddox, it's so good to meet you in person finally. You're even sexier in person, and your pictures online don't do you justice."

He towers over her, and he engulfs her with a hug as he laughs. *"Hola, Maria, es un gusto conocerte."*

She replies to him in Spanish, "Please, call me Mia."

Aw, speaking in Spanish to Mamá will win him points. Papá knows the basics, so I know he knows Maddox just said it was nice to meet her. Mamá and I hardly speak Spanish unless we are talking to each other or to my grandmother. Even then, we barely do since Papá isn't fluent. I think he knows more than he lets on, though, and tries to play the I don't know what you're saying card.

Still sitting down, watching Maddox embrace my family, a warm and fuzzy feeling comes over me and makes me smile. I look to Papá, and he smiles at me, raising an eyebrow. "We don't want to interrupt, so we'll let you two continue."

Before I can say anything, Maddox is standing next to me, slipping a hand around my waist. "We were just finishing up and heading to get something to eat. Would you two like to join us?"

I glance over at Maddox in shock, a little sad that we won't be alone but also relieved because I don't trust myself. We need time to get to know each other, and if people are around, then we won't be molesting each other.

My parents must see the look on my face because Mamá replies, "We wouldn't want to intrude on your time together." Papá moves to stand behind her with an arm around her waist.

Finally, I speak up before anyone can say anything else. “No, it would be great if you two came with us. It’ll be fun.”

Papá smiles big, pulling Mamá into a tighter embrace. “All right, let’s eat. Where’re we goin’?” Papá releases Mamá, grabbing her hand and leading her out of the studio toward the front door, with Maddox holding my hand and pulling me along with him.

God, this should be interesting. My first “real date” since college and my parents are going with us. Lord help me.

Alexandria

Dinner with my parents and Maddox is wonderful. It's like Maddox and I have been together forever with how easy it is to talk to him. He's very comfortable around my parents. The only uncomfortable part of the dinner is at the beginning when Maddox asks Papá if he minds if he dates his daughter. I almost spit my drink out but end up choking. I turn beet red in the face and hold my breath until Papá responds. I can't believe Maddox asked him that in front of everyone. Papá laughs and replies in a serious tone, "Ah, well, you know how protective I am of her. If you did anythin' to hurt her, you'd have to answer to me and about five of her security guys that are like her brothers."

Papá sits back in his chair and pauses to think about what he is going to say next while staring at Maddox. Then he continues, "But…it's not really up to me to say who she can or can't date. It's up to her. So, to answer your question, nah, I don't have a problem with it. From what I know, you're a good man, Maddox, and I respect you for askin'."

Maddox gets up and shakes Papá's hand, thanking him, then Mamá squeals, grabbing my hand. I'm just in shock, staring at Papá with a look of disbelief.

Who is this man, and what has he done with my papá?

I can't believe what I just heard. Doesn't he have a say in who I date? I always thought I needed his approval.

The rest of dinner goes smoothly, though. We all talk music, and my parents ask Maddox a million questions, but he answers them all with ease. My heart swells with joy, and the attention he gives me is unbelievable. I'm not used to someone touching me in front of my parents, or in front of anyone, as a matter of fact. I've never really been in a relationship like this. With those few guys in college, it was just dinner, movies, studying, and so forth, but they never met my parents. And it was never anything more than kissing or hugging. I still can't believe I've only known Maddox for less than forty-eight hours because it feels like I've known him forever. The way he makes me feel is indescribable. Mamá is just beaming at me, and I know she's dying to ask me details.

Once we get back to our building, we say good-bye to my parents, and Maddox and I go back to my place. Once inside, Maddox walks over to the wall of windows looking out over the city, and my phone beeps again. During dinner, it went off a few times, but I never answered it or even acknowledged it. In the kitchen, I put my clutch down on the island, and not thinking, I open up the text messages I have.

EMMETT

What are you doing today? I can't wait for our date tomorrow. Sorry for all the texts yesterday. Hope to hear from you today.

Maddox comes up behind me, looking over my shoulder at the message. Before I can say anything, Maddox looks at me and lets out a fierce growl. "Who is that? You have a date with someone tomorrow?" *Oh, shit.*

I walk around the kitchen island to give us some distance and to get some control on my emotions because I'm starting to get pissed off. I don't reply, I just look at him with a straight face, not knowing what to say. He walks toward me, clenching his fists.

Don't panic. Wait. Is he jealous, or is he mad at me?

Snapping out of my shock, I try to keep my voice soft when I speak. "Maddox, he's a friend. He works for the label and is one of my papá's protégés, and I manage him." Not knowing why I feel I need to explain, I go on. "He's just a friend, and we're going to lunch tomorrow just as friends."

Running his hands through his hair, Maddox turns to me with intense, darkened eyes. His voice is husky and full of rage when he says, "Alexandria, I don't share. I don't even usually do relationships, but I've never wanted anything or anyone more than I want you. I will not share what's mine." His words come out like a statement, or really, more like a threat. My anxiety starts to build up in my stomach, and I try not to freak out.

Fuck that. But he wants me and only me...

Fighting with my own emotions, I walk around the island to him, and I put my hands on his chest to try to calm us both down. I take a deep breath. "Maddox, we just met Saturday. You can't blame me for things that were planned before you came along. He's a friend, nothing more." I see his shoulders relax as he wraps his massive arms around me, pulling me into his chest and dwarfing my body. I freeze. *His hold. His rage. Breathe.*

Maddox's hold on me is like a vise, and I make a whimpering sound, snapping him out of his thoughts. He releases his grip a little to look down into my eyes. "I don't share well. I'm sure you think he's a friend, but I know damn well he doesn't think that way. I guarantee he's looking for more than a friendship."

Trying to change the subject, I look up at him. "Maddox, if this is going to work between us, you need to be able to trust me. You don't see me asking who is calling you or who all those slutty girls were that were with you the other night, do you?"

Wow, where did that come from? Jealous, are we?

Maddox's whole facial expression changes from being hard to soft, and he throws his head back, laughing. "Alexandria, are you jealous?"

I feel my face heat up, knowing I'm going to lose it in a second. I push him back to get out of his embrace. I turn to walk away, but he grabs my wrist, pulling me back, but I put my hand up, maintaining distance between us.

Maddox leaves the space between us, but he still stands close with a fucking full pearly white smile showing those dimples. "I like when you get jealous."

Frowning, I spit out, "I'm not jealous, but if you're going to keep questioning me about my guy friends, then I can question you about your hooker-looking friends."

Maddox laughs a full hearty laugh, which only makes me more pissed off. Once he calms down, he says, "You look so damn cute when you're mad."

His stare is so intense that I have to close my eyes. In a husky, stern voice, he commands, "Look at me, Alexandria." I swallow hard. I open my eyes to see this magnificent man in front of me, flawless skin and hair falling in his face. "You're mine, and I'm yours. After today, we are one. I'm not going to share you with anyone, and no one will have you but me."

He is looking at me with so much rage, lust, and a hunger so intense it kind of scares me.

Like he's reading my mind, he says, "I'll never hurt you. *No one* will ever hurt you. I'll protect you always. Never fear me." With that said, he lets me go. I gasp, feeling naked without his touch, letting my arms slide down my sides. Suddenly feeling exhausted from the last night and day of emotions, I lean back on the island where he left me and close my eyes.

Jesus. I feel like a hormonal teenager.

Maddox must sense my thoughts again because he turns around from the living room where he went after letting me go. In a flat, empty voice, he says, "Maybe I should go home so you can get some rest." He looks at me with an emotionless expression. I can't figure out if he wants to leave or not. Having mixed feelings myself, I don't say anything. I want him to stay with me, but then I think maybe I should have him go so I can have time to think and process all that has happened today.

I haven't moved or said anything, so Maddox walks back over to me. He's standing toe-to-toe with me but not touching me. "Alexandria, do you want me to leave?"

No. Shit.

Why is he leaving this up to me? "Do you want to leave, Maddox?" I'm still not touching him, and I'm trying to mask my emotions like he is doing.

With a big sigh, he replies, "No, I don't want to leave, but I think I should so you can have some time to think about us. Plus, I'm starting to lose control over wanting you. If I stay, I will end up fucking you, and I know that is not what you want right now. So, yes, I think I should go." Without touching me, he turns to leave.

No. Don't. I start to panic. "Wait. Stop." Maddox turns around to see the panicked look on my face. "Wait. When will I see you again? I don't want you to leave, but I agree I don't think I can control myself either..." I trail off as I stop to think.

I need to tell him because he might not want me after. I can do this. I need to tell him how I feel. Do I even know how I really feel? Fuck. I just met the guy...but the connection is undeniable.

I run my hands through my hair, pushing it back before I continue. "I just don't know how to do this." I motion between the two of us. Feeling shy, I take a step toward him. "The feelings I have for you in less than forty-eight hours scare the shit out of me, Maddox. I don't know about you, but I don't want to be away from you."

I see his eyes fill with desire, but he keeps his face straight and his jaw clenched. I continue talking while I slowly walk toward him. "Like you said earlier today, from the moment I saw you, I felt that connection, that pull toward you. I have this burning feeling inside that goes deep down to my core. I want you, Maddox. I've never wanted anyone the way I want you right now. I don't know how to explain it, but I do, and

I'm scared."

He puts his hands in his pockets, and I stop walking. *Just do it. Tell him. If he runs, then, oh well.*

"I need to tell you something before we go any further. It might change the way you feel about me." My phone starts to ring, and we both look over to where it sits on the counter.

Fuck...Not now. Shit.

Neither of us moves toward the phone. I turn my head back to look at him. I can't read his emotions. He's still looking at my phone. "Are you going to get that?" He sounds irritated.

Goddammit.

I walk over to the phone, picking it up to see who is calling. Relief rushes over me when I see it's Brant. I answer. "Hello, B. Did you get enough sleep today?" Looking over at Maddox, I see rage boiling in his eyes.

Oh God, I forgot he probably doesn't know who B is.

I put my hand over my phone, mouthing to Maddox, "It's my bodyguard, relax." Hearing Brant talk pulls me back to the conversation. "What did you say, B?"

Brant exhales, sounding irritated. "I said I heard you went out with your parents and Maddox."

"Yes, I did. I didn't call because I was with my parents, and Eli was with us."

Silence... Right when I'm about to say something to see if he is still on the phone, Brant says, "That's fine. I'm calling to check in with you about tomorrow."

Maddox is still fuming. He runs his hand through his hair while he turns away from me. I stare at him while I say to Brant, "Hey, B, can we talk about this tomorrow on our way to work? Maddox is still here with me."

Silence again. *Shit.*

Brant rasps out, “He’s still there with you right now?”

“Yes, he is. So, can we discuss this tomorrow?”

“I want you to call me when he leaves.” Now he sounds pissed off.

Sharply, I say, “I’m fine, B. I’ll talk to you tomorrow.” Then I hang up.

Maddox’s back is to me, and he’s looking out the window at the city with his arms folded over his enormous chest. Walking up behind him, I put my arms around his waist, laying my head on his sculpted back. I breathe in his masculine smell, closing my eyes and feeling him relax with a deep breath.

When he speaks, it’s with pain in his voice. “Alexandria, I’m a very demanding man. I have a temper, which I try to control. But with you, I seem to have a hard time tempering it. When I think of another man near you, I see red. I know he’s your bodyguard, but I can’t control this feeling I have to claim you as mine.”

I don’t say anything but just keep breathing in his alluring scent. Maddox turns around, pulling me into a tight embrace, and I can barely breathe. Without thinking, I just blurt it out. “I was raped when I was eighteen, and I’ve only been with one other man since.”

Holy shit. I did it. I said it. Oh, God. Will he run? Oh, please don’t run.

“Fuckin’ hell!”

Maddox’s British accent comes off stronger in his outrage. His grip becomes a vise, clutching me so tight. He starts to shake, and I try to move a step back so I can see his face, but he’s not letting me go. I lean my head back to look up at him.

I need to see his eyes so I can see what he is feeling. When I look up to see his expression, I panic. Maddox is filled with rage, his face is turning red, and his eyes are squeezed shut. Not wanting to push him, I just stay silent and wait.

A few minutes pass which feel like hours before he finally opens his eyes. He leans down so our foreheads touch, loosening his grip on me but still keeping me up against his tense body. Taking a deep breath, he lets it out before speaking. "Alexandria, I'm so sorry. I had no idea, and if I had, I would not have come on as strong as I did today. This changes everything."

Tears fill my eyes. *I knew it. He's going to leave. He doesn't want some damaged, tainted girl.*

I force myself out of his embrace, turning so he can't see me cry. "It's okay, you can go. I'm sorry I didn't tell you sooner. No one wants a broken, used girl."

Trying to mask my emotions, I wipe my eyes, but then I'm swept up in the air. I scream, and before I know it, I'm in Maddox's arms being carried, while he's muttering cuss words in Italian. He lays me on my bed, followed by him lying beside me. Tears are running down my cheeks. Confused, I ask, "What are you doing?"

Maddox stares at me, his voice mixed with anguish and anger. "Did you think I was going to leave you because of that?" Using his thumb, he wipes the tears that have run down my face.

I know my voice comes out shaky because my nerves are shot. "Yes, you said it changes everything."

Shaking his head, he leans over and kisses my forehead. "Alexandria, it changes everything with how I'm going to claim you. But, baby, I'm not leaving you. If anything, it makes me want you even more."

Closing his eyes for a brief moment, he takes a breath before he continues. "It changes everything in a lot of ways. Now I understand your father's protectiveness over you. I understand your lack of dating. Why you don't like people touching you. Why you have so many goddamn bodyguards all the time."

Tears are still sliding down my face as he kisses my lips, whispering to me, "I'm glad you told me. I'll go as slow as you want. When you're ready, I'll be right here waiting. My feelings for you are the same, if not stronger now. I need to protect you."

As he pushes my hair away from my face, I see his silver eyes sparkle with such desire and concern it takes my breath away. Running his hand through my hair, he continues, "The moment I saw you, it changed my life. All I think about is you and it has only intensified since meeting you."

He closes his eyes, leaning his head down so our foreheads touch again. He takes another deep breath while I try to swallow the lump in my throat. He looks at me with such an intense expression that I let out a long sigh. "I want this so much and will do anything to keep you in my life. Fuck, Alexandria, I don't even do 'relationships' either, so it will be a first for both of us."

Feeling overwhelmed, I reach out my hand, pushing his hair out of his face and pulling him down to kiss me. When he opens his mouth, I slip my tongue in with urgency to deepen the kiss. Tears are falling down my face, and I move my hands to his shoulders, clawing at him to bring him closer to me, wanting him to put all his weight on me. I moan into his mouth, needing more. Gliding my hands down to the hem of his shirt, I slide my hand under it, feeling his hot skin. I pull his shirt up, wanting to feel our bodies skin-to-skin, but Maddox stops me from lifting it any higher. He's panting as he says, "Alexandria..."

Anxiety is floating in my stomach while my sex throbs to be touched. I'm overwhelmed with new emotions. I know one thing, and that is that I want this man. Adrenaline rushes through my body, making me feel high and as if my body is floating. "Maddox."

Still in a daze, I put my arms around his neck and pull his hair to bring him down for a hard kiss. I moan into his mouth. Maddox rolls us so I'm on top of him again, and he breaks the kiss. I'm breathless. "Maddox, I've never wanted something as bad as I want you right now. After that night, I never thought I could feel like this for anyone. Even after Mark, I thought I was broken..."

Grabbing me, he pulls me down so I lay on his side. He caresses my shoulder. "Alexandria, not today. I want to take my time with you and cherish each experience."

Rubbing my hand over his chest, I start to trace his barbells under his shirt. I realize there is so much we still don't know about each other, but it will all come in time. Feeling exhausted, I close my eyes. "Are you going to stay with me tonight?"

He smooths my hair out of my face and over my shoulder. "I'll stay till you're asleep, but I'll be gone before morning. I don't want to piss your father or bodyguards off just yet," he laughs.

Shit, I didn't even think about that. What would Papá say if he saw Maddox leave in the morning?

"Sleep, *mi belleza*."

He slides his hand up and down my back, and it puts me right to sleep.

Alexandria

The next morning, I wake to an empty bed. Looking around the room, I notice a note on the nightstand. My heart jumps, making me squeal with joy and leaving me breathless by the time I move to the side of the bed. *My God, I've got it bad for this guy.*

> *Good morning, mi belleza. Thank you for yesterday. I can't wait to see you today. It was the hardest thing I've ever had to do, leaving you last night. I'll be in the office today to meet with your father. I'll stop by to see you. Until then, think of me. ~MM*

Holding the note to my chest, I throw myself back on my bed squealing like a schoolgirl. *Santa Maria.* I feel like these have been the best few days of my life.

When I wander into the living room to grab my cell phone, I notice I have missed texts. Sitting down on the couch, I start to read through them.

EMMETT

Are you mad at me? Why haven't you texted me back?

Okay, now I'm starting to get worried. Are you okay? Please just text you're okay.

How am I going to deal with Emmett? Do I tell him I'm seeing Maddox?

JASON

Good afternoon, Alex. Sorry for my drunk text the other day. I can't wait to see you this week. Text if you have time.

Stress starts to build in my shoulders. *Why me?* I hope I can keep my friendships with Jason and Emmett, that they don't cut me off when they find out I'm dating Maddox.

MAMÁ

I didn't call just in case Maddox was still over, but call me when he leaves so we can chat. He is a very nice man. I can't wait to hear about the rest of your evening.

I smile to myself. I love my mamá. She loves being nosy, always wanting to know the gossip. She is probably over the moon now that I have a boyfriend.

MAMÁ

You haven't called. Is he still there? Talk to you in the morning. I'm heading to bed.

Telling myself I will call Mamá on the way to work, I get up and head off to get ready. I take extra time in the shower, like I usually do every morning. But this time, I think of Maddox and how he made me feel. Closing my eyes, I touch my lips, feeling his lips all over me. The way his barbells rubbed up against my chest. I slide my hand down over my erect nipples, pinching and twisting them while moving the handheld shower head between my legs. Moaning, I pull even harder, sending pain through my nipples and down to my throbbing clit. *God, I am so close...*

I wish it was Maddox here touching me and his mouth kissing all over me. I can't stop thinking about his kisses and how he breathes down my neck and whispers what he will do to me. Letting my imagination take over, I know my orgasm is on the brink of exploding. I lean back against the shower wall, spreading my legs wider and allowing the shower head jets to work their magic. Sliding my hand down my body until it reaches my mound, I slip a finger between my folds. When the jet hits my clit perfectly, I scream out Maddox's name, wishing, imagining he was here. The orgasm lasts longer than normal. I leave the jet pulsing on my pussy while the orgasm runs through me, and I get my legs working again to stand up straight.

I take extra care getting dressed for work, knowing I'll be seeing Maddox. I put on a formfitting black skirt that ends just above my knees with some kick-ass blue stilettos and a matching blue silk button-down shirt. I leave my hair down, but I clip my bangs to the side. I smile at my reflection in the mirror, thinking I look pretty fucking fabulous.

A knock at the door startles me because I'm not used to having my own place. I head for the front door when I hear another knock, this time more forceful. When I look through the peephole, I see Brant.

Opening the door, I ask, "Why didn't you just use your key?" Once the door is open, I turn to walk into the kitchen to get my stuff.

Brant follows me. "I didn't hear from you this morning, so I didn't know if Maddox was still here or not." I look up to see he is standing with his arms folded over his chest and an eyebrow raised at me.

I laugh. "Um, no. He left sometime last night after I went to sleep."

Leaning on the kitchen island, he asks, "Seriously?"

I look back down to my purse with a giggle. "Yes, seriously. Why?"

"Are you dating him now? Your father told Beau Maddox asked him if he could date you."

Holy shit. Papá told the security team already. Damn.

I look up at Brant with a holy-shit expression. "You guys gossip more than girls do, you know that, right? What else did he tell him?"

Brant smiles. "He said Maddox is a good guy but to keep an eye on him. Since he used to be on contract with Monico, your father is trying to see what Maddox wants or is going to do."

Monico? Wait... What?

I can't hide my look of complete surprise because I didn't know any of that. I start to freak out, realizing I don't even know this man I'm dating. Brant leans forward with his hands on the island. When he sees me starting to react, he throws a hand up, motioning for me to stop. "Don't freak out. Your father likes him." Brant puts his hand back on the island. "He isn't worried about you dating him. Just be cautious with him. We don't know that much about him except that he came looking for your father and wants to date you." Brant shrugs his shoulders. "It just seems kind of weird."

I start panicking. "*Santa Maria*." My mind starts racing a mile a minute. *Oh, my God, is he using me? Does he want something from me? Is he working for Monico to find out our corporate secrets? Shit.*

Brant pulls me from my thoughts, sounding concerned. "What are you thinking, Alex? I can see your mind racing."

I bite my lip, trying to keep my voice steady. Instead, it comes out weak. "Do you think he is using me?"

Brant can see I'm about ready to lose it, so I try to look away. I hear the concern in his voice when he speaks. "Alex, it's too soon to tell. But like I said, just be cautious with him. He seems cool, but until we know—"

I cut him off, and I snap my head around. "How're you going to find out? Should I ask him?"

Brant comes around the island, placing his hands on my shoulders and looking down at me, frustrated., "Fuck no. If he's working for Monico, we don't want him to think we're on to him. Just go with the flow and have fun. We're always with you, and I don't think he would hurt you. Do you?"

I shake my head, agreeing he wouldn't hurt me. We head to the office without saying anything else. I'm so lost in my own thoughts.

Jesus. My day just went from the best day ever to being all

kinds of fucked up. Could Maddox be using me to get information for Monico? I remember Maddox told me he was in a contract over the summer. Maybe I can try to find out what he is up to without asking outright.

Once we're at the office, I get out of the car. Brant shuts the door behind me and sounds amused as he says, "So your lunch with Buff Boy. Is that still on for today?"

I totally forgot about Emmett and lunch. *Shit.*

"Yes, I'm supposed to have lunch with Emmett. Why don't you like him?" Throwing my purse over my shoulder, I turn to face Brant.

"I just don't like him. Never have, even when he was a shy geek. Just can't make myself like him."

Brant is usually good at reading people, so it makes me wonder if I even know what I'm doing with these men. Curious, I ask him, "Do you like Maddox, and what do you think of Jason?"

Still standing by the car, Brant laughs. "Alex, you don't need my approval to date guys. Even if I don't like them, I'll deal with them for you. But if they hurt you or treat you wrong, that's when they'll have to deal with me. For the record, I don't know Maddox, but I didn't get weird vibes from him when I spoke to him. And I can see in his eyes how much he adores you. Jason seems kind of fake, like he's hiding something. I don't know him, but I don't like him with you either. He isn't your type." With that, he turns and heads into the building, leaving me speechless.

Well, shit. I wasn't expecting that from Brant.

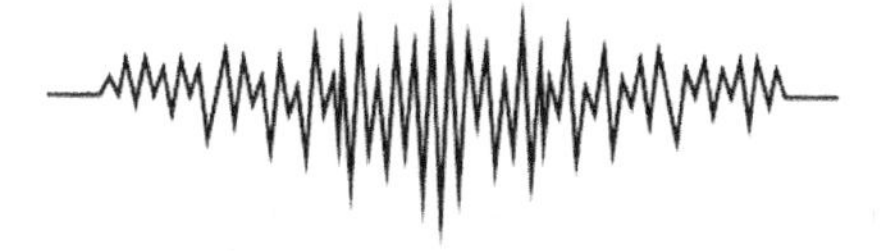

Around 10:00 a.m. I get a text from Emmett that he will be up to get me around 11:45 and that he is down in the studio working on music. I send a reply to confirm.

When I'm looking for some venues for future events, Eva buzzes me, saying there is a very yummy man out here wanting to see me and should she send him in. Laughing, I tell her yes.

Shit... I have been so busy today that I forgot to tell Eva about Maddox. I make a mental note to tell her after he leaves. Just then, Maddox strolls through my door with the sexiest smile, making me wet instantly and causing me to forget everything Brant and I discussed earlier.

Jeezus... I am one lucky lady.

Just seeing him makes my body come alive with lust and desire again—foreign feelings to me. Looking yummy is correct. Maddox's hair is still wet from his morning shower and is hanging around his face. He's dressed in faded jeans that hang low on his hips and a T-shirt that is tight on his chest but loose around the waist, making me want to put my hand under it to feel his rock-hard abs.

Gorgeous. Totally fucking gorgeous.

Leaning back in my chair, I admire him as he stalks toward me. I laugh, "Are you flirting with my assistant?"

Maddox moves around the corner of my desk, grabbing my hand and pulling me out of my chair into his wall of a chest. Before he kisses me, he says in his sexy as hell voice, "I only flirt with you, Alexandria." His kiss makes my knees go weak.

When I break the kiss, Maddox growls, looking down at what I'm wearing. With a devilish grin that makes his dimples seem even deeper, he pushes me up against my desk, sitting me on the edge while he takes a seat in my chair.

He speaks in a dominant voice. "Do you know what I want to do to you?"

God, this man and his sparkling eyes filled with passion make my sex throb with a deep pulse, aching to be touched. Taking a slow, deep breath and fighting the desire to submit to him, I try to rebel, raising an eyebrow. "No. What?"

Matching my expression, he raises an eyebrow, amused. "Alexandria, when the time is right, I'm going to show you so many new things. Explore that desperate sexual appetite I know you have, you just hide it underneath your good girl image."

He pauses to see what I do, but when he realizes I'm not moving, his face changes to a stern, hard expression. If I weren't looking straight into his eyes and seeing his silver eyes glisten, I would think he was pissed off. "I would make you lift your skirt for me, and then I would be face-deep in that sweet pussy of yours, making you scream my name. That's. What. I. Would. Do." He punctuates each word at the end, showing his forceful side and making my nipples harden against my bra, sending tingles throughout my body.

Fuck me. He's good.

I slide my hands down my skirt, itching to pull it up to challenge him. Maddox watches me intently I can see in his eyes, and it's clear from his tight grip on my chair he is trying to keep control of himself and the situation. I shift my legs, giving him a view of my wet panties.

Oh, my God, I'm showing him my panties.

In a controlled, even voice, Maddox orders, "Slide your panties down your legs and then spread them for me, Alexandria, so I can see your sweetness dripping for me." With no control over my body, I do what he asks me to. Maddox moves the chair more between my legs, not enough to touch me, just enough to have a full view of how wet I am for him. "*Jesucristo*, you're so fuckin' wet, so responsive with just me telling you what to do. You're going to drive me mad."

Jesus, I can't believe I'm doing this. Only for him. "Only for you."

Suddenly there's a knock at the door, jolting me from my erotic state. Maddox stands up between my legs. There's another knock at the door.

Wait... Shit. Is the door locked?

Then someone tries to come in, but Maddox did indeed lock the door. Relief washes over me. I go to speak, but it comes out broken. "Just a minute."

Maddox grabs my chin with his thumb and finger, making me turn to look up at him. "Alexandria, relax. I'll get the door while you straighten yourself."

Moving toward the door with ease, he adjusts his straining erection while I pull my skirt down. Sitting down at my desk, frazzled, I look up to see Maddox admiring me from the door with a devilish grin. "You ready?" I nod, and he opens the door, coming face-to-face with Emmett.

Shit. Only my luck.

The men stare at each other while Maddox stands in the doorway with his gigantic body. Emmett's face goes from smiling to murderous. Seeing both men stand next to each other, I can see the differences between the two. Maddox is big all over, starting with being a few inches taller than Emmett. But his arms, chest, and legs are all massive compared to Emmett's body which is only bulkier in the upper body.

Knowing this isn't going to go over well, I take a deep breath. Neither man moves from their stance, and Maddox has his hand on the door, gripping it with white knuckles while Emmett is just staring daggers at him.

God help me.

Standing up, I head for the door and I address Emmett. "E, why don't you come in? Emmett, this is Maddox. Maddox, this is Emmett. Please let him in."

When I say Emmett's name, Maddox's whole body tenses up and he clenches his jaw, not taking his eyes off Emmett. Both men just stand there staring at each other for what feels like forever. Once I reach Maddox's side, he pulls me to him by wrapping his arm around my waist and shifting me into his side, claiming me. Butterflies take flight in my stomach, making me feel all warm inside. I think I hear him growl, "Mine," but I'm not sure.

No one has said anything or moved, so I try again, "E, are you going to come in or stand out there all day?" *Please say something. Shit.*

I go to move back to my desk, but Maddox doesn't release me. Instead, he grips me tighter by digging his fingers into my side. Emmett looks down to see Maddox holding me, and his voice comes out husky, full of emotion when he barks, "Are you seeing him now?"

Before I can respond, Maddox answers for me, grunting each word. "Yes, she is."

Emmett fires back at Maddox. "Then why did she agree to

go out with me today?"

I feel Maddox's body tense up, making him pull me closer into his side. *Dammit. Why me?* I respond before this gets any worse than it already is. "Look, E, we're friends having lunch. My dating Maddox has nothing to do with our lunch date."

Maddox lets out a growl. "Fuckin' hell yes, it does, and fuck no, you're not."

What the fuck? Feeling my temper surface, I turn to Maddox. "You need to trust me enough that I can go out with my guy friends to lunch."

Before he can reply, I am turning back to Emmett. I see that his face is as red as fire, and the look in his eyes scares the shit out of me.

That's when I hear my saving grace. Brant walks up, laughing. "Stand down, boys. Don't have a pissing match here. Take it outside if you have to. Maddox, Luc is looking for you. Alex, call your mother. I think this little meeting is adjourned."

He stops just behind Emmett, folding his arms over his chest and waiting for everyone to disperse.

Thank you, B.

No one moves, but I look over to Brant, giving him the help me look. Maddox's grip is still tight around my waist. *Shit. Do something, Alex.* I look up to see Maddox's face rock hard, and he's clenching his jaw. I reach up to touch him, whispering, "Maddox, it'll be okay. You need to go see my papá."

Breaking his stare-down with Emmett, he looks down at me with his dark gray eyes flashing at me. I smile up at him, making him take a deep breath while closing his eyes. His facial expression eases, letting me see he's okay. "Okay, *mi belleza.*" As he leans down to kiss me, I hear a deep growl come from Emmett. Brant takes a step closer to Emmett while I try to break the kiss, but Maddox deepens it. When he pulls back, our gazes lock, and I suddenly forget everyone is around. He kisses me once more quickly before turning to walk away. When he brushes next to Emmett, he growls, "Mine," staking his claim.

Emmett is just standing there staring at me with crazy eyes and clenching his fists. Once Maddox is gone, I say to Emmett, "Do you still want to have lunch? Just as friends, though? If so, we can go after I see what my mamá wants. If you can't just be my friend, then we probably shouldn't go."

Brant must sense Emmett's rage because he moves closer to us, making it clear to Emmett that he's next to him. Without a word, Emmett turns and leaves with his fists still tightly clenched.

When I turn to Brant, I let out the breath I was holding and hug him. He laughs. "That was interesting, to say the least." I go to sock Brant, and when I pull away, Eva walks up with coffee. She notices I'm tense. "What's wrong, Alex? I just sent McDreamy in here, and now you look like someone stole your cookie. What gives?"

Brant and I start to laugh when I turn to her. "Well, if you would have hung around, you would have been able to tell Emmett I was busy and to come back. Instead, he and Maddox almost went head-to-head, and like Brant just said, had a pissing contest over me."

Eva's eyes almost pop out. "Shit, I always miss out on the fun stuff. Who won the pissing contest?"

Brant laughs, walking down the hall and saying over his shoulder, "Maddox, one. Emmett, zero."

Putting my hands on my hips, I look at both of them as I yell, “This isn’t funny, you two.” Everyone laughs while Eva goes to her desk, grabbing the phone that’s ringing, and I head off to call my mamá’s office.

Maddox

Fuck that motherfucker. I'll destroy him if he gets near Alexandria. *Fuck!* I need to get this rage under control before my meeting with Alexandria's father. But damn, I want to rip that fucker's head off. The way he looked at her makes my blood boil again. *Mine.* I don't do well with sharing, even if she says they're friends. And he apparently wants more. Jealousy is a new feeling for me, one I'm not used to and don't like having. My temper is hard enough to control, but with Alexandria, I want to inflict pain on anyone who gets close to her.

Closing my eyes, I try to calm down by thinking of Alexandria's sweet scent and the way she is so responsive to me. From the moment that I kissed her yesterday, I knew she would be my undoing and so worth the wait. Her soft, tan skin melts to my touch, her innocence combined with her want and need is a dangerous mixture. I need to take my time with her, enjoy her innocence before I corrupt her. I can see in the depths of her blue eyes and the way she responds to me that she is just as affected by our lustful encounters as I am. Just thinking about her luscious dark hair cascading down her body with all her curves makes my goddamn dick twitch to life. I adjust myself, trying to calm it down because now is not the time for a fucking massive erection.

Relax, Madd Dog. Down, boy.

Once I arrive at Luc's office, his assistant tells me to go on in and that he's expecting me. I knock on the door before walking in to face Luc. I stop in my tracks when I see a large man sitting in front of Luc. My voice comes out thick since I'm still thinking about Alexandria. "I'm sorry, your assistant told me to come on in, but I can come back." *Shit.*

Thinking I've interrupted a meeting, I turn to head back out the door when Luc replies, "Nah, Maddox, come on in. This is Beau Bagwell, my head of security."

Luc gestures for me to come and sit next to Beau, who has now stood up and is extending his hand. "Maddox," Beau says.

Shaking Beau's hand, I reply, "Beau, it's nice to meet you." I turn to Luc, shaking his hand too before we all go to sit down.

Well, this can't be good.

Luc leans forward on his elbows, pushing papers on his desk out of his way with a smile. "Maddox, I hope the rest of your night went well. Beau's here for security reasons, and we'll get to that in a bit, but we've got a bunch of things to discuss. *Capisci*? I'm pretty fuckin' blunt, as you know, and I don't fuck around. So, let's just get down to it. Why are you here, and what can we do for you?"

Luc's Jersey-Italian accent comes out thicker than normal.

Maybe it's because he's talking business with no women around, but I can tell the difference.

Fuck, I'm thinking about last night again... Focus, Madd Dog. I like him. No bullshit. No fucking around. My kind of man.

I knew this meeting wasn't going to be all that easy. Luc is very protective, and telling him what I want from his daughter probably won't go too well. Luc is known for blunt honesty, which is what I was hoping for, especially when I ask him questions about his daughter. I don't want to be fucking around, not when it comes to her and being mine.

Sitting back in the chair, I rest my hands on the arms and try to mask my thoughts. Not wanting to give away everything at once, I start with something easy. "Luc, it was great to hang out with you last night. I enjoyed getting to know you and your wife. Alexandria and I had a pleasant rest of the evening, getting to know each other as well."

Just thinking about last night and what she told me, then watching her sleep. *Goddammit.* Remembering her beauty stirs my dick again. *Fuck, keep it together, Madd Dog.*

I can't think about that shit right now; I need to focus. Shifting in my seat, I try to suppress my cock with its one-track mind, and I say, "Luc, as I told you on the phone and email, I've heard of your music, and I play your songs all the time. Once I saw your daughter at Club Monico, I knew I had to meet her."

Noticing Luc's body tense up at the mention of Club Monico, I continue, "With all the security around her, it was kind of hard to get close to her. So I…"

Luc puts his hand up, interrupting me. His face hardens as he speaks through gritted teeth to Beau. *"Vaffanculo!"* After telling Beau to fuck off, he yells, "When the fuck was Alex at Club Monico?"

He looks at me and then back to Beau. Seeing his jawline clenching as hard as it is makes it clear he's going to blow a gasket. *Hmm, he didn't know she was there? Interesting.*

Beau speaks up, clearing his throat. "It was right before she came back, and Gus and a team of six men were there with them. The girls wanted to go out before they came back. I didn't know about it till I read Gus's monthly report."

Beau pauses to see if Luc will respond. Then, he just looks over at me, and when I don't move a muscle or react, he continues, "Since there was no incident, I didn't hear about it. Alex doesn't know anything about Monico Benitez, so she wouldn't know if there was any security issue—which there wasn't."

We're all lucky Monico wasn't there.

Realizing Beau is done talking, I turn to see Luc staring daggers at Beau. *Fuck yeah, and he should be pissed.* I sit back, watching Luc and Beau exchange looks, and I know they're keeping information back. I don't blame them. They don't trust me, I get it, and I guess this is the time I should intervene. If we are going to go forward with this conversation, I want to know everything that has to deal with her. *Fuck it, here we go.*

Leaning forward with my forearms on my legs, I clasp my hands. "Okay, look, I know about your beef with Monico over your wife, Mia. I know that you know I was in a contract with him until a month ago. Before we can continue with this conversation, I need you to know I'm not here as a spy or on any business for Monico. I'm here for your daughter." *Shit, that came out wrong.*

Seeing Luc's face tense even more, I put up a hand in defense. "Luc, let me start over. I was in a contract with Monico for a couple of years DJing at his club. We're not friends" *Fuck no, I hate the motherfucker.* "I don't associate with him. I would just get a check, but I have ears. I know how much he hates you for taking Mia away from him. Everyone knows over there, but that has nothing to do with me. The night I saw Alexandria at the club, I had to meet her. Once I realized that wasn't going to happen, I had to find out who she was. And then I found out Alexandria was your daughter and how much Monico hates you, so I paid more attention, not wanting anything to happen to her. Monico was not at the club the night Alexandria was, which is probably why you didn't have any problems. If he was, I'm sure he would have done something. So…"

I lean back in my chair, looking over at Beau, whose face is a hard mask, showing no emotion at all. I turn back to Luc. "I had someone start to follow Alexandria, or at least, when she went to her last few clubs, I had someone watching her, making sure nothing happened." *Probably not a good idea I tell him it was me following her.* "I know she had security, but I wanted to hear what was going on behind the scenes, like if Monico was planning something or what people were saying. Luckily, for the most part, no one knew who she was."

Pausing, I take a deep breath, giving Luc or Beau time to intervene. When they both just sit there listening, I keep going. "I knew she was going back to the States, so I went to Monico, telling him I wasn't going to renew my contract, that I was going to go to the States to do a tour. Of course, he wasn't too happy, but he couldn't do anything. He heard about me remixing your song, which was a shock to me since no one but my internal group knew. That meant I had a leak in my group, but since then, I've dealt with it."

My blood boils just thinking of that snake Juan. He won't be walking anytime soon either, motherfucker.

Luc finally speaks up. "What did the *cazzo stronzo* say? What have you heard?" His calling Monico a fucking asshole pulls me from my thoughts of Juan.

"Luc, all I know is he flipped out on me for doing the song. I told him I did it so I could get close to Alexandria. He told me he has someone on the inside here, and he knows I wouldn't be able to get close to her, for me not to bother. That, and she doesn't date and is guarded more heavily than the president." *Which I now know why.*

Luc hisses, *"madre stronzo." Motherfucker is right.* Luc looks over to Beau for answers, but Beau just leans forward, turning toward me to speak. "Maddox, what else did he say? Any information you can provide for us would be useful. Since we have so many things going on right now, we need to know everything."

So many things? Like what?

"I told him I had to try and that she was the one for me. He told me I was stupid, but he liked the idea of me coming here to work for you. I asked him what he wanted from you, why did he have an inside man, and for what? He just laughed at me, saying it was none of my business. But from what my guys have uncovered, he wants his girls back."

Ethan found out a lot of shit about that son of a bitch.

Luc growls, standing up and pacing behind his desk, he starts rambling off a string of curse words in Italian.

For the first time, Beau shows emotions, hissing, "Which girls?" *Goddammit, they don't know?*

Irritation starts to build up inside me, so I start asking questions to get this meeting over with and go back to Alexandria. "I don't know which girls, I was hoping you would've known. I think he meant your wife, Mia, and Alexandria. I got pissed off when he said that, and I told him if anything happened to Alexandria, he would have to deal with me. I know Monico isn't an easy man to deal with, hell, most of his DJs are scared shitless of him and won't break a contract."

Beau speaks up first. "Why did he let you break your contract, then?"

Not wanting to tell them about my family connection, I just shrug it off. "I've never put up with his shit, and my contract was up."

Plus, I'm no one's bitch, and my family would kill him.

Luc stops pacing and sits down with both brows furrowed. He rasps out, "Well, I'm pretty fuckin' sure it has to do with your family bein' the Lucianos." He's staring straight at me, waiting for a reaction or for me to answer.

Fuck, he knows.

Luc sits back in his chair before explaining. "After we had dinner last night, I did a background check on your parents. Didn't think anythin' of it, but I told Beau I needed to know more about you since you told me you're goin' to date my daughter. With the way she looks at you, I knew it was serious. Then you told me your father's name was Rodrick and your mother's name was Rosa. Once I figured out your má was Rosie Luciano, I made a call."

Hmm, the way she looks at me... Wait... What?

I fire back at him, pissed off. "What do you mean, 'you made a call'?" I feel my temper rise.

Seeing my reaction, Luc waits for a second to see if I will

say anything else. With a smug smirk on his face, he replies, "I see your mother's side of the family is connected to my father's side of the family. Let's just fuckin' say your family works for my uncle. I don't involve myself with the family business. I left a long fuckin' time ago, after my parents were killed."

Well, what the fuck, that makes two of us.

"Well, you'll be glad to hear I have no links to my mother's side of the family business either. After my father died, we moved back to her hometown until I was old enough to be on my own."

I glance over at Beau, who has been quiet this whole time, just staring at me. I begin to feel frustrated and my temper starts to boil over, so I ask the rest of my questions. "Look, Luc, the moment I saw Alexandria, I knew she was the one. The connection I felt by just looking at her had me hooked. The more I've put myself in her life, the more I want to protect her from all this fucked-up shit. Especially after last night when she told me she was raped and hasn't let anyone get close to her since."

I try to simmer down my anger. I still can't believe I didn't know about this, that Ethan didn't find out. It makes me feel like shit for pushing her for sex. I wanted to kill someone last night, thinking of someone hurting her, forcing her… *Fuckin' hell.*

Luc growls, pulling me from my fucked-up thoughts. But Beau is the one to speak first, sounding surprised. "Did she tell you about that?"

Looking over to Luc, he says, "We had all those records sealed. There is no way anyone would know." Beau's shocked, looking back and forth between us. *Well, at least*

Ethan is off the hook for not finding it. Sort of.

Luc's looking just as pissed off as I feel, and he doesn't say anything. He just stares at me. Fisting my hands at my sides, I try to sound calm. "Yes, she told me last night. She thought I wouldn't want her anymore once I found out she was raped, or in her words, 'used and broken.' What I want to know is, was the motherfucker caught and dealt with? I didn't ask any details because she was already upset about telling me, but I want to know details from one of you." *Right fucking now.*

Luc is going to erupt any minute, his face red as hell. Knowing he won't be able to tell me, I turn to Beau. He closes his eyes, taking a deep breath before starting. "Long story short, she was at the festival, actually the one that's coming up next, but five years ago. Luc was out of town, and Mia took Alex to the festival. They went home before the evening events, but once Mia was sleeping, Alex snuck out with her best friend, Stella Rodriguez. We didn't have a bodyguard on Alex back then, so we got the call from Stella that something was wrong. Eli woke Mia, taking a group of men to look for Alex. Once they arrived at the festival, they found Stella with her, but Alex was still unconscious. We didn't know she had been raped or drugged until we were at the hospital. The guy was never found. Alex was slipped GHB and doesn't remember anything. The guy either knew her or cared for her because there was no force. She was found fully clothed with no major marks or evidence. He also left her where she would be found by her friends. Since we never found him, we moved Alex soon after, and she has been living in Spain ever since. She only just went out on her own a year ago, after graduation. Brant has been with her every step since the day she left the hospital."

What the fuck? He is still out there? She isn't safe. I need my team on this.

With my mind running in circles, I have to stand up. The rage is building inside me, and I feel like I'm going to burst.

Clenching my fists, I growl, "Fuckin' hell." Turning, I start to pace around my chair and running my hands through my hair. *Alexandria is not safe.*

When I stop pacing, I turn to Beau, asking through gritted teeth, "You never fuckin' found out who did it? Do you think Monico had anything to do with this?"

Fuck, even with our family connections, he never found him.

Everyone in the room is tense. Luc is still not able to talk, but he's mumbling shit in Italian when Beau continues. "Look, Maddox, we didn't know if we could trust you, but seeing your reaction, I think it's safe to say you won't hurt Alex. We don't know if it's Monico. We don't think so since it happened here in the States. Once she was scheduled to come home after graduation, she got a letter. Then when she came home from her Europe tour, we got another letter. They're sent to her at the building we live in. Then more girls started disappearing…"

What fucking letter and what missing girls? Goddammit.

"*Jesucristo.*" The urge to go to Alexandria right now is killing me. She's mine.

I rasp out, "What did the letters say? Who fuckin' knows about these letters? *And,* what fuckin' girls?"

Luc finally speaks up. "Maddox, I'm sure you know I don't trust many people when it comes to my daughter. Alex and Mia are my life. I will do anything to keep them safe, yeah. If any-fuckin'-thing happens to them, I will fuckin' kill whoever was involved. Mark my motherfuckin' words. I will find who did that to her and put them in the ground. The only fuckin' reason we're havin' this conversation is because of who your family is, and I can see the way you look at her. It's the same way I look at Mia. So, I say this with everythin' I have. If you hurt my daughter, I will fuckin' hurt you worse. *Capisci*? My daughter has been shielded from all this fuckin' madness. She has no fuckin' idea someone's after her again. I need you to know everythin' so you can be aware of her surroundings at all times."

Any other time, if he would have said those things to me, I would have been happy, but right fucking now, I only see blood.

"Who knows about this, and *what the fuck* did the letters say?" Losing my patience, I look between the two men.

Beau stands up, walking over to the counter where he grabs a folder and turns to hand it to me. I sit down before opening it. Beau explains, "We don't think it's Monico. If it were him, we believe he would've done something sooner with her living in Spain or during her tour in Europe. We definitely think he would've tried something sometime in the last five years. This is something completely different. Since the rape happened here in the States, only when she was scheduled to be back here, did we receive these letters."

Pulling out the copies of the letters, I lose my shit. *Alexandria is not safe. Mine. Fucking Mine.*

"Fuckin' motherfucker." Looking down at the typed letter in front of me makes me want to go and lock Alexandria up until I find this son of a bitch.

> *Alexandria, welcome back. I look forward to tasting that cunt of yours again. It's been far too long. I wasn't happy when you went away, but I'm glad to see you have saved yourself for me. We'll be together again soon, my love.*

I'm going to kill this sick fuck. I need to get this to my team. I need to hit something. Goddammit. I flex my hands to keep them from fisting.

I turn to the next letter, and I can't help it, I can't contain myself. I roar, "Motherfuckin' hell!"

> *Alexandria, Europe? My love, you should be here with me. I need your cunt devouring my cock. If you don't come home soon, I'll find you. You're mine forever. I've been playing, but I only have eyes for you. I was your first, and I'll be your last. I promise you, my love.*

Red. All I see is motherfucking red. My body feels numb all over like it's shutting down with so much rage and fear that I'm going to pass out. "Fuck. I want to kill someone right now. This shit is crazy. How many men do you have on her? Are there cameras in her place? Why did he wait five years to start writing again? *And* what the fuck does he mean, other girls? I want to give a copy of this to my team. Goddammit."

Luc holds his hand up to stop me from ranting. "Maddox, when Alex left five years ago, we told no one where she was goin', just that she went away for schooling. We sealed up the hospital and police records. We shipped her to our secluded villa in Spain. Everyone thinks she was away at some private school, and no one knew where she was. That's why we think it wasn't Monico because he knew she was livin' in Spain. He could have sent the letter right to her. And if it was someone else in Spain, they could've found her. We have guys working inside Monico's team, and I think you're correct he has someone working at the label here too. We don't put anythin' out there we don't want him knowin'."

Luc shakes his head. "Uh-uh. Nah, this is someone different, someone, from the States."

Beau speaks up. "Plus, we've been receiving reports of girls disappearing or getting drugged and raped over the last three years, but not enough to send us on a search. But just in the last year and a half, it has become more frequent, making us wonder if it's the same guy. The two buildings we occupy here in New York are fully secured. Both buildings are owned by Mancini Enterprises, so we've put extreme surveillance in both of them. We control the front desk, along with all video footage. No one even knows she has her own place but security, you, her girlfriends, and a select few. When she went out in Europe, we had two to four guys with her at all times, but an additional three were unseen, even by her. We don't want her scared to go out like right after the rape. She has worked through her panic attacks. And Brant is the only one she trusts when she has a panic attack. We watch her twenty-four seven. We even know you left last night around three in the morning. We have video everywhere. I have people monitoring our videos around the clock."

Jesucristo. Do they have the cameras in her place or her office? If so, they would have seen me with her today.

I interrupt Beau by blurting out, "Are there video cameras in the offices or inside her apartment?"

Beau's eyebrows furrow together like he knows what I'm thinking before he answers. "No, we have no video inside her house or her personal office. She does have some privacy but, Maddox, there is surveillance in all studios."

I change the subject. "So I'll need my team working with Beau's team. I need to know all that you have regarding these girls who are missing and anything that'll help find this son of a bitch. Now you both know I'm here for Alexandria, and I'm not going anywhere. I'll protect her at all costs."

Luc's office phone beeps, and his assistant's voice comes through. "Luc, Brant is here to see you. Do you want me to send him in, or tell him to wait?" Luc leans forward, pushing a button. "Yeah, Rachel, send him in, please." *What the fuck is he doing here?*

Luc leans back in his chair. He's stressed out and looks like he hasn't been sleeping. He runs his hands through his hair, and his voice is strained when he speaks. "Brant's here to get briefed on the new information."

Raising my eyebrow, I try to sound concerned and not pissed off. "What new information? He doesn't know about the letters?"

Luc replies in a stern but sincere voice, "Nah, the briefing is regarding you. We were concerned why you came here and your interest in Alex. Until this fuckin' mornin', we were concerned, but with all the information I found out about your family, and now about Monico, I feel better. Hope you understand, but we had to be sure you weren't the guy and you didn't have any ties to Monico. Let's bring Brant up to date so we can go from here."

Let's hurry the fuck up. I need to see Alexandria and then my team. Alexandria is not safe. Fuck.

Right then, the door opens, and Brant walks in, laughing at something Rachel must have said. As soon as he looks at the three of us, he shuts the door and turns around with a serious face, giving us all a head nod in greeting. Beau gets up, motioning for Brant to sit in his seat. Beau makes his way over to the window next to Luc.

I sit quietly, listening to Luc brief Brant on my past with Monico and what I've found out from him. When he starts to explain my family ties, I growl, making everyone look over at me. *I fucking hate being linked to my uncles.*

Running my hands through my hair, I try to keep my voice calm. "Luc, I wish people didn't know about my family ties to the Luciano family. I have no links to them. Personally, I think it is because of them that my father died. After today, please don't mention them again. I've kept that part of my life separate for many years." Luc nods his understanding.

For the next thirty minutes, we talk about Alexandria's security. I explain to them I want her with me when we're at the clubs. When I tell Luc I don't want her around Emmett ever without Brant or me around, it opens a whole new discussion, making Brant laugh. "Yes, Luc, we don't want another pissing match over her, especially in public."

Luc is looking between the two of us before landing on me with his brows raised. "What do you fuckin' mean, another?"

"I don't share, Luc, and you of all people should understand I don't want any motherfucker around my girl when they have other intentions. I don't like the way Emmett looks at her. I don't want her managing any DJs who want to fuck her. With all that I have found out in the last twenty-four hours, I don't want her alone with anyone but one of us here in this room."

I'm shocked when Brant speaks up. "I agree with Maddox. I don't like a few of the guys she manages either. I'm sorry, Luc. I know Emmett is your boy and all, but he just rubs me wrong."

Before Luc can reply, Brant turns to me. "Maddox, you're going to have a pretty hard time. She has another date this week with a promoter named Jason, and he's just as into Alex as Emmett is. Jason doesn't seem like much of a threat, but he's different. I don't know how to explain it, but he just seems…fake. Emmett and Jason already had words regarding Alex last Saturday when Alex wasn't around. I also want everyone to know I'm behind Alex in all decisions until it harms her well-being or her safety. If she wants to go out to lunch with some guy, I will be right beside her. She has come a long fucking way from being scared, and I hope you don't start taking her freedom away from her like locking her away again even with all this fucking shit going on. I know we all can work together to keep her safe, so I'm not worried. But, Maddox, you need to trust her. She is a good girl with a good head on her shoulders."

Hell fucking no, I won't let her go to lunch with some guy. She is mine.

Before I know what I'm saying, it just comes out. "First of all, she won't be leaving my side if I can help it. And second, have you ever wanted to be more than her bodyguard? Has anything ever happened between you two?"

Brant jumps up out of his chair, clenching his fists. "What the fuck are you trying to say?"

Do you want to fuck her, motherfucker?

I stay in my seat, looking amused and not intimidated by his aggressiveness at all. "I'm just asking. You're the closest person to her. I want to know what I'm up against. It's a legitimate question. Do you have feelings for her other than as a bodyguard, or have you two ever been together?"

Brant growls, "Fuck you, Maddox! She's like family, you know, like brother and sister. We are very close, but nothing like you're thinking. We've been through a lot together but never like that."

Luc stands up. "All right, guys, we're all on the same fuckin' side. We all want to protect Alex, but most of all, we need to work together and try not to alert her to what's goin' on."

Wait... Doesn't she know she is in danger? Fuck no.

That gets me to stand up. "Luc, I think you're wrong. I think we should tell Alexandria what is going on because, if, like you said, she is so independent now, don't you think she would want to know and not be kept in the dark?"

No one says anything; we all just turn to look at Luc, who's running his hands through his blond hair. His voice is tight as he struggles with emotion. "No, not right now. She's only been back a fuckin' week. Let's give it time, yeah?"

He looks at his watch. "I've got another meetin' right now. Let's all meet up later this week. Tomorrow, she'll go with Maddox along with Dominic and Izzy." We all nod our heads in agreement before heading out the door. I stop, waiting for Beau and Brant to walk out before turning back to face Luc. "Luc, we have more to talk about later, regarding her music and her future. I heard some of her original music, and she's fucking amazing."

Before he can say anything, I turn and walk out of his office on a mission to find my beauty.

Alexandria

Maddox stayed until I fell asleep again last night. Since Maddox and Brant came to get me after their meetings, I didn't get to talk to Brant about what was said or if they found out anything. I figured since they let Maddox come home with me and stay with me that it was okay.

We cooked dinner together and mostly just lay around talking. Maddox asked me a lot of questions about my childhood and living in Spain compared to here in New York. The way he always touches me, needing to have some kind of contact with my body, had my body humming. Again, he left me wanting more after only having a hot make-out session. At least he took my shirt off this time and did glorious things to me.

I wanted to talk to Brant this morning, but Sasha was with us on the car ride to work, so I didn't bring up the subject.

I tried to call and text Emmett again this morning, but he

never answered. I had also tried to call and text him a couple times after he left mad yesterday, but no luck.

I got a message from my mamá that she wanted to see me first thing this morning. I thought she wanted to talk about Maddox, but when I got to her office, a group of managers was there going over everyone's schedule. When it was my turn, she told me we're holding off on my schedule until I meet with Papá.

Leaving her office, irritated that she never explained why, I went back to my office. Now I'm working on setting up meetings for the next month, but I can't get my mind off Maddox and our time together last night. He consumes me. I never thought about what happened in the meeting, but now I'm wondering why Brant hasn't said anything to me about what was discussed in that meeting yesterday. *Are they keeping something from me? Is Maddox really here for me?*

I start to second-guess myself, and worry creeps over me with all my unanswered questions. I'm deep in thought when I look up to see Maddox walking through the door. Damn, those dimples and his immaculately sculpted body are a lethal combination of sex on a fucking stick, one I'm already addicted to. Jesus, he is a walking god.

Thank you, God, for sending him to me, please let it be real.

Relief along with desire fills my body, pushing all the negative thoughts I was just having out of my head. I lean back in my chair and giggle, saying seductively, *"Hola."*

He gives me a devious smirk. *"Mi belleza."* I instantly get wet at hearing my new nickname rolling off his lips, but the look on Maddox's face makes my insides bubble up with tingles that spread through my body. I watch him stalk over to me like he needs to be near me as much as I need to be near him. He lifts me out of my chair into an embrace, smashing our lips together, his tongue demanding entrance into my mouth urgently. A moan escapes me when I lift my arms to run my hands through his hair. I grasp behind his neck and pull him down for a deeper kiss.

Mmm, he tastes so fucking good. Maddox's hands are all over me and so demanding. *I wonder if something is wrong.*

Maddox slides one hand down, cupping the globe of my ass and giving it a squeeze before breaking the kiss and leaving both of us breathless. With a full smile, Maddox looks down and searches my eyes, for what I have no idea. "I've missed you, Alexandria."

My sex instantly throbs, wanting to be touched, and I moan out his name, "Maddox." *Please don't stop touching me.*

Maddox smiles at me seductively, and I lose my breath when his hair starts to fall into his face. I reach up, running my fingers through it and pushing it away from his face before leaning up to kiss him. I whisper, "You make me feel so many things, and it's like my body comes alive when you're near."

Heat fills my cheeks as Maddox places a soft kiss on my lips. "Alexandria, I agree and I want to take this slow with you, but sometimes it's so hard."

Maddox rubs his hands up and down my sides, caressing me, then continues, "We've got all the time in the world because I'm not going anywhere. Plus, when the time is right, one day we'll explore so many things with each other's bodies."

He leans down to kiss me, letting me know how much he

wants me and needs me, and I'm lost. Fuck, he can kiss. When he breaks our seal, leaving both of us panting hard, he rests his forehead against mine for a second before he releases me. He takes a step back but doesn't let go of my waist. "I'm going to head back to the hotel to meet up with my team. I'll be by around nine this evening to pick you up."

I look at him with a puzzled expression, "Wait... What? Where are we going tonight?"

He pulls me to his chest, wrapping his arms around tighter around my waist. "You're going with me tonight to Club Zero, along with Dominic and Izzy."

What the fuck, says who?

Stepping back to get some distance between us, I start to ramble. "I wasn't planning to go to the club. Who decided I was going tonight?"

Maddox leans down for a quick kiss, seeming humored by my outburst. "Well, Alexandria, I thought since we're seeing each other now, and most couples go places together, you'd want to be with me tonight. Am I wrong?"

He raises a brow in amusement. "I told your father yesterday I wanted you to be with me at all my gigs. I want you with me at all times if I can, but I don't want to push you too fast." Smiling at me, he waits for my response and runs his hands up and down my arms, comforting me.

Okay, now I feel stupid. He wants me with him at all times?

Butterflies take flight again in my stomach, and excitement bursts through my body. Realizing I'm just staring at him with a huge grin and haven't replied to him, I squeak out, "Yes, I want to be with you when you DJ. I will be ready at nine o'clock."

What's he doing until nine o'clock? Who's his team?

Wondering if any of those sluts will be with him makes me start to panic, and my insecurities begin to rise inside me as well.

Maddox runs his hand through my hair, looking concerned, "What's going on in that pretty little head of yours? You just got this stressed gaze in your eyes. Tell me."

Trying to shake off the images of those women around him, I don't say anything. Maddox grabs my chin, lifting my face to stare into my eyes. In a stern, dominant voice, he says, "Alexandria, tell me."

I try to move my head from his stare, but he isn't letting me budge. *Shit.* Frustrated at myself for being so insecure, I take a deep breath. "Who is your team? Are any of those girls going to be with you?"

Maddox holds my stare when he smiles, showing his dimples and beautiful white teeth. "I love when you get jealous. You're so adorable."

Huffing, I try to pull away from him, but I don't succeed and Maddox chuckles. "Alexandria, there will be no women with me tonight or any other night now that we are together. My team is my personal security team and manager, and you will meet all of them tonight. I will meet you at your place to ride with you, Brant, Dominic, and Izzy to the club, while my team follows us in their car." Maddox leans into me, dropping small kisses all over my face and making me laugh.

I'm still laughing as I say, "Okay, I'll see you tonight. Stop kissing me so I can get back to work."

When he stops placing kisses all over, he looks at me with such deep desire. I catch my breath and say in a shy voice, "Thank you. I'm sorry I overreacted. I don't know what came over me. I don't know how to do this 'relationship' thing, and I just don't want anyone touching you but me." *Touching, kissing, or even fucking sitting near you.*

Maddox's smile grows even bigger, showing more of his amazing dimples, "Alexandria, you're mine now. Since the day I saw you, I have not been with any other women. And from this day forward, I will not be with anyone but you. That is how important you are to me. Believe me, no one will be touching you either."

With a sigh, I whisper, "Okay." *Santa Maria.*

Both hands cup my face, pulling me in for a quick kiss. "Don't ever be sorry for that, and don't ever hold it in. I always want you to be honest with me and tell me how you're feeling. Okay?"

Kissing him back, I reply breathlessly, "Okay."

I walk him to the door and then to the elevator where he pulls me into an embrace, kissing me while running his hands down over my ass. When I hear someone clear their throat, I realize Ginger is walking up and watching us. I pull away from Maddox, flushed in the face, and I say good-bye. When I turn to walk away, Maddox grabs my hand, leaning in close to my ear. "Oh, by the way, I have your panties from yesterday in my pocket still. See you soon, *mi belleza*." He walks on to the elevator before I can respond, and the doors close with me staring at the most gorgeous man alive.

I knew he took them. Shit. Feeling embarrassed, anxious, and overall out of my element, I let out a deep breath.

When I turn around, Ginger is standing there with her helmet under one arm and resting on her hip. Smiling, she points to my office with the other hand. "Move. Office. Now. I need details, like yesterday."

Feeling a sharp pain in my chest, I rub it while heading into my office. Once the door is closed, I head over to sit at my desk, and I start to giggle like a little kid. Ginger's bouncing from foot to foot, not able to stay still. "Um, Alex, what the hell happened after we left?"

She throws her hands up and keeps talking. "I mean, shit, that man is all delicious with a side of fuck me hard and please may I have another. Jesus, girl." *Yes, fucking delicious and all mine.*

Thinking of my last few days, I flush in the cheeks, remembering how Maddox has stormed in my life and made me feel. I hear Ginger groan. "Alex, details now, biatch."

Laughing at her excitement, I start telling her all about our date Monday night and dinner with my parents and what happened yesterday and how he came home with me. I finish up with all the activity that happened today. She is shocked and sits down in a chair across from me. "Holy shit, Alex. You really like him, and *hello,* he totally loves you, girl."

What the... He doesn't love me. Does he? Shit, I really do like him. Could it be love?

Now I'm the one looking shocked, huffing out, "You're a crazy girl because he doesn't love me, Gin. We just started seeing each other, what, Monday, for God's sake."

Shaking her head at me and pointing her finger with a very mischievous smile, she replies, "Alex, he saw you in a club in Europe, which was months ago. Then he finds out who you are, remixes your parents' song to get in with the label, or, should I say, your father, so he can—" Ginger makes quotes in the air "*—meet you.* And then last but not least, um, the way he looks at you. Girl, he's into you, just like you're so into him."

She waves her hands in the air. "I am serious. You're so into this one. I've never seen you like this, and there have been plenty of hot men around us."

Leaning back in my chair, I smile to myself, thinking about what she said and what I want to do. I know I'm falling for him. Ginger stands up, bouncing around again and laughing. "I'm so excited for you. Finally. Well, I can't wait to hear all about your night tomorrow."

Panic rushes over me. "Gin, should I have sex with him? I mean, it feels so right, but is it too soon?"

Ginger puts her hands on her hips, turning serious. I don't say anything and let her think about what she is going to say. "Alex, you need to get laid. People have one-night stands. This is *nothing* compared to that. This man obviously cares a lot about you, so, yes, I would have sex with him. But when it is right, *you* will know. I know you have had it rough since your assault, but just follow your gut instinct or your heart. Neither one will steer you wrong. Girl, even if it is just making out, that would be good for me. He is *deeeelicious*." She springs back to her sassy self. "If you need me tonight, just call or text me."

I want him so badly. I want to do naughty things. Fuck it. I need to quit thinking and just go with it. Just breathe. Relax and have fun.

Alexandria

The rest of the day goes by pretty fast. Besides my thinking about Maddox, he texts me most of the day, checking in or texting me naughty things he wants to do with my body. It makes me come alive, and being away from him makes it worse. The need that has built up inside me is almost unbearable.

When I get home, I receive a call from Stella, who's still in Europe with her boyfriend. When I tell her about Maddox and everything that's happened with him, she promises to be home soon so she can meet him. While talking to her, I go through my whole closet, trying to find the perfect outfit, and she helps me pick out a few ideas. I decide on a short jean skirt with a tight black V-neck that shows off my breasts and some black stilettos. Since I'm not working tonight, I go for a more casual outfit because we're going to a hip-hop club.

A knock at the door sends my heart pounding in my chest.

Looking at the clock, I see it's ten minutes to nine o'clock. Either Maddox is early, or it's Brant. Glancing in the mirror again to make sure I look okay, I swoop my bangs to the side. I hear the front door open, letting me know it is Brant, and then I hear him call out my name. "In here, B." I let know I'm in the bathroom before I finish with my lipstick. Brant walks in, leaning on the doorframe and whistling while he chuckles. Grinning from ear-to-ear, I laugh. "Shut up, B."

I grab all my stuff and turn to walk out of the bathroom, but I stop when I see Brant smiling at me. I snipe at him. "What? Why are you looking at me like that?"

With a shrug, he chuckles. "Nothing, I like seeing you happy with a glow. Maddox makes you happy, yeah?"

God, yes!

I blush just thinking of Maddox. "Yes, he makes me so happy. I just…I don't know… I have this pull toward him. When he's near, I feel him."

Feeling frustrated and stupid, I snipe at Brant again. "I can't explain it. Why, what did you all find out? Why haven't you talked to me about him?"

Brant moves out of the doorway so I can pass by him. Brant follows me out into the living and kitchen area. "Alex, I get it. I understand and, to be honest, I can see a change in you. Actually, we all can, and it is great. You are finally letting yourself be you and not what you think we all want you to be. We all met with your father yesterday, including Maddox, and we talked about everything, including Monico."

Laying my stuff on the island where my clutch is, I look up at him, letting him know I'm listening and to go on. I keep my face blank, not wanting him to know how nervous and excited I am to hear what they found out.

He places his hands on the island before he continues. "Everything went well from what I know. Except your father knows now you were at Club Monico and is not very happy about that."

"Shit!"

Brant goes on. "Maddox is the real deal, and he's here for you and only you. He told your father he wants you with him everywhere while he's here in the States."

I let out the breath I had been holding. Sparks ignite inside me, and it feels like electricity is running through my body at the idea he really does want me. *Yes!*

"Alex? Hello?" Brant is waving his hands in front of me.

I shake my head and clear my thoughts. "Sorry, B, I heard you. What do you think?"

Looking down at my clutch, I start putting my things in it, keeping my focus on my task and not letting him see my reaction. "I think you should do what makes you feel good and go with your gut, because it hasn't led you astray yet."

Before I can say anything, there is another knock at the door. My heart skips, starting to beat faster and making my chest heave. Brant turns, heading to the door and opening it to reveal the man himself. Right at that moment, I know I'm done for, that I'm completely infatuated with this man.

God, he is so deliciously gorgeous.

I watch him say hello to Brant while keeping his eyes on me. He moves with confidence, like he will stop at nothing to get to me. He's wearing what I think is his usual club attire, black cargo pants with biker boots, showing off his huge leg muscles, and his shirt is like a second skin, but the gray sets off his eyes, making them a light silver-gray.

Damn. I'm falling hard for this man.

His hair is pulled back into a low ponytail, and a black bandanna is holding the loose strands back. "Hey," is all that I can muster with my irregular breathing.

Lord help me, he is fucking hot.

When he smiles down at me, I feel my panties moisten. "Alexandria, you look absolutely gorgeous."

He reaches out for me to come to him, and I give him my hand. I lean back for a kiss, but before we can get too lost in each other, Brant speaks from the door, "Okay, you two love-birds, we have to go. I'll be outside, but if you're not out in five, I'll come back in for your asses."

Laughing while he heads out of the door, I look up at Maddox, smiling. "Well, you passed B's test. I think he likes you."

Maddox grabs my hand, looking me over from head to toe. When his eyes land back on my face, I see the lust in his gaze. "Alexandria, I'm glad he approves, but yesterday, I told all of them I didn't care what they thought because I'll have you no matter what. I came here for you, knowing you're the one for me."

He only wants me... He only wants me!

Overwhelmed with emotions, I can't even speak. I just stand there staring at him with a huge smile. Maddox starts to laugh. "Come on, are you ready? We don't want to make Brant mad since he does like me."

I nod my head once. I grab my clutch, and he pulls me with him, holding my hand as we walk toward the door.

Once downstairs, I see four enormous men waiting, along with a medium-built man probably Maddox's age or younger. Maddox guides me to the group, still holding my hand, and when we approach, I start to get nervous.

I hope they like me. Will Maddox care what they think? Jesus, they are big.

When Maddox goes to introduce me to all five of them, they turn, looking me over, not even trying to hide that they're totally checking me out. Feeling uncomfortable, I look back to see Brant just a few feet back, and that helps me relax some. Maddox pulls me into his side, claiming me with a growl.

The first big guy with a bald head is a man I recognize from the club. He says, "Damn, Madd Dog, she is even more beautiful in the light." He extends his hand to me. "Hi, beautiful. I'm Austin."

Feeling my cheeks turn red, I shake his hand. "Nice to meet you, Austin."

I hear a deep growl from beside me. I look to Maddox, and I see him snarl at Austin, "Her name is Alexandria." *Wow. Okay. Possessive, are we?*

Maddox pulls me back to his side, holding my waist tighter. That's when the second guy pipes up, "Don't get your panties in a bunch, Madd Dog. He was just trying to be polite. I mean, she looked fucking gorgeous the other night when we saw her. But now, in real light, she is beautiful, so relax."

Turning to me, he extends an arm that's the size of my waist and shows me a genuine smile. "Hi, Alex, I'm Chad. Head of this dipshit's security, and those two boys over there are Ethan and Roc."

I accept his handshake with a hello, telling them they can call me Alex, before I turn to the other two men. Ethan is probably the smallest of the four, with a baby face that would melt any girl's heart for sure. Roc's name is perfect for him. He is built like Brant but probably two inches taller, and he has a scar over his jawline, making him look scary as all hell.

But his eyes…something about his eyes makes me feel he is a softie.

Warmth fills my heart knowing Maddox has a group of guys by his side that cares about him, even if he is acting like a possessive ass. My face heats up at so much attention from all of them all smiling at me.

Um, these guys are massive.

All the men are around Maddox's height, and I guess if you're going to guard someone, you should be bigger. I tell all of them it was nice meeting them, and Maddox pulls me back into his side after I greet the other two with a handshake.

The last one to step forward I'm guessing is his manager. Another growl escapes Maddox before the guy speaks. "Maddox, I never thought I would see the fucking day, but fuck me, you're whipped, brother."

Wait… What?

Looking from Maddox to me, he smiles big, extending his hand to me. "Hi, beautiful. I'm this lover boy's manager slash best friend, Isaac. Damn glad to meet you, Alex."

I shake his hand, saying hello.

Maddox growls, "What the fuck did I just say? Don't call her beautiful, fuckers."

Maddox slides his arm around my waist again with a tug. Isaac moves away from me, laughing and putting his hands up in surrender before sliding them back in his pockets. "What? You call her that all the time."

Looking back over to me, Isaac continues, "Darlin', we all thought he went and lost his marbles or had fucking gone crazy because none of us had seen you in Spain. He just started going off about you and would stop at nothing until he met you—"

Maddox hisses, "Shut the fuck up, brother."

Isaac throws his hands up again and laughs, "So, here we are." All the guys start laughing except Maddox, who's getting more pissed off.

These are his friends. Why is he getting so mad?

Leaning into Maddox, I put my hand on his chest. "Well, it's nice to meet all of you."

From over my shoulder, I notice Brant standing to the side. I motion toward him. "This is my personal bodyguard and close friend, Brant." All the guys greet him with either a hello or a head nod. Maddox tells the guys to follow us, so we all load up into the limo.

Once inside the limo, Maddox and I are alone, with Brant up front with our driver. I settle myself in next to him and ask, "So why were you so mean and tense?" Maddox doesn't reply. Instead, he just rubs his hand up and down my arm.

When I lean back to look up at him, I see the concern in his stormy gray eyes, "They have never seen me like this with anyone. They have been teasing me for months, but when they saw you, they all started talking about how fine you were, not knowing how serious I am about you. I flipped out on them. Tonight, they just wanted to get a rise out of me, but believe me, they will hear about it from me later. They are a bunch of players, and all they think about is pussy. So I don't want them thinking or talking like that about you, even if it's to get a rise out of me. No one will talk about you like that in front of me. I'm the only one who will be calling you beautiful in this group. You are mine, Alexandria. I've never wanted anything in my whole life as much as I want to have you."

Okay...definitely possessive, but kind of amazing at the same time.

Maddox continues, "The reason we have a bunch of girls with us everywhere is usually for their benefit. I told them from now on when we get back from the club, they can go out and pick up girls, but I didn't want them with us anymore."

Still looking up at him, I smile before saying, "Thank you."

Leaning down and placing his lips on mine, he whispers, "Told you not to say thank you. It's what I want, and I'm done having groupies all around me. I want only you. If they don't like it, they can leave. I only have security when I go to the clubs. Otherwise, we all just hang out as friends, or I'm on my own."

Lifting my hand up around his neck, I pull his head down to deepen our kiss. I let out a moan in the back of my throat. I need him to know how I feel.

God, I really want his man.

The more I'm around him, the more I feel my walls come down. There are a bunch of walls, and I hope he is willing to climb all of them.

I break the kiss, and when I pull away from him breathlessly, I say, "Maddox, you make me want things I have never wanted before, and my God, you feel so good."

Before I can blink, Maddox shifts me to straddle him. I cup his face with both hands and grind my hips down, feeling his massive erection under my panties.

He growls, "Alexandria, once I'm done with my set, we are leaving. Goddamn, I want to hold you next to me again. I want to be alone with you and learn everything there is about you. I hate sharing you."

Sliding both hands up my thighs and over my skirt to make it rise up, Maddox grabs my ass on both sides. He thrusts his erection hard against my sex, making me cry out, "Holy shit, Maddox!"

A tap on the window brings me out of my lust-filled haze, and we feel the limo come to a stop. Breaking our kiss, I try to hop off his lap, but Maddox grips my hips tighter. "Where do you think you're going?" he asks with a devious smirk.

Giggling, I reply, "Um, we are picking up Izzy and Dominic right now."

Shrugging and smiling with those damn dimples, he says, "So? I want you sitting on my lap."

Before I can protest, Maddox is shifting me on his lap, turning me so I'm sitting sideways then pulls my skirt down to cover my ass. "There, you're all covered. And, I can still feel you on my cock, right where I want you to be all night."

It's going to be a long night.

The door to the limo opens, and I hear Izzy squeal, "Alex, what the hell?"

She stops talking when she realizes I'm sitting on Maddox's lap. Dominic is right on her tail, pushing and grabbing her ass before saying, "Move it, Izz. Otherwise, I'm going to bite your pretty little *попка* if you don't fucking move it."

Dominic's thick Russian accent rings through the limo as he says "ass" in his native language.

Izzy giggles, moving to the other side of the limo and giving Dominic room to get in. When he realizes Maddox is in the back, he laughs, "Fuck, sorry, I didn't know anyone else was in here."

When Dominic settles in next to Izzy, he pulls her into his side, claiming her, and making me laugh at our men being so possessive. Before I can make introductions, Izzy, who can't control herself, blurts out, "Okay, so what the fuck? You must be Maddox, otherwise known as DJ Mad Max, or as they say, Madd Dog."

What the hell? How does she know people call him Madd Dog? I didn't even know that until a few minutes ago.

I squirm in my seat, and I feel his erection under my ass, making him hold me tighter to him. I look down and giggle before answering her. "Hey, Dominic. Hello, Izzy, it's good to see you too. Yes, this is Maddox, you guys, and yes, we're dating. Who called you? Ginger?"

I'm sure it was Ginger.

Dominic says hello back, while Izzy just stares at me, beaming like a kid at Christmas. Finally, Dominic pinches her, making her respond.

"Hello, Alex, and it's nice to meet you, Maddox. Sorry for the outburst, but my girl here is holding back information." She crosses her arms like she's going to pout.

Maddox laughs, saying hello back to both of them then snuggles into my neck.

Feeling eyes on us, I turn and explain a shortened version of how I met Maddox. During the whole story, Maddox is caressing me, making me wiggle on his cock and sending waves of heat to my core. By the time the evening is over, I might explode.

I think I'm having sex tonight, finally! Anxiety and passion are fighting a war in my body, but my mind is all for it. I think…

Alexandria

When we reach the club, Maddox slides me off his lap to exit the limo and then helps me out, instantly pulling me into his side to protect me. Before we head in, Maddox leans down, giving me a kiss and claiming me in front of everyone, making sure they all know we are together. The line outside the club erupts with screams from girls who are going nuts screaming, "Mad Max!" Maddox holds me tighter into his side, and we have his security team plus four of my own ushering us inside. It takes me back to the night I first saw him in the club and how the crowd was pushing me toward the dance floor when I finally caught sight of him. My life has never be the same from that day on.

I hear Izzy squealing behind me. It's madness with people screaming Maddox's name. Before I know it, we are in the VIP area and I can finally breathe again. Maddox kisses my forehead before he releases me from the vise grip he had on me. Brant grabs my elbow, turning me to look at him. "Alex, are you okay?"

From the look on his face, I realize he is checking to see if I had a panic attack with all the craziness and being pushed in the club. I freeze, totally in shock, and Brant shakes me. "Alex?"

Oh, my God, I didn't freak out. I didn't even get the tightness in my stomach. Holy shit.

Maddox must realize something is wrong because he grabs me, pulling me into his arms. "Alexandria, what is it?"

I hear Brant say, "I think maybe she is having a panic attack."

Snapping out of my daze, I pull away slightly from Maddox, turning to Brant. "*Santa Maria.* B, I'm in shock because I didn't have any kind of panic."

Smiling, I feel amazing and I continue, "Nothing, not even in my stomach or chest. I mean, nothing for the very first time." *Oh, my God, this is great.*

Brant looks from me to Maddox, who is still holding me, not understanding what's going on. Maddox gets frustrated. "Will one of you tell me what the fuck is going on?"

Brant is still in shock, and he shakes his head before addressing Maddox. "Since her assault, whenever Alex goes into a club or is in crowds, she has a panic attack. Some are big ones where I have to carry her out, and some are small where she can just take a breather and get over it. From what she is saying, tonight is the first time she hasn't had one, like, *at all.*"

Rubbing the back of his neck, he continues, "I think because she was with you holding her, she felt safe or something. Shit, I don't know, but this is a good thing."

Brant pats my arm before he walks out of VIP to meet with

the other security team. Maddox turns to me, looking into my eyes and searching to see if I'm all right. "Are you okay?" I nod my head, letting him know I'm okay with a smile.

Jesus, can it really be that easy? I'm not scared, no panic attacks, no warm feeling in my stomach besides the warmth of passion swirling in there.

Izzy comes up behind me, handing me a shot. I gladly take it and say, "To tonight and new beginnings. Let's party." I slam back my shot, and Maddox shakes his head, laughing.

Being with Maddox is a whole new experience at the club. He never leaves my side, always touching me somehow, making me feel safe and loved. Girls come and go, trying to talk to Maddox, but he is always polite and introduces me as his girlfriend and pulls me to his side. Izzy and Dominic are fun to be around. Dominic appears to like Izzy, and I'm happy for her. He seems to be just as possessive of her as Maddox is of me, always touching her or pulling her with him possessively. Izzy and I keep taking shots and dancing around. When Dominic starts to head up to the stage for his set, he grabs Izzy's arm, yanking her with him and almost making her fall. I step toward her, but she starts to bounce around him giggling. I laugh at her, and she beams back at me, waving good-bye. It makes me happy that we both have someone now. I keep glancing down to Brant, who now looks stressed out as he talks into his mouthpiece and on his phone. I feel like I should go see what is wrong, but Maddox won't let me out of his sight.

When it's almost time for Maddox to go on, he lets me know he wants me on stage with him. He says tonight's set is for me and he wants me near, which makes me even more excited for his set. The stage is set up for only the DJ and maybe two other people. But whoever is on stage is in the limelight, front and center. Usually, only the DJ is up there, but I guess tonight we girls get to hang out with our men. When my phone vibrates, I pull it out to see a text from Jason.

Shit.

JASON

Hey, Alex, at the club with your father. Shit went down tonight with Emmett and me. The second time he and I have had words at the club. This time, he flipped out and threw a punch. I wanted to let you know my side of the story, so can we talk tonight? I want to see you, but I know you're at Club Zero. If you have time, please text or call later. Looking forward to seeing you at the club and lunch.

"Goddammit." *A fight, really? Emmett is losing it.*

Maddox sees my face and walks up to me, growling, "What's wrong? Who just texted you?"

I look from him to Brant and back to Maddox. Seeing Maddox is getting pissed off, I reply, "It was one of our promoters. There was a fight at the club. I need to talk to Brant."

When I start to head toward Brant, who is standing outside of the VIP area, Maddox pulls me back into his chest. He speaks with a locked jaw and so much dominance I want to fall to my knees. "You know you suck at lying. Who texted you, Alexandria? I'm not fuckin' around."

I feel his chest rise and fall, and I know he's pissed off when I look up into his gray eyes.

Damn, he's mad. "Maddox, it was a promoter of ours."

Not letting go of me or giving any space, he says tightly,

"Who texted you, Alexandria? I won't ask you again."

Oh, shit.

"His name is Jason from Jas Entertainment. You don't know him, I don't think."

I keep my face clear of any emotions, but when Maddox reacts, I gasp. "Why the fuck is he texting you when you're not working or at the club?"

What the fuck? Seriously?

Getting pissed off myself, I try to push away from him, but I don't get very far, "Maddox, what the fuck? He's a friend who works for us and nothing more."

I look over to Brant, waving him over once he sees me. Maddox is still holding me next to him. He's trying to control his anger, while mine keeps rising. How are we supposed to trust each other when both of us are flipping out over nothing? I take a deep breath, letting it out as I look up at Maddox and cup his face to pull him down for a kiss. When his arms circle around my waist, I deepen the kiss to let him know I'm his and no one else's.

Breathe, Alex.

Brant clears his throat, alerting us to his presence. I pull away, breaking the kiss, but I stay close to Maddox. Staring into his eyes, I tell him, "Maddox, I'm yours and only yours. I do not want anyone but you, and no one will have me but you. Please trust me as I trust you." I finish by kissing him, and I hear a deep growl come from him.

I look up to see stormy eyes looking down at me. "Now, go get ready while I speak to Brant. Then we'll head up to the stage." I'm shocked when he releases me and actually moves away from me without saying anything.

I turn to Brant when I know Maddox is out of earshot.

"What the hell happened at Club Spin? Is that why you're all stressed out and checking your phone?"

Brant is masking his reaction as he answers tightly, "How did you find out?"

I put my hands on my hips, letting him know this isn't a fucking game. "B, these guys are on my team that I manage, and Jason is one of our main promoters. Jason texted me and told me about him and Emmett. Why didn't I know about the first time they had words?" I'm pissed off no one told me about it.

Brant exhales. "Alex, it was last Saturday when we all were at Club Spin, the night you met Maddox. Emmett, Ginger, and Dominic were DJing the club Jason was promoting. I guess, from what Ginger said, the two of them exchanged words and Jason pushed Emmett. But security was watching them closely, so when Jason pushed Emmett out of his face, security grabbed them."

What the fuck? I hope it isn't about me. Jason pushed Emmett?

"What was it about? Does anyone know?"

I want answers, but Brant shrugs before saying, "I'm sure it has to do with you. Tonight, Emmett swung on Jason. If Emmett is still pissed off about you and Maddox, and Jason said something, I'm sure that is what happened." Before I can speak, my phone vibrates.

Looking down, I see I have a text from Emmett. I glance around, looking for Maddox and see he's putting all his music together to head to the stage. Brant is beside me, looking at my phone.

EMMETT

Baby girl, I'm pissed off that you're with Maddox, but if you even go out to lunch or anywhere with this motherfucker Jason, I'll freak the fuck out and lose it. He's bad news, and if you knew what he says about you or what he wants to do with you... FUCK. He's going to get his ass whooped. Text me back or call me. I want to make sure you're okay and safe.

Jesus, is Emmett telling the truth? Would Jason say shit about me?

I hear an enraged growl. "What happened?"

I look up to see Maddox looking over my shoulder, reading my text like Brant and I were, only now Brant is on his phone.

Maddox is shaking with rage. "What the fuck happened?"

He's clenching his fists, making me take a few steps back. "Maddox, calm down."

He takes two steps toward me, pulling me into an embrace. I move my hands to his chest, leaning back to look up at his face and trying to calm him. "Maddox, there was an exchange of words between my promoter Jason and Emmett, our DJ, which led to them fighting. That's why Jason texted me to let me know, and you've seen Emmett's text."

Maddox still seems pissed off as he hisses, "They were fighting over you. In that text, Emmett said Jason was talking about you. I don't want you around either one of them till we figure this shit out."

My temper starts to rise. "Maddox, this is my job. I'm in charge of them, and if it's about me, I'll deal with it."

Maddox is losing control, and I see it in his eyes before he rasps out, “The fuck you will. Hell no, not without me, you’re not.”

Shit, he does have a point. I have no control over those guys.

I take a deep breath. “Fine, you and Brant can be with me. It’s probably not going to happen tonight, so can we go back to having fun. You need to get on stage.” I grab his face, bringing it down to kiss me.

Maddox deepens the kiss, sucking on my tongue with force and telling me he’s still upset. When I hear Brant next to us, Maddox pulls away. Before Brant can say anything, Maddox says through clenched teeth, “Brant, she goes *nowhere* near either of those two fucks without you or me with her, do you understand me?”

With a calm voice and no emotion, Brant replies, “Yes, I totally agree with you, Maddox. You have my word.”

What the hell is going on? I can take care of myself.

The two of them exchange looks before Brant looks at me. “Alex, your father is dealing with the problem, and we’ll all meet in the morning for an update. Now both of you, get on stage.” Without saying a word, Maddox grabs my hand, and we head for the stage.

With my mind going in a million different directions, I don’t even notice Isaac come up and start talking to Maddox, who still holding my hand. I’m so lost in thought I don’t notice they are arguing until I hear Maddox yell at him, “Do what the fuck I say. Things are different. Now get things changed.” I look up from behind Maddox to see Isaac turn beet red and walk off, leaving us next to the stage alone.

I pull Maddox around to face me when I notice he’s still seething. “Hey, what’s wrong? Please don’t be mad because of those guys from my work. We're together now. Please don't let this ruin our night."

Maddox takes a deep breath, pulling me into his massive chest before looking down at me. "Alexandria, you have no idea what rage I feel right now. I don't want any motherfucker near you. I'll hurt anyone who tries to touch or hurt what is *mine.* You're *mine*, Alexandria."

Shushing him, I pull his face down so our foreheads touch. "Maddox, no one will ever touch me again but you. And hopefully, soon you will be the only one making me *feel good.*"

Oh, my God. I can't believe I said that! Shit!

Growling, he smashes his mouth to mine, twisting our tongues around and biting my lower lip with a groan. "Alexandria, fuck, I want to be balls deep in you. You're mine, all mine."

Standing up on my tippy-toes before I kiss him, I whisper, "Yes, Maddox, all yours."

We hear someone call Maddox on stage. I wait for his intro to be over, so I stand there watching him take his shirt off when the lights go dim. I'm in awe of his body and counting down the time until I will be underneath this fine specimen of a man. *Fuck.*

When the lights flash on him, I stare at the beautifully designed tattoo on his back. The tribal ones come over his shoulders from the front, but in the middle of all the intricate tribal work is a cross. The cross starts at his neck, going down to mid-back with a flag wrapped around it. The flag is actually two flags put together and blowing in the wind. I see half of the Italian and half of the British flag, and it's truly breathtaking, with so much detail. Damn, this man is delicious.

I can't help myself, and I stand to the side of him and just admire his body with a perma-grin on my face because my heart is so full of happiness that I think it is going to explode. I love watching him with his headphones pushing his hair back, with no shirt, moving his body to the rhythm, while counting the beats to the next song coming in, and messing with the mixer. God, he is so fucking gorgeous. My eyes roam over his sculpted shoulders down the length of his torso, watching every muscle contract as he moves to the music. His legs are spread apart, bouncing to the beat and making his ass shake.

Fuck, I want to touch him so damn bad.

Suddenly, he turns slightly around to face me. He extends his arm, pointing his finger at me and motioning for me to come to him. When I start to move toward him, he turns around again, messing with the mixer and dropping in the next song. Once he finishes, he takes off his headphones. Turning around with a James Brown move, he starts to dance, making me laugh. When the next song drops, the crowd erupts and the spotlight flashes to Maddox dancing. Then I hear it. I start to laugh. "Tonight" by John Legend starts to play.

Oh, my God. Fucking unbelievable. No, scratch that, heaven.

Maddox starts dancing sexy as hell toward me, moving his arms up his body and grabbing his chest. He sings to me about tonight being the night we're going to lose control. Coming to a stop, he starts rocking back and forth, moving his pelvis in a grinding motion as he continues to sing to me, promising the best sex I've ever had, while using the most sensual, erotic voice ever.

Maddox points to my crotch, licking his lips and making me laugh. My body's so wound up for this spellbinding man. *God, I need to touch him. So fucking gorgeous.*

I can't help but start to move my hips while raising my hands above my head, but I still stay where I am. This is his show, not mine. Maddox runs his hands through his hair then down his glistening chest, sending a jolt of desire straight through my body. Maddox is smiling at me, and he takes another step toward me, moving his sexy as sin hips to the music like he's fucking me. He dances, continuing to sing and repeating he was going to be the best I ever had.

Listening to the lyrics and the meaning behind his message to me has my body igniting. I can't stop thinking about us having sex. *Jesus.* This song is perfect for us. When he reaches me, he lifts my arms above my shoulders, moving them around and thrusting his pelvis against my body while he moves me until he's eye level with me. He gives me a quick kiss. We start to dance in sync, moving our bodies together as one, when he wraps his arm around my waist, pulling me in closer and grinding on me. I feel his enormous girth moving against my leg, and I see his panty-dropping grin. He keeps assaulting me with his words, saying how he doesn't want to brag, but he's going to be my best ever, all while thrusting his cock up into me. I moan, feeling my panties soak.

Tilting my head and giggling, I tell him that he *will be* the best I've ever had. Maddox growls, leaning down to kiss my neck while repeating the song in my ear.

I'm so lost in him I forget where we are. He keeps singing, releasing me, turning me in a circle, and backing me up to his solid frame. When he brings my ass up against his pelvis, he rubs his dick against me. I close my eyes, moaning when

Maddox growls, "Fuck it, round two now."

He leans into my ear, and I feel his warm breath against my skin as he sings, his voice rough, desire dripping from each word.

The hunger in each word makes my nipples hard. He licks his lips, saying, "Goddamn, you feel so fucking good."

Still holding me, he rubs his hands over my stomach, connecting our bodies. We are moving together with his cock nudging me with each step and making my body tingle all over.

Maddox glides his hands down my thighs. The crowd's going crazy seeing him sing to me, but I don't care, I'm so lost in him nothing matters. When he turns to put his headphones back on, I think I'm going to fall with my knees going weak, but Maddox keeps a hand around my waist to keep me balanced. I pivot around, gripping his waist with my hands. I move my way around him to stand behind him, letting him mix the next song. Never breaking contact, I run my hands over his shoulders. They are slick with sweat, and I drag my hands down his rock of a torso while moving my hips against his ass. I'm gliding my hands around his waist to his front, up his abs and pulling on his nipple jewelry. That makes him grab my wrist, yanking me around to his side for a quick kiss and growling at me. While he's messing with the mixer, he starts singing the rapping part by Ludacris. He's gone completely serious while singing to me, pointing, throwing his arms between us while rapping about us being together, how we can make it through anything.

While he finishes setting up the next song, I turn to the crowd. All I can see are masses of people grinding on each other. All night, the crowd has been bumping and grinding each other. Maddox has been playing mostly baby-making music—well, that's what we call it at the label. He's truly a great DJ, able to spin any style of music and keep the crowd happy. I just keep finding more and more reasons to love him.

I make my way to the side of the stage when I see Izzy walking up, but I am pulled back as Maddox grabs my wrist. When I turn to face him, I'm shocked when he pulls me quickly into an embrace, kissing me. I panic for an instant, thinking we are on stage in front of a couple of hundred people at least. But when I hear him growl with such desire, I forget anyone and everything except us. When Maddox breaks the kiss, leaving both of us panting, he smiles, showing his dimples. "Don't go far, Alexandria. I want you by my side all night. I've got some more fun stuff planned."

Still in a daze, I hear Izzy giggle next to me, "Fuck, Alex, you two are hot as hell together."

I start laughing, but I never turn away from looking at *my man. Holy shit.* I have a boyfriend, and he's fucking amazing.

The rest of the night is like a dream. Maddox plays for the crowd, and they love him. He is so attentive to me and making sure I don't feel ignored. Izzy visits me when she thinks I need another shot, but she roams around with Dominic, never leaving him for more than a few minutes. I stay on stage, only leaving Maddox's side to talk to Izzy or one of Maddox's guys who come to check on us. They are all very sweet, and I can tell they all love what they do. When it's almost time for Maddox to be done and the last DJ heads up to the stage, I move back to give them room to do their switch. Maddox is concentrating on his last mix and doesn't see me move to the back of the stage. Before he's done mixing, he turns around, looking for me. When he sees I've moved away, he yells,

"Alexandria, get your ass back over here."

He looks pissed. *What the hell? I didn't do anything wrong.* The other DJ just looks at me confused, but he steps back, giving me room to move back over next to Maddox. I look out to the crowd and see the sea of bodies grinding and moving to the beat. Maddox doesn't look up or acknowledge me. Irritated that he snapped at me like that in front of all these people, I try to keep my temper down.

When he moves his headphones off, I look over and I hear his last song drop, "Hold On, We're Going Home" by Drake.

I smile, looking over at him and seeing a devilish grin. He leans down, giving me a quick kiss before he finishes mixing into the song.

When it drops, I just listen to the words and watch him move to the beat. All night, his songs have had some kind of meaning for us, but this song is him speaking to me. Maddox moves toward his stuff, not making eye contact with me but just singing the song, moving seductively to the words. I stand there motionless, waiting for him to look at me, but he just puts his stuff away, singing to himself with a devilish grin. Can I want him any more than I do right now? Music is definitely the way to my heart. I laugh when I hear him sing the next verse, telling me I'm a good girl and how I act so differently around him.

Maddox turns toward me, pulling me with him. He guides us to the back of the stage, letting the other DJ move in to set up. Once we're out of the way, Maddox wraps both his massive arms around my waist, singing to me and making my body come alive. I move my hands up his chiseled chest, locking them behind his neck. We don't take our eyes off each other or care who's around; he just moves our bodies to the beat. His voice rumbles deep, coming out rough and dirty.

Maddox leans down to kiss me. "Baby, you're my girl and my only one." He kisses my neck.

I can't take anymore. I need to kiss him, so I pull his head down and smash my mouth to his, demanding entrance. Maddox tightens his grip, slipping his hands down over the globes of my ass and squeezing them. He pulls me tighter against his stone-like body. I feel his rock-hard erection push against my stomach, making my nipples harden instantly.

Ay, Papi!

Jesus, this man makes me feel so many emotions it is hard to breathe. I pull away, breathless, and I whimper. "Fuck, Maddox, you're so unbelievable, and you're driving me insane. What am I going to do with you?"

Maddox leans his head back, laughing a full-hearted laugh before looking back down at me with so much passion. "I can think of plenty you could do with me."

Running his hand down to the hem of my skirt and lifting it just a bit, Maddox lets out a growl, burying his face in my neck and biting me in frustration before releasing me.

When I look around, I notice Maddox's team, along with Brant, Izzy, and Dominic. Well, I guess it's time to step out of our lust-induced bubble and get back to reality.

Alexandria

The ride home is a blur, due to having shots throughout the night along with the physical tension building up between Maddox and me. I've almost dozed off. Maddox tells me to go lie down and that he will lock up and meet me in there.

Nervously, I head to my room. With a bit of panic rising in my stomach, I start to question myself. *Are we going to go all the way? Am I going to fulfill his needs? Should I take my clothes off before he comes into the room? What if he doesn't like it?*

Realizing I'm just standing in my room in a daze, I move to my dresser and start taking off my jewelry, trying not to think too much. While taking off my earrings, Maddox's strong hands slide around my waist. He moves his head to the nape of my neck, placing soft kisses. I let out a soft moan and relax into his body, releasing some of the tension. Being in this position used to make me tense, but with Maddox, it is easily overpowered by lust.

Maddox must feel some of my stress, turning me to face him by slipping a hand under my chin and tilting it up. Looking into his cloudy eyes, I smile and take a deep breath.

Magnificent.

Swinging my hands around his neck, I whisper, "Hi."

Maddox's smile spreads across his face with his dimples at full depth. *"Mi belleza."*

While leaning down, he softly slips his tongue against my lips, letting me know he wants full access. I slowly open my mouth, granting him the connection we both need. With a moan, I pull on his neck, swaying my hips against his groin. Maddox growls, slipping his hands down over my ass and lifting my skirt. He squeezes my butt cheeks before picking me up, so I wrap my legs around his waist and feel his enormous cock rub against my already soaked panties.

Maddox lays me down on the bed, gently rubbing his hands up my body, stopping at my breasts. He pulls down my V-neck shirt, exposing one breast. Breaking our kiss, he moves down and engulfs my breast with a suck, making me cry out and lift my hips to rub against his massive body. Maddox stands up with a swift motion. Opening my eyes at his disconnection, I see him staring at me with wild eyes, and before I can speak, he says, "Alexandria, I want you so fuckin' bad." Moving quickly, Maddox takes off his shirt while kicking off his shoes.

Goodness...he is like a holy god with that body.

His pierced nipples make my mouth water. My sex throbs just thinking about sucking and biting them. I lift up, leaning back on my hands to get a better look at him. He takes my shoes off and starts to crawl back up my body, slowly caressing me, massaging me with his fingers, touching each inch of me with soft kisses.

I drop my head with a soft moan, "Maddox."

Please touch me.

Lifting my shirt over my head and throwing it to the side, he whispers, "heaven," while slipping both hands around my waist. He leans into my neck, placing soft, wet kisses. Unclasping my bra, he lays me back down onto the bed, slowly continuing his assault on me. He kisses my shoulder, over to my collarbone, down to my chest, and then finally, he sucks my nipple into his mouth, grasping the other breast with a tight squeeze.

I gasp, *"Dios mio!"*

Oh God, I can't take much more. Fuck.

I lose all my senses and go off the feeling he's igniting inside me with just a touch of his fingers. His hot, moist mouth sucking my breast has me lifting my hips, wanting more—no, scratch that, I *need* more. When he moves to the other breast, I whimper, "Yes… I need you to fill me. Please."

Please, God, please

Maddox does not take his mouth away from sucking my breast when he slides his hand down my stomach, undoing my skirt. I lift my hips, helping him maneuver my skirt down over my hips. Only then does Maddox release my breast with a pop, sending a shot of fire sizzling throughout my body. Pulling off my skirt, he leans back on his heels, staring at me with heated eyes. I instantly raise my hands to cover my breasts, regretting it immediately when I see the look on Maddox's face.

Maddox shakes his head with a growl. "Do not ever cover yourself from me, Alexandria. Your body is mine, and I think you're the most beautiful woman I've ever seen."

I release my breasts, and they fall with a bounce. Maddox gently touches my ankles, moving his hands over my shins. Pushing my knees apart and fully exposing me, he licks his lips. My breathing is heavy but changes to panting in between my moans. Wanting him to touch me, to take me, is all I can think of. With a broken voice, I say, "Please, Mad..."

He guides his hand down my thighs to my hips, touching my panties. He traces his fingers over my mound and down to my clit. I cry out, "Yes..."

Maddox slides down, placing his face inches from my pussy. I feel him breathing heavily against my skin while he keeps tracing his finger on my panties over my clit, rubbing it.

God...I can't think, only feel.

Maddox sticks his tongue out and laps at the outside of my panties. I buck my hips, wanting more, and I thrash around under Maddox, only to be pinned down. He moves my panties to the side with one finger. Once his tongue touches my pussy, I lose it altogether. "Mad, please God, don't stop." *Oh, my... I'm going to come.*

When Maddox flicks his tongue over my clit before sucking, using his tongue in a circular motion, my body hits the brink of explosion. I'm so close to having the most unbelievable orgasm of my life. When Mark and I had sex, it didn't feel anything like this. Fuck no, not even close to this feeling. Good God, this feeling is too much for my senses, sending me up to an erotic high. I start to move my hips, fucking his face. "Faster, *Jesus*...right there."

Maddox sucks hard on the swollen nub, inserting a finger slowly into my dripping wet pussy with a circular motion and sending me over the edge of ecstasy. His sensual assault has my body in a frenzy with moans and screams. My whole body spasms with the climax when he inserts another finger, intensifying my orgasm.

"*Yes.*" He drags out my orgasm by flicking my clit rapidly. "Maddy…"

Maddox slows his fingers but keeps thrusting into my sex, letting me ride the wave while moaning his own desire and sucking at my wetness.

When I feel him move away from me, I try to open my eyes, but my body is spent, slipping into the darkness. I hear a rough, heated voice, *"Dios mio, eres hermosa." My God, you're beautiful.*

The next thing I know, I wake up in Maddox's strong arms with my head on his chest. I look up to see him smiling down at me with those fuck-me dimples. Maddox caresses my arm. "Welcome back."

My throat is dry, but I squeak out, "Did I fall asleep? What happened?"

Maddox's hearty laugh has my body bouncing. "You kind of passed out after I made you come for me. It's late, and we need to sleep."

Feeling so tired, I snuggle back into his side. He places a kiss on top of my head. "Sleep, *mi belleza.*" I do as he says.

Maddox

When I hear Alexandria's breathing even out, I know she's in a deep sleep. Sliding my body out from under her, I lay her next to me. I caress her shoulder, running my hand over her and making sure she is indeed asleep.

Fucking hell. She called me Maddy. No one has called me Maddy since my má.

My cock twitches, letting me know he's still hard as a rock, ready to burst. Shifting my weight to the side only makes it worse. I slide off the bed, needing to release this pressure so I can get some sleep. The last two nights when I've left her sleeping, I went back to my hotel to jack off in the shower. And then I lay awake wishing I were still in bed with her. I'm not leaving tonight, and I don't care if I get on anyone's bad side. I head to the bathroom, shutting the door softly and hoping I don't wake her. Grabbing my cock, I grunt, "Fuck."

With the warm shower water running down my body, I close my eyes, thinking about how wet her sweet pussy was and how when she came, it exploded into my mouth. I start to stroke my cock with a hiss. "Ah!" I'm so hard it hurts, but Jesus Christ, she came undone tonight with just a few touches. I haven't even begun to explore her body.

Gripping my cock and stroking the length of it from head to shaft, I quicken the pace of my strokes. Once my tongue touched her breast, her nipples hardened instantly, making them ready to bite into.

God, her nipples are so fuckin' perfect.

Closing my eyes, I bite my lower lip, feeling my release building. I grip my cock even harder, which makes it feel like it's going to bust out of my skin it's so damn hard. I think of my fingers fucking that tight pussy of hers, her wetness dripping down my hand, and I start jacking myself faster. "Oh…yeah…"

My breathing picks up, and with my other hand, I cup my

balls. Leaning my back against the wall to steady myself, I run my hand from my balls to my chest, pinching my pierced nipple, causing myself pleasurable pain.

I hammer myself faster, thinking of her body under me, the way she thrusts her hips, fucking my face, wanting more. *"Fuck me..."*

Still pinching my nipples, I grunt with the sensations I'm inflicting on myself. I remember her crying out her release. *Yes. I can't wait to slam my cock into her.*

I start imagining Alexandria's perfect lips suctioning around my cock. "Fuck yeah, baby."

Hearing the water slapping against my body while I jack myself makes me think of slapping her fine ass while I fuck her from behind. "God, yes."

That's it. Almost…

I imagine grabbing her ass, driving deep into that sweet, tight, wet pussy. *Motherfucker…* Stroke… *yes.* Stroke… *almost.* Stroke… *yeah.* Stroke… *baby.*

The thought of Alexandria screaming Maddy while her pussy clenches around my dick sends me over. I grunt my release with my final strokes. *"Yes."*

My legs almost give out, and I'm seeing stars from the explosive orgasm. I keep gliding my hand over my semihard cock, riding it out as long as I can.

She called me Maddy.

Alexandria

Getting out of the shower, I wipe the steam off the mirror with a huge smile, thinking about how happy I am. Complete bliss, yep, that's how I'm feeling right now, totally head over heels infatuated with Maddox Maxwell.

Today marks two weeks since this spellbinding man came into my life. It feels like months that we've been seeing each other, but it's only been weeks. We've spent every free moment and every night together, completely enthralled with each other, learning every little thing we can about each other. If we're not at the club or at work, we're at my place. We talked a lot about music and what he is working on, but mostly we are holed up in my place watching movies, cooking, and having hot as hell make-out sessions, which usually end with me having over-the-top orgasms.

Maddox has completely won over my family, my friends, and if you can believe it, my security team—but most of all, me. We have had dinner at my parents' house a couple times, making my parents super happy.

When he touches me, I feel my whole body come alive. It's like he has the direct link to all my nerve endings, sending them into overdrive with each touch. It's the best feeling ever, and being with him has helped me live a little bit more and not care what anyone thinks.

He's always the one to stop us from going too far and is always the one to push us a little bit further each time too. I was worried he wasn't getting anything out of our make-out sessions, but he said he gets off watching me experience everything he does to me.

He wants to wait for the right moment to claim me, saying, *"Alexandria, when I take you, I will not be able to hold back my deep desire for you. And until you're ready to take me fully, I will wait."*

It makes me want him even more. He's very possessive of me, and most of the time I like it. But when it comes to my work or my friends, I get upset. We are still trying to get to know each other and learn how to be in a relationship. We have so much in common with music, our heritage, and our love of movies. He has traveled a lot, and when he was stuck in hotels, he would just watch movies. While I was secluded at our estate with only music to pass the time, I became a huge movie junkie.

Still looking into the mirror, I run my fingers over my lips, closing my eyes and remembering his touch last night. I run my hand down my neck and over my chest, cupping my breast and wishing it were his hand. I pinch my erect nipple, biting down on my lip with a moan. God, last night was amazing with me naked and Maddox in just his underwear. I think of sucking his nipple bars with a slight bite and tracing his tattoo with my tongue, hearing him growl. *Shit.* I open my eyes to see my face flushed, and I smile again.

My friends completely adore him when we're at the club or he stops by the label. When we talk about our music, he always tries to get me into the studio again. But things with the festival coming up have kept us both busy. I feel between Maddox, Brant, and my papa, they have been keeping Emmett and Jason away from me.

I try to explain to him it's my job, but he has made it to where Emmett hasn't been one of the DJs I manage at the club. I've tried to call Emmett, but he doesn't pick up. He replies by text to me and says sorry for not answering, but that he's busy or gives me some line of bullshit. Ginger and Izzy have seen him at the clubs and say he doesn't look good. He just shows up and DJs then leaves, or he is completely wasted and being a complete dick. His texts are coming less and less frequently lately. Mostly because he just asks if I'm still seeing Maddox, and when I reply yes, he doesn't respond.

Jason, on the other hand, I saw one night at the club. But he kept his distance since Maddox was hooked to my hip, growling at any man who came near me. Jason still texts me, or he will call when he knows I'm at work. He's still his flirty, fun self, but he doesn't like me with Maddox. He was cool with me canceling our lunch date and is always saying he doesn't like how possessive Maddox is with me.

Maddox's protectiveness has not let up, not even in the slightest. I think that is the only thing he and I don't see eye to eye on. I think I can handle myself, but he and Brant say someone needs to be near me at all times. It's not like Jason, or any of my DJs for that matter, will hurt me. Fuck, it's my job. Surprisingly, my papá is on my side regarding that and has told the boys to cut me some slack. But still Maddox doesn't leave my side if we're at a club, and if he isn't by my side, Brant or one of his guys is right there with me.

I know my attack is one of the reasons Maddox is so protective, or at least, that's what I tell myself. I feel like it has gotten worse lately with all the commotion of the festival coming up. So many people are here in town, making all the clubs really packed. I did have a slight panic attack the other night at the club. I dealt with it myself like I always do, but I know Maddox and Brant noticed. I just hate being pushed, or when it's so packed, we're like sardines in the club. I guess you could say I'm claustrophobic, but only where it involves people, not small spaces.

Pulling my shirt over my head, I shiver just thinking about being squished. *Goddammit, I need to get over it.*

It feels like months have gone by since I met Maddox, so much has happened. Since Maddox is with me basically twenty-four seven, Brant has been spending more time with Ginger and Sasha. Sasha is still here until after the festival, and the three of them have been kind of inseparable. It was weird at first when I went with Maddox and his team to the club, while those three went to another club the girls were DJing at. I think it was probably the fifth time I've been to a club and Brant wasn't with me. I felt kind of left out or like I was missing something. Ethan and Chad have been my sidekicks more often than not if Brant is busy or not around.

The thing that has me worried lately is my best friend, Stella. She is still in Spain with her boyfriend, who is a DJ for our label, but I think something is going on with her. One day I walked into Mamá's office to find Auntie Abby crying.

When I asked what was wrong, they both replied nothing. Now Stella is distancing herself from me, only asking about Maddox when we talk, sidestepping any personal questions I ask her.

I'm just so swamped with the festival, I feel like I can't keep up with all that's going on. And when I'm with Maddox, all I think about is touching his sinful fucking body. For God's sake, I need to have sex and get this anticipation over with.

"God help me!" *Will I be good enough for him?*

Shaking my head free of negative thoughts about having sex with Maddox, I think of my girls. I feel like my posse is going in different directions and we're losing the connection we all had just a month ago. Sasha and Ginger are all enthralled together with Brant, and Stella is MIA in Spain with her boyfriend. Izzy and Dominic got into a huge fight at the club the other night, and she has closed herself off, saying they will be fine, but that fight didn't look fine to me. Last is Eva, who is up to something because she has declined going out with me the last few times I went out. And when we're at work, she just talks about my relationship with Maddox, avoiding my questions about her as well.

I told Maddox last night I feel like my friends don't need me anymore, and he laughed at me, telling me they were probably giving us time together. Also, with the festival coming up, everyone is running rampant. I'm just not used to us being apart and not in each other's daily lives. I mean, for over a year, it was us girls with our security team every day. I know I'm falling in love with Maddox, but I don't want to lose my friends because I'm in a relationship.

A knock on my door jars me from my thoughts. I've been

getting ready for the club, and when I look at the clock, I notice it's only eight o'clock. Maddox isn't supposed to be back until nine to pick me up. I walk over to the door, looking out to see Ginger. I open the door smiling and about ready to comment that she's over early, but when I see her face, I know something is wrong. We're all supposed to be going to the club tonight together in a limo.

I move out of the way so she can come inside. I'm concerned, so I ask, "Gin, what's wrong, sweetie?"

Fuming, she stomps into my place. "Fuck men. I'm so pissed off right now. I mean, why me?"

Not stopping, she heads straight into my kitchen, opening my fridge and grabbing a beer with me on her tail. "Goddamn Brant and his fucking protective-stubborn-asshole way of telling me what to do."

I lean into the counter, folding my arms and laughing. She got stuck with my brute, and Ginger doesn't like men telling her what to do. She's the most independent woman I know, and she definitely doesn't take any shit.

After taking a couple of drinks, she looks over at me, pissed off. I'm still laughing. "What did he do this time?"

Placing her beer on the countertop, she throws her hands up in defeat. "I have to run some errands for my dad tonight before we go out, so I'm going to be riding my bike over to the club."

Wait... What? She is supposed to— Cutting off my thoughts, I blurt out, "Hey, you're supposed to open tonight for Maddox. Aren't you at ten o'clock, and Izzy is closing?"

Nodding her head, she takes a swig of beer. "Yes, but I talked to Izzy and switched with her because my dad really needs me to run this errand for him. And before you get all pissy with me, he called *your dad* before he called me to do this errand. He got the okay only if Izzy was okay with it, so I'm assuming this errand is pretty important."

If it were at any other club, this wouldn't be okay. But since it's our own club, we rarely post who the opening or closing DJs are since it is usually a rookie or one of our DJs from the label. The main headliner is who we advertise and promote, and it also gives the rookie or the DJ the opportunity to show us they are dedicated to us by bringing in a crowd on their own. If it were another club, they would be on the roster, and people would expect them to play at certain times.

Crossing my arms over my chest, I ask, "Okay, so what's Brant's problem?"

Ginger puts her beer down again, gripping it. "He says I can't go alone. That he's going to come with me, and I told him fuck no! If my dad is letting me go alone, then it's not dangerous. We both know my dad's like your dad and would rather me be in a bubble than put me in danger. So, I told Brant hell no, deal with it, and that I would see him at the club."

Her phone beeps in her pocket, getting an eye roll from her. "Speaking of the pompous ass. I mean, seriously, I can't handle him being so clingy. How did you deal with it?"

I start to laugh when she looks at her cell phone and reads the text. I try to sound cheerful. "Well, look on the bright side. He must really like you to be all protective bossy guy with you. He doesn't do that with any of the other girl DJs. Seriously, Gin, what is going on between you two?"

Ginger looks up, and her facial features turn lethal. Her jet-black hair is down and framing her bright green eyes. She is beautiful, but when she gets pissed, it scares the shit out of me. She squints her eyes at me, "Nothing is going on between us. We hang out sometimes. You know I do not want anything serious. I'll never let another man control me. Hell fucking no."

I put up a hand in defense. "Gin, you know I'm not one to pry, and I won't start now, but I know Brant like a brother. He's so into you, so either deal with his protectiveness or cut him—"

Her phone rings, cutting me off, and she looks down and cusses when she sees who's calling. She puts a finger up to tell me to hold on, then answers, sounding irritated. "What, Shy?"

Fuck, she can be a real bitch when she wants to.

Her face turns crimson, and she finishes her beer, heading to the trash. "Shy, shut the fuck up. I'm doing it for him. I'm getting ready to leave right now, so keep your goddamn panties on. I'll fucking call you when I'm done." I hear someone screaming on the other end of the phone, but she hangs up on him.

Jesus. Thank God I've never made her mad, and I've only seen her actually this pissed off a handful of times. Usually, it's a man. I guess her first love back home fucked her over pretty good, leaving her bitter toward men. She's a badass bitch because she was raised by a bunch of bikers and doesn't take any shit.

She heads for the front door, stopping to hug me. When I hug her tighter, I feel her relax a bit. Concerned, I pull away to look into her emerald-green eyes, "Gin, you going to be okay?"

Releasing me, she laughs, "Girl, you know me. I'm always okay." She grabs my hand and smiles. "Especially now that I got to bitch and rant about it. I got it off my mind. Now I just need to go deal with my father. I'll see you tonight at the club, and I'll text you if I need anything."

I'm a little concerned, but I know that out of any of us, she can handle herself. I close the door and head back into the bathroom to finish getting ready. Tonight, everyone will be there to celebrate the upcoming festival activities, and I'm super excited.

Maddox

With both security teams on edge due to two more girls missing from the clubs last night, it has me feeling out of control tonight. I want to tell Alexandria so bad about all the stuff going on so she understands where my protectiveness is coming from. I mean, I am usually protective, but not this crazy.

Alexandria moves into VIP, grabbing Sasha, and I try to gain control of my anxiety. I move through the VIP, nodding my hellos, but I make my way to the side so I can just watch Alexandria. She's so fucking beautiful, and she'll always be my beauty. These past few weeks have been unbelievable. The connection is one thing, but getting to know her and all her quirks make me want her that much more. Having her in my arms at night is heaven. My body suddenly heats up with waves rushing through me and making my heart hurt. I rub my hand over my chest.

Jesus Christ. What the fuck. This woman is becoming my

undoing.

A hand grabs my shoulder, pulling me from my thoughts of what-ifs. Not taking my eyes off Alexandria, I just cross my arms over my chest.

Isaac moves me out of earshot of everyone with his hand on my shoulder, but he keeps us in view of Alexandria. "She is going to be okay, Madd Dog. You can't get yourself all worked up when nothing has happened yet I know you're thinking of the what-ifs. We all have eyes on her, and nothing is going to happen."

Fucking hell. Am I that readable? I can't let Alexandria see my anxiety. I need to be strong for her.

Still looking at my woman, I hear her laugh and see her throw her head back. Fuck, she is like a goddamn goddess. Isaac laughs, "Madd Dog, I've known you all our lives. This new look you have kind of trips me out."

I tense up, worried I'm showing the rage building inside. Without turning my attention away from Alexandria, I say through gritted teeth, "What the fuck are you talking about, Isaac?"

Isaac still has his hand on my shoulder, and he's laughing as he states, "You're one lovestruck motherfucker. Never in my wildest dreams would I have thought you would have fall-en in love. I thought this girl was going to be just a conquest for you. But, fuck me, you have fallen in love, my friend."

Isaac pats me on the back then moves to stand by my side, mimicking me by crossing his arms while still laughing. I re-ply in a steady, controlled voice, "Fuck yeah, I have. She is the one for me. All mine. I will stop at nothing. I mean, noth-ing..." Drawing out the last part, I turn to face him before continuing. "Nothing will stop me from being with her and protecting her." I turn back to face Alexandria and finish, "She is mine!"

Isaac chuckles, "Yes, my friend, she's yours, and we'll all protect her for you, brother. Always." Holding on to my control and trying not to show any emotions or thoughts that are flashing through my mind, I just stand there like a tiger ready to pounce on anything that comes near *my* girl.

Alexandria never loses eye contact with me, letting me know she knows where I am. I don't partake in the drinking. Instead, I just stare at her and observe everyone in the VIP area. As I'm watching Izzy bounce around on stage, I realize Ginger is not my opener. Looking around the room, I don't see her. But then again, a lot of people are not here yet, including Luc.

When I see Alexandria moving to the music, I try to get lost in watching her move. My body relaxes with the music playing, helping me control the fire inside me that is on the brink of explosion. Being in the club and not knowing if or when he'll make his move has me so on edge I feel like a caged animal ready to strike. Alexandria moves around like a fuckin' angel, with such ease and finesse. She touches everyone she comes in contact with, using her hands when she talks, gesturing wildly, with every emotion lighting up her face. Jesus Christ, that fucking hair cascading down her back is just calling me to come and pull and tug on it. Fuck, I need to have her body and soon.

Alexandria looks over, catching me staring at her ass. I lick my lips, biting my bottom lip before smiling at her and letting her know what the fuck she does to me. Her red blouse is so fucking tight, I can see her nipples harden. My mouth waters just thinking about sucking on those perfect little raisins.

Alexandria slowly makes her way over to me while I look from her eyes to her hard nipples, licking my lips again. I glance from her nipples down her toned belly to her fucking rocking skintight pants that show every nook and cranny.

I stand still, not moving a muscle. I hold on to my self-control in order to keep from taking her right fucking here and now, and I flex my hands over my chest. When she's just a couple of inches away, I know she sees in my eyes how much she affects me. I smile down at her and suck my lower lip seductively with a growl. "I think I need to hurry the fuck up and play so I can take you home and have my way with your gorgeous body. Goddamn, Alexandria, the things I've been thinking about all day that I want to do to you tonight. Fuck."

I take in air when she smiles a full-blown smile, showing me her pearly whites. When her hands go to my waist, sliding under the hem of my shirt and making contact with my skin, I lose it. In one swift move, I turn us both, pushing her up against the wall. I place my back to everyone, hiding her in front of me before I smash my mouth to hers. I grab her jawline on both sides with my hands, holding her face still while our tongues fuck each other. Moans escape both of us, I'm rocking my cock into her, and she slides her hands up over my chest. When she fiddles with my piercings, I nip her lip with a growl.

"Alexandria, we need to stop, I'm going to lose control, and I wouldn't fucking care who sees me ravage your beautiful body right fucking here. I need to go get ready, and your father just arrived. So stay right here, and I'll be back to get you before I start. *Do not* leave this area." I kiss her again, but I pull away, leaving her breathless with a smile.

Alexandria moves to say hello to her father while I scan the area, looking for our security. When I make eye contact with Brant, I motion for him to come over. Turning back to Luc and Alexandria hugging, I wait. Once Luc releases Alexandria, he extends his hand. "Hey, Maddox, you gettin' ready to go on?"

I shake his hand with a smile. "Yeah, I'm headed up right now to set up. I'll be back to get Alexandria before I go on so she can be on stage next to me."

Right when we release hands, Brant walks up to my side with a nod to us both. "B, I'm going to head up to the stage and get set up. I'll be back to get Alexandria."

When I look at Brant, I can tell something is wrong because he glances at Alexandria and just nods again. Luc must sense it too, so he turns to Alexandria, who isn't paying attention to us but is looking over at Sasha talking to Dominic, and says, "Alex, can you go get me a drink, baby girl?"

Alexandria turns, saying yes and giving me a brief kiss before walking off. Both Luc and I turn to Brant, and I ask, "What? What the fuck is wrong?"

Brant takes a deep breath before speaking. "Nothing. It's just Ginger, she is a fucking pain in my motherfucking ass lately. She was supposed to be here by now, and I don't like that she went on this errand for her father."

Brant is looking straight at Luc, who looks pissed off.

"She's driving herself here tonight on her fucking bike. Which she told me you and her father said was okay. She's the only one right now who doesn't have protection, so I'm stressing on her. She needs to get her fucking ass here now."

Luc turns to look on stage at Izzy bouncing around. I try to think of a solution. "Do you know where Ginger is? Do you want me to send one of my guys to meet up with her? Just let Isaac know what you need. I need to go set up for my set, and I'll be right back." They both nod their heads when I take off to the stage.

Goddammit, this night needs to be over with. Got a bad motherfuckin' feeling about this. Everyone is on high alert, especially with this sick fuck out for my girl. Stressed out, I head to the stage. Once I say hey to Izzy, I set up my equipment, pulling out all my gear and headphones. When I'm done, I look around to see the stage is empty except for a couple of girls running around. I look out over the sweaty crowd of people dancing, and I try to get into the zone and feel the crowd. I bounce my head to the music, trying to loosen my body up and shake all this anxiety off, but when I look over to where Alexandria is, I become enraged.

Hell fucking no. I bounce off the stage and move swiftly across the way, not waiting on Chad, or any security, for that matter. I just see blood. *Who the fuck has their hands all over Alexandria?*

Brant steps in front of me and says, "Maddox, that's her friend Jason. I told you about him before, so do not fucking think about getting into a fight. That's why Emmett isn't here."

Pushing Brant to the side with a growl, I try to calm down, but the closer I get to them, the more I see fucking red. This motherfucker has his hands all over her. I come up behind her, snatching her from his embrace. Alexandria lets out a squeal but senses it's me when I growl. When she turns to see my facial expression, she yells, "Maddox, relax. This is my good friend Jason. You know he's one of our main promoters."

She puts her hands on my face, trying to turn me to face her so I can't keep my death stare on Jason, who is mother-fucking smiling at me. *Fucking cocky fucker.*

Alexandria moves in front of me, standing on her tip-toes to kiss me. I close my eyes for a few seconds, taking deep breaths and trying to rein in the beast inside me. Fuck. Wrapping my arms around her and hugging her tighter, I hear someone clear their throat. I open my eyes to the fucking little asshole smiling at me. *Goddamn, son of a bitch.*

Alexandria pulls away, turning to Jason with a smile. "Jason, this is my boyfriend, Maddox. Maddox, this is Jason, *my friend*."

Jason, with his fake fucking smile, extends his hand, saying hello. I just tense up, trying not to punch him. My face is so tight with tension, I hear my teeth grinding together. I don't move to shake his hand or say a word, and then Brant walks to my side, sounding pissed off. "Fuck, Jason, do you have issues everywhere you go with guys, or is it just our label?"

Jason turns to him, laughing a fake as fuck laugh, making me hiss. "Well, it has only been since Alex has been back. I usually get along with everyone, but I guess some people are just intimidated by me, but who knows?"

I take a step forward, clenching my fists. I hear Luc behind me, and he places a hand on my shoulder. "Maddox, you need to take Alex on stage to get ready."

Every muscle in my body wants to pummel this

motherfucker into the ground, but I take a deep breath and loosen my grip on Alexandria. Luc pats me on the back and steps around me, putting himself and Brant between Jason and me.

I grab Alexandria and head to the stage, leaving a huge crowd behind. I guess when I jumped offstage, everyone followed me. Once we get on stage, Dominic is with Izzy, and they don't look happy. Alexandria still hasn't said anything, but I can tell she is pissed at me.

Goddammit. I don't fucking share. No motherfucker puts his hand on her like that, especially with some sick fuck out there. Fuck no. Mine.

Izzy is looking at us with concern while I grab my headphones, trying to calm down. I take a couple of deep breaths and turn around to see Alexandria with her arms folded, staring at me angrily. I wrap my arms around her waist, putting my forehead to hers. "Alexandria, I'm sorry you're mad, and I'm sorry that I saw red with that mother—"

I cut myself off and take a deep breath, closing my eyes and not letting her move away. "I don't like people, especially men, touching my girlfriend. Hugs are okay, kisses on the cheek maybe, but fucking hands on her? *Fuck no.*"

We fight about this all the time, and she just doesn't get it. Seeing she is going to lose it, I lean down to look her straight in the face. "Before you flip the fuck out, let *me* ask *you* this. How would you feel if you were on stage and you looked over and one of my 'friends'—oh, wait, how did you say it? One of my 'slutty girlfriends'—was embracing me that way? Would *you* be okay with it? Honestly, tell me you would be okay with some girl texting me, calling me, and holding me like that."

Releasing Alexandria, I take a step back, putting some space between us and letting her know I'm just as fucking pissed off. "Now, don't answer me right this second because I know you're really fucking mad, and so am I. But think about it, and *you* let *me* know how you would feel because I'd like to know. So, when we're back in Spain or other places I have 'girl-friends,' I'll know how to act with them." I'm drawing out the words "you" and "me" so she knows I'm dead fucking serious.

Taking a deep breath, I turn around and start going through my music to try to get in the zone. I see Alexandria move to the side, still pissed off. *Relax, Madd Dog. Focus.*

Isaac comes up next to me, waiting to see how my mood is before speaking to me. "Madd Dog, you good?" When I don't answer him, he continues. "Do you want an intro with no lights, or are you just going to do your thing? I need to know regarding the lights, brother. Also, when I get everyone off the stage, we'll have security on both sides, so no one will be up here but you two."

Closing my eyes, I take a few breaths and rock my neck back and forth. I use my hands to pop my neck, trying to loosen the tension in my shoulders. When I open my eyes, I look over to Isaac. "I'm good. No intro today, I'm going to do my own thing. Thanks, brother. Keep an eye on her."

I sense her still over to the side, calming down. I don't make eye contact, but I just let her stew for a bit. I need to focus on my set, so I walk up to stand by Izzy.

Music is the key to everyone's soul I think, and if you need to make yourself happy, turn to music. Twenty minutes into my set, Alexandria comes to stand next to me, letting me know she has calmed down. I have jumped into my zone and played for the crowd. I give her a kiss, letting her know that I've calmed down too so we both can relax and start to have fun. I keep an eye on the VIP area, watching that motherfucker interact with everyone and making me hate him more. Roc and I had a conversation just by looking at each other, then he was on it and started moving toward VIP. I never have to explain myself to these guys, and we just know what the others are thinking. Isaac is staying back and watching everything from behind me, staying on stage with Alexandria. Brant and the rest of the group are around the VIP where everyone else is, so I start to zone out on the music, knowing everyone is safe.

About forty-five minutes into my set, I notice Brant is stressed about something, talking into his headpiece and looking at his phone. I motion for Ethan, who is in front of the stage, to go find out. At this point, I don't see Roc or Fuckface Jason. In VIP, I don't see Luc, just some of our group. Alexandria has moved to the back side stage with Isaac, sitting on a speaker and bouncing to the beat with a smile. Warmth fills my heart, and I can't wait until we play together so I can touch her every second.

Turning back to the decks, I begin to mix into another song with my headphones on. I start to mess with the mixer and move to the beat. I look out to the crowd, bouncing my head and smiling at everyone. The massive crowd hears my next song dropping in, and they erupt with arms in the air, swaying. I love my job.

Once I've dropped the song completely, I turn to find my next song. While the crowd goes crazy, I throw my hands in the air and jump to the beat. I do a spin, and I see Alexandria on the floor with her head on Isaac's arm. Isaac is screaming at Chad to help him pick her up.

What the fuck! Alexandria!

My heart stops and fear rushes through me. Throwing my headphones off, I charge over to them. I roar, "What the fuck happened?"

Looking her over to see if she is hurt, I grab Alexandria, pulling her into my lap. Almost crying, I lean into her ear "Alexandria… Baby… Wake up, baby. Please."

Rage mixing with fear, I start to freak out, looking over at Isaac, who looks just as panicked. "Mad, she was just sitting here, totally happy. She told me she was having fun and that you were crazy. She stood up, grabbing her phone out of her pocket, then she was looking around and passed out."

Fuck, I need to get her safe.

Without thinking, I pick her up and start yelling orders. "Where the fuck is Brant or Luc? Chad, have someone pull the limo around back. Goddammit."

Come on, stay with me. Please be okay, mi amor. *Where is Brant?*

Our security team makes a wall when Brant bends down in front of us, looking her over before yelling, "What the fuck happened?" Isaac retells the story to everyone. I'm just kissing her head, telling her to wake up, while everyone is running around yelling.

Alexandria, please, baby, wake up. Please.

Brant leans down to her ear. "Alex, wake up. It's B. You're okay, wake up." He barks out to everyone, "Did she drink anything different from any of you?"

I hiss, "No! I watched her all night. No one was on stage with us, and we didn't have anything to drink up there either. The only drink was that bottle everyone in VIP was drinking from. Where is Luc?"

Isaac comes back with her phone in his hand, and Brant takes it from him, turning toward me with a strained voice. "Luc left a few minutes ago to deal with Ginger. We need to get Alex out of here and now. Maddox, do *not* let anyone near her. I will get us out of here through the back. Just give me a second."

My body tenses on high alert, pulling Alexandria even closer. "No one's taking her from me, including you."

Brant walks off yelling into his mouthpiece. With my guys surrounding us, I don't see where he went.

Izzy rushes up, throwing her hands over her mouth and starting to freak out. She cries out, "Maddox, is she okay? Oh God, what happened? What can I do?"

Glancing around, I yell for one of my guys. "Roc, pack up my shit. Izzy, can you finish my set?"

Roc walks up, nodding at me that he got my order. I turn back to Izzy, who is still staring down at Alexandria. "Izzy, can you finish my set and I'll owe you?"

Izzy, being the overdramatic girl I've come to know, throws her hands on her hips. "Maddox, we got you. Make sure she is okay."

Both Izzy and Roc walk back to the booth to get my stuff.

Finally alone, I look down, rocking my girl. God, she is so fucking beautiful, like a damn angel. Pushing her gorgeous locks out of her face, I kiss her forehead then lean down, speaking softly, "*Mi belleza*, come back to me, baby. Wake up."

Seconds later, Brant rushes through with our guys and a murderous look on his face. It makes my adrenaline jump sky-high, so I tense up and hold her tighter. Brant starts barking orders to all of us, shouting as he points. "We're out of here. *Now!* Maddox, follow us, but hold her close to you so no one can touch her. We all need to barricade Maddox carrying her, that way no one can touch her."

He knows something. Fuck.

When Brant locks eyes with me, he says, "He is here."

I stop in my tracks, trying to register what he just said. Emotions build inside my chest, making me nearly burst as I fight the rage inside of me. I swallow hard. "What the hell did you just say? He is here?"

I grit the last part out, trying to hold my composure and not lose it when she needs me most. Brant is always in control, but just for a second, I can see he's worried when he runs his hands through his hair before masking it away. Brant barks at me, "We have to get her to the limo. Now!"

Everyone moves at once, rushing us outside. We finally make it the short distance to the back door of the limo. I slide in with her in my arms, never releasing her. I shift to the back of the limo, laying her on my lap. She's still out cold when Brant climbs in with us, closing the door behind him so it's just the three of us. He hands me an ice pack, telling me to hold it under her neck. Grabbing the ice pack, I can see Brant's eyes fill with concern when he looks from me to Alexandria. That sends a panic through my body to the core. "Brant, should we take her to the hospital? I don't see any injuries, and Isaac said he caught her when she passed out, so I know she didn't hit her head."

I slip my hand over her body, trying to feel for any bumps or any signs of trauma. Brant moves closer to us, letting out a deep breath.

Goddammit, if he doesn't tell me what is going on, I'm go-

ing to flip the fuck out.

I'm about ready to burst with anxiety. "Fuck. Just tell me."

Brant keeps his eye on Alexandria and speaks in a calm voice. "She had a full-blown panic attack. She'll be okay, we just need to get her home."

"What? Why?" A million thoughts start running through my head. She was fine on stage. *She didn't have an attack walking in.*

Brant looks pissed, his face is red with all his muscles tight like he wants to hurt someone. It's making me tense up again, and then he hands me her cell phone. "You're not going to like this, but you need to see these." He pauses. "This is why she passed out."

Taking her cell phone, I look down and see the text messages. "Mother…fucker!"

UNKNOWN

My love, you can't hide from me anymore. I'll have you again soon. Your pussy is mine. Remember that, Alex.

Goddamn, you look so fucking good tonight in your red top with those skintight jeans, showing me your perfect fucking body, just waiting for me to take you again. See you soon, my love.

Goddammit. Right under my fucking nose, son of a bitch got her cell phone number.

Brant leans his head back, trying to control his emotions. His phone must vibrate because he speaks out, looking at the ceiling of the limo. "Talk to me. Yeah, I left Maddox's guys, Austin, Roc, and his manager, Isaac, there with Dominic and

Izzy. I left the two undercover guys in place. Maddox's guys, Chad and Ethan, are behind us. Luc had already left to pick Mia up and check on Ginger. He was on his way back, but he's now on his way home to meet us." I tune him out, trying to calm down.

She's okay. She's with me. No one touched her. She's safe. Relax, Madd Dog. She'll need you. Calm down.

When Brant gets off the phone, I start rattling off the questions that are clogging my head. "How long does she usually pass out for? What are we going to do about this? Do we have any video from the club?"

Brant focuses on me, making eye contact. In a controlled voice, he says, "It depends, but this is huge for her. I use to carry smelling salts to wake her up, but she hasn't had one of these in over a year and a half. Everyone's meeting us at the studio. So when we get there, we'll figure something out."

When he's finished talking, I look down to Alexandria, caressing her hair and smoothing it out of her face. Holding the ice pack under her neck is making my arm numb. I murmur softly to her, "Baby, please, come back to me. I want to see those beautiful baby blue eyes that I love so much. Please, Alexandria, please wake up."

A rush of need builds up in my stomach. Wanting to taste her, I lean down, placing small kisses all over her face before landing on her soft, plump lips. When I hear a moan escape her mouth, all the air whooshes from my lungs, making me gasp. "Alexandria baby, come back to me."

My shoulders relax, and I loosen my grip on her, giving her space to breathe when she barely opens her beautiful blue eyes. *Thank you, God.*

Alexandria

My head is pounding, and then I hear him. Relief starts pushing my fear away because he's here. I hear Maddox's seductive voice whispering to me, but I can't understand him. Then his lips are on me. God, I love when he kisses me. It makes my heart pump faster. He calls out to me again when I try to open my eyes, but my head feels like it is splitting open. Maddox and Brant are speaking, but I can't hear what they're saying. Again, I try to open my eyes by squinting, and that's when I see those silver eyes I love so much beaming down at me. Caressing my face with a strained voice, Maddox speaks, "Alexandria, close your eyes. Rest. We're almost home. I got you, baby. Don't worry, we'll be home soon."

Closing my eyes as he tells me, I'm relieved because I don't think I could have kept them open any longer with my head hurting so badly. Maddox holds me tight against his chest, and I feel his body heat through his shirt. I know we're moving when I hear Brant ranting to a bunch of people while I'm being carried. I cling to the man I love, and I hear him growl a few times, which makes me laugh inside. My protector, always so possessive.

My head is pounding, which blocks out most of the talking. It makes it just murmurs around me until I hear Mamá gasping, *"Dios mio, mija!"* followed by my papá's enraged voice telling Maddox to give me to him. It makes my head hurt even more, so I cuddle up closer to Maddox.

Maddox's body tenses, holding me tighter as he hisses, "Like hell. No one will be removing her from my arms. Enough talking. Let me get her to bed before everyone starts yelling and screaming. Chad and Ethan, I want you and Beau to figure this out."

No one makes a sound. I only hear the elevator ding, footsteps, a door opening, and then nothing except Maddox's breathing. I feel my bed underneath me, but my fingers are woven together so tightly around Maddox's neck they're numb. I don't want to let go of my security or the warmth of his body.

Maddox shuffles a couple times, removing his shoes before moving onto the bed and lifting me so we don't break our connection. I whisper, "Thank you. Don't leave me."

Maddox settles me into an embrace, tucking me into his side and caressing me. His voice is thick with concern. "Alexandria, you'll never get rid of me. I'm not leaving your side."

Kissing the top of my head, he pulls my hair from around my face when I hear my mamá come in. "*Mija,* I'm here for you."

I feel her running her hand over my face and giving me a kiss on the cheek. I try to open my eyes, but the pain is too much. Mamá notices me wince from the pain, and she rubs my temple. "*Mija*, rest. We'll talk in the morning."

I hear her move around the room before she addresses Maddox in a motherly voice. "Maddox, thank you. I know you'll take care of her. I'm going to run home really quick to change then I'll come back over to see if you need anything. If either of you does before I come back, I've written down our home number. Also, here are some pain meds for her headache. When she can open her eyes or sit up, please make her take them. Try to get her to sit up and drink some water before she goes to sleep. I'll be back soon."

While talking to Maddox, she moves down my body and takes off my heels, rubbing my legs. Still caressing me and taking deep breaths, Maddox agrees with her and then she's gone.

We lie there in silence for what seems like forever. I'm lost in his embrace, the faint smell of his cologne, feeling his chest heave with every deep breath as he strokes his fingertips along my back and shoulder. I start to run my hand over his chest while entwining my leg with his, wishing we both were naked.

The pain starts to subside, making me feel again and bringing me back from the pain-filled haze. As my brain starts to work again, I begin to remember the night. Taking shots, laughing with everyone, Maddox touching me, Jason hugging me, Maddox mad at me, Maddox DJing, Maddox dancing, Brant stressed, and the texts. Gasping, I try to bolt up into a sitting position, but I stop at the shooting pain in my head.

Santa Maria. *He knows where I am. He's going to come for me again.*

Clutching my head, I feel it pound from the jolting movement. Maddox is right next to me, pulling me to him and soothing me while caressing my head. "Alexandria, you've had a traumatic night. Please lie back down and rest. You're safe."

I keep telling myself over and over, *I'm safe. Maddox is here. Breathe, Alex.*

Panicking, I start breathing fast from so many emotions building up inside of me. I feel like I'm going to explode as I fight to gain control, but the fear is overwhelming me. I need to push it down and take control of my body so I don't pass out again. *Breathe, Alex. Breathe.*

Maddox, reading my mind, murmurs in my ear, "Breathe with me. Focus on my chest and breathe with me. You're safe with me in your bed. Breathe."

He caresses my hair, rocking me like a baby as I start to do what he says. I follow his chest, trying to breathe with him as I place my hand on his rock-hard chest. Maddox lays us back down on the bed, holding me to him. I start to relax, focusing on tracing my finger across a tribal tattoo that runs along his collarbone.

Closing my eyes, I take a deep breath then shift myself so I'm practically lying on top of Maddox. I open my eyes, and they instantly lock on to his glistening silver ones filled with concern. I move my hands under my chin so I can rest there, staring at the most gorgeous man alive. Just looking at Maddox helps me calm the storm that is brewing inside of me. I need to tell him how I feel, but instead, I just stare at him while he caresses me up and down my torso. It sends so many emotions rushing throughout my body, making it work overtime to keep up.

I'm with Maddy. He'll make the fear go away, but he *said he* will *have me again... I'll never be safe.*

Not saying a word, we just stare into each other eyes. He traces his finger down my neck and across my collarbone to my shoulder, leaving a trail of tingling fire in its wake. Tears fall from my eyes. I'm torn with the passionate feelings Maddox is sending through my body, but the fear is too much. I feel I can't breathe, and my head starts to pound again.

Maddox rolls me onto my back so he can look down at me, whispering in Spanish, "Alexandria, *mi corazon. Yo te protegeré siempre." I am his heart, and he'll protect me always...*

Oh, my God.

I keep my eyes closed, trying to stay in the moment and not fall back into letting fear take over. I take a long, slow breath, letting it out with a whimper. "Maddy, I need you." Desire mixed with fear drips off each word like they are my last.

Please make the fear go away. Please.

I feel Maddox breathing on me, and he lowers his lips to mine, placing soft kisses over my face where tears run down my cheeks. "Alexandria, please don't cry. I won't leave your side, and I will take care of you. Please don't let the darkness take you. Stay with me."

Maddox sits up, wrapping his arms around me and pulling our bodies together to become one before he groans, "I need you too."

I reach up with trembling fingers, running them through his hair. I push a few strands away from his face, giving me a clear view of his sparkling eyes, before pressing my mouth to his. Once our lips connect, our tongues start to dance, sliding against each other while soft moans escape both of us.

Jesus. My head is pounding. Please, God, take the pain and fear away.

I tilt my head to the side, tugging on his hair and deepening the kiss. Shoving my tongue deeper, I crave more of him. While grinding down harder against his full erection, I feel my body start to warm, bringing me back from the state of shock and numbness. Breathing heavily, he struggles to speak. "Alexandria, we should stop. Baby, you had a traumatic experience. You need to rest."

Fighting with myself and my emotions, I don't reply; I just stare at him. When I start to speak, "Maddy, please…" there's a knock at the front door, and then I can hear it open. I freeze, panic and fear all rushing back into my body, and I hear my parents and a few other people.

I freak out, thinking to myself, *it's starting all over again. The fear, panic attacks, and anxiety.*

Maddox growls, pulling me to his side. "Move under the covers, but first, take these." He hands me the pain pills Mamá gave him and the water. Doing as I've been told, I take them and drink the glass of water. Maddox sets the glass down and tucks me into bed. Panic sets in and, along with the anxiety, it tries to consume me. *Please don't leave me.*

Maddox stares into my eyes, grabbing my chin and holding my gaze before saying in a husky voice, "I told you once you're not getting rid of me even if you tried. I'm going to go out there to see if they know anything. Otherwise, I'll get them to come back later so we can rest. I'll be right back. If you fall asleep, just know I'll be here when you wake. I'm not going anywhere. Now, rest."

Maddox leans over me, and his warm tongue invades my mouth, teasing me before he turns and walks out of my room, closing the door behind him and leaving me breathless.

Emotionally overloaded, my body is full of panic, tingling, and my head is pounding at the same time. I lose all consciousness, feeling numb and almost like I'm floating. Then…darkness.

Maddox

I bolt upright when I hear the scream. *Shit. Alexandria.* I fly out of bed, thinking someone is in the room, only to find no one there except her thrashing around on the bed, having a bad dream. I lunge back in bed, trying to pull her into an embrace, only to get punched square in the jaw as she cries out. *Fuck, she has a mean right hook.*

"Alexandria, baby, wake up. I have you, and you're safe." I try to pin her down, forcing her to me, so she stops thrashing. She still doesn't wake, so I shake her, saying in a dominant voice, "Alexandria, wake up."

Alexandria suddenly goes still in my arms, so I gently move her hair from her face to look into those satiny blue eyes I love. I growl when I only see a fearful darkness staring back at me. Pulling her to me, I murmur into her ear, "You're safe. We're here in your bed, and you just had a bad dream."

Trying to hold it together myself, I take deep breaths in an effort to be strong. The anger I have for whoever hurt her tries to overtake me, but I push it down, knowing she needs me. Closing her eyes, she lets out a cry while withering into me, and I begin soothing her, telling her it'll be okay and that I have her. I sit up and pull her into my lap, placing soft kisses all over her.

Feeling so useless infuriates me. *I'm going to kill this motherfucker.*

I have to ask, knowing she probably won't want to talk about it, but it needs to be said. "Alexandria, do you want to talk about your dream? I think it would help you if you did."

She slides over to my side, so we're facing each other with my hand lying on her hip. I pull her closer, giving her time to think about it. Her voice sounds strained almost like she's lost. "It's just the same dream over and over again. I'm dancing to music, feeling the vibe. Someone comes up behind me, pulling me to them, kissing my neck. And then darkness, followed by fear. Lately, I scream 'don't' or 'stop,' but I still feel the fear and the darkness."

Closing her eyes, she exhales softly. I reach up, sliding my fingers over her flawless jawline. "Alexandria, look at me." Her crystal blues still shine with fear, but I continue, "I'll do everything in my power to keep you safe and to keep the fear away. Don't let him have the power. He won't be able to get to you, and he won't hurt you again."

Again, the hopelessness I feel has my anger tiptoeing along the edge, occupying me with thoughts of killing this son of a bitch.

Pulling her into my body, I hold and caress her for what seems like hours but is probably more like minutes. She appears to have fallen back to sleep in my arms. *Mi amor.*

Holding my angel, the woman of my dreams, I run my hands over her soft skin. I gently push her silky hair over her shoulder, exposing her neck and shoulder and making my cock come alive beneath her. *Fuckin' hell.*

Needing to get control of myself, I move us, pulling her in front of me and spooning her from behind. When she stirs, she grabs my arms, snuggling into me and holding me tighter. I think I'm dreaming when I hear a soft whimper come from her. "Maddy, make it go away. Please make it go away." *Yes, baby. Yes, I'll make it go away.*

Squeezing her tighter, I feel like I'm about ready to lose my shit. Instead, I squeeze her tighter still, whispering endearments in Spanish, hoping it'll soothe her back to sleep.

Alexandria lets out a deep sigh, telling me she's awake. I rub my hand down her side, caressing her when she starts to speak. "Maddy, I'm sorry. I thought I had this under control. I don't want to be scared all the time or let him run my life. I think I'll be fine, but after five years, I was just not expecting that. I felt so powerless with the unknown and not being in control. That's what scares me the most." I flip her over, laying her halfway on my chest, and I pull her into an embrace.

I knew it. Fucking Luc. She has to know. Shit, I need to tell her. Fuck.

In a deep, steady voice, I say, "Alexandria, I have to tell you something that you're not going to like. But I'll never lie to you or keep any secret from you. And I'll never hold any information back."

Probably my tone of voice or maybe just the overall content of what I said to her causes her to bolt up, holding her head. She then focuses on me, giving me her undivided attention. "What? Tell me."

Taking a deep breath, I sit up to face her, pulling her hands into mine. I start telling her about my meeting with her father and Beau, how they were worried about Monico and me. Then I tell her about the letters, how they didn't want to tell her, but I thought it was a bad idea. Now I know if they would've told her, she probably wouldn't have had such a serious panic attack. Once I'm done telling her everything, I relax, feeling lighter. While I was talking, her face was getting redder by the minute. She's become enraged, with her hands clenching mine.

Shit...

She grinds out through clenched teeth, "Are you fucking serious? Have they known he was looking for me for over a year and didn't tell me? Who do they fucking think they are? Do they think I'm some child? What the fuck? This is my life, and they can't keep sheltering me, for fuck's sake. I knew they orchestrated my life, but this is overboard."

I sit there and listen to her go on a rampage about her father being overprotective and so forth. I just listen and let her get it all out.

God, I hope this helps. She's so alive when she's mad, so strong, so passionate. I love her. Fuck.

Alexandria

I am so mad that I do what I do best and close up, losing myself in thought. *I'm so fucking pissed off at my parents. How could they keep this from me? Brant and the boys, how could they?*

Looking at Maddox, I can see he's worried about me and doesn't know what to say or do. This is my battle with my parents, not his, and I'll deal with them tomorrow. Trying to control my breathing and calm down, I say, "Thank you, Maddy." I pull him with me down onto the bed, needing his touch.

"For what?"

Pushing his hair back from his face and touching him gently, I feel the anger and hurt subside, lust and desire taking over. "For telling me everything, for helping me with my fear, for making me feel safe, and for caring."

I shift, tugging him by his shoulders, and I spread my legs, moving him on top of me. I want to feel his weight and the heat of his body. I can't stop wishing we were naked.

I beg him with my eyes, wishing he would understand my plea. *Please take me, Maddy. God, I want to feel you inside me. Take the fear away.*

"Alexandria, you don't have to thank me. I'll always protect you, and you'll always be equal to me in everything we do. I won't keep anything from you ever again. I guess now you know why I have been so overprotective." The gunmetal gray eyes that look down at me show his hunger for me, and I can't take it anymore.

I give myself a pep talk. *Beg, make him lose control and take me. Let him cleanse me of all this.*

We stare at each other for what seems like an eternity while I run my hands through his silky-smooth hair. *Fuck...here it goes, now or never.*

Seductively, I say, "Maddy, I am ready. We've prepared me, talked about it, and now, it's time. I want you to claim me, take away all the fear and negative shit in my head from tonight and make it into one of the best nights ever. Take away his power. Please don't deny me. I'm ready. Please take—" Before I can finish, he shifts his body up, pushing into my soaked panties, crashing our mouths together for an explosive kiss.

Moaning in ecstasy, I tangle my fingers in his hair and yank him down, drawing a growl from him. The fire we've been building with all these make-out sessions has finally ignited. *God. Yes. Finally.*

When Maddox pulls away from me, leaning back on his heels, he has me whining in protest until I see him reach for his shirt. He moves off the bed seductively and throws it to the side. He then grabs his chest, tugging at one of his pierced nipples and making my sex throb. *Jesus, he's so fucking beautiful.*

Reading my mind, he smiles and says in a heated voice, "You like what you see?"

Not trusting my own voice, I nod my head, biting my lip. I'm still not moving so he'll keep touching himself. I lie frozen and watch him, but I'm suddenly jerked to the end of the bed by my ankles, and I squeal, "Maddy!"

He leans over me, placing kisses on my neck and chest while reaching for the hem of my shirt. When he goes to lift it up, I sit up, aiding him by raising my arms over my head. Once my arms are free, I immediately grab his nipples, making him hiss, "Fuck."

I sit up, not wanting to stop touching him. He moves my hair back over my shoulders when I lean in, sucking his barbell into my mouth with a soft bite. "Alexandria, I can't hold back anymore. I need to have you. I need to claim you." *Oh, God. Yes...*

My pussy instantly adds moisture to my panties. Maddox's hands slide down my back along with my hair, and he unclasps my bra. I pull back from sucking on his pierced nipple and it pops, coming out of my mouth when I release it. I tilt my head back, and Maddox brings his hands back up my back over my shoulders, taking my bra with it. Once the bra drops and my breasts bounce out, his hands are on them, teasing them, and I release a moan.

Santa Maria. *I want more…* I lift my head, and we lock eyes while I slide my hands down his chiseled torso until I reach his pants.

He's still playing with my tits while I get his pants undone, and they drop to the ground. I reach into his boxer briefs, gripping his enormous cock, and my breath hitches. *Oh God, yes.* Maddox's jaw clenches, but he never takes his eyes off me, pinching my nipples. I let out a gasp. "Take me, Maddy. *Plea—*"

Next thing I know, I'm being thrown on the bed with a feral growl. Maddox has my pants and panties off in seconds, leaving both of us panting hard. He stands over my now naked body. His voice is deep and comes out rough and full of hunger. "Grab your tits, Alexandria. I want you to touch yourself."

I grab my chest while he grabs his dick, stroking it in front of me, and letting me gaze at his whole God-given, glorious fucking body. "Fuck, Maddy, you're beautiful. Please, no more waiting."

Oh, my God. His dick is so enormous with no clothes covering it.

He circles the bed, standing there stroking his cock a couple more times before he climbs on, positioning himself between my legs.

He grabs both my legs, sliding his hands down my thighs and pushing them out farther. He sucks in his lower lip and says, "Alexandria, you're always so fucking wet for me. I want to fuck you so fucking hard, but I know I need to go slow your first time. I'm trying to keep the rage inside, but fuck me, your pussy is so wet and tight. Fucking perfect. I don't know if I can do slow."

I fire back, panting, "Fuck me, Maddox. I want you inside me now. Please. I'm so tired of waiting. I've never wanted anything more."

Maddox shifts between us, still stroking his cock as he guides it between my folds, only to then move it up over my clit. I cry out, "Oh, God."

Maddox places a hand on my hips so I can't move, and he glides his cock again over my clit, teasing the entrance of my pussy and lubing his cock with my wetness. I try to buck my hips again, but I can't move with his weight on me. "Maddy…"

He licks his lips like I'm his next meal. "You sure you're ready?"

When I scream, *"Yes!"* Maddox slams his cock halfway inside my throbbing pussy. Pain and ecstasy are all I feel when we both cry out, *"Fuck!"*

Yes! Finally, yes!

Maddox puts both hands on my knees, pushing them out again and sliding his hands down my thighs. He pulls out a little bit before he thrusts into me again, going a little bit deeper this time. Maddox hisses, "Fuck yes."

I grab my tits and twist them, feeling the pleasure shoot through my body. Maddox pumps a few soft thrusts, letting me get adjusted to his size. "Fuck me, *mi belleza.* We are made for each other with the way my cock fits so perfectly, slipping into your tight and oh so fucking wet pussy. It's so fucking hot."

Maddox bites his lower lip, watching where our bodies connect. I thrust my hips, letting him know I'm okay. "Easy, Alexandria. I don't want to hurt you, and I'm trying to control myself from jacking you."

I need him to move, so I plead, "Maddy…please, I need more."

Damn, I'm going to explode.

Maddox growls, but he grips my hips harder, grinding his nails into me, and he starts thrusting deep, long, and hard. I'm so wet that I can hear our bodies slap together with the wetness pouring out of me. I spread my legs even wider, grabbing my knees so he can lean over me. I want to give him more leverage to pound his enormous girth into me. "Yes. Faster…"

Ecstasy. Pure ecstasy. Ay, I knew he'd feel good, but this is more than I ever could've imagined.

Both of us are panting in between moans, both rising to meet our climax. I release my knees when Maddox leans back, bringing both hands down my body and gripping my tits. He leans over, smashing his mouth to mine. Our tongues start fucking each other, matching the thrusts of Maddox's cock pumping into me. I begin to move my hips, meeting him, with each thrust hitting my clit just right. I break the kiss, crying out, "Right there. Fuck yes. Don't move."

Maddox deepens his thrust, not letting up and still hammering into me. He kisses my neck as he says seductively in between each thrust, "You're perfect. My beauty. Fuck, I'm close. Your pussy is so fucking tight. Come for me."

Clenching the bedsheets and feeling my climax on the brink of explosion, I try to speak, but my mouth is dry from panting. I only get out, *"Yes..."*

Maddox leans back, placing his thumb over my clit, and that is when I see stars. When he starts to flick it and toy with it, I can't keep from bucking, screaming, *"Oh, my God! Fuck yes..."* Then it happens. I explode into a million pieces, my body tingling all over.

When my orgasm takes over, my walls clench his cock so tight. Maddox loses control altogether, pounding me like a jackhammer, gripping my hips and grunting, "Fuck! Your pussy is so tight. Wet. *Mine.*"

He bites his lower lip, looking down and watching his cock pummel my pussy. A few beads of sweat slide down his face, and then I see his upper body tense. When our eyes connect, he struggles to say, "Yes. Almost."

I reach up, twisting his nipple piercing and sending him into oblivion. He cries out, *"Fuck yeah."* I feel the warmth from him spilling his seed into me while he thrusts a few more times before slowing.

Still tingling all over, I run my hands down my face, along my neck, and down to my chest, kneading my sensitive nipples. My pussy clenches, sucking his cock in, and we both hiss with pleasure.

Maddox collapses next to me on the bed, both of us breathing hard. We just lie there quietly, riding out our climaxes. Maddox is the first to speak, rolling to his side to face me. "Alexandria, did I hurt you? Fuck, I couldn't control it. Your pussy was more than I could take. I hope I wasn't too hard on you?"

Seeing the worried look on his face, I turn to him, still breathless, "No. Not at all. That was heaven, and I only want more."

When I reach up to touch his chest, he falls back, out of breath and laughing. *"Mi belleza,* did I let the tiger out of her cage?" *Holy shit, yes. God help me.*

Maddox rolls over, still laughing, and heads over to the bathroom. I watch him move with his cock bouncing at half-staff, his muscles glistening with sweat and making my pussy throb again.

Maddox returns with a wet washcloth, and he motions for me to spread my legs. I giggle, still feeling weird about him cleaning me. The past few weeks after I'd climax from him fingering me or feasting on me, he would clean me before we went to sleep. We talked about me being on birth control and how he wanted to have nothing in between us when we finally did it. He said he wanted me to be the first person he ever went bareback with, and since I've only been with two people and have been tested, he knew I was safe. I'm still getting used to him cleaning us both. Once he is done, he climbs back in bed, pulling me into him, spooning me, caressing me. "Alexandria, you're so beautiful, and I thank God every day for you. Sleep, *mi belleza*, we have a long day tomorrow."

Kissing my shoulder, he pulls me in tighter. I whisper, "Thank you, Maddy."

We both lie there quietly, letting exhaustion take over and sending us into a deep sleep.

Alexandria

I wake up to a phone ringing. Not wanting to move, I whine, "No… I don't want to deal with anything right now."

I feel Maddox pull me tighter to his chest, and he says in a thick, sleepy voice, "Alexandria, your parents, security team, and my guys are all meeting here in an hour."

I had sex. It was fucking fantastic.

He caresses my back, running his hand through my hair, and I just try to take it all in. My mind starts to run with everything that's happened in my life these past few weeks with Maddox, Jason, Emmett, the texts, and having sex. I feel, with everything that has happened, *I am* prepared for today's events.

Surprisingly, I don't feel panicked or anxious. Maybe talking through everything with Maddox helped me, or maybe it was waking up in his arms that just overpowers the fear. I lean up on an elbow to look down into his eyes, and I see concern swirling around in those silky gray depths as he wonders if I'm going to flip out.

Instead, I smile at him before saying in a dreamy voice, "Good morning. Round two?"

Maddox's face lights up, showing me his pearly whites and my favorite dimples ever. He flips me on my back, smashing me into the bed and giving me a passionate kiss. The kiss only ignites my body, and I want more of what he gave me last night, but he breaks away, saying softly, "No round two until your family is gone. I want to take my time with you. How do you feel? Are you sore? I fucked you pretty hard."

With a pouty face, I reach up to cup his stern jaw. "I feel *amazing* thanks to you. I want more."

I pull his face down and place soft kisses all over it. With a groan, he replies in between each kiss, "Once we figure everything out…"

Kiss.

"…I promise you…"

Kiss.

"…nothing will be kept from you again…"

Kiss.

"…we'll have all…"

Kiss.

"…the time in the world…"

Kiss.

"…to please each other."

Then he grabs my face, kissing me passionately with all he has. I feel my sex throbbing, but before I can move my arms around him, he launches off me to get out of bed. "Wait! No…"

I start to pout, but I stop when I see his gloriously naked body walking away from me. He's laughing because he knows what he does to me. Maddox slips on a pair of boxers before walking away, leaving me utterly speechless.

Maddox teases me while pulling his hair into a man bun. "I'm going to cook us some food while you get ready since I won't be able to keep my hands off you. Clearly, you can't keep your hands off me. I'll be in the other room until you're fully clothed."

I'm so dazed by his beauty that I can't help but ask, "Maddox, you're so beautiful. How did I get so lucky? Why me? You're *mine*, right? I'm not dreaming?"

Maddox walks to my side of the bed, stopping right next to me. "Alexandria, you're mine, and I'm yours. *Nothing* will change that. I've wanted you far longer than you've wanted me. I'm the lucky one. Now, get up." He then leans down briefly, giving me a kiss on the lips before walking out of the room.

Thanking God, I whisper in Spanish, "No, *I'm* the lucky one…"

People start to show up around the same time, asking how I am, making small talk until everyone is here. I'm pacing my apartment, trying to busy myself while everyone else just looks relaxed, talking among themselves. My parents are talking to Beau, Gus, and Chad in the living room, while Maddox,

Isaac, Ethan, and Brant talk in the kitchen, getting more coffee.

My nerves are shot to hell. I can't wait anymore, so I walk down the two steps into my living room and stand in front of my big screen. I put my hands on my hips, not caring if I look like a spoiled brat, and I huff, "So, everyone. Can we discuss how you all kept me in the dark about my rapist? Or can we talk about what else you're keeping from me? Or what we're doing, or going to do, about him?"

Be strong. Don't show weakness. I'm pissed. Stay pissed, Alex.

Everyone gets quiet, moving into the room and giving me their full attention. "Maddox updated me on most of the stuff, but I want to make one thing clear. I'm not a little girl anymore."

Staring straight at my parents, I continue. "I can handle this, and I'd rather be prepared than have an episode like last night. If I had been aware, I might not have slipped into a full-blown panic attack." I'm not a fucking child.

I fold my arms over my chest, and Maddox moves down the two steps and comes to my side. "I want to know everything. I don't want to be kept in the dark or to be told that everything will be okay. What I do want to hear is what we're going to do about him. This is me he's after, and I don't want to hide anymore."

Maddox slides his arm around my waist, pulling me into his side and reassuring me he has my back. *God, he feels good. Safe in his arms.*

Beau is the first one to speak, walking over to me with a neutral expression on his face and handing me a manila folder. "You're right, Alex, we shouldn't have kept you in the dark. But over the last year, you've come a long way, and we didn't want to send you into a tailspin back to square one. As we can all see, you have matured a lot being gone and you can handle it. So here's what we received while you were gone."

Finally, someone talks. Don't show emotions right now. Breathe, keep it in, stay strong, Alex.

Grabbing the folder, I move over to the chaise longue, with Maddox right behind me. I sit down, pulling out the content and seeing it's the two letters Maddox told me about. Thank God Maddox had already warned me about what they said. Otherwise, I probably would have lost my shit just now reading them. Masking my emotions so they don't know I'm freaking out, I put the letters back into the folder and hand it back to Beau, not saying a word.

I can do this. I have Maddox. Breathe. He can't get me. Breathe.

Everyone is staring at me, making anxiety start to build in my stomach. Beau turns around to walk back over to the table where Ethan is sitting with a computer. Beau continues, "Alex, that's all we have from him besides your text message. Last night, we had Ethan tap into your phone and try to trace where the text came from. All we know is that it's a New York number, but it's a burner, meaning it's a prepaid phone."

Pausing, Beau looks around the room, stopping at my papá to get approval for whatever he has yet to say. Beau then turns back toward me, letting out a breath.

I start to panic, thinking, *Jesus, it gets worse. Fuck!*

"We also know over the last few years, girls have been going missing from three of the clubs around here, Spin being one of them. In the last year, we've had four girls go missing and four reports of girls being drugged at the clubs—"

Before he can finish, my mamá is crying with her hand over her mouth. I let out a deep breath, and Maddox squeezes me, letting me know he's beside me. Beau continues, "In the last month, three girls have been found raped and drugged. The reports show they were slipped GHB, the same date rape drug you were given."

I clench my teeth together, trying to hold in my anxiety, and I twist my hands together. Maddox growls. Moving to sit next to me, he pulls me into his side for comfort. Beau continues about the video or something, but I zone out. *Fuck, he's raping other girls? So, it isn't just me? But, why me? Why does he want me after all these years? I wish I could remember.*

Brant yells across the room, "Alex!" It makes Mamá and me jump and startles me out of my thoughts. I look over at Brant, who looks fucking pissed. Again, Brant says, "Alex! Are you listening? Don't zone out."

I feel Maddox squeeze me, whispering, "Are you okay?"

I snap out of it, replying, "Sorry, Beau, can you hold on a second? Are you saying he's doing this to other girls? And, why me? I don't understand why he wants me again, after all these years."

Maddox grunts beside me, and I see Papá squeeze Mamá tightly, trying to mask his own emotions. Beau walks over to me, looking down and folding his arms. It makes him look like a force to be reckoned with, but I just stare. "Alex, we think this is personal. He took his time with you. Didn't hurt you or harm you in any way."

Turning to pace the room with his arms still folded, he lifts one hand to rub his chin, trying to work out his thoughts before continuing, "*If*, and that is a big *if*, it's the same guy, this guy hurt them, dropped them in alleys or left them passed out in a club. Nothing personal like you. He must have access to someone you know, or maybe he's hacked into your stuff because he knows where you were, even if only generally, and when you were coming back."

I feel Maddox's body tense up next to me, and I slip my hand onto his thigh to let him know I'm okay. Ethan speaks up, making everyone look over to him. "Well, actually, Beau, I've tapped into her email, computer, and pretty much all her stuff, and it didn't show anything about where she was going to be last night. Also, when she was traveling in Europe, she didn't send anything with her return dates or travel plans."

I start freaking out inside, trying not to let on I am losing it. *Wait? What? He also tapped into my personal email? Who have I emailed? I've emailed promoters in Spain and here but we never did settle on dates. I always called them to finalize the dates. I rack my brain, trying to remember if I texted anyone yesterday, but I only called Stella and Izzy. No texts. Wait...shouldn't I be mad?*

Ethan is staring at me when I look up perplexed. He says, "Alex, I'm sorry to tap into your personal information. I did searches, so don't worry, I didn't go through each item. I hate to say this, but I think you might know the guy. I mean, we had a hard time finding you in Spain since you didn't have a set schedule. How can he know your schedule? Who do you talk to all the time? Can you remember who you talked to when you were in Spain about coming home or anyone you spoke to about your plans for last night?"

Think, Alex. Think. I don't talk to anyone. Fuck, I'm getting a headache.

Feeling frustrated, I look down to rub my temples while I

try to think of who I've talked to.

I have many questions my mind is in overdrive. *Men? Friends? Who do I talk to? Fuck, not men! Maddox is the first guy I've let in besides my security team.*

Before I can say anything, Brant walks up to Beau, folding his hand over his chest, and speaks up. "She doesn't talk to anyone but her girls or us. She never went on a date with anyone or even met any men in Spain. We're always protecting her or around her, making it impossible. Yes, she might have danced with some guys, but she never hung with anyone to where he would know her schedule. She never met up with anyone outside of the clubs, or anywhere, for that matter. The only men she has been in contact with have been the ones she talks to for the label, the DJs, promoters, managers, and singers."

Um, no friends. No boyfriends. No life. Sheltered. Sounds about right.

Chad steps out from behind Ethan, "Well then, I think you have your problem. It has to be someone at the label, *or* he's in contact with someone at the label. Obviously, it's not going to be her security team or her girlfriends. He's either in tight with someone at the label or works there. That's the only way he would get your information."

Everyone is looking around at everyone. Papá stands up, rubbing his head. "We have so many people workin' in that buildin', it would be impossible to figure that out, especially with the festival comin' up. It's a madhouse!" He raises his voice with irritation.

Maddox matches Papá's irritation. "We need to figure out a plan for her. Maybe set a trap? Tell certain people she will be somewhere, but really, she'll be wherever I am. We'll have undercover people in place, and we'll keep a lookout for anyone we might recognize from the label. We need to do something instead of waiting for this son of a bitch to strike again."

A phone rings, making everyone look around the room. Beau pulls his phone out. "I'm in a meeting, can I call—"

Everyone is silent for a second watching Beau. He tenses up, turning toward the door and giving Brant a look. Both men start for the door when I stand up and yell, "Wait, what's happening? What's wrong?"

Brant stops in his tracks, looking between Beau and me. Beau stops, looking like he's going to detonate any minute and barking into the phone, "I got it. Fuck, what did I just say, Wolfe? I'll find her and report back to you."

He slams his phone shut before the man on the phone can reply. Beau is beyond pissed off, so he takes a second to calm down before barking out, "B, find Ginger. *Now.* She was in the building before we came in here."

Brant grabs his phone and starts dialing, heading for the door.

What? No, not Ginger.

I cry out, shaking my head, "No…no…no… Not Ginger."

Maddox immediately pulls me into an embrace, while everyone gets to their feet. Beau hollers out, "Relax! That was her father. He has some…" He pauses, his eyes narrowing. "…things that are going down, and he needs her to check in. But he can't find her. It has nothing to do with your guy. Everyone relax. Brant will find her and bring her back here."

Relief spreads across the room, and everyone takes a deep breath.

Maddox

For the next few hours, we all talk about what we can do to lure the guy out, keeping Alexandria safe, tapping her phone, and adding more men to her security team—even though I'm not going to let her out of my sight. When Brant brings Ginger back, Alexandria seems to relax some. Ginger actually comes up with some good ideas on how to protect Alexandria better.

She won't be without me; I'm never leaving her side. Fucking motherfucker. I need to put things into place so she's always with me. She's mine. Keep her safe. Fuck.

Alexandria did well throughout the day, putting her thoughts in and agreeing with me that she isn't going to hide, that she'll be with me when I DJ at clubs. By the afternoon, we had a plan, and everyone was getting ready to head to the office to set things in motion. Alexandria was standing in the kitchen getting water, so now was the perfect time for me to talk to her father about me staying here, and her music. When I see her mother talking to the girls, I look over at Luc. "Luc, can I talk to you in private?" Everyone at the table stops and looks at the two of us, but Luc just nods.

Hopefully, she doesn't notice us walking over to the window, our backs to her in the kitchen. Her place is like one big fucking room, so it is hard to have a private conversation. I put both my hands in my pockets, trying to relax. "Luc, as I told you in your office, I don't plan on going anywhere, and I'll be staying here with Alexandria if she'll have me. I don't want to leave her alone."

I don't know why I'm asking him. Like I could ever leave her. Fuck, I love this girl.

I turn to look him in the eye before I continue. "And, to be honest, I don't want to be away from her, period. I'll do anything and everything to keep her safe."

Luc has his hands in his pockets same as I do. I try to gauge his reaction, but he masks his emotions and thoughts well. I need to get this all out, so fuck it. "Look, she's the one for me. I know we've only known each other a month, but I don't fucking care. I haven't told her yet, but I need you to know where I stand. When I saw her in Spain, I just knew. I've left everything for her. Now…" I take a big breath as I prepare to change the subject. "I want to ask you, do you have full video and sound in your home studio? Like, where you could see and hear what is going on in there from somewhere else?"

That probably came out wrong. Fuck. I'm fucking this up.

I can tell my question has taken him off guard when an eyebrow rises in question. "Yeah, I fuckin' have both, but they're not runnin' all the time. The video stream is turned on by the motion sensor, but it can be manually turned off, same with sound. The main stream goes to our main office here in the buildin' where all our cameras are monitored. Our hub is monitored twenty-four seven here, at Spin It, and at Club Spin. When I'm in the studio, I usually turn it off because I don't need monitorin', but I have it on the motion sensor most the time. Why? What do you have in mind?"

Seriously? Your daughter is fucking amazing. Probably better than you and your wife. Fuck. Hold it together, Madd Dog.

Taking a deep breath, I look over my shoulder to check on Alexandria. When I see her still talking to her mother and Ginger, I turn to look out the window. "I would like it if you could turn on both video and sound when you get back home. I'm hoping to get her in there tomorrow. I want to show you how good your daughter really is."

I turn back to face him with a stern face. "I want her DJing with me as a couple or even just her individually. Her music needs to be heard. It's even better than yours or Mia's stuff. She's that good. She's worried she won't succeed, following in your footsteps. Plus, I want her to quit managing these fucking DJs and make something of herself instead of standing behind them when she's better than half your lineup." I fold my arms to let him know I'm dead serious.

If you fucking paid attention to your daughter instead of sheltering her, you might know. Good, I've pissed him off. Wake the fuck up, Luc.

Luc's jaw clenches into a straight line. He speaks in a low growl, "I know how fuckin' good my daughter is, Maddox, I fuckin' taught her everythin' she knows."

Luc takes a step back, taking a deep breath. He runs his

hands through his hair, trying to calm down before he continues. "She never seems interested in DJin' or anythin' but the business side, so I never pushed."

He blows out a deep breath, letting his shoulders drop in defeat, then looks at me with concern in his eyes. "I'll record and watch it, then we can meet. If you think she wants to, then go for it. I just want her to be happy, Maddox. She's never looked at anyone or acted like she does with you. I can fuckin' see that, so if she loves you, and if you're truly in love with her, then I'm okay with you being here."

Luc's face turns fierce as he spits out, "But so help me God, if you fuckin' hurt her or put her in harm's way, *we* will have a fuckin' problem. *Capisci*? If she doesn't want to DJ, do not push her. I'll be watchin', and then we'll talk."

Luc turns away from me, stalking off toward the door, calling for Mia that they need to go.

Fuck yeah. Now all I need is to convince Alexandria.

I'm leaning back on the window, relaxing some and watching everyone gather their things. Isaac approaches me, smiling like he just stole someone's girlfriend and got laid. I laugh at him while he slithers over to me. "What's that grin for? Did you get laid in the last hour that I didn't know about?"

If he weren't my best friend and we hadn't grown up together, I would have kicked his ass a long time ago. Isaac is one guy you'd never want to trust with anything unless you're considered his family. Then you can trust him with your life. We butt heads a lot, but he manages all my shit that I hate dealing with.

Isaac rubs his hands together, snickering. "Well, now that you mention getting laid… What is the plan for tomorrow?

You still on for this week's events? What is your plan for us? I need to know what you need me to do."

I look over his shoulder at Alexandria. She glances up from talking to Ginger and Brant, who are getting ready to leave, with a smile that fucking has my cock twitching. Smiling back at her, I can feel my heart swell, making me ache to touch her.

I want to be alone with Alexandria. Fucking hell, I'm getting hard thinking about it.

Fuck, I need everyone gone. Right fuckin' now.

Pushing off the window, I walk over to Ethan and Chad with Isaac by my side. Once we're all together and I have everyone's attention, I start rattling off orders for everyone. "Isaac, this week's events are the same, but next week after the festival, I plan on Alexandria DJing alongside me as a couple. I'm going to talk to her tomorrow about it, so I will confirm with you once I know. Did you bring me some clothes?"

Isaac nods, so I turn toward Ethan, trying to hurry before she comes over here. "Ethan, I want you monitoring her phone, texts, calls, and emails. If it hits her phone, I want to know."

I can see from Ethan's face that he wants to say something. "What?" Ethan folds his arms, looking over his shoulder at Alexandria, which gets a growl from me. "What the fuck do you have to say, Ethan? Just say it."

My temper is on a short fuse these days. Not wanting to lose it here, I take a deep breath before Ethan speaks. "Madd Dog, she has had some crazy texts from that dude Emmett and that promoter guy Jason. They're obsessed with her. We need to watch out for those two. They're blowing her up, and since no one has replied to them and they haven't heard from anyone, they're tripping something happened to her. I'll keep an eye on her shit, but you keep an eye on your girl, especially with those two fucks."

I hold in my fury by keeping my thoughts to myself. *Fuckin' hell. That's all I need, those two dumb fucks getting in the way. No shit. I'll beat the fuck out of them if they touch her. Mine. She's mine*

"Goddammit!" I take my hair down and run my hands through it before putting it back up.

Chad steps forward, putting his hand on my shoulder, "Look, Madd Dog, you know we're all here for you, brother. Whatever you want to do, we got your back. I need to go update the boys back at the hotel. Beau is the shit, and he's actually on top of all this too, so no one is going to get past us, brother. He has even checked out those two dumb fucks, but they're clean. He says they're just guys crushing hard for her, but we'll keep an eye on her. Now relax and spend some time with your girl. We'll see you tomorrow."

Before I can say anything, they all smack me on the shoulder, saying good-bye, and we're finally alone.

Standing at her table by the window, I just watch her move around the place like a goddamn angel. I need to kiss and suck all over her body, memorizing every inch of it, claiming all of its beauty. If anything happens to her, I don't know what I'll do because she's my life now.

Her sexy as silk voice pulls me from my thoughts. "What are you thinking about, Maddy?"

Having my way with your delectable body. Fuckin' hell, I'll never get enough of this woman.

Placing a smile on my face, I stalk over to her, picking her up in an embrace. "How fuckin' amazing are you, and how proud I am of you for holding it together today."

I lean down to kiss her, and she slides her hand over my shoulders, pulling me down and letting me know she wants more. With a growl, I break the kiss. "Alexandria, go get into the shower, and I'll meet you there." I see her eyes gloss over with anticipation, and she bites her lower lip, making my dick twitch.

"Okay." Turning seductively, she sways her hips, making my balls tighten with each step she takes.

Fuckin' hell, I need to claim that ass and soon.

I move around the apartment, shutting off lights and locking all the doors before I head to my little bit of heaven. I move to turn on music, when I hear Alexandria singing in the shower. I stop to listen to the beauty of her voice. Not wanting to waste any more time, I turn the music up a bit more and start to strip off my clothes.

When I walk into the bathroom, my balls are tight, my dick is hard, and I see her washing her hair with her head tilted back, eyes closed, and humming something. I move into the shower while she's rinsing under the stream. I just stand there watching the water cascade down her silky olive skin while stroking my cock.

Alexandria steps out from under the water, running her hands over her face. She continues up over her head then through her hair, clasping her neck, opening her eyes seeing me staring in awe of her beauty. "Alexandria, I want you to grab your tits and start playing with yourself."

Alexandria's eyes glaze over. Seeing that I'm stroking myself in a slow, controlled motion, she draws in a breath, and I see her nipples harden. "Touch yourself." I demand.

Alexandria takes both hands, sliding them over her face and pushing her hair back. She then slips them down her neck seductively, grabbing both breasts and kneading them before she rebels and slips one hand down her glorious torso and over her mound to her sweet, sweet pussy.

Fuck me. "That's it. Touch yourself, baby." Stroking myself faster, I lick my lips before sucking in my lower lip with a deep-throated moan. I'm letting her know exactly what her playing with herself is doing to me.

Both of our chests start moving faster, our breathing increasing with each stroke. Alexandria's usually sky-blue eyes are now a deep blue sea color, and they're locked with mine, never losing contact. I'm so lost in our lustful stare I don't even notice she's getting closer to me until she moves her hands to my chest. The instant her fingers touch my skin, I grip my cock, inflicting pain and making me take in air with a hiss. Fuck. Alexandria whines, "Please, Maddy, let me... I want to try."

She takes over my thoughts when I see her move down my body. I slow my strokes until she moves my hands, replacing them with her hands. I cover her hand, showing her how to grip. Just the touch of her hands on my cock sends me into a tailspin. "Yeah, baby." I let out a deep moan. I know I won't be able to last long with her hands on me. I lean back on the wall and look down, watching her take over.

My God. Heaven!

Looking into her eyes, I can tell she's nervous, so I push her hair back with a tug. Needing to be certain she's okay, I ask, "Alexandria, are you sure?"

She doesn't reply but instead swipes her tongue out, licking the tip of my cock before sliding her lips over the length and engulfing it into her hot, greedy mouth. Instantly, my eyes roll back with a deep groan. "Fuck yeah…"

Alexandria hears my moans and quickens her motions, swallowing more of my cock with each suck. I grab her hand at my shaft, guiding her, showing her that grabbing it with a firm grip won't hurt me, but instead will turn me on more. When she increases her sucking, she moans her own pleasure, which in turn, has me losing control. "That's it, Alexandria. Faster…"

Grabbing her head and holding it, I start to thrust my cock into her mouth. Alexandria slips her hands up my thighs to my hips, holding on. I start out easy to see if she can take my cock fully. When she looks up with eager eyes, only to move one of her hands down to cup my balls, I grunt, "Fuck. Baby, I'm gonna come."

She moans her approval, and I hold her head firmer and start to jack myself off in her mouth.

Yes, just like I imagined it would be. So warm, so soft, fuck yes.

Alexandria hollows her mouth, sucking harder with each thrust, taking me deeper. *"Yes."*

Moaning with the slurping sound, I close my eyes. When she begins to hum with my thrusts, the vibrations send me to the edge.

"Almost, baby." Not able to control myself, I increase jacking her face. I open my eyes and look down. I see her blue eyes watering, staring back at me with drool cascading down her face. I watch my dick slam in and out of her wet mouth.

I lose it. "Fuck!" Spilling my seed into her mouth, I lean back into the wall and release my grip on her head, seeing stars.

Alexandria still pumps my cock, taking all that I have and moving her hand up and down my torso. My head still spinning, I look up at the ceiling, trying to regain control. Alexandria starts to kiss her way up my body, moaning her pleasure. "Maddy, was that okay?"

Fuckin' hell! Was it okay? Is she joking? Goddamn, I need more...

I'm so overwhelmed with my desire to have more. Still not in control of my body, I grab her by her hips, turning her around and pressing her up against the wall, making her squeal. "Maddox!"

I'm so out of control with rage, not bad rage, more like uncontrollable need and the urgency to fill her. Consume her. Claim her. Take her. Fuck her.

I pin her against the wall before leaning in to whisper into her ear, "Alexandria, I've lost all control with you."

Running my hands down her body and stopping at her hips, I bend down to my knees. I spread her ass cheeks with my hands, doing a face plant and devouring her with my tongue.

Alexandria cries out, "Oh, *God.*"

I assault her asshole and pussy with my tongue using deep strokes, and she moans, letting me know she likes it. While I'm still fucking her with my face, I reach down and start stroking myself. Fuck, I'm ready to take her again. Almost fully hard again, I stand up, placing an arm around her waist. I bend my knees slightly, lining my cock up to her already swollen pussy, and I slam into her. Both of us cry out in satisfaction. "Yes, Maddy. God, yes."

God, yes, is right! Mine.

Thinking of nothing but being connected to her, filling her,

I start thrusting, holding her against the wall. I'm so out of control I kiss and bite her shoulder, neck, ear before rasping out, "Alexandria, I have no control with you. I need to consume you. I need to fuck you hard."

Alexandria whimpers with a moan, slamming her hips back to meet my cock head on for a deeper connection. "Yes, I'm so close."

Needing to be deeper, I grunt out, "Grab the railing." I turn us, bending her over. The water is hitting my back as I slam deeper into her. "Hell yeah! So fucking hot."

When I reach around, slipping my hand between her legs and fingering her clit, she screams my name over and over again. Her pussy clenching down on my dick sends me close to the edge of my climax. I lean back to grip her ass for dear life and pound into her. With each thrust, I almost explode. One, *Jesus.* Two, *almost.* Three, *fuck yeah.* On the fourth and fifth thrust, I cry out my release.

Simply heaven.

Both of us lean into the wall, sated with pleasure. I slow my thrusts, but the wave of ecstasy continues. I lean back, running my hands down her body and cupping her ass with a couple of slower thrusts before I pull out.

Barely able to stand, I turn off the water. I pick her up and carry her to bed, neither one of us able to speak, we're so exhausted. I place us into bed, pulling her into me, spooning her, caressing her, whispering endearments in Spanish and leading us both into a deep slumber.

Heaven. Fucking heaven.

Alexandria

"Alexandria, you're mine! Motherfucker!"

When I feel myself rocking back and forth, I open my eyes.

As I try to figure out what is going on, I think, *What's wrong? Wait... what the fuck?*

I feel a huge weight on me. I try moving my arms, but I can't move. When I open my eyes, I see Maddox's flawless face looking down at me with angry charcoal gray eyes. I gasp, and a rush of fear and panic flows through me, making me freeze.

Mumbling, I try to ask, "Maddox? What's wrong?" I attempt to get up, but he has me pinned down.

Panicking, I keep thinking, *something is wrong. He looks like he wants to kill someone*.

"Maddox? What's wrong?" Still nothing. His face is strained, brows furrowed, jaw clenched, and he's just staring at me.

Am I dreaming? I don't understand. Is he sleeping? Why won't he talk to me?

I try to look around the room to see if anything is out of place. I shout at him, "Maddox! Dammit, what's wrong?"

He blinks a few times then pushes my hair out of my face, staring at me like he's in a trance. In a calm voice that freaks me the fuck out, he says, "Alexandria, do you know what I would do to anyone who tries to hurt you? I don't share, Alexandria. I don't want any man near you, touching you, or even looking at you weird. I'll freak the fuck out. You're mine. Do you understand me? Mine."

What the fuck just happened?

"Maddox you're scaring the fuck out of me." He closes his eyes and takes a couple deep breaths before he opens them again.

I try to relax, seeing his silver eyes I love so much. "Maddy, talk to me. What's going on? You're scaring me. Please."

Maddox cautiously moves off me to sit up in bed, leaning back against the headboard in nothing but boxers. I slowly move up next to him, waiting for him to explain what just happened. Then I see my phone in his hands.

Oh God, something did happen.

"Maddy, let me see my phone, please. What happened?" My voice is pleading.

Maddox flips my phone over and over in his hands. I know this can't be good because I've never seen him this outraged. I haven't seen my phone since the club, Saturday night.

Fighting with my own thoughts, I sit up, grabbing my phone from him. When he looks over at me, I can see he is fighting the urge to flip out and it's taking everything he has to keep control. All his muscles are tensed, and he's straining to keep his composure. I tell him it's going to be okay, and then I look down at my phone.

Fifteen text messages. Ten missed calls

"Jeezus." *What the fuck is going on?*

I start to look at my text messages.

After the unknown messages from the club Saturday night, I start to read.

EMMETT

Baby girl, are you okay? I just heard you passed out. I need to know are you okay. I'm sorry for being a dick. Please let me know you're okay.

And…

JASON

Hey, beautiful. Sorry I left without saying goodbye, but you were on stage. I went to a party and just got home so I'm pretty wasted, hence the drunk texting. It was so good to see and hold you, even if it was for just a brief moment. Anyway, hope to see you this week. Call me.

Oh, my God...

Feeling Maddox's intense stare, I look up to meet his charcoal eyes again, and they show me the fire brewing inside of him. Not saying anything, we just stare into each other's eyes. Maddox breaks the silence. "Scroll down to the ones from yesterday evening."

Fuck. Fuck. Fuck.

Lifting my phone, I start to scroll through the messages. I

can see most of them are from Emmett, a few from Jason this afternoon, one each from Ginger, Sasha, and Izzy, seeing if I'm okay, and then I see it.

Breathe, Alex. Breathe. I am safe. Don't panic.

UNKNOWN
SUNDAY 6:00PM
Alex, do you really think you got away? I thought you were over those panic attacks. You just made this more of a challenge. I like that, but just so you know, I can get to you anytime I want. I know everything about you and what you all have planned. You'll be seeing me soon. I can taste you now.

UNKNOWN
SUNDAY 7:00PM
Alex, my little one. If you keep avoiding me, then I might just have to play with one of your friends, and I know you would hate for one of them to go missing, now, wouldn't you? See you on video soon.

UNKNOWN
SUNDAY 8:00PM
My little one, you can't stay locked up in your place forever. Even so, do you think I can't get in there or that I haven't already been in there? Remember I'll have you one way or another. You are mine, Alex.

What! He knows my plan? Wait a minute. Video? I haven't left my place.

My mind starts racing, and within seconds, I'm bouncing out of bed, grabbing clothes. Maddox is right on my tail but not touching me. His voice sounds panicked, "Baby, I'm sorry

I lost it. I saw red when I saw those texts. Please don't be scared. I won't let anything hap—"

I cut him off. "Maddy, I'm not mad or scared. I just need to talk to Beau and Ethan." I look him in the eye, my eyebrows raised, trying to let him know that I know something. "Right now. Please call Ethan while I call Beau. Trust me, *mi amor*."

Shit, I just called him my love. Fuck, focus, Alex. Focus.

With a shocked expression, Maddox freezes in place. "Alexandria, it's three a.m. Monday morning."

Putting my phone to my ear as I walk out of my bedroom to the kitchen, I say over my shoulder, "Call Ethan *now*."

Beau answers on the first ring, and I start rambling off shit not making any sense. But before he yells at me, I stop and take a deep breath. Once I'm calm, I try to explain to him about the text messages. Of course, he already knew about them from Ethan. Since they're now wired to my phone, they see everything. I try to keep my voice down, and I run the water in the kitchen sink to make some noise just in case we are bugged or being videoed.

I explain my theory of how he knows what I'm doing. "I think either my studio is bugged, has a hidden video, or maybe he hacked into our video system like Ethan is doing to me. There are two reasons I think this. One, look at the time he texted me—six o'clock, an hour after everyone left. Isn't that kind of weird? Why didn't he text me when we got home? Second, is the video comment about seeing me on video real soon? It just doesn't make sense. The last thing he said is he knows my plan. Was he listening to us today?"

I'm standing at the sink with Maddox right next to me, just staring at me while I speak to Beau. When I'm done, I turn the water off, looking over at Maddox.

I can see the light go on in Maddox's head because his facial expression goes from rage to holy shit. He turns with his phone in his ear, calling Ethan to explain my theory. Beau cussing in my ear brings me back to our conversation and leads me to believe what I just said could actually happen. If he hacked into our security system, he would be able to see everything and hear everything except in our homes. But if he bugged or set up a camera in here… Fuck!

Shit! He could be watching now, or worse yet, he could be listening now.

Panic starts to rise in my belly. Not knowing what to do, I stop pacing and try to act normal. Breathe. *I'm safe. Breathe, Alex.*

Once Beau has calmed down and quit barking orders, I try to whisper into the phone to him, "Beau, seriously. What if my place is bugged or has a camera? What do I do?" I play with my hair in front of my mouth in case there is a video.

Beau is silent on the phone for a second, but I hear him breathing so I know he didn't hang up. I wait for him to reply. My nerves are about to explode, and I'm seriously trying not to have a panic attack.

Where the fuck did Maddox go?

When I'm about to say something, Beau growls, "Fuck, Alex. Okay, I know this will be hard, but you need to go back to bed. It's three a.m., and if you do anything out of the ordinary, he might get tipped off. Since we don't know what or if anything is inside your house, we just have to wait it out. I'll call your father and have his place scanned and cleaned. You'll keep to the plan and go over there in the morning with Maddox to work on music. We'll scan both your place and the office. So try not to freak out and just act like you two got up for a snack or something. If your place is bugged, he may have just heard you explain everything, which is fine, but we need to know. I'll have a group of guys head over to your father's place once I contact him. I'll text you when I know something."

Okay, I can do this.

When I don't say anything, Beau calls out my name sounding concerned. "Alex, are you okay? Stay calm and know he can't get to you. Maddox is with you, and we have most of the security teams here in the building. Just stay calm and try to act normal. Can you do that? I need for you to say yes."

My voice comes out weak and hoarse around the lump in my throat. "Yes, Beau. I understand. Um, Beau? Um, do you have people on all our girls? Is everything okay with Ginger and her dad? I didn't get to ask her if everything was okay."

He lets out a sigh, probably irritated with me for asking about her, but I need to know. "Yes, Brant is with her now." *Is he with her at three a.m.?* "She texted Brant earlier, saying she was going to the gym in the building. So we knew where she was, but her father couldn't get ahold of her. I guess shit went down within the motorcycle club, and they're all on lockdown. Her father is very protective of her and wanted to know she was okay. When they go into lockdown, I usually have someone on her twenty-four seven like you. Yes, I have eyes on all our girls, so don't worry. So, Alex, try to go back to bed, act normal, and let me speak with Maddox really quick, please."

Wow…he totally gave me way more information than he usually does. "Thank you, Beau. I understand. I just wanted to make sure she was okay."

If my place is bugged, at least I'm making it sound like I'm worried about my friends instead of freaking the fuck out. I start to walk toward my bedroom where Maddox is probably on the phone. I hear Beau barking orders on his side of the phone.

Shit, don't freak out. Stay calm.

I turn to see Maddox walking back into the room, phone in his hand with a grin on his face. His whole persona has changed from his rage back to the man I love. I'm guessing his phone conversation went well. I smile at him, trying to be normal and not show my panic. "Maddox, it's for you."

I hand the phone over to him. He grabs it from me but swings his other hand with his phone around my waist, bringing me into his side. I laugh up at him. "I'll be in bed waiting for you."

Maddox kisses my forehead before he releases me. Once the phone is to his ear, I walk off, leaving them, while I try not to freak out and "act normal."

Seriously, what's normal? Definitely not me. I laugh to myself because I am definitely anything but normal.

Maddox

This morning we haven't talked much, with both of us thinking about this sick fuck. Watching her out of the corner of my eye, I see the storm brewing in her head. I know she's freaking out right now, and I don't blame her. It took everything I had not to flip out into one of my fucking fits. If her place is wired with any devices, I'll lose my shit. The need to protect her is unbearable, and I don't know what else to do. I just know I can't be away from her or let her out of my sight. Today was supposed to be about us becoming one, moving forward with our future, and that motherfucker got in the way again. I should be talking to her about our future in bed, naked, and happy, not like this with her head fucked up with this sick fuck. I wish I would have been more prepared for this shit when I came here from Spain. I thought her only worry would be Monico Benitez.

Mask your emotions, Madd Dog. She's mine. She's safe.

I squeeze her hand as we exit the elevator on her parents' floor. I'm looking over my texts coming in, and we're both quite lost in our own thoughts. At least I know Luc's place was already swept last night or, should I say, this morning, and it's clean. They're finishing the office now and will move to her place. Once we get into her parents' house, we can talk freely without worry of being heard. I just need to talk to her before we go into the studio since they're leaving the video and sound on in there. Just in case he's watching her, he'll be focused on that feed. Plus, I told Luc I want him to watch us.

Alexandria opens the door, yelling out for her parents, when I grab her wrist and turn her to face me. "Alexandria, your parents are at the office, and then they'll be heading to your house to search it. We need to talk before we go into the studio. Your parents' place was already swept for devices, and they found nothing, but once in the studio, he might be able to see and hear us."

I want to punch something, seeing the fear in her eyes. I pull her into an embrace. Putting her head on my chest, I lean down and kiss the top of her head, rubbing my hands over her back and soothing her. "Alexandria, you're safe. I hate seeing fear in those beautiful eyes of yours. Fuck, I wanted this day to go so differently."

Alexandria's face stays emotionless, but her eyes tell me everything, and I start to panic.

Shit, I'm fucking this up. I need to relax.

Taking a deep breath, I pull away, looking down into her eyes that are glowing like the Caribbean Sea. My cock twitches just looking at her plump, heart-shaped lips that are calling me to suck on them. I bite my lower lip, keeping myself from kissing her. "Baby, let's sit down over here so we can talk. I need to get some things off my chest, and I also want to know what's going on in that beautiful head of yours. But first, let me get this shit out."

Moving to the couch, Alexandria says in a nervous whisper, "Oookay, what's wrong?"

I hope what I have to say will distract her and hopefully get her mind off this shit. Once I have her sitting down on her parents' couch, I turn to face her, rubbing my sweaty hand over my jeans and trying to calm my nerves. "Alexandria, I'm sorry for how I reacted last night when I freaked out. I just saw red and I was trying to calm down, but instead, I just froze up. I couldn't think of anything but finding and killing this motherfucker."

I pause to grab her hands. "From the moment I first saw you, I just knew you were the one. You took my breath away, and since then, I can't think of anything else but being with you, protecting you. I know we don't know everything about each other yet, but this connection we have is too strong to ignore. I don't want to be without you ever. I want you to be with me everywhere I go. So..." I pause again, trying to read her face for any kind of emotions, but she's just smiling and not saying a word, so I squeeze her hand. "So...I want us to start DJing together. Also, I'd like to cut a few songs with you singing, and most of all, I want you to go after your music and quit hiding behind these other fucking DJs that you can blow out of the water." I let out a breath as I wait for her reaction.

Say something. Please...

When Alexandria closes her eyes, I almost have a heart attack. My heart is pounding in my chest, my hands are sweaty, and I'm about ready to shake her when she finally opens her eyes, tears running down her face.

Panicking, I feel words start rushing out of my mouth. "Baby, please don't cry. I'm sorry I upset you. I shouldn't have asked or talked to you abo—" Alexandria puts a hand up to my lips to stop me from talking.

"I'm crying happy tears, I promise. No one has ever been so in tune with me. You see my love for music, and you believe in me. I can't even tell you how much that means to me. Until this last year with the girls, no one has ever really cared what I wanted. I know they wanted me happy, but they never really asked what would make me that way. You're the first to fight for me. I love you, Maddy." Alexandria practically jumps on my lap, kissing me.

Thank you, God.

Laughing with relief, I pull her all the way into my lap, holding her. "Alexandria, you're so unbelievably amazing and talented, I don't even know where to begin. I want us to couple DJ for a while, and then you branch out on your own, but we'll never be without each other. If you're DJing, then I'll be there supporting you, and vice versa. That's why I thought us just DJing together would be better. I know it's really soon, but I want you living with me so I can protect you at all times and we can get to know each other better, inside and out. I don't want to waste any more time or be away from you. I own places in Spain, Italy, and Scotland. I pretty much stay in Spain, but when I'm not there, I mainly live out of hotels. I want us to look to the future. I love you, Alexandria. No fucking pissant is going to ruin this for us. We'll work through this and anything else that comes our way. I'll protect you always."

Alexandria is crying in my lap, holding me around my neck. I push her hair over her shoulders and out of her face.

When I see her smile, my heart swells up and starts to burn with so much love for my woman.

My woman. Mine. Fuck yeah.

Placing small kisses all over her face, her neck, and arms, I whisper endearments to her. My dick is itching to feel her pussy clamp down around it, making me groan. "Alexandria, we need to head into the studio and work on music till your parents come home or we get a text from Beau. Once we step into the studio, it's about you, me, and the music we both love so much. Music is in both of our blood, so I want to test you and see how good you really are."

Raising my brows, teasing her, I go to tickle her, making her squirm. She laughs, "Maddy, don't, I'll pee my pants. I agree with everything you're saying. I just hope I'm as good as you think I am. I don't want to disappoint you." Alexandria bites her lower lip nervously.

I love her calling me Maddy. Wait... Disappoint? Is she joking? My God, she has no clue how remarkable she really is.

I want to shake the shit out of her. This is why I want Luc to witness her talent and hear what she has hidden away from everyone. I want her to shine because I know I'm blinded right now, and she hasn't even shown me all she has. *Fuck...* it's going to take all I have not to fuck her right in the studio. When she lets loose with her music, it'll be the true test of my willpower.

When we head into the studio, my cell phone vibrates in my pocket. I pull it out and see the text is from Beau.

BEAU

Keep Alex busy until you have heard from me. He's

> linked into our system, so he's probably watching. We've found one bug so far in the front entryway. DO NOT TELL HER until we can find out more stuff. Just keep her busy. I'll text you when we are done.

Motherfucker, son of a bitch. Keep it calm. Concentrate on her and the music. Be strong for her! I got this. She is mine.

When we're both settled into our chairs in the studio, I turn to her and laugh a wicked, devious laugh, "All right, show me what you got. Then when you're done, we'll go back and forth on the decks, playing off each other. I don't want you hiding anything you have. Right now, it's about you and me opening up to one another. I want to know about each song you show me and why you wrote or made it. I love you and am here for you no matter what. Plus, hearing all your stuff will help me figure out a song for us to make. Like I said before, I'll never lie or hold anything back from you, and I hope you'll do the same for me." I pull her chair to me, giving her a big passionate kiss before I push her back to the computer.

Give it to me. Give it all to me.

I sit back with so much excitement that it calms the storm gathering inside me enough that I can concentrate only on *mi amor*.

Alexandria

Shit. I can do this. Breathe. He loves me…

Sitting in my chair staring at the computer, I try to get my head on straight and actually attempt to process what just happened.

He wants to live with me, write music, sing, me DJ, or us DJ. Shit. Okay, I love him. He loves me. I can do this. I can show him everything. He already believes in me. Why am I so scared?

Maddox clears his throat. "Alexandria, get out of your head. Push all the negative shit away and just relax. It's just you and me here, or if it helps, just act like you're here alone. I'll never judge you or think something you did is bad. I love you for you and am here supporting you. This should be relaxing, so quit battling yourself in that beautiful brain of yours and play something."

Crossing his arms over his chest, he leans back in his chair, getting comfortable. I smile a weak smile before I turn back to the computer. Fuck, he can totally read me already. Taking a deep breath, I play the first track I have in queue. Here goes nothing.

Dios ayúdame.

After playing many of my songs and providing explanations for each, I'm finally done showing him everything. I feel so high on excitement because he loved all my songs, and he even had good input on a few of them. We bounce ideas off each other, and I can see he truly does love music and he sees things I didn't. He's good, really good, which makes me nervous to play live with him. Can I do it? I've hardly ever mixed live with anyone around, let alone played side by side with them. Anxiety starts to swirl in my stomach.

He loves me. Relax. I am good. Breathe.

We move our chairs out of the way, and Maddox starts setting up his stuff next to mine so we can go back and forth on the decks together. I just stand there fidgeting with my computer, acting like I'm doing something, but I'm just trying to calm my nerves. I jump when I hear a loud clap.

"Jesus, you scared me."

Maddox is moving around next to me with a huge grin on his face and laughing, "Are you nervous?"

Maddox turns serious while standing inches in front of me. He doesn't touch me, but he goes on a rant. "You're so fuckin' gorgeous. Listening to your tracks, seeing the passion in your eyes just makes me want you so fucking bad. When we're done here, I'm going to give you a big—" Maddox grabs his cock "—surprise and show you just how bad."

Clapping his hands before rubbing them together, he rants, "You have me so wound up. Fuck me."

My eyes go wide, my mouth drops open, and I'm speechless. My body is on high alert, ready to pounce on him like a cheetah. Maddox steps back, laughing with the most devious grin I've ever seen, making his dimples even deeper. I grab the desk, afraid my legs will give out. My clit starts to tingle, and my panties are soaking wet with such desire, it might drive me nuts before we're done.

Fuck, he just did that on purpose to distract me from stressing out. Well, shit. Now all I can think about is doing really naughty shit to him. Fuck. Focus, Alex.

"Let the games begin." Smiling a seductive smile, I take a few steps back while I pull my hair up into a loose bun on top of my head. Fucking game on. If he wants to play that way, okay with me. I have a few secrets up my sleeve too, big boy.

Maddox drops his first song and starts moving his upper body, swaying to the song "Your Body" by Tom Novy.

Once the song starts, I chuckle to myself. Playing with him, I stretch my arms over my head, twisting at my waist, and cracking my back. When I go to bend over, Maddox grunts, "Fuckin' not fair, babe. Not fair at all."

Giggling, I move to my computer. When he walks up to me and almost touches me, I put my hand up to stop him. In a wickedly teasing voice, I recite the song. But I extend my hand, pointing my finger at him to stop with a tsk-tsk, saying, "Maddy, baby, I don't want nobody… I have never wanted anybody but you…" Seeing the passion and want swirl in his gorgeous eyes, I keep my hand up, "But no touching till we're done."

I draw an imaginary line between us like in the movie Dirty Dancing. "This is your side, and this is my side." Maddox growls, making me giggle even more.

God, I love his man.

We both have the biggest smiles on our faces while we go back and forth with seductive songs, expressing our love and desire for one another. God, he can work his body, with all of his muscles moving so gracefully to the beat. I need to remind myself later to lick each of his features before devouring his voluptuous lips. I'm getting so aroused, my body is fine-tuning itself just watching his magnificent body move.

I can't believe we fit so well together. Even playing music, I can feel the connection between us. It's so unbelievable. Turning back to my computer to play my next song, I start to feel pressure in my chest like I always do when I start to think of him and me together.

This really is happening and I am so lucky to have this unbelievable man truly love me.

Maddox

I fuckin' knew it. She's fuckin' brilliant.

I can't wait to get her out there to be heard and for everyone to see. Jesus, I almost came in my pants a few times watching her mix. I'm mesmerized by the way her body moves to the beat, and the glow in her eyes shows such passion, love, and devotion to her music. She's my other half, and I can't wait to show her off, to let everyone know she's mine forever.

Watching her play with the mixer, bouncing her tight ass and wearing those fuck-me shorts, I'm ready to take her back to her place and have my way with her glorious body. I don't even think she knows how sexual she is with every move she makes while mixing. I don't think I can take much longer not touching her. If we DJ together, she has to let me touch her. My cock is like a stick of dynamite ready to fuckin' explode.

In a pained voice, I grunt, "I can't take much more of this because I need to be balls deep in that sweet pussy of yours, hearing you scream my name."

Alexandria shakes her ass, moving to the music and getting ready to drop her next song. That's when I hear it. "Is It Love," a remix of Nadia Ali's song by Avicii.

I laugh when she starts to bounce, moving her upper body to the beat and taking her headphones off. She turns around with a spin, letting her hair down, moving her hips side to side, bringing her hands up above her head, and moving toward me seductively, making every inch of my body hard. She runs her hands back up her body into her hair, but when she starts to sing, I freeze, hypnotized by her angelic voice. She's singing to me, telling me she's never felt like this before, and needing me. I can't breathe, only stand there in awe.

With her hands full of hair, Alexandria starts turning in circles, lifting her hands and letting her hair cascade down, looking even more angelic. Her look matches her voice while she repeats, "Is this love?" over and over. Fuckin' slap me, I think I've gone to heaven.

She's so goddamn sexy.

My legs don't work; they're just stuck there watching my woman dance seductively while singing. She runs her hands down her neck, over her breasts, and down her tight torso, grabbing her hips and then moving back up again. Growling, I bite my lip. "Jesucristo."

My cell phone vibrates in my pocket. With a groan, I reach

for it, but I don't take my eyes off her while she moves closer, When I pull my phone out, I look down to see a text from Beau.

Goddammit.

> **BEAU**
> Okay, we're done. We need you back here ASAP. We only found two bugs, no camera. We have more information, so we'll brief you when you get here. We're all here waiting.

Shit. Back to reality. I hope they have good information that'll help us find this motherfucker so we can get on with our lives.

I focus my attention back to Alexandria. She's standing still, moving her body to the music a few feet away from me. She's still singing to me with her hands wrapped behind her neck, just focused on me. Her sparkling blue eyes shine brightly on me, showing me what she feels—love, desire, lust, and need. She bites her lip. Her voice goes low when she tells me she's spellbound by me, and even in her sleep, I'm always on her mind. She continues to sing.

Fuck this imaginary line shit. I take two steps, wrapping my arms around her waist. I move my hands down over her ass, grabbing those perfect size globes and lifting her up. She runs her hands through my hair, releasing it from my ponytail while she keeps singing to me.

I cut her off with my mouth, and she moans the song into my mouth while my tongue dances with hers. With her legs wrapped around my body, I push her up against the wall, kneading her ass and rubbing her up against my painfully strained cock.

Fuckin' perfect.

Alexandria pulls back panting. Putting our foreheads together, she whispers, "Maddy, what if he's watching and listening? Let's wait till we get home." Motherfucker.

"Beau just texted and wants us back at your place, so we should head back." Setting her back on her feet, I place a kiss on the top of her head before I turn to collect my stuff. Trying to tame the beast inside me and the rage from bursting out of me, I keep telling myself over and over I need to stay in control around her. I grab my music case, gripping it for dear life.

We clean up our stuff without speaking, and we head back to her place. I can tell her pretty little head is worrying about what they found.

Alexandria

Breathe… What did they find? What if he has been watching me this whole time? You have Maddox, and he isn't leaving. You're safe. Relax. Breathe

Maddox and I clean up all our stuff and head toward my place without speaking. I think we are both lost in our own thoughts about what we'll find out. I know Maddox is ready to lose his shit and hurt someone. I feel safe with him, and I know he'll do anything to protect me. I see he's worried about me through the look in his eyes, and the tension in his shoulders.

Once we're in the elevator, I turn to face him with a smile. "Maddy, don't worry about me. I'm okay as long as you're near me. I see in your eyes you're trying to figure out if I'm getting ready to have an anxiety attack, so just know I'm okay."

I grab his hand, pulling him down to give him a quick kiss.

With a bigger smile, I reassure him again, "Really, Maddy, I'm okay. You make me feel safe." Turning back to face the elevator doors, I squeeze his hand with a wide grin on my face.

Maddox huffs out a laugh. "Alexandria, just so you know, you are never getting rid of me, believe that. Nothing will ever take me away from you."

He squeezes my hand, and I look over at him staring at me with the biggest smile and those fuck-me-dimples. I lick my lips, and Maddox chuckles from deep down. "Alexandria, have I told you that when you call me Maddy, I absolutely fuckin' love it? I melt every time you say it. No one calls me by that name except my má, so it means a lot to me."

My heart swells with so much love for this man I can barely breathe. I try to speak, but a knot in my throat keeps me from saying anything before the doors open and Maddox is pulling me toward my front door. Once inside, I see the apartment is full of people. I gasp, "Oh God!"

Holy shit. This can't be good. They found something for sure. Jesus, help me.

Fear… Anxiety starts to build in my stomach and my chest. Maddox moves to my side after putting down our stuff, wrapping his arm around my waist and tugging me into his side, murmuring low in my ear, "I'm with you, by your side, all the way."

He walks me into the living room where my parents are sitting talking to Brant and Gus. All of Maddox's guys are here as well, in the kitchen talking to Beau. Most of them are around the kitchen table where Ethan is working on his laptop.

Mamá calls out, "Mija!" She gets up to come and hug me,

but Maddox doesn't let go of my waist, keeping me close to him.

He must know something. I feel him tense, and he's definitely in his protective mode. Shit… This is bad.

When Papá comes to hug me, that's when I know it's bad because he doesn't even say, "Hello, baby girl." My anxiety is boiling with the suspense of not knowing.

I crack, speaking really loudly and getting everyone's attention. "So what did you find? Why is everyone so tense? What happened?"

I lean into Maddox, and he squeezes me, giving me comfort and letting me know he's right there with me.

See, I can do this.

Beau, Chad, Brant, and Ethan come to stand in the living room with us. I brace myself for whatever they are going to tell me.

I look to Beau for answers. Irritated, I huff, "What? For God's sake, just say it already." Ay, let's get this over with. Fuck.

Beau looks stressed as if he hasn't slept in a few days, with facial scruff and messed-up hair like he has been running his hands through it. Taking a deep breath, Beau speaks. "Alex, it's pretty serious. We found two bugs here in your place but no cameras. We found one bug along with a hidden camera in your office. Now, since he was in your house, we need to figure out who has had access or has been here. Obviously, seeing where the bugs were placed, he must have only come in to drop something off. So, we're going to be looking through old footage."

Maddox's grip on my waist tightens with a growl. I wrap an arm around him for support and, hopefully, also to help him calm down. Not knowing what to say, I just stare at Beau. He runs his hand through his hair before he continues, "Ethan has found that our system has been hacked a few different ways, but all of them are coming from our office computers at Spin."

Oh, my God! Wait…

When I speak, it comes out hoarse due to the knot in my throat. "So…that means it is for sure someone who works for us, and when he's at work, he's watching me on video? Where was the camera in my office?"

I start to shake, making my legs weak, so I move to sit down with Maddox. His death grip follows, not letting go. Once we're seated, Maddox goes to rub my back to comfort me. I don't even want to look at him right now or I'll break down, so I look back to Beau, waiting for answers.

I need to stay focused. I am safe. Do not freak out, Alex!

Beau moves to the couch across from me while everyone moves to settle in around me too. Beau runs his hand over his face, taking a deep breath. "Alex, the camera in your office was under your desk, pointed toward your chair."

Maddox stands up with a roar, "Motherfucker, I'm going to kill him."

Maddox walks around my chair, grabbing the back of it with both hands and trying to reel in his rage, cursing to himself. I turn my focus back to everyone across from me. My mamá has her hand over her mouth with tears falling, while my papá tries soothing her while masking his own fury. But my security team is all looking just about the same as Maddox. I take a deep breath, trying to hold it together, to be strong. He won't win.

Once my eyes are back to Beau, he continues, "Alex, we

all feel the same way Maddox does. We're doing everything to find out who this is, but at least we know it's someone within the company or who has access to the suites. Ethan has linked into all of the recording devices that are linked to the computers, so if he decides to come look, maybe thinking we didn't find all of them, we'll know right away. The good thing we do have on our side is that he knows our first plan and all that we're going to do to protect you. But what he doesn't know is our new plan."

New plan? The camera in my office, is it gone? Fuck, so many questions.

Looking around the place, wondering where the bugs were, I put my hands up to my head, rubbing my temples. I start rambling off what I'm thinking to whomever, but I need to get this out. "Okay, so the bugs in here, are they still live? Did you remove them, and where were they? The camera in my office, is it gone? Ethan, he knows that you linked to my phone and didn't care because he still texted me after everyone left. So does that mean he isn't scared you have my phone tapped? What's this new plan?"

When I'm done talking, I look up to see everyone staring at me with what looks like shock or maybe admiration. Maybe they thought I'd freak out and lose it, but whatever they thought, I obviously didn't do it. I let out a deep breath and start to have a tantrum in my head.

Yes, Goddammit, I'm staying focused and not losing it. I'm a grown-ass woman, for fuck's sake. Maybe I'll lose it later, but right now we need a fucking plan.

I blurt out, "Okay, I know you all think I'm am going to lose it, but let's get it together and get this sick fuck. I'm tired of dealing with this shit and living in fear." I take a deep breath. "Now tell me the damn plan. I'm not going to fucking break."

My mamá calls out, "Mija!"

Followed by Papá, "Ay, watch your mouth."

I look to my parents. "Sorry for cussing, but it's true. I'm an adult now, and I'm tired of being sheltered."

Brant starts laughing, followed by the rest of the group, releasing all the tension that was there. Beau leans back in his seat with a big smile on his face, and he clears his throat. "Thank fuck. Finally, I can be real with you and not have to sugarcoat everything."

Looking over to Papá, who looks like he's going to blow a gasket, his face is so red, Beau says sternly, "Luc and Mia, I'm sorry, but she's a mature woman, and I'll be dealing with her now. I know you mean well, but keeping her out of all this is just wrong, not to mention unsafe for her. I'll keep everyone in the loop, but Alex is my main concern here. I need to be able to do my job with no restrictions."

Beau looks back to me, but I hear Maddox curse behind me along with Papá, letting us know they are not happy. Beau smirks, leaning forward and resting his forearms on his legs. "Okay, let's start. Alex, when we did each search, we cut power to each floor before. So if he was looking or recording you, he wouldn't have noticed us coming. We think his main focus was you, so we left your parents' floor recording. Now, in your office, we found the camera and bug, but we have left them in place. We left them for a couple of reasons. If he heard you and knew we are looking for them, he'll think we missed them. Now if he didn't hear you, he'll think we were just doing maintenance on our system. The bugs in here we left as well, but they are disabled for now, just like we disabled all security footage on this floor. We've been doing random tests everywhere on the system, trying to make it look like a maintenance thing. So hopefully, he doesn't catch on to what we are doing, or he'll think we didn't find his link to us."

I look around the room, feeling everyone's eyes on me. Breathe, Alex. Maddox moves back down next to me, putting an arm around me again. I lean into him, looking back at Beau when he says, "We are hoping he'll contact you if he figures out we're on to him since he was obviously pissed after we all talked earlier. I'm sure he'll be texting you again. But if he doesn't, then we're still in business. He'll obviously see you're staying home today, so just go with the flow. We'll be having you say shit that will hopefully lure him out, and we'll trap him. We want you to start speaking about this week's event, hoping to lure him into a trap. We won't be beefing up your security, at least, not visibly. We want to throw him off from what we said earlier. You'll have Maddox, Brant, and whoever Maddox usually has with him on a day-to-day. We have four undercover guys who will be around you at all times. You don't even know who these guys are. The only people who have seen these men are Brant and me. We don't want anyone recognizing them or acknowledging them. We'll also have a full security team on you and on Maddox. Ginger and Izzy are going to be at the club tomorrow, as well as on Friday, so everyone will be covered."

Beau stands up. "Now with that said, we only have a little bit of time left before the security system resets, so we all need to be out of here before that happens." He turns his attention to the guys. "Okay, Ethan, Chad, who's up next?" Beau looks over to the two of them.

Shit, that sick fuck will be able to hear me here in my own house? And see my crotch at work. He was watching my crotch. What the fuck?

Holding up my hand to wait for a second, I say, "Whatever this plan entails, I want Maddox with me. Also, how do we know he hasn't linked to my cell phone like Ethan has? He could be reading my texts, correct?"

I still haven't looked over to meet Maddox's eyes, but I feel the heat radiate off him, letting me know he's still pissed off.

Ethan stands up, walking back to his laptop with a wicked grin on his face. When he turns to look at me, grinning from ear-to-ear, he says in a cocky voice, "Well, Alex, lucky for you, I'm that fucking good."

Ethan chuckles, making me laugh. He clicks on his laptop, making his screen illuminate, then looks at something before he continues, "See, I have you bugged, I have the system bugged, and now that we know he has been hacking into the system, we can detect when someone links in again."

I start to say something when he puts his hands up. "Unless the guy has had your phone in his hand, there's really no way to bug your phone. Plus, I'm linked to it now and will be looking for any connections. Now, with that said, you need to know about your phone. I have a tracking device on it, so no matter what, you always need to have your phone with you and powered on. I'll also be putting a tracking device in your purse. If you want, I can even put tracking devices on your clothes if it'll make you feel any better, but I think with the two, you should be fine. That's totally up to you. We want you to feel completely safe because you have so many fucking eyes watching you it'd have to be fucking God himself who took you without us knowing. One last thing. With both teams having undercover people, you need to have a password so if something happens and one of our undercover people has to grab you, they can say the password so you don't freak out." Ethan folds his arms over his chest all proud of himself, making me laugh.

Ay, he's good.

Feeling better about the situation and safe with all this, I take a deep breath. With a smile and trying to sound chipper, I say, "All righty, then, next on the plan."

That makes everyone laugh a full, hearty laugh, which eases the tension a bit, except Maddox, who's still tense and fuming next to me.

For the next few minutes, we go over the plan, what I need to start saying and the details of the overall goal of catching him. I pick "Purple" as my password to make it easy. My favorite color is red, but purple is close behind it. They let Maddox and me know where the bugs are so we'll be aware of them. Thank fuck they're not near my bedroom, so if we close the door or are in my bathroom, we probably won't be heard. They think since he was at the club, he didn't know Maddox was here the night before. And as he probably can't hear what's going on in the bedroom, he didn't text me until after our meeting, but no one knows for sure.

Alexandria

Once everyone is gone, I tense up, knowing that the sick fuck could be listening to us now. I start to pace around while Maddox goes downstairs to see his guys off and get more of his stuff. I feel the fear in the pit of my belly when Maddox isn't here.

I lose myself in my head with my thoughts. *Will I be able to do this with him not always by my side? I held it together today, and I need to keep being strong, but this sick fucking guy has been watching me sit in my chair and looking between my fucking legs.*

I turn to look out the window, hugging myself. *Breathe, Alex. You are stronger. You can do this*.

I keep saying my chant to myself, hoping it will sink in fully. But the fear in my stomach tells me it hasn't registered all the way. I hear the door open but don't move from where I am. Instead, I just keep staring out at the city lights. I feel

Maddox behind me even before he touches me, but when his hands wrap around my waist, I feel the electricity zing through me, igniting my body with such fierce feelings. My God, I love this man. He makes me feel so fucking alive and safe.

God, yes. Take the fear away. I need him.

Tilting my head back onto his rock-hard chest, I close my eyes. Maddox leans into my shoulder, placing soft kisses on my neck and earlobe then venturing down to my collarbone, all while whispering sweet endearments that send my emotions into overdrive. When tears run down my face, I know I'm safe and I can let my shield down. He will protect me. My saint.

A soft sob escapes me, and Maddox's body goes rigid behind me. He turns me to face him, but I keep my eyes closed. Taking a step toward me, pinning me to the window and smashing his enormous body against me, Maddox brings a hand up to my face and uses his knuckles to wipe away my tears.

Bending down, he whispers, "Alexandria, baby, please look at me. I've got you. I was so proud of you today with the way you stood your ground. Alexandria, you were so strong and completely fucking brilliant."

I chuckle, hearing his British accent peek through. He uses both hands to cup my face. When I open my tear-filled eyes, I look directly into a swirl of emotions in his wintery gray eyes staring right back at me. I wrap my arms around his waist, sliding my fingers under the hem of his shirt and needing to touch his skin. Maddox moans before slowly capturing my mouth with his, sending goose bumps down my body. Taking his time with me, he tastes my lips, nipping and sucking. Finally, he demands entrance by deepening the kiss, and moans escape us both.

Maddox slides his hands down my back, leaving one to hold me tight around my waist, while the other one slips down, kneading my ass. This kiss is so much more than just a kiss because this kiss is telling me how he feels, that he's my lover, my protector, and most of all, my fucking rock. Passion ignites inside me, so I tangle my tongue, wanting more. I pull down on his neck to deepen the kiss, and I try to suck his tongue, but I nip it instead.

Maddox pulls away, breathless. "Alexandria, I'm going to take you hard, fast, and rough right now. I can't wait."

He moves both my hands up around my neck, cupping my face. His tone changes to his seductive, erotic voice. "I need to feel connected to you and take all that fear away, along with my madness."

Maddox moves with urgency, throwing me over his shoulder. I squeal. "Maddy!"

Maddox throws me onto the bed and turns around to shut the door, locking it. Then he moves to the entertainment center, turning on music. Propping myself up on my elbows and laughing, I watch him move around the room. Thinking I want him to lose all control with me, I push him by whining, "I need you so bad."

Over the last few weeks, I have come to realize my man likes dirty talk. The way he loses control when I talk dirty makes me so wet. Sitting up when he turns around, I slip my T-shirt over my head slowly. Running my hands through my hair, I bring them down my neck in slow motion, grabbing my breasts with force. Licking my lips, I plead, "I want you inside me."

Maddox's growl is deep and lethal. "Fuck, you're so goddamn sexy." He takes his clothes off but never takes his eyes off me. I unclasp my bra, letting my breasts fall with a bounce. I toss the bra off the bed, slipping my hands back up to knead my newly freed breasts.

Maddox draws in air with a hiss, biting his lip. I beg him, "Make me forget. Clear my body of anything bad and fill it with only pleasure."

Seeing Maddox struggle within himself, I push him over by licking my lips with a moan. I sit back on the bed, leaving one hand caressing my breast, while the other one moves down my body and starts to undo my shorts.

My voice is thick with lust. "Fuck, take me now. I want you biting me and fucking me so goddamn hard I can't think of anything else."

Maddox replies, "Fuckin' hell, Alexandria…I'm going to come before I even touch you. Keep talking, baby. So fuckin' hot."

Maddox

Gripping my girth, I watch her pleasure herself while talking dirty. She sends me tumbling out of control. I tear her shorts off before I move between her legs, feeling the heat from her sex. When I feel the wetness, I can't take any more. I slide down her body, placing butterfly kisses all the way down to her mound.

Another moan escapes her with a whimper. "Maddy, please."

Slowly, I separate her folds with my tongue. I start to lick her clit like a cat licking its paw, starting out slow, but I get into a rhythm and fuck her sweetness with my tongue. Alexandria gasps, *"Jesus."*

I spread her legs wider when I feel her body tense up, letting me know she is close. I smile into her sex before sucking all her wetness and continuing to fuck her with my tongue. I want to push her to lose control like she does to me all the time. Sitting back on my shins, I push her legs up to her chest, lifting her ass off the ground and giving me more access. When Alexandria grabs her legs, I slide my hand down her abs and over her mound, slipping two fingers into her drenched sex while I admire her swollen pink pussy that is glistening wet.

"Fuck, you're so ready. Do you want to come for me?"

Alexandria hisses her approval. "Oh, fuck… Yes."

Pumping my fingers a couple of times, I move my moistened thumb down to circle her asshole. When she tenses up, I lean down, flicking her clit with my tongue and earning a deep moan from her. "Yes. I'm close."

Keeping my attention on her hardened bud, I rapidly flick her clit, rotating my tongue and sucking. I finger-fuck her pussy while moving my thumb around her puckered little ass, lubing it up.

Alexandria starts squirming around, moaning heavily. "Yes, that feels so fucking good. Please don't stop." With my free hand, I grab around her knee, pushing into her chest and trying to keep her from moving. She lets go of her legs, grabbing my head so she can fuck my face.

Moaning into her pussy and gliding my tongue over her swollen nub, I twist my hand. I circle my two fingers in her, hitting her G-spot and making her body start to convulse. When I hold her leg, she throws her body back deeper into the bed, locking her muscles while I continue my assault. She cries out in both Spanish and English, "Oh. Fuck yeah. Oh, God. Please don't stop."

She fists the sheets, and her whole body goes rigid. Sucking her swollen clit into my mouth, I move my tongue over it rapidly, pumping my fingers. Once the tip of my thumb sinks into her tight, virgin asshole, she screams her release. "Yes. *Fuck.* Yes!"

I need to fuck her... So, fucking wet.

Alexandria's body quivers when I withdraw my fingers. Not wanting to waste time, I flip her over, making her cry out my name before I lift her ass in the air.

Needing my release, I grunt, "Fuck."

My turn, baby. Fuck. She's like my drug, and I need my fix.

I grab my cock, sliding it between her folds and lubing it up from her divine pussy. Alexandria squeals, but she moans when I caress her ass. I slide my hand down to massage her swollen pussy.

My voice is filled with desire and lust. "Alexandria, do you want my cock inside of you?"

I'm about ready to go crazy, but I'm holding on until she answers. I slip the tip in, teasing her, feeling her pussy clench before I pull out, and gliding it up and down between her folds.

Alexandria grabs hold of the headboard. "Yes, take me."

Not waiting one more second, I thrust my hips forward, slamming into her. I'm so consumed I don't even hear Alexandria when I cry out my satisfaction. *"Fuck."*

Gripping her hips, I start to pump into her, speeding up the motion. Once we are in sync, I move my hands over and grab the globes of her ass. I spread her cheeks so I can slip one hand down her crack. I use her wetness to lube up my thumb before sliding it to her asshole and slowly inserting the tip, all while moving my cock with long, deep thrusts. "Your ass is so fucking gorgeous it has me always wanting more. I had to be inside you, and soon I'll take you here."

I slide my thumb all the way in, and she cries out, "Oh, fuck…"

Thinking I hurt her, I go to pull my thumb out when she moans, "Don't stop."

Getting the green light, I start to slowly massage my thumb in and out of her ass, building up the tempo to match my thrusts.

Calm down, Madd Dog. Don't come yet. Soon. I'll have claimed every inch of her…soon.

Alexandria's head falls back, her hair cascading over her shoulders as she moans. Moving my free hand from her ass cheek, I grab a handful of her hair and pull. "God, you feel so fucking good."

Alexandria grips the headboard tighter, moaning with each drive as I pound into her. Letting go of her hair, I run my hand down her body slowly. I pull my cock out almost to the tip so I can slip my hand between us, and I stroke my cock, getting my fingers wet. I tease her greedy little pussy with fast half thrusts. I don't enter her fully, just enough to make Alexandria lose herself and start shaking with desire while pleading for more. Once my fingers are lubed up, I switch hands on her asshole. My thumb comes out, and my pointer finger goes in at the same time I slam my dick into her with one thrust. I stop, fully seated within her.

Alexandria screams, "Please don't stop!" and pushes her ass back toward me.

I laugh. "Baby, what do you need?"

Without hesitation, she answers in a pleading voice, "Fuck me harder. Please, Maddy."

I grab her waist and start pumping her pussy and asshole simultaneously. Alexandria is close, begging me to keep going.

Hold on. Just a little bit more.

Alexandria is like a feral animal, pumping her ass back to meet each hammering thrust I pound into her. Both of us are moaning, grunting, chasing our releases, and my balls start to tighten up.

Fuck, I'm close... Almost.

Looking down at our bodies connected, I slow my thrusts a bit and just watch my assault on her. "Fuck, Alexandria, I'm so fucking hard watching my cock slide in and out of your sweetness."

Slowly thrusting into her, each pump going deeper, I wrap an arm around her waist. I hold her, leaning over to kiss her back.

"I need to hear you, baby." My voice is strained with desire. "Tell me. Do you like me taking you this way?"

I am desperate, needing and wanting to hear her approval. "Does this feel good? Me fucking your ass and sweet pussy at the same time?"

Breathlessly, she answers, "Yes, faster."

I slide my hand from her waist down to massage her clitoris, and she throws her head back, moaning her approval, "Oh, God. Please don't stop. Fuck, that feels so good." She pauses to push her ass back to meet my thrusts. "So deep."

I speed up my momentum, slipping my finger out of her ass so I can grab both of her hips. "Touch yourself for me. Now."

Fuck, yeah, so fucking deep. I want more.

I can't hold back, pounding into her. I only can hear our bodies slap together as moans and grunts escape both of us. I dig my fingers deeper into her hips and piston into her wet pussy. I feel my orgasm rising, my balls tighten back up, and every muscle in my body aches from the force with which I'm pounding into her.

Mine…Fuck yeah. My pussy. I'm close.

Alexandria's heat tightens around my cock, sucking it in deeper with her orgasm right on the brink.

Her voice is hoarse from breathing so hard. *"Yes."*

I lean forward, slamming into her as hard as I can as I feel my release coming. I reach under her arms, grabbing her breasts and pulling her up against my body. I hold her while I thrust up into her. I fuck her, palming her breasts with each hand and digging my fingers into her skin while she plays with her clitoris.

I'm breathless. "*Fuck*. So fuckin' close…" I slam my cock with each word. Every muscle in my body is tense and ready for my release.

Fuck. Come on. Yeah. Fuck…

Both of us are lost in passion, and sweat is slicking our bodies. Feeling her climax at its peak, I send her to the edge. My voice is thick with lust when I speak. "Come for me. I feel your sweet, tight little pussy ready to explode. Come, Alexandria."

All I can hear is Alexandria chanting yes over and over as she waits for her release. It explodes when I wrench her tits even harder, almost milking her. She cries out, "Oh, God... *Yes.*"

That's my cue to let myself go. "You like that." My body is shaking with each thrust. "Fuck, baby. You're so fucking tight." I pound into her like my life depends on it. "Oh, yeah. Right there." Being inside her sends waves of tingles all over my body, and I'm ready to combust. *"Yes..."*

Alexandria screams my name when her muscles contract like a vise grip. She gets even tighter when another orgasm rips through her, and she clenches around my cock, making me burst. *"Fuck..."*

I see stars, and both of us grunt and moan with our releases. Still pumping into her, I release her upper body, letting her fall to the mattress. Grabbing her hips, I slow my thrusts as both of our bodies twitch with the aftershocks.

Once I milk every last drop of my seed into her, I fall to her side, out of breath. I pull her to me, both of us slick with sweat and breathing hard, hushed by our earth-shattering orgasms. She runs her hand over my chest, fiddling with my nipple piercing, a thing I think she has become fixated on. It calms us both.

I start caressing her shoulder, still trying to catch my breath. In a thick, husky voice, I say, "That was so fucking unbelievable. You truly are one of a kind. I've never experienced anything like that. What we have is truly stunning. I want to do so many things to you, explore your body and make you experience pure pleasure like that all fucking day."

Fuck me, that's heaven.

Her body shivers, probably from the aftermath of mind-blowing orgasms we just had. She can't speak but instead just moans, "Mmm-hmm."

I move to slip out from under her, but she tries to protest, holding me tighter. I laugh, pushing her onto her back and looking down into her eyes. "I need to get a towel to clean us up. Then we'll order food and just relax the rest of the night in here. Where he can't see or hear us. We have a long few days ahead of us, so let's rest now."

Once we are cleaned up, food is ordered, and we're all settled into bed with her cuddled into my side resting on my chest and again playing with my piercing, I hear her breathing even out.

Thinking she is asleep, I try to relax when I hear her whisper, "I love you, Maddy."

A smile creeps across my face, and I whisper back, "I love you too, Alexandria." We both fall into silence, watching a movie.

Alexandria

Waking up in Maddox's arms is something I don't think I will ever get tired of. As I think of the sinful things we have done to each other the last few days, a giggle escapes me. I can't believe how amazing I feel—sore as hell, but truly magnificent. I'm so glad I waited and found someone who gets me. He is made for me in every way. The way he makes me feel safe, sexy, and overall like a goddess. I'm sitting in the limo on our way to the office, surrounded by security and Maddox all talking about the day, but suddenly they all stop to look over at me.

Shit, did I moan out loud? Oops, I'm caught.

Turning to look out of the window to escape the stares, I feel Maddox squeeze my leg and whisper, "Do I need to bend you over your desk today, *mi belleza*?"

Still staring out the window, not wanting to look at any of the men, I close my eyes and imagine him spanking me while

I'm spread out over my desk. It makes my sex throb. Not trusting my voice, I answer him with a moan. "Mmm-hmm."

Once we're at the building, I head up to my office. I know I should be scared or a little freaked out, but the sex last night and in the shower this morning with Maddox has me on such a high I can't think of anything else but this marvelous man. *My man.* I have the biggest smile on my face. Feeling good, I lift my head a bit higher and walk with confidence. Maddox is a step ahead of me, holding my hand and looking sinful as ever with a black bandanna pushing his hair out of his face. Faded jeans hang loosely around his waist and hug his voluptuous ass. Goddamn, this man is too fucking gorgeous for his own good in his black riding boots and black T-shirt showing off all his divine muscles. He always looks like a bad boy needing to be tamed. I lick my lips just thinking about what he does to me, the way his scent captivates me…damn. *Relax. Calm down. Stay focused.*

Our mission today is to act normal, go about our day like I don't know the cameras are there. I'm supposed to put hints out there for this week's event and see if I get a text. Walking to my office, I look around at all the people, and anxiety emerges in my stomach.

It could be any of one of these guys. What if he gets to me?

I shake my head, clearing the bad thoughts away. *Maddox is with me. I'm safe. Relax. Smile. Act normal. There's that damn word normal again.*

I'm giggling at myself and thinking about what "normal" really is when we exit the elevator, heading to my office.

The first thing I hear is a high-pitched voice. "Biatch, why haven't you returned any of our texts or calls?" I look around Maddox to see Eva with her hands on her hips, looking halfway pissed off.

I laugh, but before I can respond, Maddox pulls me into his side, hugging me before he looks to Eva. As provocative as ever, he says with an alluring smirk, "Sorry, I've been keeping her busy, fucking her ten ways till Tuesday. I thought I'd let her out of the bedroom today since it is Tuesday."

What. The. Fuck? That was hot.

Stunned myself, I look to see Eva with her mouth wide open. Brant chuckling behind me brings everyone out of their stupor and makes us all laugh. We're still standing around, though, and I don't know what I should say. We're being watched, and I don't remember if there's sound around here. Tensing up next to Maddox, I panic. "Umm…Umm… right. Sorry, it's been a long few days. I promise to fill you in, but we need to get some work done. Can you catch me up on what has been happening?" I give Eva a look not to ask questions, hoping she will understand.

Before anyone can say anything, I turn to walk into my office, followed by Maddox, Brant, and Eva. I have to figure out how to tell Eva what is going on, so I try not to freak out. Knowing the camera is under my desk, I wore skinny jeans so the sick fuck didn't have anything to see. Sitting down, I ramble about not being able to find something in my purse, but I start to scribble on a sheet of paper. Maddox and Brant come to my side to read the paper, staying out of the camera's view. Eva stops across from my desk, totally lost about what is going on. When I'm done writing, I pass it over to Eva.

My rapist has bugged my office, and there is a camera under my desk. B will explain everything to you. So leave with him and then when you come back, just play along with whatever I say. He'll explain. Sorry.

By the time Eva is done reading the note, her eyes are wide and she looks shocked. I start talking to her, asking for files for her to bring me. Brant walks her out after she says she'll be right back.

I look at Maddox, and he smiles at me, pulling me into his embrace. Letting out a deep breath, I inhale his masculine scent. I close my eyes, immediately relaxing against him.

He whispers in my ear, "Relax, you're going to be fine. I got you."

I pull away just enough to look up into his sparkling eyes. They are filled with so much love for me that I roll up on my tiptoes to give him a kiss. Maddox moves his hand down my back, gripping my ass and deepening the kiss with a growl.

Moaning into his mouth before pulling away, I say, "I need to get some work done today, so you need to be good. I've got so much to do before tonight."

With a chuckle, he hugs me tight. "Yes, I'll be gone for a bit. I need to go see your father in a few minutes. Once Brant is back, I'll take off." Pulling away, he looks into my eyes with concern. "Will you be okay?"

I laugh, taking a seat in my chair. "Of course I'll be okay. That sick fuck can't get me here. Fuck him, I'm so over this shit."

Take that, you fuck. I hope you're listening, you sick fucking pervert.

Maddox just stares at me to see if I'm being serious or just saying that for the recorder. I smile sweetly, reassuring him I'm okay before grabbing the stack of papers on my desk. He moves around my desk, taking a seat in a guest chair while I start to go over some paperwork.

See, I can do this. Deep breath. You've got this, Alex.

When I hear a growl from Maddox, I look up to see him looking at his cell phone. I'm about to ask him what's wrong when the door to my office opens and Eva and Brant walk in. I can't tell what Eva thinks since she just has a straight face. Maddox gets up, coming around my desk while he types a text on his cell. He kisses me quickly, telling me he's heading to meet with my father and he'll be right back. Eva comes around my desk toward me as Maddox passes her with a smile. I want to ask him what's wrong, but I decide it can wait. We can talk later without worrying if someone is listening.

Eva gives me a big hug, telling me she's brought me the files I asked for before releasing me and handing me a note. I look down to read it.

> *I'm sorry. I'm here for you. Just let me know what you need. Love you, and we'll talk later.*
> *=) Eva*

Brant's phone rings while Eva is walking back out of the office. I sit back down, grabbing the papers I was looking at, again trying to focus on my work. I listen to Brant's one-sided conversation. I try to figure out who he's on the phone with, but all I hear is, "Hello."

Pause. "How did you sleep?" Brant chuckles. Pause. "Yeah, I'm here in Alex's office. Where are you?" Another pause. "Okay, you remember what I told you last night, though." He chuckles again. Another pause. "Yes, so just remember." Before hanging up, he says, "Right, see you in a few."

Once he hangs up, he just looks at me with a straight face.

I'm still trying to figure out who that was. Neither of us says anything, so I go back to my paperwork while he plays with his phone.

All righty, then. I guess it wasn't something I need to know.

I'm finishing some of my work, feeling good about getting something accomplished. I look up when my door opens. Ginger bounces in, looking cute as ever in her faded jeans, gray Chucks, and an adorable T-shirt. The shirt has headphones on it that look like they are around her neck with the cord wrapping around to the back.

With a big smile on her face, she looks at Brant and then me. She's way too hyper as she says, "Hi!"

Laughing, I reply, "Hi, Gin. What's up, girl?"

She takes a seat next to Brant, putting her helmet on the ground next to her chair. Her hair is pulled up in a ponytail the way she always wears it when she rides her bike. The girl is seriously badass. Ginger drives a red and black Ninja everywhere she goes in NYC, and back home in West Virginia, she has a Harley with a custom picture on the tank of Snow White and the seven dwarfs, with her nickname "Snow" painted across it. I didn't believe it when she told me, but then she showed me pictures. When people are around, she keeps to herself and hardly speaks, but when she is around people she is comfortable with, she talks, and man, that girl can cuss.

When Ginger starts talking, I turn my attention to her. "Alex, you are coming tonight, right? I just found out your father moved me from closing set to opening because he pulled Emmett from tonight's lineup."

Jesus, what the fuck?

Shocked as hell, I ask, "What? Why would he do that and

not tell me?"

She shrugs her shoulders. "Shit if I know. I didn't ask questions." Brant is looking at her, smiling.

What the fuck is going on between these two?

When she looks over to him, he asks, "You're riding with us tonight, right?"

Ginger laughs, looking back to me. "Um, yeah. Don't I always ride with you?"

Okay, these two are definitely acting fucking weird.

Trying to figure out what the fuck is going on between them, I just sit there, watching them banter back and forth about tonight. Amused, I can't help myself and I interrupt, asking, "Am I missing something here?" Using my index finger, I point back and forth between them. They both turn to look at me smiling, when my office phone rings. *Dammit.*

Not taking my eyes off them, I grab my office phone with a, "Hello."

Papá barks into the phone, "Alex, you need to come to my office right now."

Looking at Ginger, I reply, "Yeah, Papá, I'll be right up. Is everything okay?"

I can hear him take a deep breath. "Yeah, I just need you to come up here. Please."

"Okay." I hang up the phone.

When I lean forward, I fold my arms onto my desk, raising an eyebrow and looking at the two of them. "Do either of you know what the fuck is going on? Why am I being called to his office?"

Both of them look at each other. Ginger replies first. "I just told you what I know. That's why I came here, to see if you knew what the fuck is going on. So don't look at me."

We both look over to Brant, who stands up, heading for the door. “I don’t know shit, ladies. Let’s go find out.”

Well, fuck me.

Maddox

Heading to Luc's office, I get anxious wondering what he thought of us DJing together. He must see she is fucking amazing. My dick twitches to life thinking about her that night in the studio. The way she would bounce her ass when she was mixing, her delicate fingers playing with the knobs on the mixer, and most of all, the way she would bite her lips when she was concentrating.

Calm down.

When I get to Luc's office, Rachel sends me in, letting me know he is waiting for me. When I open the door, his face is deep red and he looks real pissed off. I hesitate before shutting the door. Luc, from what I can see, is full-blown Italian, which means he doesn't take any shit, is loud, and has a temper. He motions for me to come in and sit down. When I'm across from him, I extend my hand and say in a calm voice, "Hey, Luc. Is everything okay? You don't look too hot."

Luc stands up, shaking my hand before sitting back down, still not saying a word.

Motherfucker, now what? If he isn't talking, something is wrong. Does he know about the other recording devices?

I sit down, not taking my eyes off him, waiting for him to talk. Leaning back in his chair, Luc takes a deep breath before he speaks. "Maddox, I can't explain how I feel right now. This fuckin' cocksucker has a video of my goddamn baby girl's crotch. I just fuckin' found out there are more cameras and shit linked to our system, *today!*"

His rage is rising along with his voice the more he speaks. I try to keep mine under control. The last thing we need is for both of us to lose it. We need to stay focused. I just sit there and let him vent.

"I don't know what to do. I've got so much goddamn anger built up, I feel like I'm goin' to have a heart attack."

Running his hands through his hair, he leans forward, resting his arms on his desk. I decide I will try to calm him down. The last thing I need is him keeling over with me in his office. Clearing my throat, I say, "Luc, we'll find this motherfucker. I promise you that. Alexandria will not be harmed. We'll get him."

Luc's face lightens a bit, turning a slightly less violent shade of red, thank God. After a few seconds, Luc says in a calm voice, "I saw the video of you two in the studio. I heard everythin', and you're right. She has been holdin' back from us. I've been so obsessed with keepin' her safe and shielded that I forgot about her talent."

Leaning back and taking a deep breath, he calms down even more, but his face looks pained or maybe even sad. "Maddox, when I look at you two, I see Mia and me, which scares the fuck outta me. Took one weekend and that was it for both of us. We were in love, no questions asked. I see you with my baby girl and the way you two look at each other, and I know you're in love. It scares us, don't get me wrong, but I'm happy she's finally happy. You've pulled her out of her shell. Goddamn, she can sing like her má. And you're right, she's even better than us together. I'm behind you a hundred percent in whatever you can get her to do. I just ask that you don't push her too hard."

Closing my eyes and thanking God, I let out a breath and release all the tension I was holding. "Thank you, Luc. It means a lot to me. I had spoken with Alexandria before we went into the studio that night. I told her what I wanted for us and our future, that I wanted her to DJ with me till she was comfortable with herself. We're going to make songs together and perform together. I told her I didn't want us to be apart. I explained that I would move here with her and that I have houses we could stay at, but that I wasn't leaving her. We're going to start our future."

Watching him mask his emotions, I finish with the biggest smile. "And she said yes."

Luc smirks. "I'm very happy to hear that, Maddox. I know you care for her and love her, so I'm not worried. What I am worried about is this fuckin' guy. We need to find him. Beau is goin' out of his mind. He has too much shit goin' on, and I feel he's bein' pulled in too many different directions and he's goin' to miss something. Too much shit to deal with. I'm glad you're here to protect her too."

Hmm. What the fuck else does Beau have going on that could be more important than this?

"Well, Luc, my guys are on it as well. I have my whole security team working on this just as much as Beau's men. I don't see how we can miss anything. If you let her stay with me, then we should be okay. If I'm not with her, then Brant is with her. I even left two of my guys on her floor. I have two more outside undercover. I don't think this guy was expecting me to be in the picture. He might know all your security team, but he surely doesn't know mine. We'll cover her and protect her, I promise you that."

Luc blows out a deep breath, letting his shoulders relax. I know I just gave him some peace of mind. Luc's face is serious again, making his jaw tense. "*When* we find this son of a bitch, I'm callin' in a marker with my family to have him taken care of. You're the only one who will know this, but with your family involved, you might hear somethin', seein' as she's your girl. I just wanted you to know. I've never asked for anythin' from them before, but this motherfucker is not going to exist anymore." Not taking his eyes off me, he's looking for a reaction, but I just sit there, masking the shock on my face.

He would call them. Of all people, he would call a marker into them. Hell no.

"Luc, if I don't kill him myself or take care of it, then you can call in your marker. *Believe me,* this will be taken care of. If I can help it, you won't ever, and I mean ever, have to call in a goddamn marker to them. They are our last resort. I've handled things on my own all my life without involving them. I don't need or want to start now, especially something to do with Alexandria."

I pause, getting myself together so I don't flip the fuck out and lose it on him for even thinking of calling our families. "*If*...and that is a big if, something should happen to me and he isn't taken care of, then, by all means, you can do whatever you feel is necessary." I know my face is red because I'm shaking just thinking about our family getting involved.

Motherfucking hell no. I don't need them. Never.

Luc is studying me, trying to figure me out. Looking like he's defeated, he runs his hands through his hair again. "Maddox, believe me, I don't ever want to call it in, but I will if I have to. It just needs to happen." Clearing his throat, he says, "Okay. Now, before I call my baby girl, who will be furious with me, I need you to know about tonight."

Fuck, now what?

"I've pulled Emmett from tonight's lineup. He was supposed to open for you, and Ginger was goin' to close. But instead, Ginger is the openin' set and Izzy is closin'. I did this for two reasons. Emmett has gotten into two fights with our biggest promoter, Jason, and I just don't need it tonight with everythin' else goin' on. The last thing we need is for a fight to happen around her and he slips through our grasp. Second is because Emmett and you are not cool with each other. Emmett has issues with everyone because of Alex, so I've switched all his events so he's DJing somewhere else. Tonight's the only night he won't be playin' somewhere else because it was such short notice. I've paid him for tonight and explained why he is bein' pulled. The fucker needs to get his shit together. Let's just fuckin' say he isn't very happy right now. I explained to him everythin' that's goin' on with Alex right now, and he needs not to add to her drama. He flipped out that he didn't know, and who is protecting her, yada, yada. Needless to fuckin' say, it's a good thing he isn't playin' somewhere tonight."

I think Luc is my new best friend. A huge grin spreads

across my face, letting him know I'm happy with his decision. *Thank fuckin' God.*

I know I probably sound overly happy, but I can't hold it back when I speak. "Thank fuck for that, Luc. If he had come today, I would have pounded his ass if he thought he was going to get near her. And if that Jason guy comes tonight, he needs to stay the fuck away from her too. I don't need any distractions, especially fuckheads that want to be with Alexandria."

Not happening. No fuckin' way.

Luc holds his hand up sternly. "Look, Maddox, I know you're protective of her, and I am as well, but these fuckin' guys have been workin' for me for years and would never do anythin' to hurt her. Yes, they maybe are dumb fucks and have a crush on her, but they would never hurt her. Jason's a good kid, and he will be there tonight. He and Alex have a good relationship. I hope you don't piss her off by not letting her speak to him. Deal with it however you want, but she works with them and will have to talk to them sooner than later. *Capisci*?"

Try me. Hell fucking no. Mine!

I feel my face tighten when I clench my jaw. "Luc, she won't be working with those two anymore unless Jason is throwing an event we're performing at. I don't have a problem with him talking to her, but putting his hands on her, *I will* have a problem with. So let's just focus on our main problem—the motherfucker trying to nab her again. All her other suitors I can deal with, trust me. Thank you though for pulling Emmett tonight and from all our future events. I'm grateful for that. One less thing for me to have to worry about."

Luc sits back in his chair, playing with his pen in his hands, in deep thought while staring at me. I don't move but just stare right back at him. He then leans forward, grabbing his office phone. He dials a number then looks back at me. Sounding annoyed, Luc barks into the phone, "Alex, you need to come to my office right now." Still staring at me, he continues after she has said something. "Yeah, I just need you to come up here. Please." He waits for a reply and then hangs up.

Okay, what the fuck? Why does he sound pissed?

Clasping my hands in my lap, I lean back in the chair, getting comfortable while we wait for her. Neither one of us has looked away yet when Luc breaks the silence. "Maddox, she's goin' to be pissed I pulled Emmett without discussin' it with her since she manages him. I hope you can help me out with this, and then we can discuss your future."

He grabs a pack of papers and hands them over to me. I get up to grab them. Sitting back down, I glance at the top of the page and read, "East to West Coast Tour. Top four DJs from each label."

God, yes. Now this is what we need to be talking about.

I start to flip through it, looking at all the places we would stop. The excitement begins to burst through my body because this is perfect for us to start off with. While I keep looking through it, I ask him, "When does this start? Who are you sending? Fuck, Luc, this is perfect for us. I hope she'll be willing to do it." Alexandria and me on tour, I can't think of a better way to get to know one another, away from our lives and just being us.

The door opens before Luc can answer me, with Alexandria, Ginger, and Brant walking into the room. All three of them are smiling. When Alexandria gets close enough, I pull her onto my lap. She squeals with laughter before kissing me. *Fuck yeah. Mine. All mine*. My cock twitches under her ass, wanting to be inside her.

We break our kiss when Luc clears his throat. "*Ay*, do you have to do that in front of me, for God's sake?"

Both of us laugh, and Alex turns on my lap to sit up, facing her father. Giggling, she replies, "Oh, Papá, relax. It's just a kiss."

His face is red and he's clenching his jaw. "So, what did you call me down here for?" I look over to see Ginger sitting in the chair next to us with Brant behind her with his hands on her chair.

Luc grunts, "Yeah, I asked for *you* to come…"

Ginger flinches and then starts to leave, saying, "I can leave. Sorry, I didn't—"

Luc puts his hand up, stopping her, and Brant grabs her shoulders, forcing her to sit back down. Luc speaks in a calm voice, "Gin, it's not a problem. I already spoke to you this morning, I just don't know if you want to hear it all again. *But* you need to stay here for other stuff we need to discuss." Pausing, he leans back. "I was goin' to talk to your father first…"

Sighing, he stands up, walking over to the window before continuing. "But, from what I'm learning, you girls can take care of yourselves and are damn sure old enough to make your own decisions. So…stay." He turns back to all of us with a warm smile.

Alexandria starts to shake her legs nervously, or else she is getting impatient wanting to know why he called her here. I let out a silent laugh, grabbing her hips and whispering, "Relax, *mi amor.*"

Ignoring me, Alexandria huffs out, "Papá?"

Luc sits back down, propping his forearms on his desk. "Alex, as I've told everyone here, and I hope you'll understand my decision, I've pulled Emmett from tonight's lineup."

When Alexandria doesn't flinch or say anything, he continues, "I just don't want Jason and Emmett at the same events anymore. Emmett and Maddox don't seem to get along either, so I thought it would be best if we just pulled Emmett. He was not very happy with my decision, but if he wants to stay at this label, he'll get his shit together. We do not put up with fightin' or disrespect of any kind at this label. I've paid him for tonight since it was too short notice to get him in somewhere else." Still no movement and I can't see her face. *Fucking hell. Is she upset? Goddammit.*

No one says anything for a couple of minutes before Alexandria speaks in an even tone. "I understand your decision, Papá. I'm upset you didn't talk to me or let me be in on the conversation since I'm his manager." Putting her hand up, stopping him from replying, she continues. "I said I understand. I'm very happy you switched Ginger and that you're putting Izzy as the closing set. Izzy texted me a few minutes ago all excited, so thank you."

Luc, I think, is in shock from the look on his face, with his eyebrows raised high and his lips slightly open. He plays with his pen in deep thought, probably trying to figure out who this girl is in front of him. He obviously thought she was going to freak out. *That's my girl.*

She must sense his mood as well because she laughs. "Papá, I'm not some spoiled little girl anymore. I'm not going to throw tantrums if I don't get my way. I did graduate with a business degree, and I do know what I'm doing. I would have probably done the same thing given that he has fought with Jason twice now. You just didn't give me a chance."

Ginger starts to giggle, and Brant grabs her shoulders, shutting her up. I try to hide my laughter as well. Alexandria just laid it out to him that he needs to treat her like an adult.

Luc starts to laugh a full-hearted laugh, tilting his head back and closing his eyes. When he's done laughing, he looks to Alexandria with a huge smile. His sky-blue eyes match his daughter's and only show love and admiration. "Alex, you truly are amazin', and I'm sorry I keep seein' you as my baby girl and for not trustin' you to handle this situation. I haven't been around you enough this last year to see that you have blossomed into a beautiful, independent, fascinatin' woman."

Everyone just sits there looking at Luc when he's finished. Alexandria replies in a shaky voice, "Thank you, Papá. It means a lot to me." I pull her back against my chest, kissing the top of her head.

Luc's face changes back to his stern business face, and he looks down at the papers I put back on his desk. Clearing his throat, he says, "Now… Maddox came to me the other night, askin' my permission so he can stay with you. He told me he wanted to get you in the studio and his intentions for your future."

Alexandria gasps, turning to face me. "You talked to my papá before we even went into the studio?"

Fuckin' hell

I mask my emotions, not knowing if she's mad at me or happy. I try to keep calm. "Yes, Alexandria. I wanted to let your father know I wasn't fucking around. From the first day I sat here, I've told him my intentions for you. I love you and want us to be together. I know how great you are…" I pause to control myself before I finish. "I don't want you hiding behind all these other fucking DJs when your talent is better than most."

Shit. Ginger.

I look over to Ginger really quickly. "No offense, Ginger, but *she is* hiding behind all of you, and someone needed to say something."

Ginger puts up her hands like she isn't upset. "I completely agree. I've been telling her this too."

We both look back to Alexandria who is staring intently at me with tears forming in her eyes, "So you've known all along what you wanted with me? Not after you heard my stuff?"

Goddammit. She still doesn't see it.

I take a deep breath, lifting my hand to her cheek and wiping away a tear. "Alexandria, like I said, from the first time I saw you, the connection we have is undeniable. Don't you see and feel it? I had heard from friends who heard when Ginger played your music and how good it was. Then when you played me a song, I was done for, regardless of how long we have known each other. I will never feel for anyone the way I feel for you." I pause, leaning in to give her a quick kiss. "So, yes. I came here for one thing, and that was to win you over."

She throws her arms around my neck with force, taking the wind out of me. I laugh, "Aw, *mi belleza,* what am I going to do with you? You need to believe me." Pulling her away, I wipe her eyes, and I place a sweet, passionate kiss on her lips before pulling away. "Now…listen to your father and what he has planned for us. *Together.*"

When I look around, Ginger has tears in her eye, but Brant

looks pissed off with his arms crossed over his chest. Luc has his arms crossed over his chest too, but he actually looks happy. Once we are all facing Luc again, he continues. "Yeah. He wanted me to record you two in the studio to show me what you had. I was mad at first because if anyone knew what you had, it was me. I was the one who taught you…" Luc pauses looking sad, sighing. "Well, I was wrong, baby girl. Your talent is beyond your má's and mine. You're so good, and you're everythin' in one. I'm so proud of you. It upsets me you didn't show me any of this before. When I saw you DJin', the love and happiness radiating off you were so breathtakin'. Your má and I just sat there in awe of you, baby. Your má wanted to go to you, she was cryin'. And when you were couplin' with Maddox, the two of you were beyond words. I've only seen one other couple do what you two did, and they've been doin' it for four years."

I knew it. Fuck yeah. I knew he would like it.

Luc looks over to Ginger and then back to Alexandria. "Now I need to send four DJs from our label to this East to West Coast tour. I was goin' to send Ginger, Dominic, Emmett, and Izzy. But since Maddox is here, and now you're on the team, I think we should send Ginger, you two, Dominic, and Izzy. Emmett's still a loose cannon. I've been mentorin' him for years now, but he still loses control and just doesn't get the whole club scene. He gets into too many fights with our promoters—even when Alex isn't here. It has nothin' to do with you guys, but what he did the last few events kind of sealed the deal. So, if you want to do this, we will send you away for six months. It doesn't start till after summer, so we have a month and a half to prepare and get everythin' in order. We don't have to send in final names till after the festival."

Luc looks over to Ginger with concerned eyes. "Now, Ginger, your father was not happy about you goin' traveling for a year. I know he's been dealin' with some stuff and wanted you to come home for a bit, so let me know what you want to do. If you need Beau or me to talk to him, just let us know. *Capisci*? Let him know we will keep sending him weekly or monthly reports if he needs us to."

Ginger stands up instantly, pissed off. "What the… He's *still* getting weekly reports?" She turns and glares daggers at Brant and then looks back to Luc, folding her hands over her chest and waiting for one of them to answer.

Fuckin' hell, she has some fight in her. Surprised the shit out of me.

Brant doesn't move or say a word. Instead, he just looks at her when Luc speaks up. "Calm down, Ginger. Speaking from a protective father's view myself, he is just concerned for your well-being. We haven't sent weekly reports to him in a long time. We're on monthly reports, but if you don't talk to him within a week, he freaks out and usually calls Beau or me askin' about you." With a chuckle, he leans forward. "If it makes you feel any better, I was getting reports on Alex weekly, if not daily, so count yourself lucky."

Alex jumps up now, mimicking Ginger's stance and glaring at Luc. Ginger still stands with her face as red as fire on her fair skin, but Alexandria goes off. "Papá, this is going a little overboard, don't you think? We are *adults*. You know, over the age of eighteen. Why do you need to get daily reports on me? I'm right here where you can see what I'm doing." Crossing her arms over her chest, she lets him know she is pissed off. I stand up, laughing at the two girls throwing full-on tantrums. It makes it even funnier since just a few minutes ago, Alexandria told her father she doesn't throw tantrums anymore.

Luc turns red, standing up now that everyone else in the room is standing. "For the love of God, don't you raise your voice to me. I'm your papá, and nothin' you do will ever change me worryin' about you, *especially* with this piece of crap running around. Nah, both of you need to deal with it. Ginger, your father loves you. Deal with him and let me know what you decide. Get outta my office and back to work."

Seeing how irate he is, I stifle my laughter, noticing Brant is trying not to laugh out loud either. Luc opens the door, waiting for all of us to exit. No one says a word.

Alexandria

I'm so mad at my papá. Both Ginger and I storm out of his office with Brant and Maddox right behind us, trying to hold in their laughter. I stop in my tracks with my hands on my hips. "What the fuck is so funny? Because this isn't funny! I'm not a goddamn little kid anymore who needs a fucking report card." Remembering that the sick fuck can see and maybe hear me, I clench my jaw. "I need to fucking vent outside."

I'm so fucking pissed off.

Ginger still hasn't spoken, but you can tell she's angry with her arm gripping her helmet tight on her hip. We all get on to the elevator, but instead of going to my floor, I hit the button for the lobby. I need to get shit straight.

Once we're all outside, Ginger turns to Brant. "What the fuck, B? You could have told me you were still sending reports to him. Have you told him *everything* that I do? Hmm?"

Wow, this should be good.

Brant looks at the two of us with his golden eyes and then looks back to Ginger. His face hiding all his emotions and thoughts, he mimics her stance by folding his arms over his chest. Through clenched teeth, he says, "Gin, you know I have to turn in a fucking report every fucking month. You know I report to Beau, but no, I do *not* report my personal shit. So, if you're around when I'm on my personal time, then fuck no, I don't report it." He takes a step toward her, looking even more furious. "If you're working and I'm protecting you, then fuck yes, I report it."

What the fuck? "Personal time..." Hmm, are they dating?

I'm about to say something, but Ginger takes a step toward Brant, not backing down. "Why the fuck didn't you tell me you were doing reports on *me*? Not her—" Ginger points to me but doesn't turn away from Brant and then points her finger back to herself "—but *me*."

Maddox comes to my side, pulling me into an embrace. My anger starts to subside while watching Brant and Ginger go head-to-head. I like them together, and they actually make a cute couple, both feisty as hell.

Brant closes his eyes and takes a deep breath before opening them, showing his hazel eyes. "Gin, we all just got back from the tour. I was doing a report on all of you girls. It was one big report. Your father gets a copy of the fucking report, I guess. I don't ask fucking questions. I just do my job. Now that we're back, I haven't done a report on just you because I'm with Alex most of the time. But if you're with us and I'm watching over you, then you're in my report. If you're going to flip out about reports going to your father, you need to talk to Beau and your father."

Ginger just stares at him, not saying anything. I know

she's fighting a war inside her head. I chime in, "Um, are you two dating? What the fuck?"

Both turn to look at me with daggers in their eyes, and both say at the same time, "Fuck no."

Yeah, right.

Laughing, I turn to look at Maddox and then to Brant before saying, "Okay, so I flipped out and had a tantrum because I just don't agree with reports daily, or even monthly. If something happens, I understand that. But seriously, I'm here in town now. Why the reports?" Waiting for Brant to answer, I look over at Ginger, who is now looking back at Brant.

Brant takes a deep breath, releasing his arms and running his hands through his hair. "Look, now that we have been back—" he holds his hand up "—which has only been a month, I've only written reports of the club events or what we've been doing with this stalker guy."

He takes another deep breath, looking over to Ginger. In a softer voice, he says, "I didn't know about the reports to your father because Beau doesn't tell me shit. I'm at fault for not telling you that you were in my monthly reports when we were in Europe, but all of you girls were."

Feeling bad for yelling at Brant since he was just doing his job, I say sorry as I put my hands around Maddox's waist. Brant just stands there staring at Ginger, who still hasn't changed her unhappy expression.

Maddox, who had been quiet the whole time, speaks up. "Well, the good thing here is we're all on the same page now. Things are going to change a lot with everything going on this week. And hopefully after this weekend, when we catch this motherfucker, our lives will become less stressful."

Remembering I wanted to vent about the sick fuck, I start

to shoot off questions to Brant. "So where can he hear us? Where can he see us? I need to know where and when I can talk freely. I can't handle not knowing this anymore. Like, at Eva's desk, can he hear me? I know he can see me, but where can I go to talk freely?"

Ginger is the first to speak, breaking eye contact with Brant. "In the bathroom, there are no videos or bugs. Outside, obviously, in people's offices besides yours, there is no video or sound. Anywhere there is a video for the office, there is sound. The only extra is your office, but you know about that already." Still standing tense with her arms folded, she turns to Brant. "Am I missing anywhere?"

How the fuck did she know all this?

Brant must notice my facial expression as I look at Ginger because he steps in. "Alex, I briefed her last night about all the video surveillance and bugs in your house. To answer Gin, no, you covered everything. We just need to act like normal, and hopefully, we pull him out of hiding or hear from him again."

Maddox turns me to look down into my eyes. "Alexandria, are you okay? Are you ready to head back inside, or do you want to yell at Brant some more?"

Brant curses next to us, and I start to laugh, shaking my head no. I'm done having a tantrum. I look over to Ginger, who's still mad but not saying anything. I know she's probably still enraged, but it's more toward her father than Brant, I think.

Once we're all back inside waiting for the elevator, Ginger's phone chirps. When we go to get into the elevator, Ginger, still looking at her phone, huffs out, "I've got some stuff to take care of today. I have my bike down in the garage, and it looks like I'll have to meet you all at the club tonight."

Maddox and I say our good-byes, but Brant tells us he's going to walk her down and will be back up soon. Ginger snaps her head up, narrowing her eyes at Brant and spitting out, "No! You don't have to walk me down. I'll be fine." The elevator dings, and we let it close on them standing to face each other, glaring daggers at each other.

Not dating, my ass.

Maddox starts laughing. "They need to fuck and get it over with. Fuckin' hell, that was intense." When I don't say anything, Maddox pulls me to his chest, leaning down, kissing me.

A soft moan escapes me. *God, I want this man.*

The rest of the day goes on without any drama. I play along with all the false information they wanted me to give, hoping to draw this fucker out of hiding. We receive no communication from him either. Brant returns to my office a while later looking sad and pissed off, not saying a word to me. Maddox leaves, heading over to his hotel to deal with his team of men while I finish off my day.

The only time Brant looks happy or says anything is when Sasha stops by my office before heading to the studio. Her happy, bubbly self is a breath of fresh air. She is so upbeat and cheerful, she has Brant smiling. It is nice to end my workday with her visit, but once he and I are in the car to head home, Brant's smile vanishes, leaving only his piss-poor attitude.

Alexandria

Alone in my apartment, I have time to process everything that has happened in the last few weeks while I take a long, hot bath. All my feelings for Maddox, what's going on with this psycho after me, my music, and overall what I want to do with my life. I know in my heart, even if it has only been a few weeks, I can't give up Maddox. My love for music is just the icing on the cake. I want to see where this goes with Maddox and my music.

The ringing of my cell phone pulls me from my thoughts, and I look at the time, realizing I've been in the tub for over thirty minutes. I get out and dry myself off before heading to look at my phone. I see it was my mamá calling, and I promise myself I'll call her after I get ready.

An hour later, I'm finishing my hair when I hear the door open. I call out, "B, is that you?" When I don't hear anything, I freeze, just listening. Just when I start to freak out, I see

Maddox move toward the bathroom door.

While looking me over, he leans into the doorframe. He bites his lip with a growl. "Fuckin' hell, are you wearing that to the club?"

I laugh, "What?" I look down at my tight, scoop neck red blouse which shows off a bit of cleavage, my black leather skinny pants, and red heels.

Shit. Shit. I hope he likes it.

When I look back up, Maddox is still leaning in the doorframe with a devilish smirk. "I won't be able to perform with a hard-on. Fuckin' hell, you look sexy as sin."

When he starts to stalk toward me, I put up a hand, giggling and stepping back. "Oh, no, you don't, Maddy. We need to leave, and you touching me will only end up with us in bed."

Laughing, he grabs my wrists, yanking me toward him. Smashing his mouth into mine with a growl, he devours my mouth, pushing his engorged cock against me and showing me how much he wants me. Huskily he says, "Alexandria, you drive me mad with this God-given voluptuous body."

Maddox has one hand kneading my ass while the other rubs up my back to my neck, holding me tight to his body. He tugs my hair, forcing me to look up at him as he murmurs, "I love you."

Warm butterflies take flight in my stomach and race through my body. I smile up at him. "I love you more, Maddy."

Pushing away from him, I giggle, "Now we have to go. B is waiting downstairs for us. Are your guys here too, or are they meeting us at the club?"

Maddox smiles down at me, and with a smack on my ass,

he heads out of the bathroom laughing. When I go to grab my clutch purse on the kitchen island, Maddox says from the front door, "I don't want you leaving my side tonight. I want you on stage with me while I perform. I know your girls will be there, but I want you with me at all times tonight. We don't have as much security with such short notice, so just stay with me. After tonight, all our events will be doubled with security. Brant will be protection for all you girls tonight, and I don't want to worry about you."

Wait... What?

As I walk over to him, he opens the door, winking at me. My mind is running, so I start rambling off shit. "Brant's protecting all of us? Usually, our girls have their own security. What's going on? Why are we short tonight? I mean, of all nights, this is one of our biggest events." I come to a stop in front of him. He doesn't look happy anymore. Instead, he looks pissed off at me.

Well, shit.

Grabbing my arm, he says, "That's what your father said, so I don't know. All I'm saying is, don't leave my side." Maddox pulls me out of my apartment, releasing my arm to grab my hand, then heads to the elevator, looking irritated. *Dammit.*

"Um, Maddy, what's wrong?" I ask in a whisper.

Once we're inside the elevator, he places me in front of him with my back to his chest, embracing me with both arms holding me tight. Maddox leans into my ear and whispers, "Alexandria, remember you have bugs everywhere. We have plenty of security, but they'll all be undercover. We want this guy to think he can get to you. That is why I want you by my side all night in case he tries for you. We're trying to lure him out, thinking we are understaffed." He kisses my neck down to my collarbone, and I try to relax into him.

Shit, I totally forgot.

Maddox must feel me tense because he bites my shoulder, pulling me from my nightmarish thoughts. "Quit thinking. You're safe with me. I won't let anything happen to you, but you must stay at my side while I perform. I can't be worrying about you while I play."

Closing my eyes and leaning my head back onto his shoulder, I whisper, "Okay, *mi amor*."

On the ride over in the limo, I stay quiet, lost in my thoughts while Maddox, Brant, Chad, Isaac, and Ethan all discuss the security for tonight's event and the events coming up. My mind is running a mile a minute, trying to tune them out so I don't have a panic attack and show them my anxiety. They're pretty much putting me on display and hoping he shows himself. My fear is, what if he's that good? What if he's one step ahead of us, and he gets me or one of our girls? I don't know what I would do if one of my friends got hurt because of me.

In a daze, I keep my focus looking outside. I know everyone is strung out over this and working nonstop to catch him, but I just have a bad feeling about this. I've heard everything that everyone has been saying on purpose to lure him out, but I'm still nervous. *Breathe, Alex.*

Wringing my hands together, I try to release some anxiety. Not turning my head from looking out the window, I take a deep breath before I speak to them. "So, what happens if he's a step ahead of us and I am taken? What happens then?"

The limo goes silent, and aside from a growl from Maddox, no one speaks. Maddox pulls me onto his lap, grabbing my chin and making me look into his charcoal gray eyes. "Alexandria… Do not think like that."

Feeling the tension in the limo, I turn to face all of the men, keeping my voice stern and hiding my panic. "What happens, though? Do we have a plan? I need to know if, in the next three days, I or any of my friends are taken, do you have a plan?" Maddox's grip on me becomes like a vise, locking tight.

I look straight at Brant, waiting for an answer, but Ethan speaks up first. "Alex, I have three trackers on you. Unless he strips you naked, I'll be able to find you. Your phone and clutch—"

I put my hand up to cut him off. "But what about my girls? Gin, Izzy, Eva, or Sasha, or any of the other girls from the label?"

Ethan's face is filled with concern. He's a very attractive man, but I can tell the last few days have taken a toll on him with the worry lines and dark circles under his eyes from lack of sleep. His eyes narrow, focusing all his attention on me. "Alex, all of them have tracking devices. Not as many as you, but that is because Madd Dog is overly protective."

Ethan runs his hands through his hair then shifts his laptop case on his lap. "I tried to have them carry more than one device, but to be honest, they wouldn't. Ginger is fine, and I wouldn't want to be the one to try to take her. She's scary. Eva and Izzy aren't taking this seriously and think they're fine with security and one tracker on their phones. Sasha doesn't think she would be a target since she isn't from here or from the label, but she let me put a tracker on her phone."

Oh, God, I hope I didn't come off mean or ungrateful.

When I'm about to apologize, Brant clears his throat.

"Alex, we have it covered. There are going to be eyes on you all night, and yes, eyes on *all* of you tonight. Don't worry about anyone but yourself. We have the girls covered. Everyone will be here tonight, so don't stress. You need to clear your head so you don't have a panic attack tonight."

Brant leans forward. "Alex, you have been safe all these years, so please don't start freaking out now because we kept you in the loop. You've never known of any threats all these years because we're that good. Please trust us to do our jobs."

He leans back, chuckling. "Plus, you have extra men with all of Maddox's guys and Maddox hooked to your hip. We got you."

Maddox is squeezing me, holding me firmly, but I feel his body tighten up with tension radiating from him. Taking a deep breath, I place a smile on my face. "Okay, boys. Thank you so much. Ethan, thank you, and I know you will all protect us. So now let's have some fun, okay?"

Everyone tries to relax with a few chuckles, but I see in Chad's and Brant's faces that they are anxious. I wouldn't want to be in charge, that is for sure. The limo comes to a stop in front of the club, and when the door opens, Maddox shuffles me so he can get out. He turns toward me, helping me out and stuffing me into his side, protecting me. The anxiety starts to form in my stomach at the crowd going crazy when they see Maddox, chanting his name. With flashes going off, I can't see much. I look down, but I feel Maddox's lips on my cheek. I look back up into his loving eyes squinting down at me with the most panty-dropping smile ever. I reach up to caress his face, touching his dimple. Once he places a quick kiss on me, the anxiety simmers to nothing, and I turn to see all our guys next to us.

"Okay, let's do this, boys," I say with a smile.

Breathe, Alex. I can do this. He can't take away my freedom. I am *strong. I* am *in control. I have Maddox. I have Brant. Breathe...*

Maddox grabs my ass, pulling me to him with a growl. "Mine." When the doors open, I hear more screams from the crowd, then the bass drops in and the music vibrates, shaking the windows and doors. Noticing the style of music, I know it's Izzy on the decks and not Ginger.

Hmm. I thought Gin was the opening set.

Still feeling the anxiety in my stomach, I squeeze Maddox's side, hugging him tighter. I try to listen to the music, but everyone crowds around us, screaming and trying to get to Maddox. They grab at both of us until the guys make a circle around us with the club security, and we're ushered into a VIP area. When I look up, I see Dominic and Eva bouncing around. Relief flows through me like a breath of fresh air. When I hear Eva scream, *"Alex!"* my hand loosens on Maddox's waist.

Maddox

I don't want to let her go. Eva grabs Alexandria in a bear hug, and they start chatting. Once I say hello to the guys, I start to do my usual perimeter scan. I want to know who's around us and if I see anything unusual. Everyone is on high alert tonight, even though we're all trying to act normal around Alexandria.

The crowd is jumping, and Izzy is blowing up the decks. I glance at Alexandria and see her take a shot with Eva. She looks up, smiling at me, and I smile back. When I glance over at Dominic, I sense something is wrong. His face is red, radiating heat with his jaw clenched and giving someone a death stare. When I follow his line of sight, all I see on the stage is Izzy. But behind her is Jason, standing with a few other guys watching Izzy. What the fuck? Is Dominic staring at Jason with her? Since Dominic isn't up on stage with her, they must be in a fight, but why the fuck is he so pissed? When I glance back to Dominic, he must feel me watching because he looks my way with no emotion. I give him a head nod, like, what the fuck? In return, he just nods back, but his face is still a blank mask. *Motherfucker.*

Feeling the tension in the air, I walk over to Dominic. "What's up? Are you okay, man? You look pretty pissed off. You and Izzy fighting?"

Dominic turns away from me, glaring back at Izzy and cursing in Russian, but he ends by saying, "Girls… Fuckin' PMS."

When his Russian accent is this thick, it usually means he's pissed off. We've seen a few of their fights, and it's not pretty. Izzy is a dramatic girl, and Dominic is a dominant man. They're never dull, but they've been fighting a lot lately.

Dominic finishes his drink, putting it down on the table. He gives me a nod and heads toward the stage.

Once I have my arms around Alexandria again, I seem to calm a bit and try to enjoy the night. She's safe, and we have plenty of people around. If Dominic doesn't start shit, we should be good. Tonight, everyone is in one place. But this motherfucker is lurking somewhere, so I don't think my anxiety is going to subside.

Alexandria starts to dance in front of me, swaying her hips and rubbing up against my cock, bringing him to full attention.

Down, Madd Dog…down.

Leaning down, I whisper into her ear, "You keep this up, and I'll have you bent over in the bathroom."

I kiss her neck with a slight suck that sends goose bumps over her body. Alexandria turns to me, sliding her hands up my chest and around my neck. She clasps her fingers as she pouts, "What?"

I look down at her, and my eyes automatically go to her breasts which are spilling out of that top. *Fuckin' hell.* When I look back up to her spellbinding eyes, I can see she's pushing me. Alexandria licks her lips, making my cock twitch against her body which, in return, makes her nipples harden.

With a growl, I ask, "Do you want me to spank you or fuck you really quick, and real hard, *mi belleza*?"

Two can play at this game. I slide my hands down her back and over her ass to grab her globes with a hard squeeze.

When her eyes glaze over, I know she wants what I do. She gets on her tiptoes, pulling me down so she can talk into my ear. She grabs a handful of hair and breathes, "Is that so bad?"

Goddammit, I knew we should have fucked before we came out.

My stress level and anxiety alone need some release, but the need to be inside her and fill her with my come is unbearable. It seems my little vixen wants more, and she's pushing me to see what I'll do. Obviously, the alcohol she has consumed so far tonight has given her some liquid courage.

Turning my head, I reply into her ear with a growl, "You asked for it, Alexandria." Biting her neck, I make her squeal.

I grab her hand, turning to walk out of VIP, but I stop at Brant and Chad. "B, we'll be right back. Chad, you're with us."

We turn, walking back through the VIP toward the stage. Alexandria isn't saying a word but instead giggling like a school girl. Opening the door and guiding Alexandria into the VIP bathroom, I turn to Chad. "You got me?"

Chuckling, Chad answers, "Yeah, Madd Dog, I got you,

brother."

Locking the door, I turn to prey on my feast. Alexandria giggles, walking back toward me. She must have checked the stalls because she says, "I can't believe we are doing this. But fuck, I can't wait."

I glance around. Right in front of us are a couple of chairs facing a wall of mirrors that leads to another room with three stalls. It's for the performers and VIP guests, but right now, it's all ours. I know Chad won't let anyone in here, so I focus on her.

Pure dominance takes me over, and I speak with a commanding voice. "Alexandria, turn around and hold on to the chair. I want you to watch me fuck the shit out of you."

She turns around breathless. "Okay."

I walk up behind her and our eyes connect in the mirror. I see her chest start to rise and fall faster. She's so much taller in these fuck-me red heels. Not breaking eye contact, I lean down, slipping her hair to the side so I can kiss her neck. "Alexandria, you must wear these heels more often. They get me so fucking hard and put you at the perfect height." I grab her hips hard and move a few inches closer, letting her feel my arousal.

Alexandria closes her eyes with a moan.

"Open your eyes." Alexandria jumps at my voice. The music thumps around us, making this so much more sensual. I start to move us to the music, but I move my body slightly away so I can slip her leather pants down her silky legs, releasing one foot. Noticing she is not wearing panties, I smile at her, "Hmm, my little vixen wants my cock, doesn't she? Spread your legs for me."

Moving back up her legs, I caress her smooth skin,

slipping my hand between her cheeks and sliding my middle finger between her folds. Alexandria gasps, "Oh, God… Yes."

Fuckin' hell, she's soaked. I need to fuck her, put my seed in her, mark her as mine.

When I withdraw my finger, Alexandria whimpers in disapproval. I move fast and drop my cargo pants, freeing myself. "This is going to be a quickie, but I'm going to fuck you. *Hard*. I want my come dripping from you all night."

Alexandria bites her lips but doesn't say anything. "Alexandria, do you want…" I stroke my cock with one hand. "…me to fuck…" I grab her shoulder with the other hand, holding her in place. "…you hard." I slip my cock between her folds, milking it with her arousal.

Alexandria moans with each stroke of my cock teasing her, driving her crazy. She cries out, "Fuck yes…"

Fuckin' beautiful.

On the third stroke, when my dick is coated, I thrust up, slamming into her sweetness with one hard push and making both of us cry out. Gripping her hips so hard I know it will probably leave red marks, I slowly pull my cock from her greedy pussy, positioning myself behind her for the assault I'm about to unleash.

Alexandria grits out. "Hurry, Maddy. Please…"

That's all it takes for my assault to commence. I start pumping into her, making her grip the chair harder. I slap her ass before I slide a hand up her back, moving it over her shoulder and grabbing her collarbone. I hold her still so I can jack her harder and faster. "Fuck yeah."

Alexandria spreads her legs more and leans forward, giving me more room to go deeper. "God you're so fucking wet, *mi amor*."

She shows me her gorgeous fucking ass. I slap it a couple of times in sync with my cock pounding her. Alexandria cries out, "Yes… More…"

Alexandria's tits are bouncing, so I slip my hands up her shirt and reach around, popping them out of her bra so I can grab them to hold on to, while pinching her nipples.

Alexandria screams her approval with each thrust. "Fuck yes. I'm close."

"Wait. Do not come yet." I grunt between each thrust.

Fuck me. Yeah. Come on, Madd Dog.

Jacking her like a fucking mad jackrabbit, I pound her as hard and as fast as I can. The muscles in my thighs and ass start to burn with each stretch, clenching harder. My balls are slapping against her ass, and I start to feel the tingling race throughout my body, giving me the extra high.

"Fuck. Almost, baby." My knuckles turn white, gripping her skin so hard.

Alexandria screams, "I can't. Fuck!"

Goddammit, so fucking tight. Mine.

Our bodies are slapping together, and sweat is running down my face. My body tenses up all over, knowing I won't be able to hold out much more. "Alexandria, come, baby. Come now."

Reaching around her body, I slip two fingers over her clitoris, giving it a couple of rubs and sending her into oblivion with a few more hard thrusts of my cock.

Alexandria pushes the chair away, leaning all the way forward and grabbing her ankles. I'm still gripping her hips with both hands. I start fucking her faster, out of control, her body bouncing on my cock like a fucking rag doll.

I feel like a madman, grunting curse words between

thrusts. My leg muscles start to spasm. "Yeah, baby."

Alexandria starts moaning my name with her pussy clenching down with another orgasm.

"Almost… Fuck yes."

My come shoots into Alexandria, running down her leg with each continuing thrust, making the aftermath more intense. I still move in and out of her at half-mast. I can't seem to pull out of her, like I want to stay connected forever. But a pound on the door pulls me from my ecstasy. Alexandria is still holding her ankles in her sated bliss and not moving.

We both are trying to catch our breath when I finally pull my cock from her, a gush of come following it out. Stroking my cock with one hand, I reach down with my other one, cupping her pussy and letting all the come drip onto it. Still stroking my semihard cock, I slide my pinkie and ring finger into her pussy while sliding my middle finger and index over her swollen clit.

Alexandria moans, thrusting backward, wanting more. Laughing and still out of breath, I say, "My little vixen wants more, does she?"

Goddamn, I could go again. It's never enough.

I tease her, finger-fucking her and swiping her clit, letting another orgasm rip through her. I grab her around the waist, holding her up. When I see my handiwork with the red marks all over her body from where I was grabbing on to her, I smile.

Fuck yeah, mine.

There's another knock on the door, but this time it's louder, with Chad yelling, "Madd Dog, you're on stage in five."

I pull my hand from Alexandria's soaking pussy, and she

leans up, grabbing on to the chair to steady herself. But before I let go, I make sure she's okay. "You good?"

With a nod, she smiles at me in the mirror. I walk to the sink and wash my hands before putting myself back together. Neither of us speaks, still high from our mind-blowing quickie.

I wet a towel and move back to Alexandria to clean her up. Once I've slipped her pants back up, she's looking at me with a smile.

So fucking beautiful... mi belleza.

We both start laughing while trying to fix ourselves. But there is no way around it, we both look like we just fucked, and we fucked hard.

I laugh, "Better?"

Alexandria grabs my neck, pulling me down for a kiss. "Yes, thank you." Then she turns, shaking her ass toward the door.

Jesucristo!

Alexandria

Walking back to the VIP area, I try to pull myself back together. But once we're back in view of our group, no one notices. Sasha, Ginger, my parents, and now Jason have joined our group. When Mamá sees me, she smiles big and comes toward me. But before she gets to me, Maddox turns me to face him. "Alexandria, remember, I want you on stage with me tonight. I can't focus on you running around with everything going on." I nod my head before leaning up to give him a kiss. He smiles. "Thank you, *mi amor*. I'm going to head up and get ready, but say your hellos then have one of the guys bring you up before I go on."

I hope Maddox doesn't lose his shit with Jason being here. Once I saw him staring at Jason on stage earlier, I knew I needed to do something to occupy his mind and time before he went onstage. I just hope that quickie will hold him over until the end of the night.

I grab Maddox's arm before he leaves, saying, "Be nice. It's your come inside me right now, *not anyone else's.* So be nice, please."

Maddox smiles big with a laugh. "Goddamn right, it's mine." He smacks my ass before he heads up to the stage.

Hearing my mamá laugh, I turn to her, watching Maddox walk away from us and stopping to chat with Chad before heading up to the stage. We both watch him walk away when Mamá says in Spanish, "*Mija*, he loves you very much. Your papá and I are very happy for you both."

I turn to her and give her a big hug. "Yes, Mamá, I'm very lucky to have him."

We pull away from each other but still stay in an embrace. She's so warm and carefree, which sends a sense of calm over me. She starts to ramble something in Spanish, grabbing my hand and pulling me to the couch where our stuff is. "If your papá sees you looking this way up close, he might murder Maddox. Fix your makeup, *mija*," She hands me her compact.

On stage, Maddox is DJing while I hang out just behind him with Sasha and Ginger. They both came onstage with me since I was worried Jason or some other guy would be up here and I would have no one to talk to. The night so far has been uneventful, but so much fun. Jason and Maddox both seemed to have stayed away from each other. With worrying about them, I've totally forgotten about my rapist being out there.

Jason said a quick hello when I went up to say hello to my papá, but other than that, I've had no problems.

Sasha pulls me from my thoughts. "Hey, chica, I'm going to head back over to VIP for some more drinks since Gin is getting ready to go on and your man is almost done."

Looking around, I see Ginger has moved over to the DJ booth and Maddox is bouncing to the beat, getting ready to mix into another song. Feeling a chill come over me, I grab Sasha's arm, stopping her. "Wait, let me tell Maddox I'm going to go with you. I don't want to be up here alone."

She nods, and I head over to where Ginger and Maddox are standing. "Maddy, I'm going to head back over to VIP with Sasha while you finish. I'll be with my parents."

Maddox looks over to VIP with a hard look on his face. I glance over and see Jason talking to a group of guys. I reach up and grab Maddox, nipping at his earlobe. "I'll be fine. Remember, it's been your come dripping out of my wet pussy all night."

Maddox growls, but before he can say or do anything, I walk off the stage, shaking my ass with Sasha laughing.

Leaving the stage, I feel the chill again like someone is staring at me. Looking around, I see Emmett making his way over to us.

"Oh, God. What's he doing here?"

Fuck, we need to get to VIP so we are away from Maddox when Emmett gets to us.

My arm is entwined with Sasha's while we descend the final stairs from the stage. Sasha must not have heard me because she doesn't say anything but is still laughing. I see Brant and Chad standing over at VIP with eyes on us, so they don't even see him steaming right for us.

Shit!

I try to move us away from Emmett, hoping to lose him in the crowd. Suddenly, I hear commotion with the crowd pushing, making Sasha lose her balance and almost taking both of us down. When we get our bearings, we start to move toward the dance floor as the crowd goes nuts. When I hear screams, I know it's a fight.

The crowd. Oh, God. Don't panic, just get to VIP!

When I glance back to the stage, I don't see Maddox anywhere. We try to maneuver over toward the edge, but my anxiety is starting to overtake me, and I begin to hyperventilate.

So many people. I can't see. I can't breathe. Where is Maddox? Where is Brant?

Everyone is being pushed toward the stage, so it must be a pretty big fight. Sasha is screaming while I start to gasp for air.

Breathe, Alex. Breathe.

Taking deep breaths, I close my eyes, pushing as hard as we can toward the VIP. Suddenly, a guy is thrown into us, breaking Sasha and me apart with both of us screaming each other's names.

I can do this. Don't pass out. Everyone is here. Breathe.

Like God heard my prayer, I see Sasha being thrown over Brant's shoulder and them moving toward the door.

Thank you, she's safe.

Two dark hands I don't recognize grab me around the waist, picking me up from behind. I'm in a full-blown panic attack which sends me into a frenzy of kicking and screaming. My heel connects with his knee, but the man doesn't budge.

I feel his breath on my neck, and with a grunt, he says,

"Alex, you're safe. Relax."

Not recognizing the voice, I still try to break free and keep from passing out. As we move toward the front door, I see the VIP area is cleared out.

Oh, God.

I try to scream, but I don't have enough air in my lungs from hyperventilating. The guy must sense I'm about ready to pass out.

He turns me to face him and shakes me. "Alex, I work for Maddox. I'm a ghost, my name is Ace, and the password is purple. Now hold on, I'm going to get you out of here."

At hearing Maddox's name, along with all the other security details, I try to calm down, but I still can't breathe. Once Ace throws me over his shoulder, I close my eyes and try to calm down, thinking, *Maddox, where are you?* But I fail and I pass out.

Maddox

Scanning the area in between VIP and the stage, I find Jason moving toward Alexandria. But then I see him—that son of a bitch Emmett has some nerve coming to the club tonight. He's moving fast toward Alexandria as well. My blood boils, sending me into a rage.

Throwing my headphones off, I catch Chad's eye, letting him know there's trouble with just a look. I jump off the stage, pushing the crowd and hoping to get to them before they get to her. I know Emmett's pissed off for being cut tonight, and I need to get to him before he gets to my girl.

Setting my sights on Emmett, I push a guy out of my way, only to have him grab my arm yelling, "What the fuck, man?" One punch puts him to the ground. Looking back up, I lose sight of Emmett, but I see that fights start to break out around me. When I see Jason and Emmett fighting, I move toward them, looking for Alexandria. *Fucking hell.* The music's blaring through the system, so all I hear is screaming and yelling, making it impossible to hear anything else.

Where are you, baby?

Chaos is all around me, with our men grabbing the girls from the VIP and moving them to safety, but I don't see Alexandria. Brant comes into view, but he has Sasha thrown over his shoulder. *Where the fuck is Alexandria?* Turning, I see Alexandria screaming. But when I see who is holding her, I let out a breath of relief, knowing Ace has her and will get her to safety. Just then, a fist connects with my jaw, sending me back a few steps.

Rage overcomes me, but when I realize it's Emmett, I explode, losing all control. I power into him like a pro linebacker would, taking down his opponent. Punches are being thrown all around us while we scuffle on the ground. My fist pummels him mercilessly while the crowd around me loosens up, making me aware my men are around me. With Chad holding Jason down, I know Alexandria is safe from him as well.

It isn't until Roc pulls me off Emmett that I try to gain control. Luc moves in front of me, fuming like he is ready to kill. His voice is on the edge of violent, and he has a clenched jaw. "Maddox, go outside and fuckin' take care of my girls, while I deal with all this mess."

Gus is holding Emmett down. When I look around, I see a

dozen or so other men being held down by security, with the police entering the now almost empty club. I look back to the stage where Ginger and Isaac are handling all my music stuff, shutting down everything. When I start to head toward the stage, Luc yells, "Maddox, we've got this. Go get the girls and make sure they get home okay."

Son of a bitch.

Once I'm outside, Roc guides me over to the SUVs. I see Ace striding up looking stressed. "Brother, I'm sorry. I tried to calm her down, but she was still hyperventilating. So I threw her over my shoulder, and she passed out. Brant and a few other guys took her and the other girls home. Brant gave her something that woke her up, and she flipped out again. She wouldn't calm down, just kept screaming for you." He pauses, waiting for me to say something.

Sudden pain in my chest has me taking a deep breath while clenching my fist. Roc steps forward. "What's the plan, Madd Dog? What the fuck happened in there?"

I try to reel in my anger, but before I can reply, Luc barks from the club entrance behind me, "Maddox, get to my house, along with your security team. We need to talk—and now. I'll be there as soon as I can. Let Brant know I have Ginger, and Isaac is staying with me as well."

Calm down, Madd Dog. She's okay, relax. Taking a deep breath and without a word, I get into the car.

Walking into Luc's house, I probably look like a raging lunatic with my loose hair hanging around my face. My shirt was ripped in the fight, and most of all my body is amped up with the need to feel my baby, but I don't care. On the ride over, my anger turned into need. But when I stepped into her parents' penthouse, I lost it altogether, savagely yelling out, "Alexandria—" I was cut off when Alexandria jumped me, making me stumble back.

Thank God.

Taking a deep breath, I inhale her scent, and it calms the animal in me, knowing she is safe in my arms. Holding her tight, I shush her, telling her I have her and trying to calm us both down while ignoring our surroundings. Alexandria has her head tucked into my neck with her arms clenching me with all she has. Since her face is still nestled in my neck, her voice is muffled. "I tried not to panic, but with the crowd and all the fighting, I was so worried about everyone, and I couldn't find you."

Again, I shush her, telling her I'm okay and that I have her now. When I hear a throat clear, I turn my head to see everyone is entering the house.

I carry Alexandria over to the couch, where I sit down with her in my lap. Making Alexandria tense up, I bark out, "What the fuck?" I run my hands down over her shoulders, trying to soothe her. When I look around to see all my security and Beau's team just staring at me, it only fuels my rage again.

Fucking hell, I need to relax...

Brant, who's standing next to Sasha, starts to say something, but Beau begins speaking first. "Tonight was a total shitstorm."

The look on Beau's face tells me there's trouble. Beau crosses his arms, taking a deep breath and clearing his throat before speaking, "Okay, a lot of shit happened tonight. First, when Jason was speaking to Luc, we noticed some commotion at the front door. I got the call over my earpiece to come to the front because there was a fight. When I was on my way, I guess Jason noticed Emmett and that he was pissed off, moving toward the stage. Then a fight broke out near one of the VIP booths across from ours, and that is when Jason and Emmett got into a fight, along with a shitload of other people. With Emmett pushing people to get to either the stage or Alexandria, and Maddox pushing people, it just caused a clusterfuck of fights.

"Everyone in our group is safe and okay, but the bad news is we think the fights were premeditated or fake to draw our guys out and tie up security. I think that fucked up Emmett's plan to get to the stage. Also, two girls are missing from the club, or at least, their friends can't find them. We're looking into it, but all signs lead to our guy."

Goddammit.

Before anyone says anything, the front door flies open with a very pissed off Luc entering the room, followed by Ginger and Isaac. When Luc comes to a stop, evaluating the situation, he scans the room, locking eyes with Mia. She goes to him immediately. No one has said anything, waiting to see what Luc says. Once he has embraced Mia, kissing the top of her head, he looks up. "What a fuckin' nightmare! Beau and

Chad, I need someone to go over all the videos from tonight. All angles, inside and outside the club. We need to figure out who started the fights and how he is getting these girls out."

Ginger steps forward, speaking first, "How can one guy snag two girls in one night?"

Beau replies, "We think he's slipping something in their drinks and just waiting for them to fall into a drunken state, but we don't know. We have been watching videos from prior incidents but see nothing out of the ordinary. He must know where the cameras are to keep from being noticed. We'll scan them from tonight and hope since there were so many fights, he might have slipped up."

Feeling Alexandria tense in my arms, I jump into the conversation. I need to get it over with so I can get her out of here. "So what do we need to do? I need to get her out of here and rest."

Mia steps out from embracing Luc, clearing her throat and demanding everyone's attention. "Maddox take Alexandria to her old room that is across from the studio. You both can stay the night here. I don't want my daughter staying at that apartment where he can track her." Turning to Sasha, who is still next to Brant and now Ginger, she says, "Sasha, I want you to stay here in the building and not at the hotel. So you can either stay in our guest apartment or with Ginger. Why don't you girls head home while the guys talk strategies and figure shit out? We'll all meet here tomorrow morning. We don't all need to be here for this because I know I don't want to be."

When Luc and Beau agree with Mia, everyone moves to head out, with me being the first one to go.

Alexandria

The rest of the week passed in a blur with us staying between my parents' place and Maddox's hotel. Security came up with the plan to keep me moving locations while saying I'm somewhere else, with only a handful of us knowing where I really would be. Security seemed to have doubled at both the office and clubs, even adding police. After the huge fight and the number of girls missing, Beau started actively working with the police. Everyone was on edge, so now that the festival was picking up speed, I think everyone was about ready to snap.

I went back on my anxiety pills, because I refused to let this get me down. Maddox wouldn't leave my side, which was good in a sense. But when I wanted to hang out with Ginger one night at her place and he told me I couldn't stay over, it pissed me off. Though, once he explained he needed me as much as I needed him, I caved. Plus, Maddox fucking me senseless every night has seemed to keep the nightmares away. I was worried staying at my parents' house would put a damper on our sex life, but nothing would stop him from having me. He says he needs to be connected to me, which consumes me, making me forget everything.

After the fight at the club, both Emmett and Jason have been kissing my papá's ass. Emmett said he was headed toward the stage, not toward me. Everything and everyone at the label has exploded into crazy town since the festival began. I thought I would've had anxiety when I first went to the festival, but only excitement filled me. My love for music is stronger than my fear, and I will not let fear take over.

Standing on the back of the stage, watching Maddox and my friends DJ was so unbelievable, only making me realize how much I desire DJing with Maddox. The last fifteen minutes of his set, he played some of my music with me next to him. Our debut is in a few months when we hit the road. I'm hoping getting out of town and traveling with Ginger, Izzy, and Maddox will help everyone lighten up, including me.

Once everyone finished their sets at the festival, we all came here to Club Spin, where the final after party is being held. The club is already at capacity, with a line four blocks out. Of course, I'm in VIP with my girls, dancing while REX DJs.

Maddox is up on stage with the other DJs, getting ready to go on and visiting. When he glances over, I make a kissing face, making him laugh before turning his attention back to the DJ who is talking. I can see Maddox has relaxed a little bit now that the festival is over. He still watches me like a hawk, and I have security with me nonstop, but at least he isn't hooked to my hip, not letting me leave his side.

Sasha yells from across the table, "Chica, have another shot with me." Laughing, I agree to take the shot.

Eva squeals, "Sasha, you're going to get me wasted." We all laugh and take another shot. Sasha is bouncing in her seat, drunk. I'm sad she's leaving to go back to Spain in a few days.

Brant is standing behind her, and he steps forward, whispering something in her ear and making her blush for a second.

Hmm, now this could be interesting. Does she like B?

When it's time to go onstage, Brant and Sasha come with me to keep me company while Maddox DJs. Brant is with us on stage helping Maddox watch out for me since there are other DJs from out of town running around up here. He is also up here to take care of Sasha's drunk ass. Ginger isn't here yet since she had to do another errand for her dad, which has become more frequent than I think Brant likes.

After talking to some DJs he knows from Europe, Maddox walks over to us, making me forget everyone else instantly and wanting to be alone with him again. We already had sex twice today, but the craving I have for him is lethal. Our love for each other keeps getting better and better each day, like a fine bottle of wine. Whether or not I have a crazy guy after me, I think Maddox would still be this possessive over me, which only makes me love him more. When he is possessive, it makes me feel safe and wanted in a way I've never felt, which is crazy, I know, since I've been raised with a security team always around me.

When he reaches me, he goes right for my mouth with eagerness, intent on devouring me. I reach up, clasping my hands behind his head and moaning in his embrace. Sasha makes a choking sound, saying, "Get a fucking room, you two. Fuck."

Maddox breaks our embrace, laughing. "Sorry, girl, but I need to get my fix before I go on."

Maddox pulls me into his side, hugging me and placing a kiss on top of my head. Brant just laughs, but says nothing. He's standing right next to Sasha, kind of holding her up.

Okay, what the fuck? Is he not with Ginger, or is he just being protective?

I give Brant a look, but he just looks away from me, making me even more suspicious. Maddox turns me toward Brant. "I gotta go on, but stay close to me or with Brant." With a quick kiss, he's gone, leaving me wanting more.

Sasha giggles. "Chica, you guys are so in love, it's sick."

Brant nudges her at me, and I push her back into him with a laugh.

The stage gets crowded with DJs wanting to watch Maddox mix, and when Sasha wants to go get more alcohol, I tell her I'm going to stay on stage and hold our spots. Brant looks at me with concern. I know what he's thinking; he doesn't want her to go alone, being so drunk, but he doesn't want to leave me alone.

I give him the nod. "B, go with her and watch her. I'm right here with Maddox, and if anything happens, like a fight or something, I can get to him."

Seriously, there's like twenty-five feet between me and the DJ booth, with security on both sides of the stage. Brant doesn't move until Sasha says she'll be right back and almost trips. He grabs her arm, catching her and helping her move around the speakers and wires. It's trickier than usual because we ended up moving to the back corner of the stage so we could see Maddox and be out of everyone's way.

Once they're gone, I lean back against the speaker admiring…my man, my future, my love.

Maddox

The need to have Alexandria next to me is at a record high with the club overflowing with people. The stage has DJs from all over mingling around. I know Alex is safe behind me with Sasha and Brant, but still, this uneasiness comes over me.

I start to mix in "Let Me Think About It" by Fedde La Grand and Ida Corr, a song I know she loves to dance to. Once the song has dropped, I turn around to get her attention.

My stomach drops, and I lose my breath searching the stage. She isn't anywhere to be seen; only a handful of DJs from out of town are visible. I take my headphones off, and panicking, I turn to the sides of the stage, seeing security from the club that hasn't moved. I search the VIP, noticing Sasha and Brant are up there, but still no sign of her. She wouldn't leave the stage without telling me.

I scream "Alexandria" from the front of the stage, only to have the crowd scream back at me thinking I'm trying to pump them up. I look to Chad in a panic, but when I look over to Luc and he sees my face, I throw my hands up, shaking my head. "Do you have her? She's gone."

No, no, no... Please, God, let her be in the bathroom.

Ginger

Parking my bike behind the club in the alley under some darkened stairs, I turn the ignition off, still listening to Shy flip out on the phone. Micah "Shy" Jenkins is, or was, the love of my life, and he's also a member of my father's motorcycle club. I just sit there listening and not taking my helmet off since my Bluetooth is hooked up to it, and I don't want to hang up on him because it will only anger him more.

Goddamn, I don't need this fucking shit right now. Shy is always mad at me—the story of my life. If only it were like before. I miss him.

Twisting my upper body back and forth and stretching it out from the ride, I sit on my bike and try to relax before heading into the club. Since I've been back in the States, Shy seems to be calling me all the time, mostly to just bitch at me. But I would be lying if I said I didn't like hearing his voice, no matter why he's called.

Fuck, I'm so confused about what to do.

Frustrated with my life, I lose patience with his complaining, so I interrupt him. "Shy, I don't have time for this fucking shit. I'm late, and I don't need a goddamn lecture from you right now. I just drove up, and I need to get inside. They are all fucking pissed off and worried about me being alone. Now, can I call you later when I get home, or are we done?"

When Shy starts going off on a rant, I hear the back door to the club open with a bang. Being on alert with all this shit with Alex, I freeze, not moving but just sitting there quietly listening to Shy. Suddenly, I see a hooded man walk out, opening the door of a van parked a few feet away from me, and then turning to go back inside.

What the...

No one should be loading shit up out here. That door is only used to load and unload equipment. No one really knows about this back door to the stage besides the DJs, and that van doesn't belong to any DJ I know.

My stomach starts to hurt, which usually means something bad is going to happen. I seem to have a wicked sense, and when I get that gut feeling, I don't hesitate. I've always parked my bike here because it is hidden so no one will steal it. I jump off my bike, taking a few steps back into the darkened corner. I know my bike is out of sight, but just in case, I don't want to be seen.

Shy is still bitching about me not doing something, bringing me back to the phone call. I try to shush him, but he just keeps ranting. If only I could just shut him the fuck up, but I'm frozen in the corner. Thank God I'm dressed in all black, and my helmet is all black, covering my pasty-ass white skin. Maybe I'm overreacting, and someone is just loading DJ equipment. I'm sure I don't know every DJ who spins here.

Goddammit, Brant. He is making me fucking crazy, freaking me out over everything lately. Fuck!

Shy yells in the phone, "Are you fucking listening to me, Snow? Snow, goddammit, why are you so damn stubborn?"

Hearing Shy call me by my club name pulls me from my thoughts. Feeling stupid, I start to move out of the corner when I hear noises, and then I see the big man walk out.

Shit! Oh, my God...

The man is carrying Alex over his shoulder, out cold and just dangling there. Then he lays her down in the van.

Don't panic. Fuck.

I let out a gasp. Luckily, I have the helmet so the man can't hear, but Shy does. Shy turns serious. "What the fuck, Snow? Are you okay? What the fuck is going on? Dammit, Snow. Talk to me, angel." He pauses between each question, and I can hear the concern in his voice when he calls me by the nickname only he calls me, making me want to cry.

I watch the man move around in the van, but I can't see what he is doing. I try to swallow, but my mouth is so dry. I take in a big breath, but it sounds like a gasp. Shy yells, "Goddammit, Snow, are you in danger? What the fuck, I hear you."

I hear the commotion going on in the background, which I'm sure is Shy throwing shit or fucking shit up. But either way, I'm sure the whole clubhouse is aware something is going down with me. I hear him bark orders to someone to call Beau.

Please let Alex be okay. Fuck, what should I do? God, think, Gin. Think.

Not wanting to make a noise, I just stand there. My breathing becomes uneven with my nerves shot to hell, but I keep still, not making a sound. I just stand there watching this enormous hooded man doing something to my best friend—shit, my only girlfriend since Faith died—in the back of a fucking van.

Don't think about Faith right now. You need to think. Think like Ginger "Snow" Wolfe, not fucking DJ GinGin. Fuck.

I need to get my gun, but I don't want to make a noise. The man closes the van, looking up and down the alley. I hold my breath and pray he doesn't see me or my bike. When he finally jumps into the driver's seat, I take a breath.

Shy must be trying to listen because he is completely quiet. Then he says, "I hear you breathing, Snow. I hear a car door. I'm right here, angel."

The van starts up pulling out of the alley. I jump onto my bike and start it up, just going on instinct. Shy says, "I hear a car, your bike. Snow…" He says my name in a growl.

The van stops at the end of the alley, so I cut Shy off, yelling, "Goddammit, listen to me. Oh, God, Shy!" The last part sounds panicked.

Shy yells, "What the fuck is going on, Snow?" He's punctuating each word, trying to rein in his anger.

Damn, he is fucking pissed.

"Shut the fuck up. Listen. P-l-lease."

My "please" comes out shaky, letting Shy know I'm freaking out, so he goes quiet. "Shy, please, I can't explain everything, but I just saw someone take Alex in the back alley and throw her into a van. I was hidden, but I'm going to follow them. I need to call Brant and Beau. Please don't give me any shit and let me call them."

When the van turns the corner, I start my bike and head down the alley.

Shy is quiet for a second before speaking in a calm but stern voice. "Fuck. Snow, you fucking call me right back after you call them. I'm on my fucking way there. Fucking motherfucker. Please be safe, angel."

I pull out of the alley, seeing the gray van up the street at the light. My voice is still shaky. "Shy, please don't. I'll call the security team and lead them to where he's taking her. I have my gun and will stay back, so please don't worry. You won't be able to get here for several hours. It's not worth it to drive all the way for nothing. Brant and the team are here. I'll call you back."

Even more thrashing and men yelling goes on in the background, but all I hear is Shy breathing hard.

Fuck, he's pissed off.

A shiver runs through my body. Shy says through clenched teeth, "Snow, you're worth everything to me, angel. I'm coming for you whether you like it or not. If I hear one more fucking thing about this motherfucker Brant protecting you, I will fucking snap. It's time for you to come home to me and quit fucking around. I'll be there as soon as I can. And, Snow, please be safe. I can't lose you."

God, why now? This won't be good.

Tears are welling up in my eyes, but I hold them back. *Stay strong. I'm a fucking Wolfeman.* Before I can reply, he hangs up, leaving me overwhelmed and scared. Instantly, I call Brant, but it goes straight to voice mail. Then I try Beau's cell, but his goes straight to voice mail too.

Dammit. Someone answer their fucking phone.

Trying Brant again, this time, he answers on the first ring

with music blaring in the background. "Gin, I can't talk right now. We can't find Alex."

Hearing his voice, I lose it and scream into my helmet so he can hear me, "B, she was taken. She's in a van, and I'm following it."

Panicking that he can't hear me, I scream again, "Brant! Can you hear me? Alex was taken. I'm following the van."

When Brant starts cussing, it sends waves of relief flowing through me. Brant tells me to hold on. Maneuvering my bike, I stay a few cars behind, trying to keep far enough back so I can just see the van.

Brant will come. Alex will be safe. We have to save my best friend. I can't lose another best friend. Fuck. I start to repeat it over and over in my head to keep myself calm, but then I remember.

Fuck. Shy's coming for me. Focus, Snow-Ginger. God-dammit!

I stay on the phone, waiting for Brant, and concentrate on staying far enough back to keep an eye on the van but not be seen. I hear Brant yelling to Luc, Chad, Maddox, and whoever else is there. I can tell Brant is running by his heavy breathing, and once the music fades away, I know he's outside when he says, "Gin, baby, are you all right? Where are you? Tell me everything." I speed up once the light changes, telling Brant everything that just happened and what direction I'm headed.

Brant's barking orders to get the cars. Suddenly I hear Maddox flipping out, and with everyone screaming, I can barely hear anything, just men yelling. I stay on the phone, waiting for them to calm down. Brant is talking to Maddox, telling him what happened. Maddox doesn't understand how he got to her, so I yell at Brant to let me talk to him so he can work on the cars and I can calm Maddox down.

Once Maddox has the phone, he yells, "What the fuck happened, Gin?"

Taking a deep breath before talking, I say in a calm voice, "Maddox, I was parking my bike on the back side of the building in the alley that leads to the back of the stage. No one ever goes in or out that way, so it probably wasn't considered by security, but that is how he got to her."

Maddox starts cussing. "Gin, was she hurt or struggling?"

I hear him breathing heavily, so he is either running or going to have a panic attack. Trying to keep him calm, I answer in a soothing voice, "No, it looks like he drugged her because she was passed out and fully clothed. She must have been onstage, and he just snagged her from behind, maybe. I don't know. Who was onstage?"

Maddox pauses before he speaks. "She was sitting on the speaker by the back of the stage. There were a couple DJs, but they were all still there. Fuckin' hell! This is my fault. I wanted her up there with me. I thought she was safe. If something happens to her…"

He cuts himself off, and I know he is fighting his own demons right now, but he is pissing me off talking like that. "Don't fucking talk like that, Maddox. I'm right fucking here, and I will protect her. I have my gun, and I'm right behind them. Nothing is going to happen. Just get your fucking ass here. Ethan can track my fucking phone, so let's get off the phone, and you hurry the fuck up."

Maddox answers in a pained voice. "I just found her, Gin. Please don't lose her. I'm coming to get her. Please don't lose her." Then he hangs up.

My phone rings again. I answer it on the first ring, and I

hear Brant sounding like he's in pain, "Baby, please be careful. I'm coming. Don't engage unless you have to, but please just don't. We're all in the cars headed your way. Ethan has you on a tracker. Maddox's grabbing his bike at his hotel and heading your way. He will probably get to you a whole hell of a lot faster than we will. Stay safe, baby, I'm right behind you."

I can do this, goddammit.

When my phone rings again, it is Luc this time. "Gin, how're you doin', hun?"

Luc's calm with his dominant voice, and it soothes me, making me feel everything will be okay. Just like my dad's voice does when he is concerned.

I come to a stoplight. Sitting up to stretch and release some tension in my shoulders, I answer, "I'm okay. We are heading into the Holland Tunnel. It looks like he's going toward Jersey City, maybe? I don't fucking know. I wish he would just fucking stop. He's probably going to see me tailing him soon."

Taking a deep breath, Luc stays calm. "We're all behind you, so wherever he's going, hopefully, we'll be able to catch up with you soon. Gin, please don't do anythin' stupid. I can't lose both of you. Just tail them, and we'll find you. Oh, and, Gin, you should know your father is on his way with the club. He isn't too happy."

Luc sounds pained and stressed out, but my heart swells, knowing he cares about me and is taking the time to deal with me while his daughter has been taken.

Dammit, Shy.

"Thank you, Luc. I will try to get my dad to change his mind. He doesn't need to come out here. I won't do anything stupid, but I can't lose her either."

Luc laughs, "Yeah, I don't think that's fuckin' gonna happen, hun. I know I'd be here as fast as I fuckin' could if it were Alex in your shoes."

Once we hang up, I try to calm down so I can call my dad. Before I do, I see the van slow down. I try to stay back, but the guy changes lanes, taking a sharp turn to exit and making me slam on my brakes to make the exit.

Goddammit. Motherfucker, I was just made.

Alexandria

Darkness. Fear. And the smell of gasoline. Gasoline? I realize then that this isn't a dream. The sounds of horns mixed with the song "Creep" by Radiohead blare through the speakers.

Breathe, Alex. Calm down and think.

I try to remember what happened. My mind is foggy, but I remember being at the club, dancing, Maddox DJing, the hands over my face, pain, and then complete darkness.

Oh, God. I was drugged and taken.

This isn't a dream. I was actually taken! I start to hyperventilate, but then I take deep breaths, trying to calm down. My eyes are covered. I see flickers of lights but nothing else.

Don't panic. Breathe, Alex. Remember the training. Breathe.

Feeling the motion of the vehicle and seeing lights flicker, I know I'm in a van or an SUV of some kind. When I move my arms and legs, a razor-sharp pain shoots through my body, but most of the pain is coming from my head and shoulder. I whimper in pain, biting down on the cloth shoved into my mouth, and I try to keep from making too much noise. My wrists are bound together behind me, but my legs are loose. Taking deep breaths, I tell myself to stay calm because nothing good will come if I'm in a full-blown panic attack and I need to be in control.

Focus, Alex. Breathe. Brant, Maddox will come for me. Oh God, Maddox.

Thinking of Maddox, I close my eyes, letting the tears escape, only to dampen the cloth over my eyes. When I roll my body over onto my back, that is when I feel a body beneath me. I scream, but it comes out muffled with the fucking gag in my mouth. Realizing there is another person bound next to me, I panic. *Please don't let it be one of my girls.* I try to move closer, but the pain in my shoulder keeps me from moving too far. Feeling the person's hands that are bound, I notice they are large hands, a man's hands.

The vehicle slams on its brakes, making both of our bodies roll forward. I cry out in pain, but again, it's muffled by my gag. I hear horns honking along with grunts coming from the front.

Oh, God. Are we in a car chase? Maddox!

The car is making a bunch of sharp turns, and we hit several bumps, each one sending shooting pains throughout my body. I can't hold back the tears. The pain is becoming too much, and I feel like I'm going to pass out. Sweat is beading up on my forehead, and I cry out again for help, only to hear muffled sounds. When the car comes to a halt, jolting me forward, I land halfway on the other person. My face becomes wet lying on this other body.

Is it blood? Sweat? Water? Why isn't he moving?

Suddenly, the door opens to the side. I struggle to move away, crying out, only to have a pair of hands grab my legs, pulling me toward him. My kidnapper doesn't say a word; he just grunts when he throws me over his shoulder, and the pain becomes so unbearable, I pass out.

Ginger

Goddammit. I knew he was going to see me tailing him. He thinks he can lose me in these warehouses, but good luck with that, motherfucker. When I turn the sharp corner, the van is stopped right there in front of me, making me slam on my brakes and lose control of the bike.

Jesus Christ.

I've been in a crash before, so I react fast, laying the bike down and hoping not to crash into the van. Taking the first hit to the asphalt, which burns like hell, I roll and pray. When I stop rolling, I lie there still, hoping the guy doesn't get out of the van.

I say a silent prayer when I hear the van peeling out and taking off. Taking a deep breath, I lie there and evaluate my injuries. I try to roll over, but my shoulder and leg that hit the ground first are scraped up pretty bad. *Dammit to hell.* I roll over and push myself up onto my knees using my good arm, but feeling my leg and shoulder, I cry out in pain.

You need to get to Alex. Don't lose her, Gin. Hearing Maddox's voice in my head, I force myself to push the pain aside because I need to get up. *Push through the pain.* Rocking back on my heels and standing up, I let out a deep breath. Once I'm up, I take a second to gather myself before I grab my bike with my good arm and use the good side of my body to push my bike up. Once it's up, I throw my bad leg over, praying it'll start and that it's not too fucked up. I take another deep breath. I got this.

Push through the fucking pain. I must get to Alex. My prayers are answered when the sound of my bike's engine starts. Then I'm off.

After a few turns, I see the big warehouse in the distance with the doors open and the van inside. I slow down, trying to keep the bike quiet so they don't hear me approach. I park the bike a building over so I can sneak up.

I am a goddamn Wolfeman. Fucking suck it up and deal with this piece of shit. Hearing my Dad's voice in my head, I try to summon his energy. *Daddy, where are you?*

I hear the big warehouse doors closing, and I crouch down to hide just in case he looks around. It feels like forever before he gets the door low enough for me to move to the side door. Once the overhead door is closed, I wince, pulling myself up the door to listen. I hear the van door open followed by a few grunts, and the van door shuts again.

That is when I hear him. "I'm going to fucking kill you…" I open the side door slowly, slipping in, only to see two big stacks of crates. I lower myself and crawl, or, really, I drag myself behind them.

I hear Alex's muffled voice say, "Jason?"

Jason? She said, Jason. Holy shit. It can't be.

I try to peek around the crate, but they're even more stacks of crates. Jason speaks, "Alex? Is that you? What the fuck? We've been taken."

Alex cries out in a muffled voice, "Jason? Why?"

I can barely hear Alex, so she must have something in her mouth.

What the fuck... Was Jason kidnapped too? I didn't see him. It might be a setup.

I pull myself up slowly to stand up and start to shuffle around the crates when I see Jason sitting next to Alex. Both are tied up, blindfolded, but only Alex is gagged. I try to move closer, but I hear noises coming from the other side of the van. I crouch down, waiting until I can assess how many people are here. Then I see the man who took her. He pulls his hood off, and I finally see his face.

Son of a bitch...Emmett!

Alexandria

Jason? How's Jason here? What the fuck is going on? I don't understand.

The pain in my shoulder is throbbing to the extent of almost making me pass out again. I think I dislocated it. When I hear footsteps, I whimper, and when I feel a pair of hands caress my face, I start to cry out.

Jason hears me and growls, "Goddammit. If you hurt her, I'll fucking kill you."

When the kidnapper moves away from me toward Jason, I try to cry out to warn Jason, but it comes out muffled. "Watch out, Jason."

Silence. I try to calm down, but I hear Jason huff out, "Are you serious? I fucking knew you were up to something, Emmett. Why?"

Emmett? Holy shit. What? It has been Emmett all along. Rage builds inside of me, and I start to scream, still blindfolded and gagged. I hear Emmett laughing and making his way back over to me, taking my blindfold off and removing the gag. Overcome with anger, I flip out. "Emmett, are you fucking kidding me? What the fuck do you think you're doing? Why?"

Emmett's malicious laugh echoes through the warehouse. He takes a step back to Jason, pulling a gun out from behind his back. I scream, but Jason just sits there, staring Emmett straight in the eyes.

Emmett says viciously, "You couldn't stay away, could you? Did you think I was going to let you get your fucking hands on my girl? Do you know I was the first to take her sweet virgin pussy? I've been in her life for over eight years and have been watching her blossom."

What, eight years? He has been following me for eight fucking years. Shit.

"You've been trying to fuck up my shit for the last couple years now, trying to get me busted when I slipped those girls the roofies. Only, I was smarter and a few steps ahead of you. Now you'll pay for it, and you'll be blamed for Alex's kidnapping. All signs lead to you, motherfucker."

He turns to look at me, and Emmett's face softens with a smile. "Baby girl."

Emmett starts walking around me, running his free hand over my body and shaking his head in disapproval. "I told you I'd find you, anytime and anywhere. No matter what your Papá or your lover boy said, you'll always be mine, forever."

My body starts to shake, overcome with rage. I don't even panic but go on the defensive, hammering out questions. "E, why? When did this all start? Why me? Why wait all these years?"

Emmett moves to stand behind me, and with one hand, he

caresses my cheek, sliding my hair over to one shoulder while holding the gun in the other hand. Emmett's laugh comes out sinister, and he leans into my ear. "Alex, you have been my obsession for eight fucking years. I've been working with your father for seven years because I wanted to get closer to you. Seven fucking years, I have been his bitch just to get closer to you, and what did he do? He shipped you off to fucking Spain. Well, Luc will pay, I promise you that. Things are in motion to pay him back."

"Santa Maria! No! Please, Emmett, I'll do whatever you want. Just don't hurt anyone."

Jason finally speaks up. "Emmett, let's work something out."

Emmett is still leaning over with his face in my hair, smelling it and running his hands through it.

Jesus, he's fucking crazy. How did we not see this? Fuck. I need to stall him until Maddox and Brant find me. Please, God.

Emmett stands up straight and moves to stand in front of Jason, crossing his arms with the gun pointing at the ground. I watch as they stare at each other. I can tell Emmett is thinking hard with his jaw clenched together.

Shit. Fuck. Please don't hurt Jason. Please.

Emmett turns around and stands back in front of me. "Alex, I'm going to take you in the back. I don't think you'll want to see your good friend here die, do you?"

I cry out, "No, please, Emmett. Don't do this."

Emmett puts the gag back on me, muffling my cries. He goes to lift me by grabbing my bad arm where my shoulder is dislocated or broken, but when he grabs me, I cry out in pain. So much fucking pain, then darkness.

Ginger

When Emmett grabs Alex, she screams out in pain before passing out, and he throws her over his shoulder. Goddammit. Where are the fucking guys? I start to panic. *I can do this. I've been trained to do this. Pull it together, Snow.*

Jason starts yelling, "Put her fucking down, Emmett. I swear to God, if you hurt her, I'll..."

Emmett growls, cutting Jason off. "You'll, what? You think you can hurt me? Who do you think you are? You're a dead man. Say your last fucking prayers because when I get back, we'll have some fun before I kill you slowly."

Shifting Alex, Emmett turns to walk away. *Shit! Goddammit!*

I take a step out from behind the crates. Raising my good arm, I point my gun at him and shout out, "Put her fucking down right now, Emmett."

Emmett freezes, looking up and making eye contact, only to smirk at me. He laughs, turning back toward the chair Alex was sitting in, but he doesn't turn his back to me. He moves behind the chair, lowering her down the front of him and into the chair. Before she can slip out of it, Emmett grabs her shoulders, putting pressure on them to keep her sitting upright since she is still passed out cold.

Never taking his eyes off me, he chuckles with a chilling laugh. "I should have fucking known you wouldn't stay down, bitch. I should've made sure you were dead. It won't happen again, I promise." His gun is half drawn, and an evil grin spreads wide across his face, creeping me the fuck out.

I take a few more steps closer to him. "Emmett, drop your gun right fucking now. I don't want to shoot, but if you don't put it down, I will."

Jason yells, "Fucking shoot him, Ginger. He's a piece of shit that rapes girls and drugs them to have sex with him. Fucking pathetic if you ask me." Jason spits in Emmett's direction.

Goddamn, this fucking guy has a death wish.

Emmett laughs, but he doesn't lower his gun. He moves a couple feet around Alex and just stands there in front of Jason, who is between us. I take a couple more steps closer, ignoring the pain in my leg and shoulder.

Emmett is taunting me, "Come a little closer, Ginger. Please join the party."

We both have our guns drawn with Jason between us. He hasn't said a fucking word. *Think, Gin. Just relax. Hang on until the guys get here.*

Before I know it, Emmett jumps to the side, and in seconds, he's blasting his gun at the same time I do. I jump out of the way when Alex screams, and Jason jumps up, screaming, "No!" He gets in front of Emmett's gun and goes down. I hit the floor hard, still unloading my gun in Emmett's direction. I feel my head split in pain all the way down my body. Emmett goes down too, but I can't see if he's dead. Pain starts to consume me, leaving me light-headed, so I lean my head back on something. I think I can hear Jason or maybe Emmett moaning.

Fuck, is he dead? God, please don't let Alex be hurt. Please God, not again.

I try to sit up, but the pain is too much. I try to roll over, but even more pain jolts through my body, making me feel faint. I lay my head back down, and everything starts to go black. *Alex!*

Maddox

We arrive at the warehouse and see Ginger's bike. Once we're off our bikes, we hear gunshots. *Fuck. Please God, no*. Rushing the warehouse, we flip open the side door to see three people on the ground. I hear Alexandria crying from behind a chair on the ground. *Thank God she's alive.* When we move closer, I see Jason and Ginger both bleeding from gunshot wounds, but neither is moving. I look over to see a trail of blood. I motion for Austin and Roc to handle Jason and Ginger, and Chad goes to follow the blood trail while I head to Alexandria.

When I reach Alexandria, I pull her gag out to hear what she is saying. She cries out, begging me, "Maddy, please. Please save them. Please, they protected me. Please..." She can barely move, and she breaks down in my lap. When I unbind her hands, she screams out in pain. I can see her shoulder is messed up, but I don't know if it's broken or not. She tries to get up again but falls back down, crying in pain.

Goddammit. "Alexandria, don't move. You're hurt pretty bad. Please sit still and let me look." Alexandria shakes her head no, sobbing and looking over at Ginger and Jason.

Son of a bitch.

"Alexandria, lean into me, love. I'll carry you over there. Then you need to let me check you out. Hold on."

I reach around her and lift her up to carry her over to Ginger. I place her next to Roc and Austin, who are working on Ginger.

Alexandria cries out, "No. No. No. Please don't die. I need you. Please."

Austin is on his phone with 911 while Roc tries to stop her bleeding. I look over to Jason and back to Roc, who just shakes his head no. "Fucking hell!" Alexandria holds Ginger's hand, crying and telling her to hold on. I bend down and try to help Roc, but I hear Chad holler my name to come quickly. Still high on adrenaline, I jump up, grabbing my gun, and I head toward Chad. I find him dragging a large body toward us. *Goddammit.*

When I reach him, I see who it is. Emmett. "Motherfucker! Is he breathing?"

I point my gun at his face. When he looks up at me, he smiles, and before he can say anything, I punch him. I hear the door open and the rest of our group flooding in. Luc searches the area and sees Alexandria. He rushes over to her, but she won't release Ginger's hand, still sobbing uncontrollably. Brant freaks out once he sees Ginger as well, pushing everyone out of his way. He lifts her head yelling at her to wake up. Fuck, I have never seen him lose control before.

When I walk around the corner, I yell out for Luc. When he looks up, I give the nod, letting him know he needs to come follow me. When I turn around, I hear Emmett laughing. I try to hold back the urge to kill him, well, at least until Luc sees him. From where Luc is standing, he can't see who it is, but I know he is going to freak the fuck out. Emmett was his golden boy, and all along, he was right under his nose. Fuck, I should let him kill the motherfucker.

When Luc is on his way over, I shout, "Brace yourself, man. It's not gonna be good." Luc is tense all over with all his muscles flexed and bulging out like he is getting ready for a cage fight.

Luc looks down and sees it's Emmett, and he loses all control. I step back to give him room to do what he needs to do.

Luc's enraged. "I fuckin' loved you like a son." Luc lands a couple of punches to Emmett's face. "You fucked me over, and you fuckin' took my baby girl's virginity against her will." Luc kicks him in the balls and ribs. Then everyone goes quiet when they see Emmett laughing.

He looks up, laughing at us with blood dripping out of his mouth, "She was so worth it. She's mine and will always be mine. From the day I met her, she was always the one, and fuck you for taking her away from me. You'll get what's coming. She will alwa—"

A gun goes off, making everyone jump back and pull their guns, only to find Alexandria holding the gun with one hand. She unloads what is left in the clip into Emmett.

What the fuck? Where did she get that fucking gun? Son of a bitch, she can shoot.

Through gritted teeth, Alexandria spits out, "I'm *not* yours anymore, you sick fuck." I let out a deep breath before moving to her side and taking the gun from her hands. I pull her into an embrace, holding her arm in place.

Fuck, is it bad that I'm so fucking turned on right now? Mine. All mine.

The ambulance and the police arrive a few minutes later. They load up Ginger right away, and thank God, she's still breathing, but it's faint due to the amount of blood she is losing. Brant is telling Alexandria he's going in the ambulance with Ginger, but Alexandria is trying to fight them. The paramedics are trying to hold Alexandria down when Luc steps in, calming her down.

Chad yells my name, so I head over to him while Alexandria talks to her father. Walking over to Chad, I see his face, making me clench my jaw. He knows something, and by the looks of it, I'm not going to like it. *Motherfucker, now fucking what?*

In a growl, I ask, "What now?"

Chad and the gang just shake their heads, but Chad points to the big metal shipping container. "That motherfucker is lucky he's dead. Take a look for yourself, but hold your nose. It smells pretty bad."

Chad tells Roc to get the police. I walk over to the container, opening the door only to find four more dead bodies of young girls around the age of twenty-one and all with the same features as Alexandria.

"Jesucristo!"

Chad is moving down toward a hallway off to the side of the warehouse. He points. "Emmett was dragging himself this way, as you can see. This is where I found him, but I think he was trying to get over here."

We all head over to a long hallway with about six doors.

We each start to open doors, only to find empty beds in each room. But in the last two rooms, we find two girls knocked out and chained to the beds. *Fuck.*

Chad is helping one girl get unchained while Austin checks her vitals. I make my way over to the other room, and the police come running down the hall. I stride into the other room where Ethan is holding a girl in his lap, rocking her. He nods that she's okay and he has everything under control when I hear a gasp from behind me. I turn to see Alexandria with her shoulder wrapped, holding her hand over her mouth.

Tears are building up in her eyes, and she speaks in a cracked voice. *"Dios ayúdame!" God help me.* "They all look like me. These are the girls who went missing from the club last week. Oh, my God."

I see the panic in her eyes, so I move to try to embrace her. "Alexandria, this is not your fault. Emmett was a sick motherfucker, and this was not your fault." I hug her tight, but she starts to sob again. I continue to rub her back, and I kiss her head. "I love you, *mi amor.* I thank God you're okay. If I would have lost you…"

Alexandria pulls back, crying. "This is all because of me. He couldn't have me, so he fucking tortured these girls. If something happens to Ginger, I don't know what I will do. She is one of my best friends."

I look down at her with sympathetic eyes. "Alexandria, you can't blame yourself. He was a sick fucking guy. Ginger will be okay. She's in good hands. Let's get you out of here and head over to the hospital."

Moving Alexandria into my side while we walk back to the ambulance, I look around for her father. "Where's Luc?"

Alexandria replies, "He went with Brant and Ginger. He's

her next of kin until her father gets here. Plus, he knew you'd be riding with me in the ambulance."

We reach the ambulance, and they start to put Alexandria on one of the stretchers. I see Austin is on his phone, so I walk over. He gets off, not looking too happy. "That was Isaac, he's tripping out. They said three other girls went missing to-night, but they're not here. So I don't know if Emmett was working with someone or what, but it doesn't look good." *Fuck, is there someone else after my girl?*

I try to act calm because I know Alexandria is watching me right now, and I don't want to add to her anxiety. In a low voice, I say, "Well, go and let Chad know what's going on. Have someone monitor this place. We need to get someone over to Emmett's house and search it before the cops do. You know the drill. We leave nothing untouched. I'm heading over to the hospital with Alexandria. Call me with updates and have one of your guys get Ginger's and my bike over to the hotel."

Alexandria is quiet when I climb into the ambulance. I grab her hand and lean over to kiss her. Soft sobs escape her as I caress her cheek, wiping away the tears. "Everything is going to be okay. Hold on, we'll be there soon. Don't worry. Ginger is going to be okay."

Alexandria

Riding in the back of the ambulance, all I can think about is Ginger. *Please let her be okay.* I don't know what I'll do if I lose her. She protected me, and Jason died for me. Fuck, if only I could have talked Emmett down or something. *Emmett was a psycho. He was a serial killer.*

I'm trying to talk myself out of feeling guilty, but I'm not doing a good job. I could have done something, couldn't I? *Jesus, those girls.* I can't get them out of my mind, but when the EMT sticks me in the arm, that pain brings me out of my trance. *Shit. Fuck, that hurt.*

The EMT rewraps my shoulder and arm to my body and tells me I have dislocated it pretty badly. I may even have a fracture, but we won't know until we get X-rays. He'd just given me a shot for the pain. *Great, knock me out. Fuck.*

When we arrive at the hospital, they unload me and head into the emergency room, where Papá is standing right inside on his phone. His face is as red as the blood on his shirt. He barks out, "Wolfe…just fuckin' get here. She's in surgery right now, and it'll be a few more hours before we know anythin'."

When Papá puts his phone back in his pocket, he turns to see us approaching. He squeezes the hand I extend to him so tightly I gasp. "Papá, it's going to be okay."

Not letting go, he groans, "I almost lost you, and he was right under my nose the whole time."

I lean back on the gurney with tears in my eyes, and I try to tell him about the girls. "Papá, it got worse after you left…"

He looks down at me and then over to Maddox. "What do you mean after I left? What did you do?"

Papá looks over, keeping his glare on Maddox. I reach up, pinching his chin and turning his face to look down at me. I take a deep breath before I try to speak in a calm voice. "Papá, the girls…" I start sobbing, not able to finish.

Maddox rubs my leg, trying to calm me down, and finishes for me. "Emmett was a serial killer. We found girls' bodies in an old shipping container, and we found rooms with beds in them. Then we found two girls alive, still chained up to beds."

Papá's grip on my hand tightens. "What are you sayin?"

Maddox moves his hand, placing it on the back of my neck before continuing. "What we're trying to tell you is the girls who went missing this week from the clubs were found tonight. Two were alive, and two were dead, along with two other unidentified girls."

Papá releases my hand, taking a step back in shock. Maddox replaces Papá's hand with his to comfort me before he speaks. "We have our teams working on it right now, searching Emmett's house and looking for any known relatives.

There's more…" Papá's head snaps up with a murderous look on his face. Maddox continues, "There were three more girls reported missing tonight from the club, and they were not found in the warehouse. So, either someone was working with Emmett, or he did something with them before snagging Alexandria and Jason."

I cry out. "What?" *No, not more girls.*

Maddox leans forward, kissing the top of my head. "I found out right before I got into the ambulance."

God, I love this man. He's so strong and loves me. Fuck, what did I do to deserve him in my life? I squeeze Maddox's hand with a small smile.

I look over at Papá standing there in shock, not moving. I'm about to reach for him when he bursts out, "*Madre stronzo!* I can't fuckin' believe this shit. All along this *cazzo* was right next to me the whole fuckin' time."

Papá runs his hand through his hair, and I can tell he's trying to keep his temper in check but failing. I just lie there not saying anything, just letting him take it all in, when a nurse comes over to take me back to have my shoulder checked out. Maddox and Papá start to go with me, but I tell Papá to stay and wait for news about Ginger. I tell him I'll be okay, and Maddox will get him if I need him. My head starts to get heavy from the pain medicine the EMT gave me.

Just as we're heading down the hall, a nurse comes out, asking for Papá. "Mr. Mancini? You're Ginger Wolfe's relative, correct?"

Papá turns immediately, rushing to her. "Yeah, I'm her guardian until her father gets here."

The nurse stops, and all of us gather around her. That's when I notice Brant. He looks like he just saw a ghost and is in shock. *Jesus, he looks worse than me.* Brant's hair is always short and neatly groomed, but since all this has been going on, he has let it grow some. Right now, it's a mess. He is as white as a ghost, and his eyes give him away, letting me know how much he cares for her.

The nurse's voice snaps me out of my observation. "Okay, well, she's still in surgery and will be in surgery for quite some time. She pulled through the first part of the operation well, where they stopped the bleeding and removed three bullets. One from her right shoulder, one from her right leg, and one on her right side near her ribs. She lost a lot of blood from the bullets, but she has a whole series of injuries we think came from what looks like a bike accident. They are working on her left leg and left shoulder. They look to be broken and with some pretty bad road rash, like she went down hard on her left side. She has some swelling in the brain, we are monitoring that as well. I'll know more details regarding the leg and shoulder when they are done, but she's stable and doing well so far. I'll be back when I know more."

We all say "Thank you" at the same time, and when the nurse leaves, we turn to each other.

I start to cry when Maddox leans over onto the stretcher to hold me in an embrace. "Alexandria, see? Everything is going to be okay." Maddox places a light kiss on my forehead, and I close my eyes, absorbing his love with a moan in response.

Opening my eyes, I see Brant and Papá talking. Brant is flexing like he's going to freak out on Papá. I want to go to them, but the nurse starts to push me toward my room. Maddox sees my concern but tells me, "Don't worry, baby. Your father is telling Brant what we just told him about the warehouse. Give him a few minutes. I know this is hard on both of them. Having Emmett right under their nose, and they didn't know—it's a hard pill to swallow."

Taking a deep breath, I lean my head back on the pillow and look up at Maddox. "Maddy, I love you so much. Thank you for coming after me."

He squeezes my hand, "*Mi amor*, I would be lost without you, so you need to get used to me being around because I'm not going anywhere. And I will always come for you."

I lean back and think about what Maddox said. He's right, and I knew my papá wouldn't handle it well. But Brant almost lost both of us girls too, and he's my security. I can only imagine how he's feeling right now. Brant stomps off out the emergency room doors, clenching his fist. Papá turns back to us with a strained expression, running his hands through his disheveled hair.

Not able to hold in my tears anymore, I start to sob. Maddox rubs my head while we roll down the hallway. Once I'm settled in my room, the nurse tells us the doctor will be in soon, then she leaves us. The door closes, and Maddox sits on the stretcher, facing me. God, he is beautiful. Even looking as worried as he does, he is still stunningly handsome. He reaches up to caress my face when the door opens and in walks Brant.

Letting go of Maddox's hand, I reach for Brant and am sobbing by the time he gets to my other side. He leans down to embrace me, trying to calm me down. "Alex, it's going to be okay. You're safe now, and that fucking bastard will never touch you again."

He's rubbing my back, trying to soothe me, and I pull back to look up into his face. "B, they all died because of *me*. If I would have lost Gin too, I don't know what I would have done."

Brant's face tightens and his jaw clenches when he grips my hand tighter. In a murmur, he says, "I don't know what I'd do if I lost her either." I look up and see his sparkling golden eyes. *Jesus, he really cares about her. Shit.*

"B, why didn't you tell me you two were seeing each other?"

He laughs, and it's a full-hearted laugh, looking from me to Maddox. "Alex, we're not dating. That woman is so complicated, it drives me insane. It's not like I haven't tried to tie her down, but she's just untamable. If I had my way, we would be together, but she said she isn't ready."

We both laugh because we both know our Ginger is her own person and so headstrong. *God, I love her.*

The doctor walks in, and Brant lets us know he will be back to check on me. All I want to do now is sleep, but instead, I get to deal with my pain.

Ginger

I hear people yelling and loud beeping sounds. *Fuck, the pain.* The fucking pain is all over my body. Holy shit! It hurts. I let a moan escape me, and then I hear more commotion. I hear men arguing. *Where am I, and why can't I open my eyes?* Then it's silent, but the loud beeping continues. *Try to remember: Shy, the club, Emmett, Jason, Alex. Oh, God, is Alex alive?*

Beeping. Loud beeping. Blackness.

I hear an angel, and I feel her touching my hand, but the loud beeping is still here. God, the pain. The pain is still here. Fuck! Then I hear her voice again. "Gin, please come back to me. Please. I need my best friend." *I can't open my eyes.* Fuck, it hurts. *Is that Faith or Alex? Where am I?*

Fuck the pain and that loud beeping. *The fucking beeping needs to stop.* I still hear her voice and then silence.

I feel rough hands on my arm, caressing me. I feel his breath on my neck. *Am I imagining him*? Is it really him?

"Angel, come back to me. I can't lose you. I love you, Snow. It's always been you."

Shy. He came for me. I need to open my eyes. Am I dreaming? Fuck the gods, damn pain. Why am I in so much pain? I feel his lips on me, placing small kisses all over me, and then he lands on my lips. Fuck, I have missed him. I have missed his smell and his touch. The pain is too much. Fuck, the beeping again, then darkness.

"I'm not fucking leaving, not until she wakes up." *Brant...he's here for me. Wait, was I dreaming about Shy? Are Brant and Shy here together? Shit, this isn't good. Please let me open my eyes. Why can't I open my eyes?*

I moan in frustration, and the room goes quiet except for that fucking beeping. *Am I dreaming?* Then I feel hands all over me, on my arms, legs, and one on my head. *Fuck, who is here?* I have to be in a hospital. I feel more alert this time, but I can't open my eyes, and then the darkness consumes me again.

I hear her voice... *My angel.* When I go to move my hand, I feel someone holding it. I squeeze, hoping they will feel it, and I hear a gasp. "She fucking moved. Snow? Angel? Do you hear me?" I moan in response since I can't seem to talk.

Then my angel talks, "Gin, it's Alex. Please open your eyes." *Alex is my angel's voice. Fuck, she is good.* I try to open my eyes with a flutter. The pain shoots straight through my head. Fuck, I let out another moan, and the fucking beeping starts up. *Dammit.*

"Angel, you need to relax. You're okay. You're in the hospital, but you need to relax. You had a bad fall, hitting your head. Snow, please relax. We're all here for you. Just know you're okay and safe. Angel, we got you."

I feel a tear slide down my face. *My boys are here. I'm truly safe.* I try to grab his hand again, hoping he feels it, letting him know I heard him. "Angel, I felt that. I know you can hear me. Rest, Angel, we're not going anywhere." Joy fills me before the silence.

Alexandria

I sit there watching Shy, this big-ass scary biker, hold Ginger's hand. *Jesus, this man is fucking fine as hell. What was Gin thinking, leaving him?* I'm finding all kinds of things out about my girl these days. Ginger and I are so much alike it is scary. We both keep so much inside, secret from the world. Ginger is like two different people. You have this amazing, stubborn, funny, mad-talented DJ, and then you have this badass biker chick who will beat the shit out of you and has a club of men that bows down to her.

The mayhem that has happened over the last few days has been crazy. Brant and Shy are about ready to kill each other over Ginger. Her father and my papá went head-to-head until her father met me. I cried to the big-ass biker and told him everything and that she is one of my best friends. I guess it softened him up a bit. I think he's still going to ream Ginger's ass when she wakes up. He's one scary fucker.

Ginger is heavily sedated because she fell after getting shot, hitting her head pretty good, and had some swelling. It's been three days that she has been out of it. I know she can hear us just with the little signs here and there. When Shy stormed through the door, followed by ten men, I understood why they all call her Snow White. She was raised by all these men, and she's their princess. I fucking love it, and now I know why Ginger is so badass. These men would kill for her, and I just don't understand why she left. I don't know what's going on between her and Brant or her and Shy, but I would hate to be her when she wakes up to two angry men. I'll be here to help her out, for sure.

That leads me to Maddox and me, and we're doing really good. I had a pretty badly dislocated shoulder with a hairline fracture, along with a concussion. I was put in a sling and given lots of painkillers. They kept me overnight to make sure my head was okay. Halfway through the night they just released me because I kept sneaking out of my room to check on Ginger. So I have been camped out in Ginger's room ever since, and no one is getting me to leave, not even these wolfman bikers.

Maddox was by my side until I was released, but I refused to leave the hospital. He was very leery of leaving me since I was so upset about Jason dying and Ginger being in the hospital. I cried myself to sleep the first couple nights.

Maddox and his team have been helping in the investigation. They still haven't found the other missing girls. With Emmett gone, I think everyone feels my life isn't in danger anymore, so they have been giving me some leeway. I only have one bodyguard instead of ten. Maddox fought with me for a day, trying to talk me into going home with him, but I said I needed to stay here for when Ginger wakes up.

Jason's death was big news. A bunch of clubs canceled their parties out of respect for him, and this weekend is his funeral with a huge party scheduled for Saturday night in honor of him. I'm doing pretty well, considering everything that has happened. Crying and releasing my grief those first few days helped me, along with Ginger's improvement each day. I'm ready to move forward with my life and follow my music career and pursue my relationship with Maddox. With him by my side, I have more courage and self-esteem than ever before. I just need my girl here to wake up.

Shy moving pulls me from my thoughts, and he sits back down next to the bed, still holding her hand. I start singing again, trying to wake her. Lately, it seems when I sing, she tries to wake up. Shy closes his eyes, leaning back in the chair. Shy is the complete opposite of Brant. Brant has more of a body builder type body with upper body muscle, hazel eyes, clean-cut hair, and is an overall pretty boy, I guess you could say. Shy, on the other hand, is all bad boy. Jesus, the man reeks of sex on a fucking stick. He has light golden-brown hair in a shaggy length that curls up in the back and hangs slightly in his face. Tattoos peek out of his T-shirt that is under his leather cut, and goddamn, he's ripped all over. Even his forearms are muscular. His pants hang just right, showing off his rock-hard ass, and believe me, I have looked a few times since he has been bending over, whispering in Ginger's ear. It's right there, so fuck, I should look, right? I think I'm attracted to him because he reminds me of my Maddy boy. Except, of course, my man is probably three inches taller. Since Maddox isn't here and Ginger is sleeping, I'm taking the opportunity to check out her man since she didn't tell me he was this hot. I mean, she told me about her one true love. But, fuck me, Ginger, why did you leave this fine-ass specimen of a man behind? Don't get me wrong, I love Brant like a brother, and he's one badass motherfucker, but they're like complete opposites. I don't get it. *Dammit, wake up, Gin. I need you, girl.*

I'm trying to write a song, but I'm way too preoccupied and I just can't seem to get anything down. I look up from my paper, and I see Ginger's eyes flicker open.

I jump off the windowsill, holding my shoulder but still singing, or more like half humming. Shy must hear me jump down because he opens his eyes then jumps up himself. We both stand on either side of her bed, and when I grab her other hand, Ginger's eyes flicker open again.

I gasp, and Shy whispers in a sexy, sinful voice, "Angel, you here, baby?" Ginger squeezes both of our hands. Shy and I look up at each other, smiling, before we look back down to see her amazing green eyes looking back at us.

"Welcome back, girl. We have missed you!" We both get a squeeze from her again. I push the call button, and within minutes, a nurse rushes in, followed by Brant.

Well, shit. This should be interesting.

Alexandria

4 Months later

Lights are flashing all around me as I lift my head to see the wave of people throw their hands in the air when I drop my first song. My heart is pounding with excitement, filling up with so much joy. I start to bounce while I play, with the mixer adding effects. The club we're at in San Francisco is one of the top one hundred clubs in the world. Our group has packed the place with a sea of people moving to the beat.

When I feel arms slide around my waist, I don't panic because those days are a long gone. I know it is Maddy coming up to bounce around while I mix. We've been DJing for three months on the road. Things between Maddox and me have only gotten better. Our love for each other is stronger and hotter than ever. Daily, he pushes my limits in everything I do, making me love him that much more.

We took time off after everything that happened. Once Ginger was released, Maddox wanted me to go with him to Italy to see his mom and then make a stop at his house in Spain to regroup before we headed out on our tour. He was worried I was holding back my emotions and that killing someone would affect me sooner rather than later. I kept telling him I was fine and that I finally had closure on something I hadn't had control over. Not knowing what happened to me or who did it was the main source of panic I had. I still get panic attacks when we are in a tight crowd, but that has to do with being claustrophobic.

Ginger was released to her father after she woke up. He took her back home to heal from all of her injuries. She wasn't too happy about that, but her father can be very scary. When a woman named Storm came to visit Ginger, she cried, which shocked me because I'd never seen her cry. She has always been a badass in my eyes, and was usually yelling at people.

After Storm came, Ginger quit fighting about leaving with them. I didn't make a fuss or ask any questions because I knew she'd tell me when she was ready. I mostly stuck by her side so she knew I was there for her. Whenever I'd go to leave and try to give her time with her visitors, she would get pissed and tell me to sit my ass down. I think we both were leaning on each other for emotional support.

When the fight broke out between Brant and Shy, I didn't know what to do but worry about Ginger and her head injury. Instead, Ginger just sat up in bed and yelled for both of them to get the fuck out, and she didn't want to see either one of them. Brant just walked out, looking torn and hurt, but Shy rounded on her, telling her she needed to think again if she thought he was going to leave her side. She told him to get the fuck out of her room, or she would call her father in to remove him. He left the room, but he stayed planted outside her door like a watchdog.

Since she left, we've talked almost every day, and our talks are mostly how pissed she is about not DJing with us. But next week, she'll be finally joining us in Los Angeles for the last three months of our tour. I can't wait, and I miss my friend.

Maddox, who is still behind me, moves in closer to me, rubbing his cock against my ass and slipping his hands to my waist while thrusting into me. I laugh, turning around to push him away before using my finger to tsk-tsk him, telling him no. I draw an imaginary line between us before I turn back around, laughing. The music is so loud I can't hear him, but I bet my life that he's crossing his arms and growling at me. I'll pay for that later tonight with a good old spanking.

I start to bounce around again, and the crowd loves us. We play-fight on stage all the time and perform for the crowd. We love it. The way the crowd loves us and our music just fills my soul with a happiness I have never felt before. Maddox moves next to me, getting his music ready to go on next.

When I see Brant and Gus telling Sasha something in VIP, I can tell they're giving her shit about something. Ginger might not be here, but Sasha has given these boys a run for their money. She's just as fearless. Brant came with us on tour after Ginger left. He was a mess and wanted to get back to work.

Gus and Brant are the only two security guys from my papá's team, but we have all of Maddox's men with us. My papá said regardless of how many men Maddox had, he will always have one of his guys with me. I was shocked when Gus wanted to come with us, but he said he has been protecting us girls for so long, he would feel weird doing anything else.

Izzy and Dominic are with us as well on tour, even though they don't hang out much. They always slide in before they have to DJ and leave right after. Maddox says to leave them alone, that they're still trying to figure each other out and build their relationship. I don't agree, and I think they fight way too much.

When Maddox's team crashed Emmett's place, that was when we realized Emmett and Dominic were roommates. At first, everyone thought he was in cahoots with Emmett, but during the investigation, it was proven that Dominic had nothing to do with it. Every night that something happened or girls went missing, he was always with Izzy. Since then, Dominic has kept his distance, feeling we still blame him for what Emmett did.

The police investigation ended after that since they had no leads and the girls they found in the rooms confirmed by a photograph, that Emmett was the only one who came into contact with them. They didn't know who took them as they had been drugged. We couldn't figure out what he was doing with them. We do know he had sex with them and kept drugging them. All we could come up with was that he would use them, acting like they were me, and then dumped them once he'd drugged them up too much.

Finally, after all of the madness ended, we could all breathe again. Maddox stopped being so overprotective and possessive. I guess he felt better knowing Emmett was dead. Our relationship has only blossomed, getting better and better every day.

When Maddox turns from me, he slips his shirt off, making the crowd go nuts. He throws his shirt at me, flexing his muscles. *Jesus, this man lights my fire every time. Fucking gorgeous.* I bite my lip with a devious smile. Things with Maddy are never boring and I know they never will be.

The End

Coming soon…

Ginger

Book Two - Spin It Series

Alexandria: The Playlist

"Da Bump" by Mr. V, Miss Patty

"Satisfaction" by Benny Benassi, The Biz

"Like A Roller" by Tomcraft

"Tonight" by John Legend, Ludacris

"Hold On, We're Going Home" by Drake, Majid Jordan

"Your Body" by Tom Novy

"Is It Love" by iio featuring Nadia Ali

"Let Me Think About It" by Ida Corr, Fedde Le Grand

"Creep" by Radio Head

"I Know What You Want" by Busta Rhymes, Mariah Carey

"World, Hold On" by Bob Sinclair feat. Steve Edwards

"Put Your Hands Up For Detroit" by Fredde Le Grand

"Show Me Love" by Robin S

"My Joy" by Quentin Harris, Margaret Grace

"Playing With My Heart" by Jose Nunez, Shawnee Taylor

"Destination Calabria" by Alex Gaudino feat. Crystal Waters

"Infinity 2008" by Guru Josh Project, Klaas Gerling

"All of Me" by John Legend, Jason Agel remixed by Tiesto

"Better Off Alone" by Alice Deejay

"Call On Me" by Eric Prydz

"Blame" by Calvin Harris, John Newman

For more songs, follow the *Alexandria* playlist on Spotify:

bit.ly/AlexandriaPlaylist

About the Author

Crazy, outgoing, adventurous, full of energy and talks faster than an auctioneer with a heart as big as the ocean... that is Angera. A born and raised California native, Angera is currently living and working in the Bay Area. Mom of a smart and sassy little girl, an English bulldog, two Siamese Cats and a fish named Red. She spends her days running a successful law firm but in her spare time enjoys writing, reading, dancing, playing softball, spending time with family and making friends wherever she goes. She started writing after the birth of her daughter in 2012 and hasn't been able to turn the voices off yet. The Spin It series is inspired by the several years Angera spent married into the world of underground music and her undeniable love of dirty and gritty romance novels.

Acknowledgements

Over the last three years, so many people have had a part in making this book a reality so please forgive me if I miss anyone.

First and foremost, I want to thank my family but most importantly my parents. They are my biggest fans and supporters. My mom has and will always be my biggest cheerleader and my best friend. She is always pushing me to do better and is always asking what I need to move forward. With daily phone calls to keep me grounded, I don't know where I would be today without her. Also, a big thank you to my Aunt Debbie for always being there for me and always being up for traveling with Mom and me.

To my first group of beta readers: Marlena S., Katie J., Sarah F., Jeriann O., Tawnya R., Christine F. and Heather E. who got the raw, unedited, fucked up version with over ten thousand grammar errors and still read it all those years ago, told me I had a story to tell and for pushing me to do more with it, thank you!

Marlena Salinas, my partner in crime and soul sister. I could be here all day listing all the things you have done for me throughout the years. You are my spiritual ground, and you always help me lighten my soul when it is full. You've been my main support throughout writing this book, helping me develop Alexandria's story and even helping me write my damn biography. I am so thankful for your true friendship. I love you Mar.

Katie Joaquin, my lifetime friend, without you I wouldn't have been introduced to this world of smutty books. Between you and Sara sharing book recommendations, how could I not become addicted? I knew from the first time you and Dave took me to my first book signing in San Francisco I was hooked and wanted in.

To all my guy friends who read parts of the book (yes, the sex scenes) and gave me advice from a male point of view: J.Saliani, L. Elliott, J. Fay., R. Foley, N. Llama and my best friend J. Franklin, thank you.

To my bitches: Melissa S., Evie L., Erin C., Camisha C., Dawn B., Rebecca R., Lisa V., and Nicole F. you have listened to me bitch, cry, laugh and lose my fucking mind but no matter what you have had my back and lifted me up. With all my heart, thank you.

Jennifer Ramsey, thank you for listening to me ramble on our late night phone calls. From helping me decorate my house, character building or just letting me vent, you are always there for me. I pray one day we can meet in person but no matter what you are a sister for life because seriously if you can keep up in a texting conversation with me while I've been drinking (not making any fucking sense) you are my soul sister. Love ya girl!

To Author Chelsea Camaron and Author Nicole Edwards and so many other authors, thank you for helping to guide me in the right direction with all the questions I throw at you, holding my hand, guiding me and overall walking me through this whole process.

Author Leela Lou Dahlia, girl I probably would have had a nervous breakdown if it wasn't for you and our voice messaging. You have helped me so much and guided me along step by step. Love ya girl!

Author Chelle Bliss, my secret sister. You have been so amazingly awesome with the book recommendations and helpful hints. I will be forever grateful for your friendship and love. Meeting you on the Book Splash, 2016 Cruise was epic. I will never forget it, both you and Brian will always have a place in my heart.

Author Harper Sloan, girl you have been an idol for me for years. From meeting you in San Diego 2015 to Book Splash 2016, you've sealed the deal of your awesomeness in my eyes. You have such a big heart and give so much to everyone. You have helped me and guided me whenever I have asked or needed it, and I can't thank you enough for that. You and your bestie, Author Felicia Lynn, have both been there for me and I am grateful for your friendship. You two are so much fun and all the love and support you give people is truly a blessing.

Gina Kast, thank you for helping me put together my logos and graphic ideas throughout the years. Jessica Quintal, thank you for all the years we have been doing photo shoots together. You have always captured the most gorgeous shots. Love you both

To my editors, Lisa Hollett, thank you for ripping off the bandaid and putting everything into perspective for me. Teaching me and guiding me in the right direction of being a better writer. Thank you so much for being so awesome and always answering me when I needed help. Emma Mack, thank you for helping me calm the storm.

Kate Newburg, my one stop shop girl! Thank you for understanding me and making my dream come to life with the website, graphics, and formatting. I am so glad you were there to hold my hand through this process, and I can't wait to start on the next one.

To my book splash (2016) crew. The trip that put this all into motion. April R., Dawn R., Scheva H., Michelle W., Lindsey B., Kim H. and most important my exit buddy Nicole F. This trip came during a very dark time in my life, but you bitches came to my aid and helped me rise above and have a great time. All the friendships that were formed on that trip are life long, and I thank you, girls, for your love and support.

To my resting bitchface sisters- I love how close we've all become, with the support to say and do whatever we want. Thank you, Alice S. and Rachel Z. for inviting me into this group. To Pam B., Susan O., Carla N., Lisa D., Debi N. and all 69 of you bitchfaces, I just can't express how much I enjoy all of you. I love you, girls.

Andy B. & Angie D- You two have been my life line. All day texts and voice messages, planning, building and making this happen, you've been my rock, and I couldn't do it without you. Thank you for all you do.

To my angels, thank you for all your support and helping me build my dream. I love my group, and it just keeps getting bigger… let's keep it going!

To all my friends, family and readers that have pushed me and supported me through these past three years, I just want you all to know I love you and thank God every day for you. Without your love and support, I wouldn't have been able to finish this book. I know I am forgetting people and I am sorry for that, but just know I am so thankful for everyone that had a part in making this dream a reality.

With Love,

Angera Allen

Made in the USA
Middletown, DE
29 April 2022